❦   ❦   ❦

He advanced until a faded white column was behind her back, until the dusty red bricks of the gallery were pressing against her legs. Resting his hands on either side of her head, he moved closer, so close that he could feel the heat where her hips cradled his. He could feel the soft warm puffs of her breath against his chin. "You're not too smart, little girl, are you?" he asked, his voice tauntingly low. "You keep playing with fire, you're going to get burned."

She didn't back down. "Maybe I like living dangerously."

"You don't know shit about danger, honey."

"I know you," she retorted. "You seem to think that you're dangerous."

"I don't think. I *know*."

"I think you're all talk. I think your reputation as the big bad boy is all bluff and no substance. I think—"

He covered her mouth with his, biting her lower lip. She made a startled sound that quickly turned to a soft moan, vibrating through her and into him. He felt it all the way through, and it made him throb . . .

❦

Marilyn Pappano
In Sinful Harmony

WARNER BOOKS

A Time Warner Company

WARNER BOOKS EDITION

Copyright © 1995 by Marilyn Pappano
All rights reserved.

Cover design by Diane Luger
Cover photograph by Herman Estevez
Hand lettering by Carl Dellacroce

Warner Books, Inc.
1271 Avenue of the Americas
New York, NY 10020

W A Time Warner Company

Printed in the United States of America

First Printing: June, 1995

10 9 8 7 6 5 4 3 2 1

Chapter One

Summertime in Louisiana.

It was five o'clock in the afternoon, and the temperature was as high, as blistering, as it had been at noon. Celine Hunter hated summer. She hated watching the heat rise from the streets, hated feeling the asphalt give underneath her sensible low heels, hated the sweat and the languor and the listlessness that accompanied the endless summer heat. It all combined to make her feel restless. Achy. Itchy. And she didn't even know why.

She walked down the main street of town, periodically shifting the books she was taking home from one hip to the other. When she got to the house, there would be damp spots on the spines where they'd come in contact with her sticky skin. Her dress, sensible cotton befitting a small-town librarian, would be damp, too—already was, in fact, where her hair fell like a heavy, confining cloak nearly to her waist. Maybe this was the summer when she would get it all cut off, she mused as she crossed a street. Maybe this was the summer she would stop being sensible and start driving her car the mile and a half to work.

Maybe this was the summer she would run away from Harmony, Louisiana.

She liked her hometown, liked it just fine, but there were

times when, God help her, she never wanted to see it again. When she wanted to jump into her car and take off. When she wanted to leave everything behind—her clothes, her furniture, her job, her family and friends. When she wanted to be free.

She turned at the last street before the road curved out of town. It was a broad street with uneven sidewalks and towering oaks that created a shady canopy overhead. Two blocks up it turned to dirt. Three blocks beyond that was Miss Rose Kendall's house and, next door, the smaller place that she rented to Celine.

Switching the books one last time, she crossed the road when the sidewalk gave way to a dirt path. She was feeling vaguely uneasy, as if a storm were about to break. She wished one would, a violent storm with lots of thunder and lightning and blinding rain. It wouldn't do anything for the heat, except maybe make it worse, but it might help the way she felt. It might wash away some of her discomfort. It might make her feel more grounded. But there wasn't a cloud in the sky or a breeze in the trees. Everything was calm. Everything except her.

Rounding a bend in the road, Celine saw the houses ahead. Miss Rose's was most distant, not too large, not too showy, but suitable for the matriarch of Harmony's founding family. Celine's was little more than a cottage and stood on the near side of the broad lawn. There was a wide gallery on three sides with screens to keep the mosquitoes and gnats at bay, and a tangle of overgrown azaleas that labored valiantly to cover every inch of the foundation.

"House" was a generous description for the third structure, situated ten yards behind Celine's house. It consisted of one large, airy room with rows of ten-foot-tall windows, a tiny bath tucked into one corner, and a narrow, rickety porch that extended all the way around. Miss Rose used the building for storage. Celine had been in there more times than she could count, putting away this item, digging through boxes for that one. It could be a lovely place with its high ceiling and slowly whirring fans, with its walk-through windows and wooden floor, but mostly it was just dusty, empty, hot.

One mailbox, located at the side of the road midway between the front two houses, served both residents. Celine stopped in front of it, carefully pulling the door open. The aluminum box had withstood many a drive-by battering, and it showed the scars—a dent here, another there, an off-center tilt, and a crooked door. After every heavy rain left them with soggy mail, she suggested they replace it with a newer, tougher version, but Miss Rose always demurred. There was a certain charm to the crooked post, and the honeysuckle vines that wound round the box covered the worst of the dents and perfumed the air with such sweetness.

Sliding the mail between the top two books, she crossed the grass and climbed the steps to her porch. After unlocking the door, she stepped into the blessed darkness of her living room. She had closed the blinds and drawn the drapes before she left in the morning, trying to keep the temperature down so she could delay turning on the air-conditioning until it was absolutely necessary. These days, it was getting necessary about two minutes after she walked in the door.

She set the books on the table, turning them so the damp places on the covers could dry, then went into her bedroom. It was as neat as the rest of the house, as neat as the library where she worked. She was compulsive, her sister Vickie said, bordering on obsessive. But what choice had she had, growing up in a family of the most irresponsible people in the world? Someone had had to bring order to the chaos that was their lives. Someone had had to see that the laundry got done, the dinner cooked without burning, the car keys found when lost. Someone had had to keep their absentminded father on track, had to see that their dreamy mother made it from day to day. Since Vickie had inherited the worst traits from both parents, that had left only Celine.

Sensible Celine.

Levelheaded Celine.

Reliable Celine.

Her parents, her sister and her friends had all meant the words as compliments, but she hated them. She had always wanted to do something rash, something reckless. Just once in her life she wanted to do something totally unlike herself. Just once she wanted to surprise the hell out of everybody. But opportunities for rash and reckless behavior didn't often present themselves in Harmony, and certainly not to sensible, reliable librarians.

She opened the curtains, letting the evening sun into the room, and immediately felt the temperature start to climb. After kicking off her shoes, she removed her pantyhose, then her dress. She stood in front of one window, wearing only a plain cotton bra and an even plainer cotton slip, and stared out at the scene that had greeted her every morning and every night for the last six years. She needed a change. She needed some excitement. She needed to run away.

She didn't know how long she'd stood there, seeing what she was used to seeing—empty white guesthouse, pale blue sky, and lush green growth—and not what was actually there. The guesthouse wasn't empty, though, not this evening. All those tall windows were open, and standing at one was a man, vague, lean and shadowy, looking out. Looking at *her*.

In spite of the heat, chill bumps formed on her arms, and her skin crawled. There was something threatening about the man, something dark and hardly restrained, even though he stood absolutely motionless. She couldn't see his face clearly enough to make out his features, but undoubtedly he was a stranger, and he made her feel unsettled with his mere presence.

Maybe he was a phantom, conjured up by her restlessness. Maybe if she blinked, he would disappear. She did blink, and he was still standing there, still unmoving, still watching her.

With a shudder she stepped away from the window and removed a cool summer dress from the armoire. She would ask Miss Rose about him, would find out if the old lady had invited someone to visit and had forgotten to tell Celine about it. If he were a stranger to Miss Rose, she would call the sheriff and have him send out a deputy to chase the man away.

If he weren't a vagrant, a bum who had happened on a nice, empty place to stay a while? If he were a guest who rightly belonged in the guesthouse? Unease fluttered through her at the thought. She didn't care for unexpected guests, and she knew without a doubt that she especially didn't care for this one. No matter how she claimed to crave change and excitement, dangerous men weren't for her. The sooner he was gone, the better.

Will Beaumont stared out the window, watching as the woman crossed the lawn, watching until she disappeared inside Miss Rose's house. He'd heard the whispers in town today, had felt the stares, had seen the curiosity. He had known he couldn't return to Harmony without attracting attention, and so he had asked the trucker who'd given him a lift to let him out right in the center of town, and he had carried his battered old suitcase with him right into the restaurant at straight-up twelve o'clock for lunch. They wouldn't ignore him, and so he'd done one of the few things he did well: he had deliberately drawn their attention to himself. He'd given them plenty of chances to look, to speculate, to remember.

But somehow Celine Hunter had missed out on the gossip. She hadn't expected to see him here. If she had, she never would have opened those curtains. She never would have stood there half-dressed. She never would have let him look.

Did she remember him? Probably not. She'd been just a kid when he'd left Harmony. But *he* remembered *her*—not even a teenager, awkwardly tall, all long legs and graceless. He had met her when he'd gone out with her older sister a time or two, until her folks had put a stop to it. No parents in town had wanted him around their teenage daughters, and the Hunters had been no exception. Vickie hadn't been any great loss, but his pride had suffered anyway. Back then, about all he'd had was pride.

Today he didn't even have that.

Turning away from the window, he looked around the room. Miss Rose had offered him his old room, complete with air-conditioning, in her house, but he'd taken this place instead. He had always liked the big windows out here. It was as close to being outside as a room could be. He wouldn't feel confined here.

Tomorrow he would clean up, he decided. Move the boxes to one end, rearrange the furniture, sweep up the layers of dust that covered everything. For tonight the clean sheets on the bed were all he needed. It would be nice to sleep in a bed again. It would be nice to have a temporary home again.

If only it weren't in Harmony.

When he had received Miss Rose's message last week, he had ignored it. He had sworn sixteen years ago that he would never return to Harmony, and he hadn't, although he'd been a hundred places like it. Small, closed towns that welcomed no strangers—places where people watched every move a man made, where suspicion and distrust were about all a man like him would find. Restrictive places. Suffocating places.

With the message had come guilt, and it had eaten away at his resolve. With no family ties, no obligation or duty, Miss Rose had taken him in when he was scarcely ten years old. She had fed him and clothed him and loved him at a time when his own mother had found him unlovable. She had taught him the value of hard work and the meaning of honor. She had given him pride. Wasn't it time he gave something back?

And so, knowing that nothing had changed, that the distrust, the suspicions, and the lies would still exist, that no one would welcome him except Miss Rose, he had come home. He'd known the moment he'd made up his mind that it was a mistake. He'd known he would regret it. He had known that Harmony, Louisiana, was the last place in the world he wanted to be, but he had come anyway—for Miss Rose.

Across the yard he heard the sound of a screen door banging. He watched as Celine crossed the grass, appearing in one window, then disappearing briefly before coming into view in the next window. She moved with purpose, her strides long, her shoulders erect. She had grown up since the last time he'd seen her. She looked like a completely different person—a woman instead of a child.

At that thought, an image of her in front of her window formed in his mind—plain lingerie, creamy skin, long thick hair—and his mouth curved in a smile. She was definitely a woman.

Halfway across the yard, she slowed her steps, then turned toward the guesthouse. What did she have to say to him? Hell, there were generally only two things women said to him—warnings or invitations—and he didn't want to hear either from little Celine Hunter. He didn't want to know that she had grown up to distrust him, to hear that she believed he was after Miss Rose's money. He sure as hell didn't want an invitation into her bed. Not even if it did look from here like a mighty comfortable place to be.

She knocked at the door, even though it was open, even though she could see him through the mesh of the screen. He remained where he was, leaning against a stack of dusty boxes, silently watching. After a polite moment, she opened the screen door and stepped inside. "Hello, Billy Ray."

There was something about a Southern woman's voice, something in particular about *this* Southern woman's voice. Even cool and guarded, it was sexy. It slid along his skin, seeping underneath it, making him think about blatant invitations, about lust and need and hot, steamy sex. It made him remember how good it could be. It made him remember how long it had been.

"I prefer Will," he said, hearing the need in his voice, feeling it grow in his body.

She acknowledged that with a slight nod that made her hair swing. Such long hair, heavy and looking as fine as silk. It would startle her if he touched it, if he tested its texture, and in a moment he just might do it, if for no other reason than to get her out of his house. But for now he was content merely to look.

"How long are you staying?"

"As long as Miss Rose wants."

She nodded again, then glanced around. "She was planning to come out here and clean tomorrow. I told her I would do it—"

He interrupted her. "I don't want your help."

Another nod, another shimmer rippling through her long, long hair. Damn, he wished she would leave. He didn't like her intruding in his space, didn't like the awareness she was creating, didn't like the heat she was bringing. Didn't she remember what kind of boy he had been? Didn't she suspect that the man he had become was just as wild and a hell of a lot more wicked? Didn't she realize that he could destroy her the way he had destroyed everything good in his life since he was ten years old?

She shifted to lean back against the doorjamb, cushioning

the position with her hands behind her. "Do you remember me? I'm—"

"Vickie Hunter's kid sister. You used to wear pigtails and braces, and you were flat as a board." Shifting his gaze lower to her breasts, he smiled, deliberately letting her see the threat in it, then added, "You've grown up."

When he raised his eyes to her face to see her reaction, he found she was looking at him evenly enough to make him uneasy. If she were half as innocent as she appeared, *she* should be uneasy, wary, ready to flee at the first move he made. But the expression in her eyes was calm, steady, knowing. As if she could see past his words. As if she could see inside him.

"You've been gone a long time."

"Not long enough."

"Is that your opinion or everyone else's?"

"Both." He wasn't interested, damn it, he wasn't, but he asked anyway. "What's *your* opinion?"

"That all hell's going to break loose when Raymond finds out you're back."

Will scowled at her observance. Raymond Kendall was Miss Rose's only son. When the old lady had taken him in, Raymond's objections had been the loudest, the most vehement. He couldn't bear to see his mother spend one penny of the precious Kendall money on a worthless kid like Will. Let the state track down his mother and make her take him back, Raymond had insisted. Let them place him in a state home. Let him live on his own. He would have preferred any solution over seeing Will in his family home, over watching Miss Rose treat Will like one of her own.

"I'm surprised it's taken him this long to come out."

Celine shrugged. "He's in Baton Rouge. He's not expected home until this evening."

And all hell *would* break loose then. Raymond's fireworks would light up the night sky. Will wasn't worried. He'd had more than a few run-ins with the man in the eight years he had lived here. He had handled him when he was a kid. He had no doubt he could handle him now.

He regretted it for Miss Rose's sake. She was over seventy years old, too old to be subjected to any more of Raymond's tiresome tantrums. Still, she had known what she was getting into when she had asked Will to come home. She had known it wouldn't be easy, and she had wanted him here anyway.

"What kind of reception am I going to get from everyone other than Raymond?"

"Depends on whom you see." Celine shifted positions, but didn't come closer. She was acting so calm and cool, Will realized, but she was also damned near hugging the door. She wasn't going to get any closer to him than was necessary.

So maybe *he* would get a little closer to *her*.

"Most of the parents, no matter how old their daughters, are going to be a little cool," she continued. "Most of the younger women will be friendly, and most of their husbands will be hostile because their wives are friendly." She paused, briefly considering the wisdom of what she was about to say, then said it anyway. "The Robinsons won't be happy. Neither will Jared."

The Robinsons. Pretty Melanie, her hardheaded, narrow-minded father and her clinging, insecure mother. He had known they would probably still be here. He just hadn't wanted to give them any thought. "Who is Jared?"

She opened her mouth, closed it, then finally spoke. "Jared Robinson. Melanie's son."

Will almost smiled, giving her credit for avoiding the obvious answer. *Your son.* Was she giving him the benefit of the doubt by not saying it, or did she merely think it best not to push him too hard on this first meeting?

Other than his father, no one had ever placed much faith in him. His mother had been quick to believe whatever anyone else had said, and his teachers had rarely even asked for his side of the story when he'd gotten into minor squabbles or fights at school. Miss Rose had stood by him as much as she could, but not even she had believed him about Melanie Robinson. Own up to your mistakes, she had counseled him with a look of disappointment in her sharp blue eyes. Accept responsibility for what you did.

Melanie's father, accompanied by the sheriff, had phrased it more bluntly. Either marry the girl or go to jail. After all, she was just sixteen. A minor. Jailbait.

No one had cared to hear Will's side on that issue, either, and the few who had listened hadn't believed him. Miss Rose hadn't believed him. Prissy Celine, standing safely way across the room, certainly wouldn't believe him.

"And what about you?" he asked, lowering his voice, making it silkier. "What kind of reception am I going to get from you?"

She glanced away, out the window, and thoughtfully considered his question before looking at him again. "That depends, too."

"On what my intentions are?" He grinned. "If you're worried about Miss Rose, don't be. She asked me to come back, and that's the only reason I did." Then his grin turned nastier. "And if you're worried about yourself, don't bother. I don't mess with little girls, and no matter how much you've grown, in the ways that count, you're still just a little girl."

He expected at least a blush, but she simply gave him another of those long, even, too-perceptive looks. "Why did Miss Rose ask you to come back?"

"You'll have to ask her that."

"I did."

"And what did she tell you?"

"The same thing you did: not to worry."

Will merely shrugged. Truth was, he didn't know why the old lady had wanted to see him again. They had spent several hours talking this afternoon—she'd passed on all the gossip about the people he'd known here and had told him all about Celine, and he'd told her mostly bullshit. There hadn't been much about his sixteen years away that was worth telling, and so he had lied. He had made his life sound better, more respectable, prettier, than it had actually been. He had lied.

He suspected she had known it.

Across the room, Celine lifted her hair so the still evening air could reach her neck. "It's been a hot summer," she remarked, her voice unconsciously as sultry as the heat.

"And it's bound to get hotter still. July and August are yet to come."

Her eyes grew shadowy, giving her a mysterious air, reminding him of places along the water, dark places where even the midday sun couldn't penetrate. "People tend to get disagreeable when it's hot like this. Don't forget that." Her movements as easy and natural as the river's flow, she slipped out the door and down the steps. Will moved to the nearest window and watched her until she was out of sight. A moment later the banging of the screen door signaled she had reached her own house.

Had those last words been a threat or a warning? It wasn't likely that Celine Hunter would be offering a warning, unless she thought it might make him leave town. No, in any conflict between him and the folks in town, she could be counted on to side with them, with the people she'd grown up knowing, with her parents and her friends.

And no one could be counted on to take his side. Not even Miss Rose.

He had to remember that.

Raymond Kendall arrived shortly after dusk. He parked his big Lincoln Town Car on the shell driveway beside Miss Rose's house and climbed out, pausing long enough to give each of the three houses a malevolent stare. The only lights on were in Miss Rose's. Celine preferred darkness for her evening ritual of iced tea on the screened porch, and the guesthouse where Billy Ray—where Will Beaumont was staying was as dark as her own.

She raised the glass to her forehead, wiping the droplets of condensation across her hot skin. The sun had set awhile ago, but the heat hadn't relented much. If she had any sense at all, she would be inside, where the air-conditioning could cool her skin and calm her fever, but she was too restless to be trapped inside four walls. As sticky as it was, she felt . . . not comfortable, but less troubled. She felt less disturbed out here.

She watched Raymond climb the steps to the wide gallery outside Miss Rose's house, then knock at the door. It annoyed him that she insisted on that courtesy. This was his childhood home, and when she died, it would belong to him. He would like to take ownership now, Celine knew—not that he would actually live there. No, when he had married Frannie

Dumont, of the New Orleans Dumonts, her daddy had built them a fine new house on the other side of town. Miss Rose's house was a poor relative compared to their place.

Raymond just liked being in control. He thought that being president of Harmony National Bank, along with being the only man in the Kendall family, made him naturally superior to the others. He wanted to handle Miss Rose's money, her property, and all her personal matters.

Tonight he would demand answers to the questions Celine had asked more gently this evening. *You asked Billy Ray Beaumont to come back to Harmony? You invited him to stay here? Why did you do that? Why did you want to see him?*

For all his anger and all his demands, he wouldn't get any more of an answer than she had. Miss Rose could be the most stubborn woman in the entire world when she took it into her mind to be, and when it came to Will Beaumont, she was downright ornery.

Celine sipped her tea, grimacing at the taste. Melting ice had diluted it until it was as weak as colored water. Mercy, she was tired of the heat, and, as Will had pointed out earlier, July and August were yet to come. It *was* bound to get even hotter. She doubted he was referring to the weather when he'd said that. Tempers were going to get hot. There was probably already a little fire burning inside Raymond. And Jock Robinson would likely erupt like a volcano when he heard that Will was back. He'd never forgiven Will for seducing his little girl, for getting her pregnant and then running off without marrying her. He had ruined Melanie, according to Jock. He was responsible for every bad thing she'd done in her life since then.

Celine thought that was just a convenient excuse for not accepting any responsibility himself for the way his daughter had turned out. Granted, having a baby a few weeks after her seventeenth birthday couldn't have been easy for Melanie, but thousands of other girls had gone through it, and most of them had managed a whole lot better. Most of them hadn't dumped their kids on their parents because they were too selfish to care for them any longer. Most of them hadn't run off with the first guy—and the second and the fifth and the fifteenth—to ask. Most of them hadn't devoted their entire lives to good times and fast living.

Snagging a wicker hassock with her foot, Celine drew it closer, then propped her feet on it. She should go inside, shower, and get ready for bed. She shouldn't be sitting out here in the heat, waiting for a clue as to how things were going inside Miss Rose's house and thinking far too much about Will Beaumont and the lives he had affected.

She hardly even remembered him from before. Naturally she'd heard Vickie talk about him, mostly in hushed whispers, describing things that had made little sense and held no appeal for the naive adolescent she had been. What girl in her right mind wanted a boy to put his tongue in her mouth, to touch her in those places, to try to sweet-talk her into doing things she wasn't supposed to do?

Mercy, she had been young.

She remembered clearly enough the fuss when their parents had told Vickie that she couldn't see him again, how her sister had cried as if her heart were breaking, how she had threatened to sneak around and see him anyway or to run away from such horrible people. That had resulted in the most severe punishment either of the Hunter girls had ever received—which wasn't saying much, since their parents were by nature easygoing and accommodating—except when it came to Billy Ray Beaumont.

By the time Vickie had gotten off restriction from the incident, Will had been seeing Melanie, who had promptly gotten pregnant.

Celine sighed softly. She wished the wind would blow and some rain would fall. She wished summer would pass and the cooler days of autumn would arrive. She wished Will Beaumont would pack his ratty bag and go back to wherever he'd come from before he did too much damage to the peaceful life in Harmony.

Most of all, though, she wished she had the courage to be like him. She wished *she* had the courage to leave Harmony and never come back.

Across the lawn came the slam of a door, then Raymond stalked down the steps. There had been a time, Celine remembered as she watched him in the thin light from the floodlamp, when she had thought he was the kindest, handsomest man she had ever known. Every time she'd gone to the bank with her mother, he had called her by name and tugged at her braids, and she thought that someday when she was grown up she would marry him. The fact that he was already married to Frannie Dumont had been inconsequential to her then; and by the time she'd been old enough to care, she had already set her sights on someone kinder, handsomer, and fifteen years younger.

When he turned away from his car and started across the lawn, she wondered if he were coming to her house, wanting her help in influencing his mother. Even though she agreed with him, even though she knew in her heart that Will Beaumont's leaving would be best for everyone, she didn't want to talk to Raymond. She didn't want her evening, upset enough as it was, further unbalanced by an angry conversation with him.

But he wasn't heading for her house. He turned toward the back, toward the guesthouse, toward Will Beaumont. Celine could see about a third of the back house, including the front door, from where she sat. Nosy and unashamed of it, she watched.

Raymond banged on the door loudly enough to startle her, even though she was expecting the knock. No lights came on. For a moment there was no response at all. Then Will Beaumont appeared.

The floodlamp, situated close to Miss Rose's house, didn't reach that far. There was only moonlight, and precious little of that, to light the scene, but it was enough to see Will. It was enough to see that he was wearing jeans and nothing else. It was almost enough, she thought fancifully, to see the sweat that surely must coat his exposed skin.

"What the hell do you think you're doing?" Raymond demanded, his voice thick and taut with emotion. Will's return had shaken up his secure little world, and he didn't like it one bit. It made him angry. It made him afraid, and it showed in his voice.

That was a mistake. Celine had realized quickly in their

brief meeting that displaying emotion with Will Beaumont was as dangerous as showing fear to a wild animal. Just as an animal would attack someone whose fear was palpable, Will would use it to his advantage. If he had realized exactly how uncomfortable he had made her, he would have deliberately pushed, deliberately taunted her.

She couldn't understand Will's reply. All she heard was the low, controlled rumble of his voice. Whatever he said, though, further enraged Raymond. "We had an agreement, but, hell, I should have known better than to trust a Beaumont." He muttered something that sounded nasty and vicious. "Whatever your plans are, you can just forget them. You're not getting anything from my mother. Do you understand? You're not going to leech off her anymore."

Again Celine couldn't make out Will's reply. It was probably something cocky, though. It would certainly fit his stance—one shoulder against the door, holding the screen door open, arms folded across his chest, one ankle crossed over the other.

It would fit his personality, too. She'd seen his expression when she'd mentioned Raymond earlier. There was no love lost between the two men, but Will was here, and as long as Miss Rose had a breath in her body, there was nothing Raymond could do about it. But there was something Will could—and would—do. He could rub Raymond's nose in it. He could be as obnoxious and arrogant and mocking about it as he was rumored to be. He could fuel the older man's anger. And he could take some perverse satisfaction in doing so.

"Let me tell you this," Raymond said. Then, abruptly, he lowered his voice. Threats were more effective delivered in quiet tones, Celine thought uncomfortably, and they were always safer without witnesses to overhear. Raymond was unaware that he had an audience, but he was being careful anyway.

Good. She didn't want to be drawn into this. She didn't want anything at all except a little rain, a little cool weather, and a little more comfort.

But things weren't going to get comfortable around here

for a long time, she suspected. She had felt the approach of a storm this evening—the uneasiness, the prickliness, the tension—but the sky had been clear. Now she knew she'd been looking in the wrong direction.

There was going to be a storm, all right, but it wasn't going to come from the heavens. It wasn't going to bring wind and thunder and cleansing rains. This storm was more likely from hell itself.

And at the center of it stood Will Beaumont.

Raymond backed out of the driveway with a spray of shells, then shifted into gear and shot off down the dirt road toward town. His fingers clenched the steering wheel, flexing, then relaxing. He wished it was Billy Ray Beaumont's throat he was gripping so tightly.

The bastard had promised never to return to Harmony. He had given his word, and Raymond had paid for it with cold, hard cash. So many years had passed that he'd almost forgotten the younger man. He'd forgotten that he hated him. He had forgotten the problems Beaumont had caused the family in general, and him in particular.

Then he had returned from a meeting in Baton Rouge this evening, and Frannie had told him the news. She had relished the telling, hadn't been able to wipe that smile from her face the whole time. *Billy Ray Beaumont's back in Harmony, and he's staying with your mama.* It had amused her, until he had pointed out what it probably meant. If Beaumont had come home, then he must want something, and the only thing here for him to want was the Kendall money. He was a con man and a thief. If he couldn't persuade Rose to hand it over, he would just take it, and where would that leave *them*?

Raymond had some money of his own, along with the salary the bank paid him, but it wasn't enough. There would never be enough money in the entire state of Louisiana to satisfy Frannie. His mother was old; she couldn't have too many years left, and she had a *lot* of money. Raymond wasn't even sure how much, because she jealously guarded that information. But she had property all over the parish—hell, all over the state—and she had more accounts and investments than he could even begin to guess at, and when she died, it would all be his and his sister Meredith's, provided that Billy Ray Beaumont didn't steal it all away.

When Raymond had reminded Frannie of that, it had wiped the smirk off her face. She had sent him off to talk some sense into his mother with her blessing.

He must have been out of his mind with anger. Talk *sense* into *his* mother? There had never been a man alive who could make her do anything she didn't want to—not her daddy, not Raymond's daddy, and sure as hell not Raymond himself. She had listened to his arguments, had nodded her head in understanding, and then had told him to mind his own business. Whom she took into her own home was none of his concern. Will Beaumont—she had always called him Will instead of Billy Ray because his old man had—was none of his concern. But she was wrong; Beaumont *was* his concern. More his than anyone else's in town.

About to turn onto the street that led to his house, he made a U-turn instead and headed back downtown to the sheriff's office. He hadn't made it more than ten feet inside the door when Mitch Franklin stood up from behind a desk and raised his hands, palms outward. "I heard the news."

"And what the hell are you going to do about it?"

"Nothing I *can* do. The boy hasn't broken any laws—not yet, at least."

"What about that complaint against him from the last time?"

The sheriff gave him a chiding look. "We can't go back sixteen years, Raymond. No warrant was ever issued because Miss Rose wouldn't allow it then, and she won't allow it now. Besides, the satute of limitations comes into it now." His smile was thin and, damn him, the slightest bit smug. "It's expired."

"So what are you going to do? Just sit around and wait for him to rob my mother blind?" Raymond dragged his fingers through his hair. "By the time you find out about it, he'll be long gone again, and this time he won't be found."

Franklin sat down again. "What do you want me to do?"

"Run him out of town. Make it clear he's not welcome here."

"I don't remember the Beaumont boy as being stupid. I

imagine he already knows he's not welcome here. And as long as he's staying out at your mama's and minding his own business, I can't run him out of town.''

"But you can make it real uncomfortable for him here. You can find out where he came from. You can find out where he's been. You can find out what kind of trouble he's been in since he left here.''

Franklin folded his hands over his stomach. "That I can, and I can have a little talk with him. But unless he causes some trouble, I can't lock him up and I can't run him off.''

Raymond scowled at him. "Oh, he'll be causing some trouble,'' he said darkly. "You can count on that.'' He started to leave, then turned back. "What about Jock Robinson, Sheriff? You know there'll be problems there. What are you going to do about it? Lock up Jock and let Beaumont go free?''

"If Robinson doesn't have any better sense at his age than to go looking for a fight—''

Raymond interrupted him. "Seems like maybe we need us a new sheriff around here, you know, Mitch? Somebody who'll take care of the people who pay his salary and rid the town of the trash that drifts in.'' The warning given, Raymond's voice became harder, more insistent. "You look around and find out what Beaumont's been up to since he left here, and you let me know. Understand?''

The sheriff gave him a mocking salute. "Yes, sir, Mr. Kendall, I understand.''

They really did need a new sheriff, Raymond thought angrily as he left the station. Franklin had too much education, too much awareness of right and wrong, and too little understanding of justice. He'd never been the kind of guy to do what you expected of him, anyway, and since his wife's death a year ago, he'd become even more unpredictable. But one problem at a time. First he would get rid of Billy Ray Beaumont. Then he would take on the sheriff.

Will awakened Saturday morning only hours after he'd finally fallen asleep. He was lying on his stomach on the edge of the bed, his face against the sheet, his right arm over the side, his fingers brushing the wooden floor, and there was the most god-awful racket in his head. He hadn't drunk anything stronger than Miss Rose's lemonade last night, and no matter how sweet and tart it was, surely it couldn't have this kind of kick.

Then he realized that the sound wasn't in his head. It was coming through all the open windows. It was a lawn mower. A lawn mower, for God's sake. At six-thirty on a Saturday morning.

He rolled over in bed, finding a pillow and stuffing it beneath his head. The mower engine needed tuning. Its coughing, irregular buzz was an annoyance that pounded behind his eyes. He rubbed them with both hands, then scratched the growth of beard that stubbled his jaw before sitting up.

The air in the room was heavy with the promise of another hot, humid day. The ceiling fans overhead stirred it, offering a slight breeze but no relief other than cooling the sweat that covered his skin. Even his hair was damp and sticking out at odd angles until he combed it down with his fingers. Summertime in Louisiana could be hell on a man if he cared enough to mind. This morning, Will decided, he didn't care.

He shoved the sheet back and got out of bed, reaching for the jeans he'd discarded last night. Buttoning them, he crossed the room to the window where the engine noise was loudest. If it was Miss Rose out there pushing the mower, he would have to take over and finish the job for her after giving her the kind of talking-to she'd always given *him* growing up.

If it was Celine . . . His smile felt rusty and unpleasant. If it was her, he would find a comfortable place to sit and watch.

It *was* Celine, with the penchant for long skirts and shapeless dresses that hid whatever charms nature had granted her. But this morning the concealing clothes were gone. She wore a pair of shorts that exposed legs longer than he would have imagined and a thin little top that was soaked with sweat and clung in all the right places. Her hair was in a thick braid, the early-morning sun giving it a dull sheen, and her eyes were hidden behind dark glasses.

She looked good, good enough that he could lay her down

right there in that fresh-cut grass and do all sorts of wicked things to her. But if he even tried, she would run screaming the other way. Wouldn't she?

He got a glass of tepid water from the bathroom sink, then went outside and sat down to drink it. It was the kind of lazy summer morning he well remembered, already warm, the rising sun's rays filtered by live oaks and tall pines, the dew already drying on the flowers—roses, hollyhocks, and gladioli—that perfumed the air. The steps were still in the shade, offering a few degrees of relief from the heat; but when the sun cleared the sheltering trees, it would be as hot here as anywhere else. As hot as hell.

He knew exactly when she noticed him, when she slowed her steps behind the mower and tugged at her shorts, when she pulled her shirt away from her sticky skin. Her attempts at modesty didn't do any good. Covering an inch or so of those legs still left plenty to admire, and when she let go of her shirt, it did exactly what he would, given the opportunity— molded itself to the soft curves of her breasts and the flat expanse of her stomach.

When she reached the portion of grass that separated her house from his, she couldn't ignore him any longer. Releasing the handle that kept the engine running, she came to a stop and took a seat nearby on the steps. "Sorry if I woke you, but in this heat the mowing has to be done early in the morning or late in the evening, and there are fewer bugs in the morning."

"Why doesn't Miss Rose hire someone to do it?"

"She says they don't take proper care of the grass and her flowers." Celine moved her braid from one side to the other, then wiped the back of one arm across her flushed face. It was a simple gesture, one that pulled her damp shirt taut across her breasts and made Will's throat go dry. He gave himself a silent warning. When he started thinking about sex with an old girlfriend's baby sister, it had been too damned long between women. Don't worry, he had told her last night. *I don't mess with little girls, and . . . in the ways that count, you're still just a little girl.*

But, just as he had lied to Miss Rose yesterday, he had lied to Celine last night. She *did* have cause for worry, because while his head might acknowledge that she was too young and naive, his body didn't give a damn. His head could recognize honor, right, and wrong, but his body cared only about hunger and need; and right now he needed to be inside some woman. Inside *this* woman.

Shifting from a position that had become too open and uncomfortable, he took a sip, then offered her the glass of water. "Drink?" When she hesitated, he grinned. "I can get you a clean glass if you'd feel safer not drinking after me."

Holding his gaze, she took the glass from him and drank deeply from it. So Miss Celine couldn't resist a challenge, he thought, filing that information away. A person's weaknesses were always good to know. It made dealing with her easier. With a woman like her, he might need all the advantages he could find.

She held the glass out to him, but he gestured for her to finish the water. She had just lifted it for another drink when he casually asked, "What did you think of Raymond last night?"

His timing couldn't have been better. She damned near choked. If he'd wanted an excuse to touch her, he had it— a couple of pats on the back wouldn't be inappropriate, and who knew where it would go from there? But he didn't want to touch her.

Yeah, and if he reminded himself often enough, he just might start to believe it.

She removed her glasses and looked at him, and for the first time he could see the color of her eyes. The woman had drab brown hair and nothing-special pale skin, but her eyes were the prettiest green he'd ever seen. He never would have guessed it.

"I wasn't eavesdropping," she said stiffly.

"No, of course not. You always sit outside in the dark when Miss Rose has company."

"I usually do sit outside in the dark," she clarified.

A creature of habit. He had already learned that from Miss Rose. She'd told him plenty about dear Celine, who was as honest as the day was long and twice as reliable. She was an efficient woman—what librarian wasn't?—who didn't like disorder. Well, he was bound to bring more than a little disorder to things around here. Set-in-her-ways Celine would just have to learn to deal with it.

"He said you'd had an agreement." She was watching him curiously. "What did he mean?"

Will shrugged and lied. "Who knows? Raymond and I never saw eye to eye on anything in our entire lives." Before she could press for a more satisfactory answer, he turned the conversation to her. "Celine. What kind of name is that?"

"It was my great-grandmother's name."

"It's kind of prissy, isn't it?" He saw her stiffen, and he laughed. "I think I'll call you Celie. That's better suited for a little girl like you."

She set the glass down between them, then stood up to her full height. A couple of steps below him as she was, it put him right on eye level with her breasts. Although the action was unintentional, she couldn't have found a better way to remind him of just how grown up she was. "Excuse me, Billy Ray," she said, her tone bland. "I have work to do."

He watched her go, the smug grin fading from his face with each step she took away. Her use of his old nickname was deliberate, a reminder of who and what he was. In high school he hadn't been considered good enough for the elder of the Hunter girls, and sixteen wasted years later he sure as hell wasn't good enough for the baby.

Well, he didn't need any such reminders, especially from her. He had learned two things from his experience with Melanie—avoid the innocent type, and don't go looking close to home. He'd had the misfortune to draw female attention his way since he was thirteen, and coming back home hadn't changed that. If he needed a woman, he could find another easily enough.

He carried the glass inside, shaved, and finished dressing, then headed for the big house. Miss Rose had invited him for breakfast to be served promptly at seven o'clock. In all his life he had never eaten as well as he had under her roof. She believed good food fed the soul, and she had fed his for eight years. It had seemed like forever. It hadn't been long enough.

The good times in his life had never lasted very long. Somehow he had always managed to screw them up. Of course, he hadn't done anything wrong with Melanie, but it was still his fault. If he hadn't deliberately cultivated such a wild reputation for himself, maybe someone would have heard him when he said he wasn't responsible. Maybe someone would have believed him.

He crossed the lawn to Miss Rose's back door, aware of Celine pushing the mower around and around in ever-smaller squares, but he didn't look at her. The last thing he needed before facing Miss Rose's sharp blue eyes was to rouse an itch like that.

"You're late."

"Yes, ma'am," he agreed, even though the big clock over the stove showed a few minutes until seven. If Miss Rose said it was past seven o'clock, it was, no matter what the clocks said.

"I see you've met Celine."

"Yes, ma'am." He glanced from her to the kitchen table. It was set with three places. Apparently in exchange for mowing the lawn, prissy Celine got a free breakfast—a more than fair exchange when it was Miss Rose's cooking. She would also get the dubious pleasure of sitting across the table from him when she was all hot and sweaty, looking as if she'd just enjoyed a few hours of steamy passion.

No, correct that, he thought with a grin. The pleasure would be all his.

"Can I help?" he asked, offering as he always did and knowing she would turn him down as she always did.

"You can pour yourself some orange juice and have a seat."

He took the juice, cold from the refrigerator, but ignored the chairs in favor of leaning against the counter out of the way and watching her work. She was efficient, keeping an eye on the waffle iron, two skillets on the stovetop and the biscuits in the oven all at once. She reminded him of a tiny bird, all aflutter, not settling for even a moment. He'd eaten many breakfasts at that table with her just like this, cooking, cleaning, and puttering behind him.

"What is it you want from me, Miss Rose?" His voice was gentler than it'd been in a long time. There weren't many people who made him feel gentle. None of the women in the last sixteen years of his life had brought out that particular emotion.

The old lady glanced at him, her blue eyes and white hair reminding him of a cloudy summer sky. He had never known either of his grandmothers—his father's mother had died before he was born, and his mother's mother had never cared to meet her daughter's family—so Miss Rose was the closest he'd ever found. When she died, as she inevitably would, he would be alone. There wouldn't be anybody left to care about him, no one to find disappointment in his failures, to regret what he could have been, to mourn what he had become. He would be utterly alone.

"It's a beautiful day. Let's not spoil it with such talk."

Her answer didn't sit well with him. Was the request she had to make so repugnant that it could ruin a hot summer day? He'd been wondering for days now exactly why she was calling him back home. His mind had come up with possibilities: that she was sick, that she'd learned the truth about Melanie, that she needed some help that only he could give her. But since his arrival yesterday, he'd discounted all of them. She wasn't sick, and she certainly didn't seem to have any qualms over her failure to trust him about Melanie. And as for that last idea . . . Hell, there was nothing he could do that a million other people couldn't do better.

"It's a fair question, Miss Rose," he pointed out, earning a narrow-eyed look from her. "You tracked me down—"

"Which wouldn't have been so difficult if you had kept in touch with me after you left here."

"And you asked me to come—" He almost said home, *almost*, but he caught the word and choked it down, "back. I did. Now the least you can do is tell me why."

"Don't be so impatient," she admonished. "You haven't even been here long enough to relax and unpack. Don't fret, Will. I'll tell you what you want to know . . . all in good time. Now why don't you step outside and call Celine? By the time she washes up, I'll have the food on the table."

He knew it was useless to argue with her, useless to try to force a response that she didn't want to give. With a sigh, he left his glass on the counter and went out the back door, approaching Celine as she maneuvered the mower around the steps of the guesthouse. Unaware of his presence, she backed up and right into him, her bottom coming into close contact with his groin. Before he even had a chance to enjoy it, she jerked away, letting the engine die, and gave him a withering glare that he could feel even with her eyes obscured by sunglasses. "What do you want?"

He smiled innocently. "Breakfast is ready. Miss Rose says come on in and wash up."

"I'll be there in a minute."

Last evening he had been surprised by her calmness, until he had realized that she wasn't going to dare get close to him. Now he knew it was an act. He made her uncomfortable. He got under her skin, like an annoying splinter that was just below the surface, just out of reach. He fully intended to keep annoying her, to keep tempting himself.

She left the mower where it was and headed for her own house. Will had hoped she would wash up in Miss Rose's kitchen, where he could watch her splash cool water over her heated skin, where he could witness the effect of mechanically cooled air on her breasts. He wanted another excuse to lust. He needed another reassurance that nothing would come of it.

Shoving his hands in his pockets, he waited near the side door that led to the cottage porch. According to Miss Rose, Celine had been living in this house for nearly six years. The old lady had a habit of taking in strays. He hadn't been the first, and Celine probably wouldn't be the last.

Briefly he tried to picture her inside. In her long modest dresses with her long hair somehow restrained, she would fit right in with the old house and the old furniture. He could picture her fitting all too well in the old iron bedstead that filled half the bedroom.

The door around front alerted him to her return. She had changed from shorts into one of those damnable skirts, had traded the grass-stained tennis shoes for rubber thongs, and had put a white shirt on over the cotton tank top, buttoning only the bottom half. She had already washed up, too. The tendrils of hair that framed her face curled damply, and wet spots had already soaked from the top through her outer shirt.

"No need to get all covered up on my account."

"I didn't," she replied smoothly. "Miss Rose doesn't care to get too casual. She still dresses for dinner, you know."

Of course he knew. He had endured many a meal in dress shirt and tie before the old lady had decided that a clean T-shirt and clean hands were the best she could realistically expect from a wayward ten-year-old. "Do meals come with your rent?"

Celine gave him a long look. The question seemed innocent enough, but with Will, who could tell? She'd heard her father tell her mother once that Billy Ray Beaumont had been born knowing more than most people learned by the time they were thirty. And *she* was still two years shy of the mark.

"Sometimes she invites me over for breakfast or Sunday dinner. And sometimes when it's particularly hot, she fixes a batch of—"

"Homemade peach ice cream," he finished for her. "When I first left here, I used to have dreams about her peach ice cream."

"So why didn't you come back?" she asked directly. "Was it because of Melanie? Or Raymond? Was that your agreement with him?"

He scowled a little too fiercely. "I told you I never agreed with him about anything."

Celine stopped at the bottom of the steps that led to Miss Rose's screened back porch. "Having an agreement and agreeing with someone are two different things. You're playing with words."

As quickly as it came, the scowl disappeared and was replaced with a look that couldn't be anything less than a leer. "Maybe you'd prefer that I play with you," he suggested, his voice silky soft. "That could be arranged, little girl."

Somewhere deep inside she was disappointed by his evasion, but she didn't let it show. Instead, she merely raised one brow mockingly before turning and climbing the four steps to the porch.

Chapter Two

Sunday morning in Harmony was given over to church. The only businesses open were the grocery store downtown and the gas stations along the main street. Everything else was quiet except for the many churches in and around Harmony.

Celine slipped into her heels, then checked her reflection in the cheval mirror opposite the bed. The dress had been a gift from her mother, muted peaches, corals, and greens on a white background of finely woven linen—something pretty, Annalise had said, to set off her eyes.

Her intention had been a little more than setting off her daughter's eyes, Celine knew. Her mother was afraid Celine would never find a husband, not when she spent her work hours in the library and her free time out here. The fact that she wasn't *looking* for a husband was irrelevant to Annalise. She was a Southern woman, and it was every Southern woman's duty to find a mate for her daughters, whether they wanted one or not.

Still, the dress was pretty, even if the only time she ever wore it was to church, where she wasn't likely to find a man of interest. But if she wanted a man of interest, she need look no farther than her own backyard.

To Will Beaumont.

Grimacing at her reflection, she picked up her handbag

and left the bedroom. Miss Rose would be waiting on her gallery, as she'd waited every Sunday for the last six years. The Hunters and the Kendalls attended the same church, so she always gave the old lady a ride. After church, if Raymond and Frannie had other plans, Celine would bring Miss Rose home and sometimes have Sunday dinner with her. Otherwise, Raymond chauffeured his mother home while Celine had dinner with her own family.

Miss Rose was waiting, but not in a comfortable chair on the porch. She was standing in the grass midway between all three houses, her attention directed to the steps of the guesthouse. "You sure you won't come with us?" she was asking as Celine came down the side steps.

Will was sitting in front of his door, much as he'd done yesterday morning, looking as sleepy and disreputable and wickedly handsome as he had then. His grin was wide and just a little bit mocking, but there was nothing but respect in his voice as he replied, "Yes, ma'am, I'm sure." His gaze shifted from Miss Rose to Celine as she joined the older woman. "Good morning, Miss Celine."

In spite of his declaration yesterday morning—*I think I'll call you Celie*—he hadn't done it yet. She was grateful. Celie was her own secret name for herself, one that she had always coveted for her own. She had even once asked her mother to start calling her that, but Annalise had just laughed and told her not to be silly. Celine was a perfectly fine name, good and sensible for a good and sensible girl.

But at thirteen she hadn't wanted to be sensible. She wasn't certain, if Will started calling her Celie, that she would ever want to be sensible again.

"Good morning." She sounded stiff and unfriendly, but she couldn't help it. "Miss Rose, we're going to be late."

"Well, if you won't change your mind . . ." Miss Rose paused, and Will gave a shake of his head. "I'm going to Raymond's after the service. The back door's unlocked, and there's turkey and ham in the refrigerator for sandwiches."

"Maybe I can persuade Celine to join me."

"No," Celine replied abruptly, and his grin grew even wider. "I've got plans." Touching Miss Rose's arm, she turned toward her car, parked on the far side of the house.

They were halfway into town when Miss Rose spoke. "Maybe I should go on home after the service. I can have dinner with Raymond and Frannie any time."

"I think Will can amuse himself for a few hours."

"I worry about that boy."

Celine's automatic response was to remind Miss Rose that, at thirty-four, he was hardly a boy, but she held it back. To a seventy-something-year-old woman, thirty-four was barely grown. "He can take care of himself."

The look Miss Rose gave her was tinged with acerbity. "Of course he can. He's been doing it most of his life. But that doesn't mean it wouldn't be easier if he had someone who cared about him."

Celine felt a shade guilty. Miss Rose was right. Will *had* spent the better part of his life with no one to count on but himself. Even his own mother had let him down. But did that excuse the way he behaved, the outrageous things he said and did, the way he treated others? Did that account for his running out on his own son?

She couldn't say. She'd always known that her parents loved her, no matter how ditzy or empty-headed they were. Even through all the times when she had felt like a parent herself, organizing and running the family because they couldn't, she had been certain of their love.

Will had lost that certainty of being loved when he was ten years old, when his father died and his mother disappeared.

The First Baptist Church was located a block or two from downtown Harmony. It was a big redbrick building with white columns and arched stained glass windows. With the possible exception of St. Michael's, it was the largest church in town, and it was where society, such as it was in a town like Harmony, worshiped.

Miss Rose left Celine at the door and joined her family on a pew near the front. Celine's own family was a few rows behind them. Ordinarily, she would join them, sitting between Vickie's two boys to keep them from fussing and fidgeting throughout the service, but this morning she chose instead to sit at the back.

Her mind wandered all through the prayers and hymns and the pastor's drawn-out sermon. It seemed such a peaceful scene, filled with peaceful people, but appearances were all too often deceiving. Raymond looked as if he didn't have a care in the world. Jock Robinson was his usual quiet, remote self, but she knew he must be brooding over Will's return. And Jared Robinson . . .

He was fifteen, as quiet as his grandfather, as attractive as his mother, as unpredictable as his father. He spent a good deal of time in the library, looking for something that he seemed unable to find elsewhere. Answers? Knowledge? A way out of this town?

How ironic that, just as Will's mother had abandoned him as a boy, so had his son been abandoned. Jared hadn't been more than seven years old when Melanie had left him at his grandparents' house for a few days and had never come back for him. She had visited from time to time—always in the company of a new man—but she'd made it clear that she wanted no permanent place in her son's life. That must be a difficult burden for Jared to bear. Celine felt sorry for the kid.

Why had she no sympathy to spare for Will, who had received not the same treatment but worse? she wondered cynically. At least Melanie had left Jared with loving grandparents. At least she did occasionally return to see him. Will's mother had just left him, period. He'd been alone for days before his abandonment had finally come to anyone's attention, and, in the eight years he had remained in Harmony, he had never seen her again.

It was just hard to feel sorry for someone who looked at her the way he did, for someone who was so cocky, so insolent, so bold. For someone who knew exactly what he wanted and took it, with no regard for the consequences.

Jared was an innocent child. Will had never been innocent.

She wondered what Jared thought of Will's return. Did he have any curiosity about the man who had helped bring him into this world? Was he anxious to meet him, to be acknowledged by him? Or was he bitter? Had Jock's anger and resentment rubbed off on the boy? Did he blame Will, as the Robinsons did, for everything that had gone wrong in his and his mother's lives?

The end of the sermon came as a surprise to her. She hadn't heard a word the preacher had said, and she felt more than a little guilty. Still, guilty or not, she decided to make a quick escape before the handshakes and the after-church socializing—and before the inevitable questions began. She could get in her car and go for a long drive. She could follow the winding road to New Orleans and have dinner alone in the Quarter. She could take the nearby interstate to Baton Rouge and beyond. But she couldn't put off facing her family and friends forever.

So she smiled and greeted those who wanted to talk and begged off the only subject they wanted to talk about. She worked her way slowly out the door and inched across the lawn toward her car. She was safely there when Raymond Kendall called her name.

"I assume he's still there," he said flatly.

Celine unlocked her car, then opened the door so the heat could seep out. "Yes, he is."

"Have you found out yet what he wants?"

"I haven't been trying."

"Well, why don't you?"

She gazed across the roof of her car from Raymond to his wife, standing at his side. They were an attractive couple, both in their mid-forties but looking ten years younger. Being able to afford the best could do that for you. It didn't seem quite fair, though, that such intense selfishness and greed didn't show somewhere on either face. "It's really none of my business, Raymond."

"I'm offering to make it your business."

She simply waited.

"I'll pay you to keep an eye on him and Mama, to tell me what's going on."

"You want me to spy on them." He was more unbalanced by Will's return than she had realized. He usually had more finesse than this, more charm. It didn't matter how charming he was. What he was suggesting was out of the question.

Something in her tone must have alerted him, because he suddenly smiled engagingly. "Now I wouldn't call it that, Celine. But you must realize that my concern for Mama is overriding—"

"Yes," Frannie interrupted, giving him a sharp look. "We want you to spy on them. We'll make it worth your while."

Again Celine looked at them, waiting.

"Miss Rose is old," Frannie continued. "Her judgment isn't always the best, and, of course, she's always had a soft spot for Billy Ray, who's always had a soft spot for easy touches. We're trying to protect her, Celine. Caring about her the way you do, you understand that, don't you?"

She should get in the car and drive away, but, damn it, Frannie had a point. Miss Rose *was* extraordinarily fond of Will, who wasn't, based on his reputation, the most trustworthy man in the parish. Yet Will had assured her that she had no cause to worry on Miss Rose's behalf, that he was here only because she had asked him to come.

Will had also assured her that she had no reason to worry for herself. Had that been before or after he'd commented on how she'd grown, before or after he'd given her that stripped-naked look?

Oh, she would keep an eye on them, all right. She would watch every move Will Beaumont made, and she would try to find out why Miss Rose had brought him back; but she wouldn't do it for Raymond and Frannie, or their money. She would do it because she did care about Miss Rose, and because she didn't trust Will.

"I'm not interested," she replied evenly. Climbing into the car, she slammed the door on Raymond's protest, started the engine, and backed out of the parking space. Her parents were already gone, she saw with a glance toward the corner where they always parked, and Vickie and Richard were loading their three kids into their own car. One encounter down, one more to go.

Her parents would be curious about Will, but having married off the susceptible daughter and confident of the other's eminent sensibility, they wouldn't believe the Hunter family had any reason for concern. Vickie's husband, Richard, wasn't native to Harmony and wouldn't understand all the fuss over one less-than-respectable drifter.

Celine wasn't sure what to expect from Vickie, though. After only a couple of dates, she had been convinced that Will was her first great love; and the way the relationship had ended had added some small measure of significance, some thin layer of drama, to the romance. If their parents hadn't interfered, Will would have soon grown tired of her as he had of every girl before her, and he would have moved on. Because their parents *had* interfered, she had been able to convince herself that she had also been his great love, that something special and different had been brought to a premature and tragic end. Grown now, a wife and a mother, Vickie still felt a need to believe in something special and different.

The Hunter house was on a quiet, tree-lined street three blocks over from the church. Originally white, it had gone through a series of changes over the years—from pink to pale blue, kelly green to salmon, sunshine yellow, and drab brown—to match her mother's current mood. Judging by the soft gentle shade of peach that colored it now, things must be looking up in Annalise's life.

When Celine walked in, her father was in his favorite chair with the Baton Rouge newspaper, and her mother was in the kitchen, putting the final touches on the dinner she'd started before church. "You were almost late today."

Celine took an apron from the hook on the kitchen door and slipped it over her head, tying the ties loosely around her waist. "We made it before the service started."

"Things must be pretty stirred up out there."

Her mother had always referred to Celine's house as if she were languishing somewhere out in the back of beyond instead of a mere mile and a half from downtown Harmony. *Why do you want to live way out there?* she had asked when Celine had come home after graduation to take the library job and Miss Rose had offered her cottage for rent. *You have a perfectly good room right here.*

A place of her own was the one thing Celine had been looking for all her life: a place that got dirty only if *she* dirtied it; a place where everything stayed exactly where she'd left it; a place that was neat and orderly. Her parents had driven home from church less than ten minutes earlier; but when they got ready to return for this evening's service, they would first have to search for the car keys. Her mother was wearing her glasses right now, but soon she would take them off, only to find them later in the refrigerator or the dishwasher or tucked into one of the planters around the house. Celine had had enough of that sort of chaos growing up. She wanted privacy now.

"No, actually they haven't been," she replied evenly. "It's been so quiet, you'd hardly know anyone was there."

"But he is staying out there, isn't he?"

He. Will was such a popular topic of conversation lately that a person didn't even need to mention his name. *He,* in that angry or interested tone of voice, made it perfectly clear whom they were talking about.

"Yes, Mama, he is."

Celine took over cutting out the biscuits on the floured counter so her mother could start the gravy. She'd cut out only three fat rounds when Annalise prompted, "Well? What do you think?"

"I think everything's been exaggerated all out of proportion. I think the folks in this town are just too incredibly nosy for their own good. I think everyone around here needs a hobby of some sort."

Her mother laughed softly. "We can always count on you to put things into perspective, can't we? I wish Vickie had even a tenth of your common sense; but she was always the romantic, and you were the realist."

Celine jabbed the biscuit cutter into the dough with more force than necessary. She'd been the realist because they had given her no choice, but didn't they realize that *she'd* had dreams, too, that she had also wanted romance?

She had wanted to be Vickie—not as vain, not as silly, but she had wanted some portion of her sister's dreamy, romantic nature. She had wanted the permission Vickie had always been granted, the permission *she* had always been denied, to not be realistic.

The slam of the front door indicating the Jourdans' arrival interrupted her thoughts. The boys, four and six, were fussing as they always did, and three-year-old Amy was exclaiming loudly over something or other. Celine knew her sister well enough to know that Vickie, who generally avoided the kitchen when there was work to be done, would be back here, eager to gossip, in a matter of minutes, and she wasn't disappointed. Trailing Amy behind her like a shadow,

Vickie came through the swinging door less than three minutes later.

Amy pressed past her mother and headed straight for Celine, tugging with grimy hands at the hem of her dress. "Wanna' help," she demanded, imperiously raising her arms to be picked up.

"Not this time, sweetie." Celine transferred the biscuits to the baking sheet, spread more flour on the counter, and prepared to roll out the next batch. At her feet, her niece was preparing to throw a full-fledged temper tantrum.

"Oh, for heaven's sake, Celine, let her help," Vickie said, lifting the girl onto the counter, where she promptly grabbed a handful of flour and patted it over her face.

This was her only niece, Celine reminded herself, the only daughter of the sister and brother-in-law she loved. It wasn't Amy's fault that she received no discipline from either parent or her grandparents, that she, like her brothers, was a first-class brat. Celine loved her best from a distance.

Vickie made no pretense of helping, but leaned against the sink where she could watch Celine. "So . . . tell us about Billy Ray."

"There's nothing to tell." Celine scooted Amy back, then rolled out the dough. It wasn't easy, keeping both hands on the rolling pin while two smaller hands tried to undo her work.

"Well, he is living there, isn't he?"

"For the time being."

"Why'd he come back?"

That was the million-dollar question, on everyone's minds, it seemed. "I don't know."

"Haven't you even seen him?"

She thought of their brief meeting Friday evening, of their even briefer conversation Saturday morning—*I think I'll call you Celie*—and his suggestion before breakfast. *Maybe you'd prefer that I play with you. That could be arranged, little girl.*

With an innocent expression and a clear conscience, she lied. "He keeps pretty much to himself."

So far this morning, she thought grimly as she transferred

the biscuits from the counter to the pan for baking, she had sat in judgment of others, had sworn, and now, right in front of her mother, her innocent little niece and God, she had lied.

Church certainly hadn't done her much good this morning.

Will had never been much of a churchgoer, not since his father had died. He had been close to his father, and losing him had been almost more than he could bear. It had put an end to his interest in church. A God who would take his father's life when he was still so young and had a son to rear wasn't anyone Will wanted to know on a personal basis. Of course, later, he'd gone regularly with Miss Rose because it was expected of him, but he'd felt nothing but disdain for the people there. The folks who wore their fine clothes, paid their tithes, and prayed out loud and long were the same folks who thought he was a bad influence on their children, who didn't want him around their daughters, who agreed with Raymond that Miss Rose should have let the courts place him in a state home.

Still, it might have been interesting, walking into church this morning. Just seeing the looks on the hypocrites' faces would have been worth whatever discomfort he would have felt.

The afternoon was passing slowly. It was hardly two o'clock when it seemed as if it should be at least six or seven. He wished someone would come home—either Miss Rose, who he knew from experience would settle into her old battered recliner for an afternoon nap, or Celine. He wasn't picky. He didn't care which one.

It wasn't that he was lonely. He was used to his own company. Moving around the way he had for the last sixteen years, he'd never made any friends—just casual acquaintances, distrusting bosses, and women. Clinging women, tough women, manipulative, bitchy women. There had been the ones who'd wanted him because he was new, or because they thought he was dangerous. Some had been intrigued because he wasn't acceptable; others, because he looked mean, or because they wanted to make some other guy jealous. Too many women, too many reasons.

But he'd never had a woman like Celine Hunter.

Damn right he wasn't lonely, he thought with a grin. He was just horny as hell, and all for the wrong woman.

Leaving the shade of the live oak, he headed for the storage shed around back. If he sat there thinking about how much he wanted Celine in bed, she wouldn't have a chance when she finally did come home. He would drag her off, consequences be damned. Better to put his time and energy into something more constructive, like working on that ancient mower she had used to cut the grass yesterday.

He was searching for the tools he knew Miss Rose kept somewhere in the shed when a voice, quiet and authoritative but not threatening, called his name. Coming out of the shed, toolbox in hand, he saw the man, wearing brown trousers and a tan uniform shirt, then the car parked out front. A sheriff's car.

He felt a sinking feeling in the pit of his stomach. He'd been rousted by more than a few law officers in his lifetime, most of them restrained and all business, a few just waiting for an excuse to exercise a little excessive force. It was hard to tell about this one.

"Remember me? Mitch Franklin?" He loosened the tie around his neck, then began rolling his sleeves up. "I was a deputy when you left here before."

Will didn't remember. Because of Miss Rose, he'd tried to avoid run-ins with the cops back then.

"Raymond Kendall asked me to come over and have a little chat with you."

Bending, Will set the toolbox on the ground so his hands would be free. Just in case it was necessary. "What favor are you going to do for Raymond? Send me on my way? Tell me I'm not wanted in your parish? Or does he have something a little more involved in mind? A trumped-up charge or two, maybe?"

"What Raymond wants doesn't matter much to me. Like I told him, as long as you stay out here and mind your own business, there's nothing I can do."

"And what if I go into town? What if I decide to visit some old friends, old hangouts?"

"You don't have any old friends here, Beaumont. You go

into town, all you're going to run into is people who don't want you here."

"People like Raymond." Will paused. "And Jock Robinson."

The sheriff nodded. "Word around town is that Jock damned near took his house apart when he heard you were back. If he gets the chance, he'll take *you* apart."

"He can try." Will's attitude was cocky, but it was a bluff. He had no doubt whatsoever that Jock Robinson could do a hell of a lot more than try. He was bigger, stronger, heavier, and he'd been feeding off his hatred for Will for sixteen years now.

"I don't want any trouble, Beaumont, not from you and not because of you. Find out whatever it is Miss Rose wants from you, do it, and then get out of Harmony. It'll be better all around." His piece spoken, the sheriff turned to leave. Fifteen feet away, though, he turned back as if he'd just remembered something. "By the way, Billy Ray, where was it Miss Rose finally found you?"

"Alabama."

"Exactly where in Alabama?"

Over the sheriff's shoulder, Will saw a familiar little blue car pull into the driveway beside Celine's house. Futilely he wished she'd been ten minutes slower, or the sheriff ten minutes quicker. He wished she didn't have to see the sheriff here, obviously on official business. He wished she wouldn't think what, of course, she would. "A little town called Walker."

The sheriff glanced around as Celine got out of her car. She was watching them curiously, and he dipped his head in her direction. "One other question, and then I'll let you get back to your business."

His muscles stiffening, his stance growing rigid, Will waited.

"If you were to leave Harmony today and head back to Walker, Alabama, would they let you stay?"

"I don't believe they could stop me," he replied, then very softly added, "yet."

Satisfied, the sheriff nodded, then left. When he passed Celine near her house, he nodded again and offered her a respectful greeting. She watched him leave, then slowly approached Will near the shed. "What did he want?"

"To talk."

"About what?"

He bent to pick up the toolbox again, then fixed an annoyed frown on her. "If it concerned you, he would have told you."

She glanced at the road, empty now, then back at him. "Was he here because of Raymond?"

"He was here because of *me*. He wanted to talk to me. Now mind your own business, Celie."

Grabbing the lawn mower with one hand, he pulled it backwards across the lawn to the nearest shade tree. He didn't look back at her as he dropped to his knees on the spongy ground and opened the toolbox, searching through rusty and ill-cared-for tools for the ones he needed. Maybe if he pretended to ignore her, she would go away. Then he could work on truly ignoring her.

"What is it about you that bothers Raymond so much?"

"Go ask Raymond."

"I'm asking you." She came closer until her feet were in his field of vision: slender feet in shiny stockings and white shoes. Slender feet that led to slender ankles and long, long legs that could wrap their way right around a man and pull him in so deep that he would never get free . . . provided he was fool enough to try. A wise man would just stay there, lost inside her.

He picked out a wrench, then tossed it back into the box and got to his feet. "You're a bright little girl, aren't you, Celie? You can figure it out. Raymond is a Kendall, and Kendalls are mighty important people around here. Beaumonts have never amounted to shit. He never liked having me live in his family home. He didn't want me sitting down to dinner just like one of them, sitting in their antique chairs, eating off his great-grandma's china. He didn't want his mama treating me like one of the family. He didn't want me to start thinking that I *was* part of the family. He didn't want me to forget that I was just another charity case, just one more of Miss Rose's throwaways."

He had moved closer to her while he was talking, so close that he could look right into her pretty green eyes. So close that he could smell the fragrance of her perfume. So close that he could see each tiny rise and fall of her breasts as she breathed.

And he moved closer yet, wanting her to retreat, to forget her questions and think about her safety and get the hell away from him. But she didn't. She held her ground and quietly disagreed with him. "I don't think that's all of it. Your coming back has unsettled him. You've made him uneasy."

"I make a lot of people uneasy," he answered softly.

Before she could even draw breath to respond, he raised his hand and pushed a strand of her hair into place. She was wearing it down today, straight down her back. He touched it with the back of his hand so he couldn't easily recognize its texture or silkiness, and he didn't linger over it.

"I make *you* uneasy, don't I, Celie?" he murmured.

She held his gaze for a moment, her eyes clear, her lips parted. Then she broke the contact and looked down. They were so close that if she took a deep breath, her breasts would brush his chest. If she relaxed her stiff posture one bit, their bodies would touch. Chest to chest, belly to belly, hips to womanly soft hips. Just the thought was making him hot, and the nearness was making him hard. In another moment the swelling of his erection would be impossible to hide. In another moment she wouldn't have to move to bring their bodies together. He would do it himself.

"He offered me money."

Jerking his gaze back up, he saw that she was watching him again. Her expression was serious, her voice unintentionally provocative. For a moment his mind was muddled. Money interjected into his thoughts of steamy, hot sex struck a discordant note. "Who offered you money? For what?"

"Raymond. For watching you."

He took a step back. "Watching me?"

"For spying on you. For reporting back to him about you."

Another step back brought him up against the mower. He pushed it out of the way, then wrapped his fingers around the handle. "And what did you tell him, Celie?"

"My name is Celine."

"I like Celie. It suits you."

"It suits a child, and I'm not a child. I'm twenty-eight years old."

He grinned even though he had to force it. Even though the last thing he wanted to do right now was talk. Even though the only thing he wanted now was to crawl inside her. It wouldn't be hard—unzip his jeans, pull down her stockings, brace her against the tree and slide deep inside. She would be wet and tight, and he would be achingly hard. It would take no more than that for him to finish.

Wrong thoughts. Wrong woman. Damn it, she would always be the wrong woman for him.

"You're a real woman of the world, aren't you?" he taunted. "Tell me, Celie, how many lovers have you had? Two? One? None?"

She repeated his earlier words to him. "Mind your own business, Billy Ray."

He knelt beside the mower again and once more started sorting through the tools. "So what did you tell Raymond?"

"That I wasn't interested."

"In his plan? His money? Him?" He glanced up and grinned, then looked away again before their eyes could connect. "Or in me?"

"He doesn't trust you."

"No, ma'am, he doesn't, which is just fine." Again he looked at her, but this time he was serious. This time he made sure she saw it. "Because I'm not trustworthy. You turn your back on me, Miss Celie, and I'm liable to take everything you hold dear." He paused for his words to sink in, then gave her a hard look. "You've been warned."

"Is that why the sheriff was here? Was he warning you?"

Damn the woman, she was persistent. Had he actually thought a moment ago that she might run away? She didn't have the sense to do it. "Why the sheriff was here was my business."

"Are you in trouble?"

At that he tilted his head back and laughed. "Honey, I've been in one sort of trouble or another for most of my life."

"Are you in trouble *here*?"

"How could I be in trouble here? I've only been here a

couple of days, and I haven't set foot off Miss Rose's property since I got here. Exactly what is it that you think I might have done in that time to attract the sheriff's attention?''

Celine moved farther into the shade. She was hot, her pantyhose were clinging to her like a second skin, and her feet were starting to ache in the low-heeled sandals she wore. Since Will was obviously determined to be difficult, she should follow her earlier instincts when she'd seen Sheriff Franklin's car and go inside her house where she could ignore everything else. Where she could strip out of her clothes, take an aspirin for this headache, and sleep the rest of the afternoon away, the way Miss Rose did most Sundays.

Stubbornly she stayed where she was. "A man like you attracts attention even without doing anything," she said flatly, and Will gave her a wicked smile that made her stomach clench so tight that it hurt.

"Why, Miss Celine, that sounds almost like a compliment.''

Ignoring him, she continued. "Everyone at church wanted to talk about you. Even my family was curious.''

"Even your family?" He tilted the lawn mower back, then weighted the handle with the toolbox. "You say it as if that's unusual. As if they're above gossiping like the common folks, I don't remember the Hunters as being any different. They were just as prejudiced and judgmental as everyone else.''

"My sister was especially curious.''

"Your sister . . . Oh, Vickie.'' He removed the blade from the mower and examined it, then tossed it at her feet. "How long has it been since the blade's been changed?''

"I don't know. Awhile.'' Bracing her hands behind her to protect her dress, she leaned against the tree. "Vickie's married now. They have three kids.''

He didn't reply, but the look he gave her spoke volumes. Vickie could be married with children, or she could have turned green and grown antennae. He couldn't care less. Did he even remember her sister? she wondered. Friday evening he had given the impression he did, and he had certainly seemed to remember *her*. Maybe he really had. Or maybe Miss Rose had given him the information he'd needed in the hours before she'd come home.

"All the girls you went to school with are married now," she continued, watching the back of his head as he worked. His hair was black and cut short, and it looked softer than her own. The color was pure and gleaming, the texture silky, the style careless but flattering.

"Is that another warning?"

"Another?" she echoed. "Was the sheriff warning you, too?"

Sitting back on his heels, he gave her a long, exasperated look. "The sheriff was doing what sheriffs and police chiefs in small towns like this always do with strangers. He was making sure I understood the way things stand."

He sounded so stiff and annoyed that she wished she had dropped the subject. Before she could start feeling too bad, though, he conjured up that arrogant grin again. "The more interesting question, though, is why you're warning me off the ladies in town. Are you afraid I'll upset your friends' easy, complacent lives?" The grin got bigger, and his voice got softer. "Or do you want me for yourself, Celie?"

She pushed herself away from the tree and walked over to stand right beside him. "You know, Will, it's not so much that people here want to dislike you," she said with a calmness that she might never feel again. "It's just that you don't give them any other choice."

She walked away then, aware of his gaze on her back until she reached the privacy of the porch. Inside the house she walked through the gloomy living room to the bedroom, where she closed the shades before she began undressing. The headache that had started at her parents' house was pounding now, doubled in intensity after only a few moments with Will.

He was obnoxious. Arrogant. Too handsome for his own good. Too handsome for *her* own good. And, damn it all, he was probably right. She probably *had* pointed out the marital status of his old girlfriends for selfish reasons. Maybe she had wanted to place everyone else off-limits so that she would be his only choice when he went looking for a woman . . . as he inevitably would.

As if *she* had anything to offer a man like him. She hadn't answered his question about lovers earlier, but he'd guessed right the first time. Two men in twenty-eight years. Neither had been exciting or particularly sexy or particularly talented—and neither of them had been particularly impressed with her. The first had left her for another woman—*another woman*? She would have laughed if she hadn't been afraid she would choke on it. Her sister certainly qualified as a woman, and she had done very well as the *other* woman. The second man Celine had become involved with had simply left her, period.

Will was exciting and sexy, and there was no question that he was particularly talented. He was too comfortable with his body not to be, and too experienced, too sensual. He could make a woman feel things she hadn't even thought of. He could give new meaning to the concept of arousal, of wanting, of needing. And he could break her heart.

She draped her dress across the chair in the corner so she would remember to take it to the cleaners this week. Encounters with her niece usually left her dirty or stained in some way, and today had been no exception.

After washing down an aspirin with a cup of warm water, she turned on the ceiling fan, ran a brush through her hair, then stretched out across the bed. She needed a few hours of undisturbed sleep. A few hours of blissful sleep to allow her body time to heal, to give her mind a chance to relax. Then she could face life again.

His grandparents were fighting again. Jared Robinson retreated into his room, as he always did, and closed the door on his grandfather's shouts and his grandmother's grating whine. He loved them, and he was grateful to them for taking him in and giving him a home when his mother had decided she didn't want him anymore; but there were times when he wished he were far, far away. As his father had always been. Until now.

He sprawled across the bed, his hands under his head, and watched the progress of a spider as it traveled across the ceiling. When he had first heard the news Friday that Billy Ray Beaumont was back, he had been curious and, though he was ashamed to admit it, a little hopeful. Maybe Billy

Ray had come back for *him*, the son he had never acknowledged, the son he had always sworn wasn't his.

Yeah, right. He'd been an idiot for even thinking it, much less hoping for it. Beaumont had been here three days now, and he hadn't tried to see Jared. He hadn't tried to contact him. He hadn't shown any interest in apologizing for all the trouble he'd caused him.

If Billy Ray were any sort of man, his grandfather had said, he would have accepted responsibility for Jared. He would have married Melanie; and even if that had ended in divorce, he would have helped support his kid. According to Grandpa, Billy Ray was to blame for everything wrong in the last sixteen years.

The spider overhead reached the light fixture in the center of the room and became still. Most people rarely looked overhead. They wouldn't even notice it there. That was how Jared felt sometimes—unnoticed, overlooked.

It wasn't anybody's fault that Melanie wasn't cut out to be a mother; she'd just gotten pregnant too young, Grandma had explained. She hadn't had time to be a kid, so being a mother was harder for her. Jared knew that wasn't entirely true. At fifteen he had better parental instincts than his mother ever would.

She was selfish. She drank too much, experimented with too many drugs. She slept with whoever wanted her, and she took money for it. She drank and cussed and just generally didn't give a damn about anyone but herself. Jared had simply gotten in her way—he had realized that at an early age. It was hard to go out drinking all night when you had a kid waiting at home, to attract men when you were spending your money taking care of a kid instead of yourself. It was hard to hold on to a man when you had a son, especially one whose silence was taken for insolence.

For all her faults, though, she was his mother. He pitied her, and he resented her, but he also loved her, as much as he was able.

Billy Ray Beaumont was a different story. He had faults, too, more than Melanie could ever be accused of. He'd made an art out of selfishness. She had told him once when she

was drunk and feeling sorry for herself how she had begged
Billy Ray in front of her parents and old Miss Rose to tell
the truth, to admit that he was the father of her baby, and
how he had stood there, just as cold and mean as you please,
and flat lied. He had left town rather than admit it.

And now he had come back. Not because he was feeling
guilty or remorseful. Not because he wanted anything to do
with his son.

Rolling onto his side, Jared pulled a photo album from the
nightstand drawer. Most of the pictures in it were old. Melanie
had loved having her picture taken, until she'd seen one that
showed how poorly she was aging. Years of drinking and
sleeping around, of hard living and hard men, had taken their
toll on her. Rather than give up her lifestyle, she had given
up the photographs.

She had been pretty when she was young—the prettiest
girl in town, his grandfather liked to boast, and it must have
been true. Golden-haired and blue-eyed, she'd had a delicate
look about her, almost angelic. He could understand why
Billy Ray Beaumont and all the men who had followed had
been drawn to her. She had been warm and funny and quick
to laugh. Even her pouting—something she'd done far too
much of—had been adorable.

Billy Ray had changed all that. He had made so many lives
hell—Melanie's, Grandma's and Grandpa's, and Jared's,
too. Everyone had suffered except *him*.

Letting the album close, Jared turned to watch the spider
again. He had reached the opposite wall now and was slowly
climbing down across a New Orleans Saints pennant to a
poster of Jared's favorite rock band. He waited until the spider
had cleared the poster, then rose from the bed, stealthily
approached the wall, and, with one quick movement, pressed
his thumb against the spider, trapping it, squashing it, leaving
a dark stain against the white wall.

Yeah. Now that Billy Ray was back, he just might have
to pay for what he'd done.

The heat was relentless.

Will sat on the gallery that fronted Miss Rose's house, a
tall glass of lemonade in hand. He was as sweaty as the glass,

his clothes sticking to him, drops of perspiration trickling down his spine, making him uncomfortable. She had invited him inside when he'd joined her here a few minutes ago, but he had politely refused. It wasn't much cooler there—the air-conditioning hurt the old lady's joints—and at least out here it was bright and sunny.

Out here he would see Celine when she came home. It had been four days since their last conversation. Since then he had caught only glimpses of her, and those only because he'd watched. He stood at the window each morning, waiting for her to leave for work, and he waited each evening for her to come home. If she was aware of him, she didn't let it show. But that was all right. *He* had more than enough awareness for them both. Three of those four mornings, he had awakened with an itch that had swollen into an all-out erection just at the sight of her. That rich, thick hair, those long swirling skirts that hid longer, lean legs, the unconscious sway of her hips as she walked, the soft curves of her breasts, the throaty sound of her voice as she called across the yard to Miss Rose—damn it all, it was almost enough to make him come right there at the window without so much as a touch, a caress, or even a look from her.

The heat was relentless, all right—and most of it came from *her*.

"If you'd like to go out somewhere, you're welcome to use my car," Miss Rose announced.

Will gave her a sidelong look. She had never volunteered the use of her car unless she were right beside him in the front seat. It wasn't that she didn't trust him, she had always insisted. It was just that the car meant so much to her. It had been her last gift from Wynn before he'd died. It was solid as a tank, guzzled gas the way a body guzzled fluids in this summer heat, and looked brand-new after some thirty-odd years.

"Thank you," he replied. "But I don't imagine I'll be going anywhere." As the sheriff had pointed out, he didn't have any friends here, and as Celine had been so kind as to make clear, all the girls he'd known growing up were married. Although she certainly didn't seem to expect anything so honest and decent as morals from him, he wasn't going to mess around with another man's woman. There was no surer way to get himself into trouble.

He finished his lemonade and refilled the glass from the pitcher on the table, then settled back. The wicker creaked comfortably beneath him, but the comfort disappeared when she broke the silence between them.

"Have you ever been happy, Will?"

Of all the things she could have asked him, that was the one he least expected. Happy? Of course he had been before his dad died and, to a lesser extent, during the time he'd lived here. But happiness was something he'd grown away from, like being a kid and having few responsibilities and living for a good time. It wasn't something he'd given any thought to as an adult. Finding work, a place to live, and food to eat had been the focus of his adult life. Surviving. Being happy hadn't entered into it. He wasn't even sure he was entitled to it.

But he relaxed and gave her a charming grin and lied. "Sure, I have. I've lived my life the way I wanted to. What more could I ask for?"

"Have you? Being a drifter—that's the life you envisioned for yourself growing up? You wanted to move from town to town, never staying long, always living alone, never having anyone to help you when you were in trouble?"

His face flushed. He'd had plenty of trouble, all right. On more occasions than he wanted to remember, circumstance or prejudice or suspicion had landed him in a jail cell. Most of those times he had been guilty. A few times he hadn't. A few other times there had been no crime. He had simply been locked up on principle, as sort of a preventive measure. He'd looked mean or lazy or no-good, and he'd had a record. In some of the backwater towns where he'd been, that was enough for a trip to jail.

Miss Rose didn't know about any of that. She was referring to more honest kinds of trouble: needing work, getting sick, being hungry. If she knew that he'd been in jail as recently as a few weeks ago . . . he wasn't sure what she would do.

"You never wanted to settle down, to have a home or a family of your own? You wanted to be greeted with suspicion everywhere you went? You wanted to sleep on park benches or under bridges or in fleabag hotels?'' She shook her head gently. ''I don't believe that. Don't forget that I helped raise you. You were smart. You worked hard. You had pride. The Will I knew could never be happy settling for the life you've lived.''

''Things changed, Miss Rose,'' he said flatly. The day Melanie Robinson had decided that he should be the father of her baby, that he should pay for the crime without having the pleasure of committing it first, his life had changed. The day Miss Rose had been faced with a choice—of believing Melanie or him—and, making her choice, had looked at him with such disappointment, everything had changed. Forever.

''So change them again. Settle down. Find a job. Find a pretty girl and make an honest woman of her.''

Her choice of words stung. *Make an honest woman of her.* That was what they'd wanted him to do with Melanie. Even though he wasn't responsible. Even though he'd never done anything dishonorable with her.

''I am what I am,'' he said with an uneasy shrug. ''A home, a job, and a woman aren't going to change that.''

''I don't understand you young people,'' she said with a sigh. ''You could have so much, yet you settle for practically nothing.''

He wondered what poor unfortunate was being lumped in the same category with him. Then, following her gaze to the road, he got his answer. Celine. *Find a pretty girl and make an honest woman of her.* Would Miss Rose be disappointed in him again if dear Celine was the pretty girl he found? With his reputation? When he had no intention of marrying anyone? When all he could do was hurt her?

If Miss Rose had even the vaguest idea of the lust he felt for her good neighbor Celine, the sheriff wouldn't have to worry about running him out of town. The old lady would do it herself.

He watched Celine follow the dirt trail to the mailbox. She moved slowly because she was probably tired after a day's work, and she'd just walked a mile and a half in near–hundred-degree temperatures. Not because it gave him plenty of time to appreciate her rounded hips and full breasts and the swing of her long hair. Not because just watching her pricked at his skin and made him sore all over. Not because it was sexy as hell.

She took the mail from the box and sorted through it. When Miss Rose called her name, she looked up, waved, and smiled. The smile slipped just a bit when she saw him.

"Put your things away, then come join us for some lemonade," Miss Rose invited.

Celine hesitated only a moment, then, smiling tightly, accepted the invitation. Leaning back comfortably, Will watched her until she climbed the steps onto the screened porch of her own house; then he glanced at Miss Rose. "And what could Celine have instead of settling for practically nothing?"

"The same things you've given up. A family. A home. A more fulfilling life. Do you know she has a college degree?"

He hadn't known, but it didn't surprise him. Weren't librarian types supposed to be bookish and intelligent? But they weren't supposed to be pretty. They weren't supposed to be sexy. They weren't supposed to have hair practically to their waists or a mouth that looked just kissed or a body to make a man weak.

"Four years of working and studying, and she comes back here for what? To run the library. And all because of one unhappy romance."

That last part made all the nerves in his body tighten. He wanted to demand details, but Miss Rose would clam up if she realized that she was gossiping. He hadn't overlooked the fact that Celine had refused to answer him Sunday about her lovers. Maybe he had asked the wrong question. Instead of how many men she'd been to bed with, maybe he should have asked how many she had been in love with. Even if the very idea did make his jaw clench and his teeth hurt.

But Miss Rose had said all she intended to for the time being. Excusing herself, she took the lemonade pitcher inside to refill it. While she was gone, Celine came out of her house and joined him on the gallery. Will scarcely gave her a chance to seat herself in the wicker chair across the table from him before he spoke. "You look hot, Miss Celine."

Her cheeks were already pink. His remark made them pinker. "It's a hot day," she responded, the coolness of her voice inversely proportional to the temperature. "Where is Miss Rose?"

"Getting more lemonade. How was business today at the Harmony Public Library?"

"Business is always good when the weather's like this. The library is cool, the kids get out of the house without having to play in the heat, and the mothers get a few hours of peace."

"And does your sister send her three kids for Aunt Celine to watch over while she gets some peace?"

"Thank God, no." She answered thoughtlessly, then regretted her honesty and tried to explain. "Vickie's kids are too young to be left alone like that. Matt is only six, and the little one is three. It wouldn't be appropriate."

Unless Vickie had changed significantly since he'd known her, it wouldn't be the first thing she'd done that was inappropriate. She had always been up to something or other in high school. The few times he'd gone out with her, she'd been the most hellish tease. She had thought she was being coy and enticing, that playing hard to get was the way to go with him. Instead she had only irritated him. If her parents hadn't intervened, he would have given her one more chance to drop the act, and then *he* would have dropped *her*. Sex had been too easy to come by back then to waste time trying to coax someone like Vickie into it.

Someone like Celine, though . . . that would be worth his while. Taking the time to seduce her properly and thoroughly before he even laid a hand on her would be the best time he'd ever had. And laying his hands on her would be even better. Better than he would ever deserve.

Chapter Three

Miss Rose pushed the door open and came out, carrying a silver tray. Will took it from her, setting it on the table before sitting down again. There was the lemonade pitcher, filled to the brim, a glass for Celine, saucers, and a plate of soft, round butter cookies. "What are you dressed up for, Celine?" the old lady asked as she perched on the edge of her seat and served the sweets.

Given a chance, Will would have commented on her clothing. Instead of a typically full skirt, she was wearing knee-length shorts in pale creamy linen, a print blouse with a nearly off-the-shoulder neckline, textured hose, and ballet slippers. Shorts had come a long way from the bermudas and cutoff jeans of his youth, he thought appreciatively, and Southern women could certainly do them justice.

"Vickie and I are having dinner together this evening. Richard's keeping the kids."

"Where are you going?"

"Baton Rouge. Vickie's due to pick me up any minute now."

That brought a frown to Miss Rose. "Since you're ready, there won't be any need for her to get out of the car."

Celine leaned across to pat Miss Rose's hand. "You know the only reason she asked me to dinner this evening and the only reason she's picking me up. I promise, she won't stay but a minute.''

"Maybe I'll just send Will on an errand."

He was looking from one woman to the other. It was easy enough to guess Vickie's reason for the invitation—she wanted to see *him*. What wasn't so easy was understanding the emotions here. Neither Celine nor Miss Rose seemed happy about it. Miss Rose, in fact, was downright hostile. Was Vickie under the mistaken impression, as she'd been years ago, that he was hers for the asking? Did Celine think he was going to play on old relationships to shake up her sister's marriage? Was Miss Rose afraid he hadn't yet learned how to handle himself when he had settled on an affair?

"She's just curious, Miss Rose," Celine said softly, giving him an apologetic look. "Everybody is. He's been back nearly a week, and no one's talked to him but you, me, and Raymond."

She left the sheriff off her short list. Will appreciated that. He had decided against mentioning Franklin's visit for the time being. The only thing reporting it could accomplish would be to make Miss Rose worry, and she'd already done enough worrying over him to last a lifetime.

"Maybe I should go into town," he said with a grin. "Stake out a place on the grass in front of the courthouse where everybody could come and look. I could even talk to the ones who have enough nerve to come close."

His teasing fell flat. It angered Miss Rose, and Celine looked sorry again. He would have preferred anger from her, too. It sat more easily on his shoulders than regret.

"That's enough, Will," Miss Rose said sharply. To Celine, she commanded, "You tell that sister of yours to stay home where she belongs, with that husband she wanted so bad that she stooped to—" Abruptly drawing in a deep breath, she closed her mouth in a firm line and simply sat there scowling.

His gaze shifted to Celine, who was staring down at the half-eaten cookie left on her plate. Exactly what had Vickie done to marry this man? Trapped him, the way Melanie had tried to trap *him*? But that wasn't really such an awful thing. Thousands of women had done it, and the men involved were just as much to blame. That wasn't enough to explain Celine's discomfort.

Before either woman decided to break the silence, the subject of their conversation arrived, parking on the edge of the road in front of Miss Rose's house. He had never seen two sisters who looked less alike. Celine was tall and willowy; Vickie was short and voluptuous. Celine's hair was long, brown, and controlled; Vickie's was moussed, teased, and sprayed within an inch of its life, and the color, a brassy red, was undeniably bottled. Celine moved gracefully and graciously; her sister's gait was awkward, thanks either to the unstable shell walk or the three-inch heels.

Celine was desirable, Vickie wasn't.

She had the sense to greet Miss Rose first, reaching for her hand, exclaiming in a too-loud voice how *nice* it was to see her, patting her on the shoulder. The old woman just glared at her, mumbled something about seeing to dinner, and disappeared inside, letting the door close with a bang behind her.

Vickie rolled her eyes upward in amused condemnation of the old woman's disapproval, then smiled. Her mouth was like Celine's—full, forming a perfect Cupid's bow—but her lipstick was too bright, clashing with the vivid hue of her hair and the bright green of her dress. "Well, well, Billy Ray Beaumont, you are a sight for sore eyes," she declared, her voice sultry, her open arms inviting.

Will remained where he was on the settee, his position effectively blocking her from coming as close as she would like. She still managed to kiss him, though, leaving a smear of bright red lipstick on his cheek that he wiped off with Miss Rose's white damask napkin.

"You wouldn't believe the stir you've created in town, Billy Ray," she said, taking the seat Miss Rose had vacated. "Why, if I didn't know you better, I'd think you had holed up out here deliberately, just to keep us all wondering and guessing."

He restrained the urge to remind her that she *didn't* know him better and, instead, repeated the first words he'd spoken to her sister nearly a week ago. "I prefer Will."

It took her a moment to understand. She was pretty, but

her head had always been empty. Of course, there were times when empty-headed women served a fine purpose, but most of the time they were boring. He would be bored now, after only two minutes, if Celine weren't sitting across from him.

"Oh, of course. I guess Billy Ray's a little juvenile for a grown man." She gave him a long look. "And, my, you *have* grown."

It was funny how meanings could change. A week ago he had made the same remark to Celine. He had meant it as an insult, a warning, a weapon to distance himself from her, but she hadn't taken it any of those ways. Vickie had meant the words as a compliment, maybe as a reminder of the times they had shared, but they felt like an insult to him.

"We've got to get going," Celine said, rising abruptly from her seat.

"Oh, don't be in such a rush," Vickie admonished. "I don't often get a night out, and I intend to enjoy it." Looking back at Will, she smiled coquettishly. "To the fullest."

She was going to kill her sister, Celine thought silently. She'd always wanted to be an only child. It certainly would have saved her a lot of grief if Vickie hadn't been around when she was growing up, or especially when she was in college and in love. It would save her some embarrassment if she weren't here now.

It would save her some jealousy, too. God help her, it was so easy to be jealous of her sister. She had been everything Celine had wanted to be, had had everything Celine wanted to have. Even now, Vickie had this unflagging belief that Will still found her attractive. Celine wished she could be certain of her own appeal for him. She wished she didn't have the feeling that he was playing games with her, amusing himself until a woman came along—not a *little girl* like her.

Vickie was definitely a woman, and she was making no effort at all to hide the fact.

Celine wished Will would make some excuse and go inside so they could leave. She couldn't pull Vickie away, not as long as he was listening to her nonsense, not while he was giving her a serious, damn near smoldering look. If he kept that up, she fully expected her sister to burst into flames or disappear in a puff of smoke.

Maybe she was embarrassed for nothing. Maybe Will liked that kind of breathy my-aren't-you-a-strong-handsome-man routine. Maybe he *was* still attracted to Vickie.

Slowly he got to his feet. Both sisters watched the movement, Vickie with undisguised hunger, Celine with carefully guarded fascination. Only once in their lives had they both found the same man attractive. It had almost destroyed their relationship and had caused unbearable tension in the family. How ironic that the only interest they had shared since that event was another man. How frightening. How depressing.

"I've got to see if Miss Rose needs any help," he said, edging toward the door. "Enjoy your dinner, ladies."

Vickie watched until he was inside and the door was closed; then she gave a soft, dreamy sigh. "Oh, my. If he doesn't get your blood pumping, honey, you are beyond hope. No doubt about it."

"Shall we go?" Without waiting for an answer, Celine started down the path to Vickie's car. Her head was starting to hurt, and the pain wasn't going to go away on the trip to Baton Rouge. Maybe she should beg off. Vickie's real goal had already been accomplished. She had seen and talked to and even kissed Will. Tomorrow she would spread the word around to every one of her friends, no doubt embellishing it here and there, making the encounter seem far more than it had actually been and probably completely removing Celine and Miss Rose from the picture. She didn't have any further need for her sister tonight.

Instead of making an excuse, however, Celine climbed into the car, fastened her seat belt, and tilted her head back. Eyes closed, jaw set, she prepared herself for the verbal onslaught about to come.

"Isn't he just about the handsomest man you've ever seen?"

"Yes, he's very attractive."

"Attractive?" Vickie laughed. "Honey, he could raise the dead. And that body! Funny how some people stay so hard and muscular and others get soft and weak."

Her sister could never be credited with much subtlety. Richard had put on a few pounds over the last seven years. It came from sitting behind a desk all day, eating rich, tasty lunches at the restaurant, and indulging in the sweets Vickie was constantly making for the kids. Will *was* hard, but his life had been hard. No doubt he'd known more than his share of hunger and had done more than his share of hard labor.

"So what do you think about him?"

"About Will?"

Vickie gave her a chiding look. "No, about old Mr. Simmons down the road. Of course about Will."

"He's an interesting person."

"He's an interesting person," Vickie mimicked in a prissy voice. "If you didn't look just like Great-grandma Hunter, I'd swear to God that you were adopted. How could any woman who describes Billy Ray Beaumont as 'an interesting person' possibly be *my* sister?"

Celine finally opened her eyes and glared across the car. "What do you want me to say? That he's handsome as sin and probably twice as wicked? That I lie in my bed at night wondering how to get him in it? That I'd like to get my hands on whatever he's got in his jeans?"

Hearing herself, she winced and looked away. All those things were true, of course. They just sounded as if they'd come from her sister's mouth instead of her own.

Vickie apparently thought so, too, if her laughter was anything to judge by. When her amusement faded, she reached across and patted Celine's hand. "There's hope for you yet, honey."

"What does Richard think of your fascination with Will?" Celine asked, drawing her hand away.

"What Richard doesn't know won't hurt him."

Celine's smile was thin and bitter. The Vickie Hunter Jourdan philosophy of life. *Don't tell Mama that I'm going out with Billy Ray. What she doesn't know can't hurt her. Don't tell Daddy that I scratched up the car today. By the time he sees it, he'll think Mama did it, and what he doesn't know can't hurt him. Oh, Richard, don't bother telling Celine just yet that you've been seeing me on the side. What she doesn't know . . .* Her sister was pretty, vain, selfish, and flirting with amoral.

That was the tough part for Celine. Vickie honestly believed what she was saying. She saw nothing wrong in lusting after

Will as long as her husband didn't know. She'd seen nothing wrong in lying to their parents or in beginning an affair with the man her sister was going to marry. If she hadn't gotten pregnant with Matt, who knew when she would have stopped or at least come clean with Celine? After Celine and Richard were married? Maybe on their wedding day she would have announced, "Oh, by the way, Celine, Richard and I have been lovers ever since you brought him home to meet the family last Christmas. Hope you don't mind."

One thing was certain. Vickie had never felt a moment's remorse—not over the lies to their parents, nor over getting pregnant by Celine's fiancé only three months before their wedding date. Certainly not over betraying Celine's trust.

She had no principles. She was lacking a conscience, but she was so open about her dishonesty that people tended to forgive it. When she went home to her husband tonight, she would be so genuinely attentive that Richard, who knew firsthand how she had maintained her relationship with Celine all the while she was seducing him, would be shocked to discover that she might be seducing someone else.

"Have you ever had an affair?"

"Since Richard and I got married?" Even now, when she was speaking about a time that had been unbearably painful for Celine, there was no sign of guilt or regret in her eyes. "No. I haven't met anyone worth the effort." She smiled lasciviously. "Until today."

"You would risk your marriage, your future, and your children's future for an affair with Will Beaumont?" Distaste, jealousy, and pure, momentary dislike for her sister left a sour taste in Celine's mouth.

"Billy Ray would be worth risking almost *anything* for. You should see his—" Breaking off, Vickie gave her a smile. "Well, we won't get crude here. I'm sure that, even with the life you lead, you can imagine exactly what I'm talking about. Just let me say it's impressive."

She made the last word sound dirty and raised more questions, more dark emotions, to join the ones already swirling in Celine's mind. Had Vickie and Will been lovers back in high school? The thought somehow shocked her, even though it was a logical assumption. Will had certainly had his share of girls, and Vickie had been nearly eighteen when they'd dated. Celine had gone to school with more than a few girls who'd started when they were fifteen. She had felt like an oddity of some sort when she'd finally given up her virginity to Richard at the grand old age of twenty.

The involvement of sex would explain their parents' uncharacteristically strict punishment when they'd uncovered Vickie's lies. It would explain the way she had acted afterward, moping around as if her life were over, as if she would never find another boy to replace Will. It explained why she was so sure he would welcome her back into his life sixteen years later. It made Celine sick even to think about it. She didn't want any man that Vickie had already had.

Oh, a little voice contradicted inside her, but she *did* want Will. No matter who'd had him first, no matter who followed after.

She didn't speak again until they were parked in the lot outside their favorite seafood restaurant. Vickie was checking her makeup in the rearview mirror when Celine abruptly asked, "Do you love Richard?"

The look her sister gave her was incredulous. "Why, of course I do."

"You know he would be hurt if you had an affair."

"*If* he found out." Vickie's supremely confident smile returned. "And if he did, honey, I guarantee I could make him forget all about it. I mean, it's not like I'm considering leaving Richard for Billy Ray. Things have changed in Harmony but not *that* much. Billy Ray is fine for some hot and hard sex, but no woman in her right mind would get *involved* with him. He's just a Beaumont, and Beaumonts in this town . . ." Her shrug was a silently eloquent echo of what Will had told Celine more bluntly last weekend. *Beaumonts have never amounted to shit.*

She got out of the car, welcoming the heat to chase away the chill of anger. So Will was just a Beaumont. And who the hell was Vickie? A Jourdan by marriage, but her husband wasn't even from Harmony. Richard's family ties were in a broken-down town that could be Harmony transplanted to Mississippi. A Hunter? There was nothing prestigious about that. Their father was a laboratory version of the absentminded professor. He was a chemist at one of the factories on the nearby Mississippi River, a brilliant man who could lose his car in the parking lot at the grocery store. Their mother was a dreamer who fancied herself an artist, who changed the paint on the house as easily as other women changed clothing, who had never created anything pretty other than Vickie, anything useful other than Celine. They were known in town as the flakes, the oddballs, the parents in need of parenting. Their parents had been oddballs, too. No one in town expected reliability, stability, or common sense from any Hunter but Celine, and she was explained away as a throwback to the no-nonsense great-grandmother whose name she bore.

So what, she wondered with a scowl, did Vickie find in that background that made her better than Will Beaumont?

Dinner was more bearable. Her attention diverted from Will, Vickie flirted with the maître d' who seated them, the boy who served them hush puppies and tea, and the waiter who took their dinner order. She caught Celine up on all the local gossip, including the little tidbit that Melanie Robinson was supposedly returning from New Orleans to discuss the little matter of child support with Will.

How was she going to get child support from a man who didn't have a job and didn't own a thing but his clothes? If Vickie's source was accurate, Melanie would soon learn the meaning of the old saying about squeezing blood from a turnip.

"Jared doesn't look a thing like him," she remarked.

"No, he takes after his mama. You remember Melanie, don't you, or were you too young to notice when she left?"

"I remember her. She was very pretty."

Vickie gave an unladylike snort. "If you like the fragile flower type. I never cared for Melanie myself."

Of course not. A pretty woman rarely cared for the competition, and Melanie had been just that in high school. It was Melanie to whom Will had gone when he'd stopped seeing Vickie; Melanie was the one he'd gotten pregnant, even though he'd denied it.

"She was a snooty bitch," Vickie continued, unaware of Celine's amused smile. "She always hinted at things, but never came right out and said them, like she thought that keeping secrets made her mysterious or something. She used to hint that she had this really special boyfriend but would never say who. She hinted that she was sleeping with Will but never actually admitted it until her folks found out she was pregnant. Boy, that was a shocker.''

This was the kind of conversation Celine could handle. She couldn't get jealous over Melanie Robinson's long-ago affair with Will when she'd never really even known the woman—especially when, at the time, she'd been too young herself even to fully understand what sex was. "What was so shocking?"

"Him getting her pregnant. He was careful about that, you know. He made it clear that nobody was going to force *him* into marriage." Vickie's laugh was more of a giggle. "The way he was with girls, if he hadn't been so careful, he probably would have gotten trapped long before he was sixteen."

Trapped. That was an ugly word, especially coming from Vickie, who had been well into her third month of pregnancy when she and Richard had finally gotten married. "Nothing's a hundred-percent effective except abstinence," Celine replied mildly.

"Yeah, and abstinence isn't even in Billy Ray's vocabulary," Vickie said with an indecent grin. "Hooray for that."

Quickly becoming uncomfortable again, Celine shifted in her seat. "He asked you to call him Will," she quietly reminded her.

"Hey, it's just a name. He was Billy Ray for a long time. For the best times."

"It is just a name, but it's *his* name. He has a right to be called by the name he prefers."

More serious than she'd been all evening, Vickie studied her for a long time. Celine carefully kept her expression blank and her gaze steady. Vickie could look all she wanted, but she wasn't going to learn anything.

"For a while, I thought maybe you'd given up on men. It's been a long time for you, hasn't it? But I guess even *your* blood must get stirred up from time to time. I'll tell you what. When I'm through with Billy Ray—sorry, with Will, you can have whatever's left. And believe me, honey, whatever it is . . ." She finished with a lecherous smile and a promising drawl. "It'll be well worth waiting for."

Closing time at the library was five o'clock, but because of a steady influx of kids all day, Celine knew she wouldn't get out before six Friday evening. There were books to re-shelve, magazines to restack, newspapers to refold. Even though janitorial services weren't part of her job description, she would also empty the trash, sweep the floor, and wipe down the tables. Those tasks couldn't wait for old Mrs. Gallier's biweekly cleaning the following Wednesday.

She was on a step stool in the tiny reference room when someone spoke her name. The voice, young and thin, startled her, so that she nearly fell. "Jared," she exclaimed when she turned to see him. "I thought everyone was gone."

"Sorry I scared you. I—I wanted to talk to you, to see if you—if you could get a book for me."

. She came down the ladder to stand in front of him. At fifteen he was already nearly six feet tall. His mother was petite, only an inch or two over five feet, but his father was a foot taller. But height seemed to be the only thing he'd inherited from Will. He was surely his mother's son, with blond hair, blue eyes, and fine bone structure. His personality, though, seemed to come from neither of them. He was quiet, withdrawn, introverted. He got along well enough with people; he just seemed to prefer the company of books. He was always reading, always studying. Maybe that would be a way out for him. A college scholarship could open up an entire new life for him, one to be lived far away from here.

"Do you have the title and the author's name?" she asked, leading the way to the counter up front.

"No, ma'am. I—I was hoping you could find that out for me."

"Okay, that's no problem. What topic are you interested in?"

He glanced around the room, briefly met her eyes, then looked away again. "DNA fingerprinting," he blurted.

Celine had already written his name on a pad at her desk. Now her pen hovered over the paper, not quite touching, not quite ready to begin the D. "DNA fingerprinting," she repeated hesitantly.

"The use of DNA for identification."

Slowly she began writing. "Interesting subject." She wasn't a science-minded person, but even she had heard a little on the matter. DNA was proving invaluable in solving crimes.

It was also of great help in proving paternity.

She wanted to ask Jared if that was his goal, if he wanted to find evidence to back up his mother's claim, to prove once and for all to the people of Harmony that Will Beaumont was a liar. She wanted, too, to offer him sympathy, to tell him she understood that growing up in a small, close-knit town without a mother or a father was difficult. She wanted to ask him what he thought about Will's return. Had he expected his father to acknowledge him in some way? Or had his grandparents infected him with their hatred for Will? Did he, like everyone else, want Will to leave town and never come back? Everyone except Miss Rose. And Vickie. And herself.

But she didn't ask him anything at all. If he wanted to talk, she would listen, but she couldn't bring up such a personal subject.

"I'll look into it first thing Monday morning," she said, sticking the note to the phone on her desk before offering him a smile. "Is there anything else I can do for you?"

"No, ma'am, that's all. Thanks, Miss Celine." Ducking his head, he took the books she had checked out for him earlier from the counter and left through the double doors.

Celine sank down on the edge of her desk. She felt sorry for Jared. Will and Melanie had known what they were doing when they decided to have sex. They had known the consequences they faced. But Jared had never been given a choice about being born, and he hadn't had much of a chance since then.

It must be hard for him, knowing that his father had come back after a sixteen-year absence and that his return had nothing to do with *him*. She was positive Will hadn't made any effort at all to contact Jared. If he had, Jock would have stopped him, and everyone in town would have heard the details.

Beyond mentioning the Robinsons to Will that first night, she hadn't brought them up again. But this weekend she would. She would tell him that he owed his son something— a meeting, a phone call, something to show that he knew he existed, that he *cared* Jared existed. She would *make* him do something.

Returning to the reference room in back, she finished the filing there, then moved to the cart of books she'd left between stacks. As soon as she'd taken this job from Miss Russell, the retiring librarian, she had made it her policy that reshelving was her job, not the patrons'. People who understood the Dewey numbering system well enough to locate books on the shelves somehow forgot how to find their proper places for return. In the long run it was easier for her to put everything away than trying to find misshelved books.

She worked methodically, leisurely, enjoying the peace of the empty library. Like Jared, she got along well enough with people, but she, too, often preferred the company of books. She liked the places they took her. She could live vicariously through the pages of a book. She could experience all the things missing from her own life—adventure, romance, danger, excitement, love—without the risks. Books were safe.

She had just returned a book on the history of baseball to the shelf and was reaching blindly for the next one when her fingers brushed something warm and solid and definitely human. Unlike the incident with Jared, though, she wasn't startled this time. She knew instinctively whom she would see when she looked.

As lean as he was, Will seemed to fill the aisle. So often when she'd seen him, he had been comfortably slouched, leaning against this box or that step, looking, by turns, lazy and deceptively harmless or wicked and dangerously appealing. This time, though, he was standing erect, his shoulders back, his chin level. His hair was neat and short, his jaw clean-shaven, his clothes clean and pressed. He didn't look shiftless or untrustworthy. He didn't look like the drifter she knew him to be or like the thief and con man he was rumored to be. But wasn't that the trick for a con artist? Not to look like one?

His hands were resting on the books remaining on the cart,

the left one underneath hers, and he was looking at her, his mouth unsmiling, his dark eyes intense. For a long time she simply looked back; then, forcing herself, she removed her hand from his and picked up the next book, glancing at the number on the spine.

"I thought the library closed at five."

"It does. I didn't have time to reshelve everything before then." She walked along the shelf, searching for the call number, only to realize that she'd been standing right in front of it when she'd picked up the book. "What are you doing in town?"

"Miss Rose is having dinner with Sophy Michaud. She asked me to drop her off. Sophy's son is going to take her home later."

She slid the book into its place, then reached for another. He had already picked it up, though, and was holding it out. "I'd forgotten. She and Miss Sophy get together every other Friday for dinner and a game of cards."

She continued her work, the stack slowly dwindling, squeezing between him and the cart when necessary, maneuvering the cart around the corner into the next aisle. "So you have a free evening tonight," she remarked as she stretched to fit one thick book into a thin slot on the top shelf.

"Unless you want to fill it."

Quickly she glanced at him to see if he was teasing. He wasn't. "I can't."

"Just dinner. I won't ask you to take your clothes off or anything like that."

Again she gave him a sharp look, expecting one of those arrogant grins, but he was serious, so serious that he almost scowled. Will Beaumont was asking her for a date, and he looked as if he hated doing it. *Thanks for the ego stroke*, she thought with a hint of resignation.

Reaching past her, he pushed the books to one side so she could fit the thicker volume in. "I guarantee I'll be at least as good company as your dinner companion last night."

"Did you sleep with her?"

Hearing the echo of her words, Celine realized what she had so bluntly asked and her cheeks turned deep red. Hadn't Vickie already made it clear that they'd been lovers? Why in the world did she want confirmation from Will? Besides, it was none of her business. If he'd had sex with every single woman in this town except her, it was none of her business.

"I'm sorry," she murmured ashamedly. "Forget I asked that."

Finally he did smile, and the look in his eyes lightened. "Curious, Celie?" he asked, his voice deliberately low and sexy. "You been listening to bad talk about me?"

She wedged another book into place with more force than required. Talk, he'd said. Not gossip. Not rumor. But not necessarily truth, either. Just as the seductive tone of his voice had been intentional, so, she suspected, was his choice of words. He didn't want to give her an answer either way. He wanted to make her wonder . . . and damn him, she would.

"So what about dinner?"

"I told you, I can't."

"You have other plans?"

If she told him she was going out, she would have to do it. If she told him someone was coming over, she would have to find someone who would. If she told him she simply wasn't interested, he would know she was lying. "Don't you know it's impolite to badger someone who's turned you down?"

He laughed. "Being polite never was one of my goals in life. Besides, I rarely ask." Finally came the grin she had been waiting for. "I rarely need to."

The next four books were all located on the top shelf. Retrieving a stool from the end of the aisle, she pushed it over and stepped into place. One by one Will handed her the books.

"What would it cost you? One evening? A few hours of your time?" he cajoled. Sensing that she was weakening, he again used that seductive voice that made her nerves quiver. "Come on, Celie. It's Friday night. Put on something nice and have a little fun."

She seized on the least important part of his invitation. " 'Put on something nice'? What's wrong with what I'm wearing?"

Will looked at her dress—pale peach cotton, the top part fitted, the material clinging to her breasts, her arms left bare.

The waist hugged her own waist, and the skirt was full and swirled almost to her ankles. It was pretty enough. The color flattered her, and from the waist up it certainly did her justice. But that skirt. . . . "What's wrong with it," he replied, "is there's too damned much of it. If it ended here . . ."

He shouldn't do this. He shouldn't touch her. He shouldn't even get close. But he did. He moved closer, filling one hand with folds of fabric. The other he slid beneath her skirt. He waited, his fingers curved around her calf, giving her a chance to stop him. The muscles beneath his hand tensed and trembled, and she opened her mouth, but she didn't say anything. She didn't tell him to stop. She didn't slap his hand away. She just looked down at him, her green eyes opened wide, giving him a sort of startled, skittish, frightened-doe look.

He knew exactly how she felt, what she was thinking. It felt good, but it was dangerous. Did she suspect how dangerous? Did she know that he could take her right now, that he could lay her down right here on the floor like some paid-for whore without even a twinge of guilt?

No, that wasn't entirely true. If he could treat her like a whore, if he could use her, then walk away, he would do it. He would forget that she was innocent, that although she was only six years younger than he was in age, in experience there was a lifetime's difference between them. He would forget that she could be hurt, that she deserved better.

But he couldn't forget. He couldn't escape the guilt, even for so simple a touch. And he couldn't ignore the need.

Slowly he glided his fingers upward, taking her skirt with them. Her leg was smooth, her skin warm. She would be that way all over—smooth, warm, and soft. Little girl soft. Womanly soft.

He meant to stop at her knee, maybe just a little above, but he wanted to feel more than that. He wanted to stroke her everywhere—her legs, her breasts, her back, her ribs. He wanted to wrap his arms around her and pull her to him, to feel her body hot against his. He wanted to slide his fingers inside her, to gauge how hot and wet and tight she was, and to kiss her there, to taste her, to taste himself on her. God, wanting her was damned near killing him. And not taking her was going to finish the job.

The tips of his fingers reached the lacy edge of her panties, and he became still. A slight shift to the side, and he could touch her. A little maneuvering, and he could fill her with whatever she could take. But how long would he have to pay if he did?

For a moment he remained as he was. Then, dragging in a deep breath, he let go. He let her skirt fall back into place, covering her panties, her hip, her muscled thigh, her calf. With one soft swoosh of fabric, everything was safely covered.

Except his erection.

Damn, he thought as he turned away. He had developed entirely too close a relationship with his hand since he'd met this woman.

Leaving her there, looking dazed and bewildered and too damned appealing, he went to stand in front of a bulletin board, pretending to study the notices pinned there. Finally, behind him, she came down from the stool and began putting away the last few books. He followed her progress without turning his head, listening to the rustle of her clothing, the tap of her shoes on the tile floor, and the slide of book cover against cover.

"I need to take out the trash and run the sweeper," she said from somewhere behind him, her voice subdued. "Then we can go."

He opened his mouth to renege on his invitation, to tell her that he had changed his mind. The last thing he needed was to spend the evening with her. In fact, what he really needed was a quick trip to New Orleans. For the price of a nice dinner with Celine, he could buy himself a much more productive hour or so with a Bourbon Street hooker.

He had never gone that route before—paying for sex. He'd never needed to, and he didn't need to now. If any woman would do, he could call Celine's sister Vickie and get it for free. But any woman wouldn't do. Screwing some prostitute or Vickie or one of the other girls of his youth would only take care of the immediate problem—the hard-on he had right now. It wouldn't satisfy his hunger. It wouldn't make him stop wanting Celine. It wouldn't make him quit imagining her naked and underneath him, her long legs wrapped around him, her long hair tangled about their bodies. But it would make him more of a bastard than he already was. It would make him even less suitable for her than he already was.

So instead of telling her no, instead of doing the wise thing and putting her off, insulting her or maybe even offending her so she would stay away, he offered to empty the trash for her. While she got the sweeper from the storage closet at the back of the library, he gathered the garbage from the gray metal wastebaskets scattered around the big room and carried it out back to the Dumpster in the alley.

For a moment after dumping the trash, he just stood there, leaning against the warm, rough brick wall, letting the evening sun seep into his bones. He wished he hadn't given up smoking ten years ago. His lungs craved the poisonous pleasure cigarettes had given him, and his nerves needed the relaxation they had always brought.

Failing that, he could use a stiff shot of whiskey. There was a bar a half block down the street, a liquor store a block in the opposite direction. But liquor didn't relax him. It usually made him mean, and that was one thing he didn't need help with.

Wishing that he had never received Miss Rose's message, that he had just pleaded guilty to whatever charges the police in that little Alabama town had had in mind for him, that he had asked the chief to lock him up without a trial and to throw away the key, he drew in a deep breath, opened the door, and went back inside.

He hadn't expected coming home to be easy, not after sixteen years, not after the way he'd left. He just hadn't expected it to be so damned hard.

Raymond Kendall watched his mother's car go by from his office window on the bank's second floor. Seeing Beaumont behind the wheel intensified the frown he was already wearing. If Mitch Franklin was any kind of sheriff, he would have Billy Ray picked up for that. Naturally the bastard had Rose's permission, but in the time it took the sheriff's office to track her down to verify that, a couple of deputies could teach him a lesson that he wouldn't forget. They could fix his pretty face so that no one—not even the women around town who hadn't even laid eyes on him yet but were already panting over him like bitches in heat—would be able to look at him.

But Franklin wasn't much of a sheriff at all. If Raymond suggested that he do his job as he should, the way all the sheriffs before him had, he would probably arrest *him*.

"So what did you find out from the police in Alabama?" he asked, turning when the car was out of sight.

"Beaumont was arrested about two weeks ago on charges of breaking and entering and burglary. The police suspected he was running a scam on the old ladies in town, widows mostly. He would get a job with them, find out what they had worth stealing, get to know their routines and then—allegedly—clean them out."

"So why did they let him go?"

"No evidence. He did work for each of the women, odd jobs and such, and the burglaries always took place shortly after he left their employ. But his fingerprints were never found anywhere they shouldn't be, he didn't have any of the stolen property in his possession when he was arrested, and he didn't have any money that couldn't be accounted for from his jobs."

"But you know he was guilty."

Franklin just looked at him.

"It's the same thing he did to my mother sixteen years ago. She trusted him. He had access to her house. He knew where she was at any given time, and he knew where she kept her valuables. He robbed her *and* me, and you people let him get away." Raymond sat down behind his desk and leaned back comfortably in the big leather chair. "I bet if you contact the police in all the places he's been, you'll find he's been doing the same sort of thing ever since he left."

"He does have an arrest record, but there's nothing major on it." The sheriff removed a folded computer printout from his pocket and scanned it. "Vagrancy, public drunk, petty larceny, a couple of assaults stemming from barroom brawls. He's a bum, Raymond, that's all. That doesn't make him dangerous. It doesn't make him a threat."

"He's a thief," Raymond corrected him. "And around here, Sheriff, thieves sometimes get shot."

Franklin returned the printout to his pocket, then stood up.

"If he gets shot in *my* parish, Raymond, there'd better be signs of forcible entry, his fingerprints all over the place, and the stolen goods in his possession." Taking his hat from the other chair, he nodded politely before taking his leave.

Raymond sighed in exasperation, then abruptly began clearing his desk. The bank didn't close until six o'clock on Fridays, but no one would care if he left a little early. Hell, he was the president. He was entitled.

Saying good-night to the employees he passed, he made his way outside and to his car. The leather seat was hot. He could feel it burning through his summer-weight suit. When he got home, he would swim a few laps in the pool, he decided, then have Mae fix him a tall, cool drink. That would improve his disposition.

The house he and Frannie shared on the north side of town was his pride and joy. It was the biggest, prettiest, fanciest house in the entire parish. There wasn't a place in Baton Rouge upriver or in New Orleans downriver that could compare. Frannie's daddy had spared no expense.

The house rose out of Spanish moss–draped live oaks. It was white, built in the Greek Revival style with massive columns and majestic lines. It looked as if it had been standing in that spot forever, as if it had seen the nation grow up around it. The wood inside was cypress, mahogany, and cherry, the wall coverings were silk, the furniture antique. The house required a live-in housekeeper whose sixteen-year-old niece often helped out, and care of the broad lawn in front and the extensive gardens out back kept a staff of three busy.

The Kendalls had always been important in Harmony, but since the destruction of the family home by fire more than a hundred years ago, they had lived sedately. They hadn't flaunted their money. They had settled for comfortable rather than ostentatious, for modesty rather than pretension. This house made up for that. It would stand forever, and even though it had been built with Frannie's family money, it would always be known as the Kendall place. Long after every last one of them was gone, the name would live on in this house.

He changed clothes and headed for the pool. Thanks to

the unyielding heat, the water was lukewarm. Still, with the sun slowly setting and the ghostly breeze that drifted across the lawn, it was refreshing.

He was finishing his tenth lap when Frannie joined him. Even at forty-three, she had a body well suited to a revealing maillot or barely there bikini, but she preferred the sleek, high-necked tank suit of serious swimmers. The legs weren't cut to the waist, and the clingy fabric all but flattened her breasts against her chest, but Raymond liked it. Seeing her in it always turned him on because she looked so athletic, so hard and strong. He liked strong women.

They swam side by side without speaking for lap after lap. Finally Frannie lifted herself onto the side, then stood up and wrapped a towel around her waist. Seeing Mae come out of the house with their drinks, he followed suit.

"Are you getting some exercise or working off your frustration?" Frannie asked as she settled at one of the tables beside the pool.

"What makes you think I'm frustrated?"

"Because the weather is hot, the economy is miserable, and Billy Ray Beaumont is still around."

"I saw him today," he admitted with a scowl. "In town."

"With your mother or alone?"

"With Celine." He'd always had a soft spot for the younger of the Hunter girls. He remembered when she was a kid with that gorgeous rich hair always forced into braids. Her sister had been an early bloomer—brash and bold and unappealingly available—but Celine had taken her time. It had been a slow process, but she had gone from tall and gawky to one of the most sexually attractive women he had ever seen. The transformation had been so gradual that it had startled him. Time after time she had been in the bank, tagging along behind her mother, dirt smeared on her face, and then one day he had looked at her and realized with the impact of a sudden blow that she was provocative, enticing, *hot*—and absolutely unaware of it. The fact that he'd been certain she was a virgin had made her effect even more powerful.

But he had never done anything. She had been too young. He had been married. Once she'd gotten a little experience under her belt, she'd lost her appeal. It was the innocence

that had made her sexuality so intense. Richard Jourdan and
the men who had come after him had taken that innocence.

"You think he's screwing her?"

He turned his attention back to Frannie. "I don't care who
he's screwing. I just wish he was doing it someplace else."

She shifted in her chair, stretching one leg out so her foot
rested in his lap. "For as long as I can remember, you've
disliked Billy Ray. Why is that?"

"The fact that he tried to rob us blind isn't sufficient?"

"He only took a few hundred dollars. Besides, that was
just before he left. What about all those years before then?"

"It was closer to a few thousand," Raymond corrected
her. "And that's not counting what he stole from Mama."

"I think that's what you resent most—what he took from
Rose." Wagging her foot from side to side on his thigh, she
smiled teasingly. "And I'm not talking about a few pieces
of jewelry."

He was starting to get annoyed, but he knew better than
to show it. Frannie would take it and run if she knew. "And
what are you talking about?" he asked, setting his glass down
and taking her foot in his hands, massaging her heel and the
graceful taut arch.

"Her affection. You were all grown up and out on your
own. Miss Rose needed someone to love, and she chose Billy
Ray. She didn't give birth to him. She didn't have to accept
what she got. She *chose* him."

"Bullshit. She was fulfilling her Christian duty when she
took him in." He gave the words he'd heard his mother use
so often a sarcastic twist. "Hell, his own mother didn't even
want him. Mama was just doing what was expected of her."

"Maybe it started that way. But she loves him like a son.
Even if you are her only *real* son." Frannie loosened her
towel, then propped her other foot on his lap. The tank suit
clung smoothly to her body. There were no bumps or bulges
underneath, no protruding bones, no stretch marks or sagging
muscles or flaws of any kind. Her body was as beautiful and
firm as it had been twenty-five years ago.

They had met in college at a fraternity party. He had been
horny and had gone looking for a virgin because he had
liked their innocence, their inexperience. And he had found

Frannie. She'd had more to offer him than the one-time pleasure of virginity—although she'd had that, too. She'd had
an insatiable hunger, a willingness to try anything, a cruel
streak that even now could get him hot.

Best of all, she'd had a rich father. Not just comfortably
wealthy like his family, but *rich*. Obscenely so. They had
been married for twenty-one years now, and he'd never gotten
bored with her. He had never stopped loving her. Hell, sometimes it almost frightened him how much he loved her.

"What I think of Beaumont doesn't matter," he said impa-
tiently. "The question is how do we get rid of him."

"I'm not sure there's any reason to bother—at least, not
until we find out what Rose wants with him. Someone like
him, who hasn't stayed more than a few weeks at a time in
any one place, isn't likely to hang around here long."

"Are you kidding? Mama will give him a place to live,
feed him, and buy him whatever he wants. He doesn't need
a job, doesn't need any money, doesn't have to do anything
but lie around in *my* home and be taken care of. He'd be a
fool to give that up and hit the road again."

Frannie acknowledged his point with a thoughtful nod.
"When your mother comes over for dinner Sunday, why
don't you talk to her, work on her? But for God's sake,
Raymond, use a little charm this time. Don't put him down.
She's as protective of him as she is of you and Meredith,
maybe even a little more so because of his background. Your
insults will only anger her."

Grudgingly, he admitted that she was right. Somehow he
had to learn to control his hatred for Billy Ray, at least around
his mother and Celine. He had to give the impression that he
meant Beaumont no harm, that he was naturally concerned
for their welfare. After all, given the man's reputation . . .

His slow smile had nothing to do with the intimate probing
his wife's foot was doing between his legs.

Billy Ray Beaumont had always had a wild reputation, but
that was all it had ever been. Talk. Rumor. Supposition. Even
when he'd been accused of breaking in here, of stealing from
this house and from Rose's own house, she had refused to
believe it. He was a good boy, she had kept repeating to the

sheriff all those years ago. If he had taken her jewelry and Raymond's things, it was because he had needed the money, because he was scared, because he'd felt pressured to run away. Surely he had the intention of paying them back some-day. He wasn't a thief, she had insisted.

But now Billy Ray had more than just unfounded accusations. Now he had an arrest record. He had convictions. Rose might be inclined to accept his stealing from her, because she was a forgiving sort of person and, as Frannie had just pointed out, she did love the bastard. But she wouldn't tolerate his victimizing others, especially other old women who had trusted him. Soon he would get rid of his mother's soft spot.

And this time Billy Ray would never come back.

They crossed the Mississippi River at the Sunshine Bridge and headed to a small restaurant on the west bank. It was one of Celine's favorites, but a place she rarely visited. It seemed fitting to come here with Will, who rarely asked for dates. He had promised her better company than she'd had last night. Even in this quiet, irritable mood, he was providing that.

The dining room was dimly lit, the background music soft, the dinner guests few at this early hour. There was an intimate feel to the place that made her restless. She should have asked for bright lights and fast food, but a change of scene wouldn't change the way she felt. Nothing would, she suspected, short of being naked in bed with him—and that was something he didn't seem particularly interested in.

She was aware that he got aroused around her sometimes. The evidence was difficult to overlook, especially when it brought to mind the nasty inflection her sister had used last night. *Impressive.* It certainly seemed to be. Still, his arousal was accompanied by reluctance. He thought she was too young. Too naive. Too inexperienced to be worth his time. He was probably right.

They gave the waitress their order, then sat in uneasy silence for a few moments. Will surely could talk when he wanted—people like him, who lived the way he had for the last sixteen years, needed the gift of gab—but tonight he seemed only to want to brood. She might as well give him something to brood about.

"Did you, by chance, see the blond boy leaving the library before you arrived?"

He shook his head.

"It was Jared Robinson, Melanie's son."

He scowled at her.

Celine hesitated. What she was about to do was wrong. She never told anyone what others read, never discussed a patron's interest. But this was a special case. If divulging Jared's confidence led to Will's acknowledging him, that would make it right, wouldn't it?

"He wanted me to get a book for him."

"Fancy that—wanting a book from a library. What's this world coming to?"

"He wanted a book on DNA."

He was quicker than she had been. He realized Jared's interest immediately. "He's wasting his time," he said flatly.

"Why? Because you're never going to admit it?"

"Because there's nothing to admit."

She spread her napkin across her lap, then smoothed the creases. "Is it that simple for you? You really don't feel any obligation toward him? Any responsibility?"

"You're not listening to me. Jared Robinson is *not* my responsibility. He's *not* my son."

Celine felt a little disappointed and a whole lot annoyed. He had lied sixteen years ago. Why had she expected him to tell the truth now? Unless he *was* telling the truth. Unless he had always told it.

"How can you be so sure?" Her voice quavered just a bit.

His was as steady as his narrow-eyed gaze. "The same way I can be so sure that you and I don't have a kid out there somewhere."

"But you and I—" She broke off when the waitress returned with their drinks. When they were alone again, she continued. "You and I have never made love."

"Exactly." He gave her a wicked grin. "Not that I would be averse to getting more than my hands underneath those clothes of yours."

Ignoring his challenge, Celine sat back and gazed at the opposite wall. So he claimed never to have had sex with Melanie. *Never*. That was a pretty good indicator, then, that he hadn't fathered her child. *If* he was telling the truth.

She considered it, studying both sides but unable to decide which one was right. She wanted to believe him. She wanted to believe he was too good to turn his back on a kid who needed him, to treat his own son the way his mother had treated him. She wanted to believe he was honorable enough to accept responsibility for his actions, to put his duty as a father ahead of his desires as a man. She wanted to believe she was drawn to a decent man.

But she had nothing to base that on. He had warned her himself that he couldn't be trusted. He had taunted and teased and mocked her every time she'd seen him this past week. He had refused to give a straight answer to any question she had asked. He had lied and evaded and avoided. Yet she wanted to believe him.

"Why would Melanie lie?"

"Maybe the father was someone her parents disapproved of," he said, with a shrug that declared he didn't care.

"More than they disapproved of *you*?"

He didn't seem offended by her disbelief. "Maybe he was too old for her. Maybe he was married. Maybe he'd taken off and wasn't coming back. Maybe she never knew who the father was." Then his expression turned sour. "You think Melanie didn't have anything to gain by lying, don't you? And that I did."

Her face grew warm with a blush. "You did go out with her."

He leaned closer, not stopping until his face was only inches from hers. To anyone else in the restaurant, it would seem intimate, a perfect position for whispering sensuously indecent propositions. But no one else in the restaurant could see the cold, angry look in his eyes. No one else could hear the threateningly low tone of his voice.

"After this evening, I can legitimately say that I've gone out with you, too. Does that mean that if you turn up pregnant in a few weeks, I'm responsible?" The corners of his mouth curved up in a smile that held no warmth. "Are you really

that naive, Celie? Didn't any of your boyfriends teach you
what happens between a man and a woman? Don't any of
those books in your library explain how a woman gets pregnant?''

She swallowed hard, saying nothing, and he leaned closer
still, invading her space, daring her to back away—which
was exactly what she wanted to do; and so she remained
perfectly still, so still that she could feel his breath on her
cheek. ''Maybe you need some private lessons, Celie,'' he
murmured. ''I guarantee I can teach you everything you ever
wanted to know. Just let me warn you: I don't make love,
little girl, and I don't have sex. I fuck, pure and simple and
hard. If that's what you're wanting, you come to me and I'll
oblige you. But if you want more than that, you're panting
after the wrong man.''

Quietly, calmly, still without moving, she considered her
options. She could slap him—although a physical response
was silly and liable to bring like retaliation. She could push
him away and leave. She could pretend the last few minutes
hadn't happened. She could even accept his invitation. *Come
to me and I'll oblige you.* It just might be worth whatever
self-respect she would lose in the process. Or she could bluff
her way through.

''I'm a little confused here,'' she said, her voice too husky.
''Am I supposed to be offended, insulted, or aroused by that
little speech?''

There was a flash of surprise in his dark eyes that made
her smile. Will Beaumont was rarely caught off guard, and
she had just done it. And *that* answered her question. His
words—his use of that one blunt word in particular—had
been meant to offend or insult her. If she came knocking at
his door one of these sultry hot evenings asking for a tumble
in his bed, he would probably send her scooting the other
way—and not because she was too young or too innocent or
too naive.

He was aroused. He just didn't intend to do anything about
it.

Now she had to figure out why.

Chapter Four

The waitress brought their dinner and refilled their glasses, maneuvering close to Will, giving him an appreciative smile, brushing against him. He returned her smile with a long, lingering look that seemed to satisfy her, but his mind was elsewhere.

Damn Celine. She was too smart for her own good. Those damnable green eyes of hers could see right through him, and that wasn't a feeling that sat well with him. He was used to being the mysterious one, the misunderstood one, the private one. But she saw too much. She saw that he wanted her. She saw that he couldn't let himself have her. She probably even saw that his need for her was becoming a living, breathing obsession. Could she see that he could destroy her?

"Even if you aren't Jared's father . . ."

Back to that again, he thought grimly. "I'm not."

"You still need to see him. To talk to him. He deserves that much."

"He deserves it from his father. Not me."

"But he believes you *are* his father. He believes that you seduced his mother and got her pregnant, that you left home rather than accept your obligations to him and Melanie. And now you've come back and everyone is gossiping about you and him and Melanie, and you haven't shown even the slight-

79

est interest in meeting him. He deserves at least that small bit of attention from you, Will.''

He didn't want to admit that she was probably right. At this point in the kid's life, the question of who his father really was didn't much matter. Who he *believed* was his father was what was important. Jared must feel neglected. It was one thing to be abandoned and ignored by a parent who went on to other places—as Will's mother had, as Jared's own mother had. It was another entirely to be ignored by a parent who was living only a few miles away.

''And what am I supposed to say to him? 'Sorry, kid, but your mother lied. I'm not your father'?''

''I don't know what you should say. But if you attack Melanie, he's going to get defensive.''

''Even though she dumped him?'' He couldn't remember ever getting defensive in his own mother's behalf, ever being sorry that she was gone. Even when he had watched her pack, when she had explained that she was leaving and never coming back, when he had realized that she was leaving him alone there in the house with little food and no money, he hadn't been sorry. Scared as hell, yeah, but not sorry. He hadn't felt even a moment's regret when he had watched her walk away for the last time.

''She's his mother.''

''And that explains everything.'' He shook his head. ''You *are* naive, aren't you?''

She uncomfortably turned her attention to her dinner. He ate, too, but he watched her. It seemed that that had become his favorite pastime lately.

After his suggestion at the library—and the graphic manner in which he'd made it—she had changed clothes when they stopped by her house. Now she wore a white skirt, slim and snug and ending inches above her knees, along with a filmy, dusky blue blouse that left her long throat and her arms and a generous portion of her shoulders bare. It was as revealing as her usual clothes were concealing. It was exactly what he'd had in mind.

Finally she glanced at him, the look in her eyes hesitant. ''I'm sorry. I forgot about your mother,'' she said quietly.

Apologies made him uncomfortable. He didn't make them,

and he received them so rarely that he didn't know how to accept them. "She's easy to forget," he replied with a shrug.

"When was the last time you saw her?"

"The day she left. Twenty-four years ago."

"She never contacted you? You never tried to find her when you were older?"

"Why would I do that?"

She looked bewildered. "Because she's your *mother*. She's your only family."

"And she didn't want me, not ever. Not just when she left Harmony, but before that. It went way back to before I was even born. She never wanted to be a mother. And you think I should go looking for her?" He smiled lazily. "I guarantee you, if she didn't want the kid I used to be, there's no way in hell she's going to be interested in the man I've become."

"And you don't miss her."

"No. Paulette was just excess baggage in our family. My daddy and I got along fine without her. After he died, it didn't matter whether she was around or not."

"You called your mother by her name?"

"That was what she wanted."

Celine's smile was crooked. "As old as I am, if I called my mother Annalise to her face, she would kill me."

"As old as you are?" he mimicked. "Twenty-eight going on nineteen. You're such a woman."

Her smile faltered briefly, then grew stronger, knowing, secretive. He wished he could read her as easily as she read him. He wished he knew what was responsible for that mysterious smile. He wished he could take that smile—womanly, sensual, taunting, enticing—and keep it with him for the nights when he needed it.

It was still light when they left the restaurant. Still hot. The sun had set, coloring the western sky in shades of pink and purple, and the nightly chorus of insects had already begun their performance. A cloud of gnats hovered in the parking lot, forcing them to make a small detour as they walked to the car. This close to the river—the Mississippi was only a few hundred yards away on the other side of the high levee that obscured it from sight—summer always meant bugs.

It wouldn't even be nine o'clock when they got home, Will acknowledged as he backed out of the parking space. An early end to another unsatisfying evening.

It was a short, silent drive back to Harmony. The first street on the right led to Miss Rose's house. The first one on the left led to the old Beaumont place. He hadn't been there in years, and he would wager Celine had never seen it at all. Not that she would be impressed by it. The Beaumont farm had never been much to look at, even in the best of times. The first Beaumonts had squeezed a living from the land, one of them even supporting seven children. Will's father had been the first to give up farming and take a job in one of the factories instead. He'd made a living wage and supplemented it by leasing the unworked farmland to a neighbor.

The farm had been one of the few details Paulette had seen to before she'd taken off. She hadn't made any plans for the care of her son, but she had sold the farm, probably for a fraction of its worth, to that same neighbor. The desire for something new, something better, had been too strong for her to wait. He wondered if she'd found it. Heartless as it sounded, he didn't care.

He felt Celine's look as he turned to the left. She was curious, but she didn't ask him where they were going. Of course, she knew she was as safe out here with him as anywhere else. If he was going to come on to her, he would take her home to the comfort of her bed. Just in case she said yes. He was pretty sure now she would. *Damn.* He'd picked a fine time in his life to develop principles.

The road was a straight shot except for a curve around one giant live oak. Slowing a quarter of a mile past the oak, he turned into the driveway. It ended ten feet in at a fence.

He shut off the engine and the headlights, then got out. The night was alive with tree frogs, crickets, and the rustle of a soft breeze, and the rich, damp smells seemed intensified by the darkness. They brought back sweet memories of playing in the woods, splashing in the creek, digging in the dirt with his father. The first ten years of his life had been the happiest, just him and his father and, nearly forgotten in the background, Paulette. Then his father had died, and his life had gone to hell.

After a moment Celine joined him at the front of the car. "Is this where you grew up?"

"Yeah." The house had been straight ahead fifty yards. Shingled and tin-roofed, with six rooms, a deep front porch and a rickety back stoop, it hadn't been big or fancy, but it hadn't been poor, either. Now it was gone, its location marked only by the flowers growing wild in what had once been well-tended beds. Paulette had loved flowers, and his father had planted plenty of them for her—violets and daffodils, camellias and lilies, zinnias and roses—and in the lower-lying marshy areas out back, irises, yellow jasmine, and passionflower had grown wild. They'd given the place a beauty it lacked on its own and had sweetened the early-morning and late-evening air with their heavy fragrance.

Now the house was gone, torn down and carted away, and the arable land around it had been planted in sugarcane. Only the hardiest of those flowers remained.

"There was a creek back in those trees where we used to go fishing. Over there"—he gestured off to the right—"was my father's vegetable garden. Even though he couldn't make a living from farming, it was still in his blood, I guess. Every spring we planted a garden big enough to feed our family and then some. And the best wild berries in the whole damn parish grew over there."

"Does this land belong to you now?"

He glanced at her in the fading light and chuckled. "Hell, no. I don't own anything I can't put in a bag and take with me when I move on."

"And you do that a lot."

He rested one hand on the warm hood of the car. The stance turned him toward her, a little bit closer to her. That, plus shoving his free hand into his hip pocket, kept him from reaching for her. "I don't suppose I've stayed anywhere longer than a few months since I left here."

"That's a lot of places," she murmured.

A lot of places, a lot of unfriendly faces. Miss Rose had been right yesterday. That wasn't the life he would have chosen for himself. He had always thought he would finish high school, get a job in one of the factories like his father, and eventually settle down. Instead he hadn't even finished school—Melanie's announcement had come in March of his senior year—and he'd never found a steady job, and he hadn't even thought of settling down. He'd been alone and on the move for so long now that he wasn't sure he could settle in one place.

"How do you live?"

"Day by day. I pick up work when I can. I'm stingy with the money when I can't."

"They say you're a con man."

"They do, do they?" He shifted more comfortably against the car. "When I was in school, they used to say that I could sweet-talk a virgin right out of her clothes—and they were right." His grin was cocky. "Lucky that you aren't a virgin."

She moved to stand in front of him, forcing him to look at her. The light—a soft afterglow from the sun, the pale luster of the rising moon—was gentle on her face, making her too damned pretty. "You enjoy being arrogant and obnoxious, don't you? You appreciate your reputation as a hellraiser, a bad boy, someone who can't be trusted with women or money or anything else of value. You like making people like Raymond afraid of you. You like trying to scare me. But it's all an act, isn't it? It's a shield you hide behind so no one can know what you're really like, so no one can see if you have feelings that get hurt or pride that gets wounded. You've hidden behind it so long that you don't even know yourself anymore, do you?"

He stared at her, his throat tight, his mouth dry, a sick feeling in his gut. Then he forced out the harsh words to contradict her. "I know exactly what kind of person I am. I know what I've done. I know what I've felt and what I haven't felt. I know what I'll do in the future. I know what I'll do to you if you're not careful." He paused for a heavy moment, then said softly, "I'm not hiding from anything, Celie. But you are. You're seeing things that don't exist. You're giving me credit for qualities that I never had and never wanted. You're playing with fire, little girl, and you're going to get burned. Remember that, and when it happens, don't come crying to me. Don't expect me to give a damn."

After a moment, she turned away and walked around the car. He felt the slight shifting as she got inside, then heard the closing of the door. He stood there a few minutes longer, then, with a weary sigh, he slid behind the wheel, started the engine, and drove home.

At the steps to her porch, Celine turned and thanked him politely for dinner, then went inside. So damned polite, he thought with a scowl as he headed for the big house. Mrs. Hunter had surely done a good job of raising her little girl.

The back door was unlocked, and lights were on down the hall. Miss Rose was napping in the recliner, her head tilted slightly to one side. He crossed the room quietly, intending to put the car keys on the table beside her, then leave again; but just as he reached her, she woke up. She wasn't at all startled to see him.

"You're home early."

He shrugged. "So are you."

"Sophy and I are old women. We don't have as many late nights as we used to." She studied him a moment, then gestured toward the nearest chair. "Sit down."

"I don't want to keep you up."

"I think I can hold my eyes open a few minutes longer," she said drily. "Sit down."

"Yes, ma'am." He seated himself in the wing chair.

"What did you do with yourself this evening?"

"I had dinner across the river."

"Alone?"

"No." He wanted to leave it at that, but, like his dinner companion, Miss Rose's gaze was too sharp, too knowing. "With Celine."

"She's a good girl. That family of hers is as loony as a mud hen, every one of them, but Celine's got a good head on her shoulders. She takes after her great-grandmother. The first Celine and my mother were good friends. That woman single-handedly kept the family going. Celine had to do the same thing for her own family. Her father is an eccentric who married a kook, and her sister—" She gave him an admonishing look. "Well, you know Vickie. From the time Celine was a little girl, she made sure the bills got paid and there was food to eat. She's such a responsible girl. Even now she'll call her mother to remind her to pay this bill or run that errand or take care of this business."

Will hooked his fingers tightly together. He didn't want to hear a list of Celine's virtues that would surely lead to a politely phrased, subtle, but firm reminder that he wasn't the kind of man a paragon like Celine needed in her life. "How is Meredith?" he asked, then inwardly winced at his abruptness. Nothing subtle about *him*, was there?

"She's fine," Miss Rose replied as if his question wasn't unusual. "She still lives in Houston, she still has three dreary children, and she still thinks that dull man she married hung the stars in the sky."

"They've been married a long time." He hardly remembered Meredith. By the time he had come to live here, Miss Rose's daughter had already been married and living in Texas. There had been annual Christmas visits and occasional summer visits, but he'd had little contact with her or her husband, and he'd had nothing in common with her curiously well-mannered children—two girls with long hair that fell in perfect long curls, who wore lace-edged dresses and never got dirty, and a boy who didn't know how to throw a baseball and had no interest in fishing, tramping through the woods, or picking on his sisters.

"Thirty years." She gave a dry laugh. "And *I* thought it wouldn't last." After a moment, she folded her own hands together and asked, "How does it feel to be home again?"

He tried to avoid an honest answer. "You know, this part of Louisiana's no different from rural Mississippi, Alabama, and Georgia. Living in those places is almost like being here."

"Except that those places aren't home to you," she chided. "Harmony is."

That was true, he silently acknowledged. In the brief time that he was in town today, he'd begun to suspect that maybe he had missed the place. Maybe that was why he'd spent so many years in similar towns, where being a stranger had as often as not gotten him into trouble. God knew, he could have done better for himself in some city—Atlanta, maybe, or Nashville—but the few times he'd moved into a city, he had quickly moved right back out. Even unwanted, he'd felt comfortable in places like Harmony.

He'd felt at home.

"I haven't seen anyone I used to know except Raymond and Vickie."

"You need to get out more. A lot of people have moved away, but I'm sure some of your old friends must still live here. Let's see . . . George Martin's still here, and Davis Armstrong and that Peterson boy."

They *had* been friends—George, Davis, and Mark. Too often when he thought about growing up here, he forgot that he'd had a few friends. Mostly he remembered the girls who had been attracted to him for all the wrong reasons and the adults who had given him any number of names to live up to or down to.

But what would he have in common with a grown-up George, Davis, or Mark? They were settled. He probably never would be. They were probably married, accepted, if not respectable, members of the community. He would never be that, either. The only thing they'd really had in common sixteen years ago was a fondness for liquor, trouble, and girls. Nowadays he did his drinking alone, he got into more than enough trouble on his own, and all the friends in the world couldn't do a thing about the itch he had for the girl-woman in the cottage on the other side of the lawn. Besides, he wasn't going to be staying long enough to bother with renewing old friendships. Or building new ones.

"When am I going to find out why you brought me here?"

"All in good time," she replied, the same answer she'd given him last week. Then she testily asked, "What's your rush? You have something better waiting for you back in Podunk, Alabama? Or are you just ready to find someplace new to light for a week or two?"

"Just curious," he retorted just as testily. "You bring me three hundred miles because you need to see me, because there's something you want me to do, and then you refuse to tell me what it is. You would try the patience of a saint, Miss Rose."

"I don't try Celine's patience at all, and that girl's about as close to a saint as you'll find around here."

Rising from his chair, he started toward the door, then stopped near her. "I won't stay here forever," he said quietly.

She gave a soft sigh. "I know, Will."

For a moment he studied her, trying to tell if her disappoint-ment was in him or herself, in her own expectations. Bending, he brushed a kiss to her cheek, the way he'd done when he was ten years old. "But I'll stay long enough to do whatever it is you need."

Smiling dimly, she patted his arm. "Good-night, Will."

Laissez les bon temps rouler.

Melanie Robinson knew only six words in French, and that phrase contained five of them. *Let the good times roll.* That had been her motto for fifteen years, since she'd taken a hard look at her life so far and realized that it wasn't going to get much better. She'd been seventeen, alone, a high school dropout and mother of a baby she had never wanted. Jared's father wasn't going to marry her. She wasn't going to finish school, as her parents had wanted. She wasn't going on to college, as she had wanted. She wasn't going to make any-thing at all of her life, not with the mistakes she'd already made, so why bother trying? Why not devote herself to having fun?

She had tried. She had indulged in every sin she'd ever learned about in Sunday school. She had lived for the mo-ment, satisfying every whim, every hunger, only to find her-self starving again a short while later. She had eaten too much, drunk too much, screwed around too much, experimented too much. She had gone through money and men and her family's understanding, and she had lost everything—her son, her future, her heart, her pride. She had suffered all these years, and so had her parents. So had Jared.

Now it was time for a trip back to Harmony. It was time that Jared's father paid for their problems.

Leaving the sofa, she began dressing for the evening. Her apartment was tiny, a third-floor walk-up in one of the seedier sections of the French Quarter. When she had first come here, she had found the entire Quarter so exotic and exciting that she hadn't minded the shabby surroundings. Now, she admitted in a moment of rare honesty, she fit in perfectly. She looked as shabby, as used up and discarded, as this neighborhood.

Soon she would go home. She would leave this dismal place behind, for a while at least, and she would once again be her parents' little girl. She would see her son—God, how she missed him!—and forget the sordid life she had lived. For a time she would pretend that things were different, that she hadn't gotten pregnant, that she hadn't been abandoned, that she hadn't in turn abandoned her son. She would pretend that she was a daughter and a mother to be proud of.

She wouldn't stay long. She had tried before, but always the very sordidness that repelled her now had drawn her back. She would start to miss the men, different ones as often as she pleased, and the booze and the occasional drugs. She would miss the freedom. She would resent the constraints of pretending to be a worthy daughter and mother. She would sink back into the hopelessness that held her.

But before she left Harmony once again, this time—like that very first time—she would make sure Jared's father paid. She didn't care how he came by the money—if it was his own or if, as before, he stole it. All she cared was that he *did* get it, and a lot of it. She would make him pay dearly to get rid of her this time.

Saturday was just too damn hot to do anything but sit, Celine thought, and today outside was almost as cool as in. The air conditioner was laboring to cool the cottage, but it was a tough job for a system older than Celine herself. At least out here on the porch a breeze was blowing.

Unfortunately Will was there also, sprawled shirtless in the hammock stretched between two trees behind Miss Rose's house, right in Celine's line of sight. Even though he hadn't so much as twitched a muscle since she'd come outside, she couldn't ignore him. She would give a year of her life if she could, and five years if she could quit wanting him.

Maybe even ten, her sly voice whispered, if she could have him. If she could convince him that she wasn't so innocent or naive; that she could weigh the consequences and choose to risk them anyway; that his warnings had been sufficient; that whatever happened, she would deal with it without expecting anything from him.

He had one bare foot on the ground. Jeans, faded and snug, gloved his long legs and narrow hips, looking hot and uncomfortable and sexy as hell, making *her* hot and uncomfortable. He seemed to be asleep, although how anyone could sleep in this heat escaped her. The temperature would have to drop ten degrees to be bearable, thirty to reach comfortable.

It was nearly noon, and she had accomplished next to nothing. Will had appropriated the job of mowing, finishing three-fourths of the yard before she had even awakened this morning. What little cleaning that needed to be done inside could wait until this evening, when temperatures might be a little cooler. Miss Rose had been closed up inside her own house all morning, uninterested in chatting or anything else.

Maybe she should go visit her family, she thought, then immediately vetoed the idea. Sunday afternoons with them were enough most times, and Sunday afternoons with Vickie's family were often *too* much, especially now that her sister had seen Will again. She didn't want to see any more leering looks, didn't want to hear any more vulgar comments. She didn't want to let her jealousy of her sister grow any stronger.

Miss Rose came out the front door, carrying a quilt over one arm and a large woven basket. She set them at the bottom of the steps and walked halfway to Celine's house. "Go and get Will for me while I back the car out, will you, dear?" she called.

It wasn't necessary, Celine thought grudgingly. Miss Rose could yell across the yard at him as easily as at *her*. But she got to her feet without protest and went down the steps. "Going out?" she asked politely.

"Oh, yes, we're having a picnic."

A picnic on the hottest day of summer. She didn't envy him as she crossed the grass under the midday sun. Stopping at the foot of the hammock, she started to speak, only to be interrupted by him.

"I've got an idea, Celie," he murmured, his voice low and husky, his eyes closed, his smile nothing less than wicked. "Why don't I unfasten my jeans and you lift up that skirt and climb up here on top of me?"

"I've got a better idea," she replied, wrapping her fingers around the woven rope beneath his foot and swinging the hammock gently. "Why don't I give this thing a push and dump you facedown in the dirt?"

His laughter was clear and unexpected. "I've been there before. It wouldn't be anything new." Finally he opened his eyes just a bit, his dark lashes screening them. "But I've never been down and dirty with a woman like you. It has possibilities."

"Miss Rose wants you."

"So I heard." With a grace that she envied, he rolled to his feet, setting the hammock swinging. Now he was standing in front of her, so close that she could see the beads of sweat caught in the swirling dark hair that covered his chest and belly. "Why don't you come along?"

"I'm sure she packed only enough food for two."

"You can have mine. I'll just feast on you."

She held his gaze for a moment, then slowly smiled. "One day, Will, you're going to make a remark like that, and I'm going to take you up on it. Then what are you going to do?"

Just like last night, she had caught him off guard, but he recovered quickly. In a low, sexy, intimate voice, he murmured, "I'll teach you things you haven't even begun to imagine, little girl."

Little girl. Who was he reminding of her unsuitability? she wondered. Her? Or himself? Not caring, she replied softly, "You'd be surprised what I can imagine."

"You'd be surprised what I can teach you."

For a long time they stared at each other. Celine's throat was dry, her muscles all fluttery, her entire body achy. If Miss Rose weren't waiting, she thought numbly, she would make a pass at him. For the first time in her entire life, she would do something bold, something reckless, something totally out of character. But Miss Rose *was* waiting.

"You'd better go," she recommended hoarsely.

"You might as well come along. You're going to be hot and dissatisfied here."

"I've lived an entire life being dissatisfied. I think I can last another afternoon."

Before he could reply to that, she turned and walked away. She was almost at her house when Miss Rose, behind the steering wheel of her big black car, leaned across the seat and rolled down the window. "Come along, Celine," she called. "I want you to see this, too."

"See what?" she asked, slowly veering toward the car.

"It's a surprise. Come on, get in. I have plenty of food."

"Thanks for the invitation, Miss Rose, but I—"

"Come on, Celie," Will seconded, coming up behind her and catching her arm. "Get in." He steered her toward the car, ignoring her glare, practically pushing her into the front seat. After tossing his shoes into the backseat, he pulled the T-shirt he carried over his head and tugged it down, then climbed in back.

Instead of turning around and going toward town, Miss Rose headed east. The dirt road wound through acres of Kendall property, undeveloped woodland that Raymond wanted to sell to one of the corporate farms and Miss Rose wanted to keep wild and natural. Being the stronger of the two—and the sole landholder—Miss Rose had won for the time being; but Celine had no doubt that once the old lady was gone, all these trees would be sold to some logging company and the land cleared to make way for more sugarcane. Just what this parish needed.

They'd gone only a few miles when Miss Rose slowed and made a careful turn into a brick-column-flanked drive. Celine couldn't remember ever noticing the driveway before, but then she couldn't remember the last time she'd come this way, either.

The lane was dirt, soft and silty, and the weeds that grew in the center brushed the bottom of the car. A half mile in, the dense growth of trees gave way to what had once been a grand manicured lawn, and sitting square in the middle of it was a house.

Even though it was in a sorry state of disrepair, it was beautiful. Great patches of stucco were missing, revealing faded red brick underneath. The pillars, once white, had been stripped to bare wood and brick by the elements and years of neglect. The glass panes in the windows were broken and boarded over, the shutters hanging loose or completely fallen, the big double doors in front kicked in. Upstairs, on the front and one side, sooty smoke stains cut a wide swath from each window, each burned-out door.

"This is the old Kendall family home," Miss Rose announced when they were all out of the car.

"I've always heard that it was destroyed by fire," Celine remarked.

"Damaged. Not destroyed. It's been empty longer than I've been alive, but it's still solid. I'm going to restore it." She looked from Celine to Will, standing beside her, and smiled triumphantly. "And I want you to do it."

Will gave Miss Rose a long, steady look before shaking his head. "I can't."

"Of course you can."

"I don't have the background or the knowledge for something like this."

"You're good with your hands."

"So's a typist or a hairstylist, but that doesn't qualify either one for this kind of job."

"You'll be fine. All you'll have to do is help supervise the crew."

Swallowing, he looked from her to the house. Some of the small things he could handle, but anything more complicated than carpentry or a little masonry work was way out of his league. "I'm not qualified," he repeated. "Let Raymond handle it for you."

Both responses came at once—a choked-back laugh from Celine and a disgusted snort from Miss Rose. "Raymond has probably forgotten that the place even exists; and if he did remember, he would insist on bulldozing it down along with everything else on the land." She glanced at the house, then sighed softly. "Raymond has a great fondness for the Kendall name, but he has no respect for the family history. He would take one look at this house, and his banker's mind would go to work. However much it would cost to restore it would be too much, in his opinion. Why spend family money on *this* house when he has a big, beautiful *new* Southern mansion of his own to live in?"

"And maybe he'd be right."

She gave him a hard look. "You siding with Raymond? I

thought pure orneriness alone would make you take a stand against him.''

He had been looking at the symmetry of the house—the columns, the windows, the doors, all perfectly matched. Now he turned to stare down at Miss Rose. ''Is that why you brought me back here? To take a stand against Raymond? To play me off against him?''

''Of course not. The house has little to do with the matter. This is something I intend to do whether you help me or not. I just thought you might be getting bored sitting around the guesthouse all day. I thought you might like something to occupy your time.''

Scowling because he *was* in need of some hard, physical labor, he turned away and crossed the grown-over lawn to the steps. The gallery was eight feet wide and ran all the way around the house. Only a few feet above the ground and lacking a rail, it was made of dusty red brick laid in a herringbone pattern. As he walked in a slow circle around the place, he noticed a brick here, two there, a few more up ahead, that had crumbled and needed replacing.

The four faces of the house were virtually the same, except for the French doors on the sides and the ornate double doors in front and back. All four sides were in sorry shape. All four held the potential to be beautiful again. It would cost a fortune to restore it. It would infuriate Raymond, who was already unhappy enough with his presence.

But he knew Miss Rose well. She *would* go ahead, regardless of his decision. After all, he did know enough to recognize substandard work, and how to keep an eye on the crew. He could learn the rest. There must be a ton of books out there on restoring old Southern mansions to their past glory, and he just happened to know a librarian who could get them for him.

Completing the circuit, he leaned against a front pillar. Miss Rose and Celine were waiting at the top of the steps, watching him. ''How do you know this place won't collapse at the first strong wind?'' The Louisiana climate was hard on grand old houses like this. It was unforgiving of neglect.

''I've already had an architect and several engineers look at it. They assure me that, although there's significant damage, it's structurally sound." Miss Rose drew herself up to her full height, all five feet four inches of it. "Work starts a week from Monday. Will you be here?" she demanded.

Slowly Will grinned. "I'll be here."

"Good." Then her shoulders rounded just a bit, and she fanned herself with a handkerchief from her pocket. "Oh, dear, it's warm today, isn't it? Celine, be a darling and get the lunch from the car. I do believe I'll leave you two here to enjoy it alone and return to the house. This heat drains something from an old lady like me."

Celine opened her mouth—probably to protest, Will thought—but Miss Rose didn't give her the chance. "Would you like me to come back for you in a few hours or would you rather walk home? It's only about a mile through the woods. Will, you know the way, don't you?"

She hurried them along, handing the quilt to Celine, the basket to Will, then sliding behind the wheel and driving away before either of them could stop her. "Maybe one of us should have gone with her," Celine said, her expression shaded with concern.

He didn't share her worry. When Miss Rose wanted something, she used whatever advantages she could to get it, including her age and her health. In spite of her fragile appearance, she was one of the strongest women he'd ever known. "There's nothing wrong with her. She got what she wanted, so why stay out any longer in this heat?"

"She *is* a tad manipulative," she conceded.

"A tad? That's like saying Raymond's a little greedy or I'm a little reckless or you're a little pretty."

She gave him a sharp look, then swept her gaze around the yard, searching for a good place to spread the quilt. She settled on a patch of grass beneath a live oak. Will followed her, setting the basket down to help spread the quilt.

"Do you think she's crazy?"

Sitting down, he watched her unpack their lunch. "For wanting to restore the house? Why shouldn't she? She can afford it, and it's important to her."

"But it's going to cost a lot of money, and she's in her seventies."

"Meaning what? That she won't be around long to enjoy

it?'' He snorted. ''As cantankerous as she is, she's going to live to be a hundred.''

''Have you done any restoration work?''

''I've helped build new houses and repair old ones.'' Then he shook his head. ''I don't know anything about this kind of work.''

She unpacked fried chicken, boiled shrimp on ice, potato salad in an insulated container, a dish of sliced tomatoes, gooey brownies, and two tall tightly capped bottles of ice water, one flavored with slices of lemon, the other with lime.

''Raymond isn't going to take this quietly, is he?'' he asked after she'd dished up the meal.

''Raymond doesn't take anything quietly,'' Celine replied. ''He won't stand by and do nothing while his mother spends his inheritance on a house that he's erased from his memory.'' She sighed softly. ''He told me once that this house had burned down nearly a hundred years ago. I had no idea it was still here.''

''Like Miss Rose said, damaged but not destroyed. It happened when Wynn's grandfather was living here.'' He remembered the story well, had heard it years ago on a day like this when Miss Rose had brought him over here for the first time. They had walked through the big house, and she had talked and he had listened. The strangely empty rooms, big and shadowy, had seemed to echo her words, bringing her tale of vengeance eerily to life. That day, for the first and probably last time in his life, he had believed in ghosts.

''Do you know the story?'' Celine asked, her gaze shifting from the house to him. ''What happened?''

''Jefferson Kendall's wife, Wynn's grandmother, had died and left him with four children to raise, so he went looking for a replacement in New Orleans. The woman he found was from a prominent French family that was down on its luck. She was beautiful, outgoing, and about twenty-five years younger than he was. But it wasn't a happy marriage. For the first time in years she finally had some money again, but she was stuck up here in Harmony where she couldn't spend it. She missed the parties and the social life, and she wasn't any too thrilled with a husband old enough to be her father.''

Silently Celine offered him the two bottles of water. When

he shrugged, she took the lime water for herself, ignoring the glasses Miss Rose had packed and drinking straight from the bottle. He watched her for a moment, then swallowed hard and looked away.

"So what did she do?" she prompted.

"What any beautiful young woman with a tired old husband would do, I guess. She found herself a lover—one of the men who worked for Jefferson, one of the *young* men—and she wasn't any too discreet about it. She brought him right into Jefferson's house. He came home one afternoon and found them in bed together, and, in a jealous rage, he set the room on fire. He claimed afterward that he had intended to kill himself in the fire, but somehow he managed to survive unharmed while his wife and her lover died. After that, he wouldn't allow any repairs done on the house. He built the house down the road, moved the kids in there, and put this place off-limits to everyone. He left it here to fall in on itself."

Celine was moodily silent for a moment, her attention on the upper floor where Jefferson's wife had died. Was she thinking about the unhappy woman? Did she fancy, as he had years ago, that she could hear her tears, her screams? Could she feel her fear?

"How do you know all that?" she asked when she finally looked at him again.

"That's the kind of story Miss Rose told me when I was a kid. No nursery rhymes or fairy tales for me."

She wiped her hands on a napkin, then leaned back against the tree. "It's a sad story," she said with a sigh. "Jefferson must have loved her a great deal to feel so betrayed by her affair, to take such drastic action against her."

"I doubt that love entered into it. Possessiveness, maybe. Dominance. Control. Revenge. Pure old meanness. She'd made a fool of him, and men don't take lightly to being made a fool of, especially by someone they bought and paid for."

"Has anyone ever made a fool of you?"

"Nope." He tossed his napkin into the basket, then stood up and gazed down at her. "And no one ever will."

Leaving her without a backward look, he approached the house again. This time he entered through the gaping portal where the back doors should have been. He found them inside, splintered and lying in pieces on the floor.

The entry hall was twenty feet wide and ran the length of the house front to back. The floor was wood, the ceiling high, the signs of decay everywhere. Each of the downstairs rooms was the same—darkened by the boarded-over windows and filled with debris, shattered glass, crumbling plaster. A mouse scurried across the drawing room floor as he entered, and a bird swooped from its nest high in the chandelier.

He was studying the cracks in the black marble fireplace when the hall floor outside the door creaked. He'd known Celine would eventually come inside. Maybe he would offer her a tour of the house, ending in one of the upstairs bedrooms—not that there would be a bed left behind, and certainly not one in any condition to use after nearly a hundred years. But maybe the suggestion of a bed, and the suggestion of what they could do on it, would be enough.

One day, Will, you're going to make a remark like that, and I'm going to take you up on it.

God, he was tempted to find out if she was bluffing.

And if she wasn't?

She'd been warned. She knew exactly what she could expect from him. She knew exactly what he wouldn't give her. She was an adult. If she willingly accepted those risks, didn't that free him from blame, from guilt? Hadn't he done all any decent man would do in warning her? Wouldn't it be all right for him to have her? No. It wouldn't.

She came into the room, walking in a slow circle around the perimeter, taking note of the faded stenciling that decorated the walls, the elaborate moldings too high for vandals to reach, the plaster medallion, about half of it missing now, that was centered on the ceiling. "I bet one of the rugs in Miss Rose's house came from this room," she remarked, joining him at the fireplace.

"Probably."

"I wonder if she intends to live here."

"I doubt it, unless she's planned some extensive renovations along with the restoration. The house doesn't have a kitchen or bathrooms. It was never set up for electricity or plumbing, and heating and cooling it would cost a fortune."

"Maybe she plans to give it to the state, to make a museum of it."

"Or maybe just once before she dies, she wants to see it the way it was intended to be."

Resting her chin on one hand, with the other she traced a pattern in the dust on the mantel. "You said you'd worked on houses before. Was that what you did all the years you were gone—construction work?"

"I did a little of anything you can imagine," he replied with a grin. "Including begging, borrowing, and stealing."

She didn't smile. "That's what con artists do, isn't it?"

He blew his breath out in an exasperated sigh. "The only people I ever conned were women, and I never took anything that they didn't give willingly." His voice dropped a tone or two. "Nothing that *you* wouldn't give willingly, too, Celie, if I decided to ask for it."

She didn't back down or look away or forget the subject. "So what kind of work did you do?"

Swinging away, he crossed to the double doors leading into the parlor. Called pocket doors because they slid into the walls, turning the two smaller rooms into one large room when open, they were hand carved, heavy, and in decent shape. Refinishing was probably all they would need, he thought, rubbing his hand over the fine wood.

Finally he gave her an answer. "I built houses and laid bricks. I picked up trash in a state park and washed dishes in diners from here to the East Coast. I drove a tow truck and pumped gas and swept floors and fixed cars and picked cotton. I worked as a security guard—that's a joke, isn't it, Miss Celine?—and I dug ditches and for a while I cleaned rich people's swimming pools. I also parked rich people's cars, and from time to time I screwed rich people's lonely rich daughters when they needed someone in their beds. When *I* needed a bed, period."

When he slid the doors apart, she left the fireplace and walked past him into the parlor. "There's nothing wrong with honest work," she said quietly, annoying him all over again.

"I'm not apologizing for the way I've lived. I'm not ashamed of anything I've done." But that wasn't entirely true. Every one of the nights he'd spent in jail, every one of the times he'd stolen he'd felt ashamed. But he'd done what he had to to survive. He hadn't had much choice.

Now he had. For a while, at least, Miss Rose was housing and feeding him and giving him work. In return he had to be on his best behavior.

That reinforced the answer to his earlier question. Celine was still off-limits. He could watch her, talk to her, even make outrageously suggestive comments to her. He could want her until he thought he would die from it. He could screw any other woman in the state of Louisiana and pretend it was she. But he couldn't screw her.

They walked through the rest of the downstairs in silence, then made their way to the next floor. The staircase was made of cypress, prized for its resistance to rot, and was still as solid as when it was built. Whichever Kendall had built the house had placed a high premium on quality materials and workmanship. That would make the restoration a little easier.

Outside on the upper gallery, Celine faced west, staring through the trees. "I've always thought it a shame that we live within a mile or two of a river like the Mississippi and the only place we can actually see it is from Sunshine Bridge."

"Take that levee down and we'd see it all right—right inside our houses."

She responded with an agreeing murmur, then turned toward the corner room. The scorch marks discolored the walls and had burned away the windowsills. She could see inside from the gallery, Will knew, because he had stood there himself more than twenty years ago and peered through the glassless window.

"It doesn't look as bad as I expected."

"The fire was put out pretty quickly. The drapes burned, and the upholstered furniture and the bed. That was where he started it—the bed. Miss Rose said they were asleep, that they woke up in flames. She said their screams haunted Wynn's father's dreams for months afterward."

"What a terrible thing to do to another human being."

"Passion can be a terrible thing."

"Passion?" she echoed. "Down there you were calling it revenge. Meanness."

"Passion refers to more than lust, Celie. You look at another man right now the way you look at me, and I might get jealous. But if you belonged to me, if you were my own beautiful little wife, all mine, and you looked at another man that way, jealousy might turn to rage. Who knows what I'd do then?"

Celine swallowed hard. He was speaking hypothetically, of course, putting himself in Jefferson Kendall's place. He wasn't saying that there was anything special about the way she looked at him. He wasn't implying that he cared enough to be jealous. "You wouldn't set me on fire," she disagreed, her throat tight.

His smile was strangely erotic. "I think I would. I'd make you burn. I'd make you forget any other man existed. I would touch you in places you've never been touched, in ways you'll never be touched. I would make you need until you begged, until you pleaded, until you thought you would die, and then I would bring you such satisfaction that you would weep. I would create a hunger in you that no one else could feed, that no one else could satisfy." This time his smile was taunting, promising, slightly threatening. "I would punish you with pleasure."

Trembling deep inside, she took a step toward him, then another. Even though her heart was pounding, even though her blood was so hot that a damp sheen covered her skin, even though her entire body was throbbing with just the kind of need he had described, her hand was remarkably steady when she reached out and laid it flat against his chest. "Punish with pleasure," she echoed. "I like the sound of that."

She didn't know which was hotter—his skin beneath the thin cotton of his shirt or her palm. It was a sure bet, though, that the humid heat of the day didn't even begin to compare to their own steamy heat.

She expected him to push her away, to make some comment about her innocence, her inexperience, or her unsuitability for him. She expected a scathing insult, mockery, or some other small cruelty. She didn't expect him to stroke her hand gently, to spread her fingers so that she touched more of him, to press every bit of her palm against him, to lay his own hand on top to hold it there.

She didn't expect his soft, soul-weary sigh.

After a moment he wrapped his fingers around her wrist. In a movement so quick that it left her breathless, he pulled her hand away and twisted her arm behind her back, using the leverage to yank her close. His body was hard, and so were his voice, his eyes, his words. "Maybe you've fooled me with those big eyes and those innocent ways of yours. Maybe you're really a whore at heart. Maybe you don't deserve anything better than getting fucked in the dirt."

"And maybe you're a coward, Billy Ray," she replied, calling on every ounce of courage she could scrape up to challenge him. "Maybe you're afraid to risk anything better than getting fucked in the dirt."

She could feel his anger, dark, shuddering, frustrated, but she wasn't afraid. He wasn't hurting her. His hold on her wrist remained firm, but not tight. "Don't play with me, Celie. I've given about all the warnings you're going to get."

Offering him an innocent smile, she leaned so close that she could see the shadows in his eyes, and softly, deliberately seductively, she whispered, "Promises, promises, Will."

He stared at her—shocked? dismayed? repulsed?—then dropped her hand and stalked away. She wanted to call his name, to do the taunting this time herself, to go after him, but she remained where she was. There was a limit to how far she was willing to go, a limit to how far he was willing to let her.

His steps were heavy on the stairs and the wooden floor in the entry. There was no door to slam or, she was sure, she would have heard that, too. In a moment, he appeared in the yard, his strides long, his tension palpable even from a distance, and a moment after that, he disappeared into the trees.

She wasn't concerned as she turned away from the railing. Even if she didn't know the way through the woods back to Miss Rose's house, she could follow the driveway and the dirt road out front. It would take longer, but it would get her safely home.

Before she followed the route he'd taken, she cautiously approached the front bedroom, staying a safe distance back from the scorched floorboards. The story Will had told her was interesting and sad, and the people, long since gone, were too easy to pass judgment on. A part of her couldn't blame Jefferson Kendall for wanting to punish his wife. Marriage vows deserved some sort of respect, some honor, and she had betrayed hers.

She walked slowly through the house and down the stairs. Without Will at her side, she felt the emptiness now, the loneliness, the ghostliness. It was a sad place—painstakingly built, lovingly cared for, then callously abandoned because of one man's rage, one man's passion.

Underneath the live oak, she packed away the last of their lunch, then shook out the quilt and folded it. She was bending to pick up the basket when Will's voice came from behind her. "I'll take that."

He was leaning against another tree some distance away, his stance casual except for the arms folded over his chest. She knew enough body language to interpret that with her eyes closed. *Keep away.*

"You didn't have to come back," she remarked as she approached him. "I can find my own way home."

He moved away from the tree and took the basket. "The trail is this way."

Calling the path they followed a trail was a generous overstatement. It was a good thing she trusted his sense of direction, because once they were surrounded by the dense growth, she couldn't even find the sun in the sky to check their progress.

Soon, though, they came out of the woods and into a wide clearing bisected by railroad tracks. The tops of the rails gleamed in the midafternoon sun. To the left they curved to the southeast until eventually they reached New Orleans. To the right they ran straight, running along the edge of town, snaking their way north to Baton Rouge and points beyond.

"Was he punished?" she asked, catching up with Will, matching her strides to his.

He frowned down at her before realizing that she meant Jefferson. "By the law? No. He was a Kendall."

"So was she."

"But only by marriage. The circumstances of her death were covered up. Officially she was taking a nap when a candle ignited the bedclothes—although no explanation was given for why she was using a candle in the middle of a sunny summer afternoon or how the candle moved from the night table to the bed. As for the man, he was reported to have disappeared after helping himself to his boss's riches.''

''Which was true in a sense.'' She picked her way across the gravel railbed, then followed him into the trees again, sighing softly at the comfort their shade provided. ''So Jefferson got away with it.''

''I don't know. He was rumored to have gone mad a few years later, supposedly driven crazy by guilt over what he'd done. Brutally murdering two people could do that to you, I suppose.''

''I can't believe I've lived here all my life and never heard this story.''

''It *was* a hundred years ago,'' he reminded her. ''Besides, Raymond wouldn't like having Kendall family history treated as common gossip.''

When the trail widened, she moved to walk beside him. ''Have you seen him lately?''

''Not since that night when you were eavesdropping.''

''The night he said that you two had had an agreement. You never did tell me about what.'' She tried to sound innocent because she knew her remark would annoy him. He had denied any sort of agreement with Raymond, but she didn't believe him. She was undecided about his claim that he wasn't Jared Robinson's father, but she had no doubt whatsoever that he had lied to her about Raymond. She had let it slide for a week, but as long as she was being pushy this afternoon, she might as well nag him about that, too.

''You know, Celie, I can't think of much in my life that's any of your business.''

She stopped walking and waited for him to stop, too, and turn to face her. When he finally did, she said, ''This town is my home, and these people are my family and friends. You're causing trouble for them—for Miss Rose and Raymond, for Jared and his grandparents, for Vickie and her family, for me. That makes it my business.'' After a pause in which he remained silent, she continued. ''Did you promise him that you wouldn't come back here? Did he help you leave? Did he keep Melanie's parents away from you until you got away?''

She waited, one long, hot minute after another, but still he said nothing. Damn him, he was too good at keeping secrets. But that was all right. If there was one thing working in the library had taught her, it was how to use all her resources. Will might never tell her anything. But Raymond would.

Chapter Five

———•o•———

Sunday dinner was over, the kitchen cleaned, and the Hunter house relatively quiet. The men were in the living room watching baseball on TV, and Annalise had taken the three kids into the backyard to play in the wading pool there. Celine and Vickie sat at the corner kitchen table that doubled as their mother's workspace, a pitcher of tea between them and a horde of strange little ceramic goblins, their mother's latest creations, keeping vigilant watch over them.

"Has Billy Ray asked about me?"

Celine had been dreading this question, this conversation, all day. She had almost decided to skip church and stay home to avoid it, but had decided that wouldn't be such a great idea, not with Will in the guesthouse out back.

"No," she replied flatly, disapprovingly. "He hasn't."

"I wish I had remembered to tell him my last name. Of course, he can find that out from you. You will tell him when he asks, won't you, Celine?"

Lowering her voice so no one outside the room could overhear, she said sharply, "You're a married woman, Vickie. Have you forgotten that?"

"How can I when you keep throwing it up at me?" She rolled her eyes heavenward with a put-upon sigh, then her lascivious smile returned. "That's part of the fun, you know?

106

It makes it a little bit more wicked. More sinful." She picked up one of Annalise's creations, wrinkled her nose at the ugly face, and set it down again. "So . . . have you seen him since Thursday evening?"

Celine bit back the desire to tell her that he'd taken her to dinner Friday night, that they'd shared lunch and a little intimate conversation yesterday, that he had been watching her, moody and intense, from his window when she'd left for church this morning. But it was none of Vickie's business. Her relationship with Will—if she could call it that—was no one's business but theirs.

"He keeps to himself."

"I expected him to get in touch with me by now." Vickie fluffed her hair. "Of course, he probably realized that Richard would be home over the weekend. I'm sure he'll find some way to reach me later."

Clenching her fists beneath the table, Celine gracelessly changed the subject. "We're starting a children's story time at the library Wednesday. Maybe you can bring the kids. I think they'll enjoy it."

"How long will it last?"

"A half hour to an hour, depending on how attentive the kids are."

Vickie's smile came slow and sweet. "Hmm. Sounds perfect."

Celine stared at her. "Don't even think it. Don't you dare bring those kids to the library and leave them with me so you can go out with another man. If you do, I swear I'll tell Richard everything."

The smile remained in place but changed subtly, becoming cooler. "And I'll make sure he doesn't believe you. I'll tell him you still have feelings for him. I'll tell him you're making up lies to punish me for marrying him when you wanted him for yourself. I'll tell him you never got over your jealousy that he preferred me over you. And he did, Celine. I know you like to think that I seduced him, that I gave him no choice, that I stole him right away from you, but you're wrong. From the moment we met, he quit loving you. He quit wanting you. He just had to find some way to get rid of you."

Celine wet her lips, but her short, shallow breaths dried them again. It wasn't enough that she had to listen to Vickie's crude talk about the man Celine wanted, but now she had to hear her brag about the man she'd already taken from her? "Vickie—"

"Did you know that we made love that very first night? That when Richard sneaked into your room around three o'clock that morning, he had already been with me?" Her expression was amused—not malicious or threatening or hurtful, but *amused*, damn it. "Did you know that he used to skip class to be with me? That sometimes I drove up to the school and we did it in your bed while you were gone?"

"What did I do to you?" she whispered stiffly, feeling numb deep inside. "What did I ever do to deserve this?"

"I did you a favor, honey," Vickie replied, her tone sincere. "You weren't in love with Richard, not really. You were just infatuated because he was the first guy you'd been to bed with. I guess you really believed all that garbage we heard growing up about only sleeping with the man you loved. You wanted to go to bed with Richard, and so you convinced yourself that you were in love—"

Celine didn't want to hear anything else. She didn't want to hear Vickie attempt to justify what she had done. She didn't want to know her only sister could be that selfish, that stupid, that amoral. Pushing back from the table, she walked out in midsentence, ignoring Vickie's, "Hey, where are you going?" She said an abrupt good-bye to her father and Richard, left the house and called a second good-bye to her mother out back, then got into her car and pulled away from the curb. She wasn't quick enough, though, to avoid seeing Vickie hurry out of the house or to miss hearing her name.

So it had all been for her own good: Vickie's affair with her fiancé, her betrayal, Celine's heartache. It had all been a favor done for her out of the kindness of Vickie's heart. The mere suggestion made her feel sick inside.

She was nearly home before she noticed the car in her rearview mirror. Vickie's car. Damn it, she would strangle her, she swore, before she would listen to another word out of her stupid, empty head.

She was home and on her way inside when Vickie raised

a cloud of dust with her sudden stop. "Celine, wait!" she called, hurrying around the car.

Reluctantly she stopped on the porch, the screen door between them. "What do you want?" she demanded coldly.

"Oh, honey, I'm sorry. I shouldn't have said those things. I didn't realize—"

Celine jerked the screen door open again and stepped into the doorway, leaning her shoulder against the frame there. "You're sorry you said those things?" she echoed. "How about being sorry you *did* them? Haven't you ever felt even the slightest remorse for what you did?"

"Well . . . Celine . . ."

She swore silently. The look on Vickie's face was a familiar one: total lack of understanding. She didn't feel remorse because she didn't see anything wrong with what she'd done. She had seen a man she'd wanted, and who gave a damn that he was engaged to someone else?

Her sister didn't search long for something to say. In less than thirty seconds, Celine would bet, her mind had started to wander, and it wandered in Will's direction. "Is that where Billy Ray's staying?" she asked, gesturing toward the guesthouse with its open windows and door.

"You are incredible, Vickie."

Hearing the disgust in her voice, Vickie looked back at her. "I told you I was sorry for what I said at Mama's, Celine. But you know what happened was for the best. He wasn't right for you, and you certainly weren't right for him."

Celine stared at her. "It probably was for the best. We probably wouldn't have been happy together, but that's not the point. My God, you're my *sister*, Vickie. That's supposed to *mean* something to you. *I'm* supposed to mean something to you. Damn it, I've had casual acquaintances who showed more consideration for me than you ever have."

"You mean that stuff about not dating each other's old boyfriends. I never did see the sense in that. If I met a guy that I liked, what did it matter who he used to date?"

"There was no 'used to' involved here. You met a guy you liked who happened to be engaged to marry *me*, and you didn't think twice before jumping into bed with him. You didn't even have the decency to come to me. If you guys had wanted each other so badly, I would have stepped aside. I would have given his ring back to him and canceled the wedding. But you didn't do that. You sneaked around behind my back, you lied to me, you pretended that nothing was going on . . . until you got caught. Even then you couldn't say you were sorry."

Vickie's voice when she spoke was soft, sympathetic. "Do you think you're still in love with him, Celine? Is that the problem?"

She wanted to cry. She wanted to pull her hair and stomp her feet in a tantrum the likes of which she had never experienced. Better still, she wanted to slap some sense, some compassion, some decency, into her sister. She wanted to just slap her, period.

In the end, though, she simply sighed. "You don't understand, do you? You never will." Shaking her head, she said flatly, "Go home, Vickie. Go away and leave me alone."

For a moment Vickie stood motionless, her expression bewildered and chastened, like a small child who had been punished and didn't know why. Then she took a step forward. "I really am sorry I upset you, honey."

Celine just stared down at her, and after another moment Vickie turned and walked away. When she reached her car, she called, "I'll talk to you later, okay? And I'll bring the kids to the story hour Wednesday. I'll stay and help out, all right? Okay, Celine?"

The hopeful note in her voice made Celine feel ill. Still, she didn't respond.

Around the corner on the screened porch, slumped way down in a wicker chair and motionless, Will watched Vickie drive away. Slowly the sound of her car faded and was replaced with another, closer sound, this one slow, arrhythmic, hollow. The angle of the chair's position made it difficult to see, but when he twisted his head far enough, he could see Celine leaning against the flat white post, tilting her head forward until her forehead banged with a thud against the wood.

When she had arrived a few minutes earlier, he had intended to talk to her, to coax her into spending a little time with him, to torment himself a little further. When her sister had unexpectedly shown up, he'd decided to stay hidden and unnoticed. Now that Vickie was gone, that was probably still the best course of action. Their conversation hadn't left Celine in the best of moods.

But, her forehead resting against the wood, she opened her eyes and saw him. He sank a little deeper in the chair, but she didn't look away. Finally he felt compelled to speak. "Banging your head against the wall usually tends to be a painful and futile exercise."

"You've tried it before?" she asked drily.

"Not voluntarily, but I've met a few people in my life who took great pleasure in bringing my face into contact with immovable objects such as walls and parking lots. I didn't usually enjoy it."

Slowly she moved, letting the screen door bang behind her, and approached him. "Been sitting there long?"

"Long enough." He moved his feet from the chair in front of him so she could sit down. She was dressed for church, wearing a pretty flowered dress with a heavy crocheted lace collar. Like all her other clothes, it made her look innocent, fresh, wholesome. Too good. Maybe that was what bothered him about the clothes, and not the fact that her long legs were usually covered, her full breasts too often concealed. Maybe he saw the simple garments themselves as a reminder to stay away.

"I keep telling myself that I love my sister, I really do." She folded her hands primly in her lap, sighed deeply, then laughed. "But I swear, there are times when I could kill her."

"There are times when she probably deserves it."

He wanted to ask what man had been unfaithful to her with her sister, what man she had loved enough to want to marry. He wanted her to answer Vickie's question, the one she had brushed off. *Do you think you're still in love with him, Celine?*

Was that why she was twenty-eight, the prettiest woman he'd seen in a long time, for damn sure the most desirable woman he'd seen, and still single? Was that why she buried herself in the library? Why she spent all her free time out here with no one but Miss Rose for company? Because she was pining away for the fiancé Vickie had stolen from her?

He didn't ask. Asking would embarrass her, and he didn't have the right to know. Unless he were offering her something in return, he didn't have a right to ask for anything from her.

"Were all the good people of Harmony in church this morning repenting their sins?" he asked instead.

"All the usual ones. You should go sometime and see for yourself. Show all those good people that God still works miracles."

"I don't care much for religion. I never figured out how going to church on Sunday absolves you of guilt for all the sins you committed Monday through Saturday."

"Not everyone at church is like that."

"Enough are. I guess they're balanced out by the occasional folks like you and Miss Rose." Grinning, he added, "Miss Rose says you're the closest thing to a saint Harmony has."

The comment didn't amuse her, as he'd expected. Instead, she looked pensive, regretful. "Just for a little while, I think I'd like to be a sinner instead."

His grin faded slowly. That was something he could help her with. He could teach her more about wicked living than anyone else around. But he would surely be damned if he did.

She slipped her heels off and stretched her long legs out, crossed them at the ankle. "Why did you come back to Harmony?"

"Miss Rose asked me to."

"But why did you come? You got away from here. You were free for sixteen years. Why did you come back?"

He could give her a flip answer or no answer at all. Instead he offered the truth. "She raised me for eight years. She took me in when no one else wanted me. I owe her something."

"Do you think she brought you back just to work on the house?"

"I think letting me work on the house is just a ploy to keep me busy and out of trouble." He hesitated. When she had asked him before about Miss Rose's reason for bringing him home, he had refused to answer, had refused even to admit that he didn't know. Now he did. "She won't tell me what she wants. She just says I'll find out in good time."

"Maybe she was just lonely for you."

The suggestion made him uncomfortable, but he hid it. "She doesn't strike me as being lonely," he said drily.

"There's a difference between being lonely and being lonely for a particular person."

Didn't he know it. When he was ten years old, and twelve and fourteen and sometimes even now, he had missed his father, and all the company in the world couldn't have changed that. Later he had missed Miss Rose, and working for other elderly women, ladies who reminded him of her, hadn't satisfied that need. Now it was Celine who had gotten under his skin, Celine whose presence he hungered for, whose voice he wanted to hear, and there was no way any other woman in the world was going to satisfy him.

"You and your words," he drawled, preferring mockery over admitting how truly well acquainted he was with loneliness in all its forms. "I've never met anyone who's as picky in their speech as you are." He shifted in the creaky seat. "Who do you get lonely for, Miss Celine?"

She didn't need even a moment to consider it. "Not who. What. Where. I'd like to go away. To see other places. To live among people whose names I don't know, whose family histories I'm not familiar with. I'd like to live someplace else, anyplace else, besides Harmony, Louisiana."

That surprised him. She seemed better suited to life in Harmony than anyone else he knew. The pace, the intimacy, and the familiar old comfort were all a part of her. When he did whatever it was Miss Rose wanted and moved on, whenever he thought of home, he would think of Celine, right here in this house. "Just yesterday you were defending this town and its people to me. Now you want to run away from it?"

"For a while. I just feel . . . empty here. Dissatisfied."

I've lived an entire life being dissatisfied. That was what she'd told him yesterday. Maybe her emptiness, her dissatisfaction, had to do with the man she and Vickie had talked about. Maybe it had to do with being betrayed by your sister and being twenty-eight and not married and having no children.

Maybe it came from needing a man who could make her hot and horny as hell. A man who knew how to satisfy her. A man like him.

No doubt he could give her more sexual satisfaction than any man who came before or after. The electricity between them was such that they just might not even survive it. But that was *all* he could give her—that, and disillusionment. Disappointment. Pain.

"So why don't you pack your bags and go? It's not so hard."

She gave it a long moment's thought, then leaned forward, picked up her shoes, and got to her feet. At the door, she turned back and smiled faintly. "It is for me." Then she unlocked the door, went inside, and shut him out.

After finishing Mae's excellent dinner, Raymond escorted his mother and his wife into the parlor, where he poured sherry for them and bourbon for himself before sitting down. He was silently congratulating himself for hiding his impatience to tell Rose his news about Billy Ray Beaumont when she spoke in that acid-sharp way of hers.

"I suppose this"—she held up the crystal glass—"is to prepare me for another lecture about Will."

Frannie was sitting close to his mother on the sofa. Giving him a warning glance, she reached across to pat the old woman's shoulder. "That's not fair, Miss Rose," she chided. "You make it sound as if Raymond's got a vendetta against Billy Ray."

"That's a good way of describing it."

Raymond laced his fingers loosely around his glass. "Mama, I don't like Billy Ray, and I never have. I've never tried to hide it. But you have to understand my concern. Taking a ten-year-old kid with no family into your home is one thing. Welcoming a grown man with a questionable background is another altogether."

"I don't have any questions about Will's background," she said stubbornly.

He struggled not to show his frustration. "Maybe you don't, but I do. Sheriff Franklin does."

Her gaze narrowed on him. "It's Mitch Franklin's job to be suspicious. And it's your job to mind your own business."

Frannie intervened again. "Miss Rose, we're just worried, that's all. You live out there away from everyone else, just you and Celine. If you aren't concerned with your own safety, at least consider Celine's."

Raymond almost groaned aloud. Thanks to years of expensive schooling and generations of wealth, Frannie normally knew exactly the right thing to say and do in any circumstance. But to suggest to his mother that Beaumont might present a danger to the Hunter girl, when she already suspected that they were probably sleeping together, was just plain stupid.

"The only thing Celine might risk by living so close to Will is her heart," Miss Rose said coldly. "And at her age that's a risk she can certainly afford to take."

"Her heart," he repeated, "along with anything else he's able to pocket. And speaking of what he might steal . . . remember when he robbed *us*? Remember how positive you were that he meant to return our property? Remember how you convinced the sheriff not to go after him because you *knew* he would pay us back just as soon as he was able?" He waited, but she said nothing. She just got stiffer, more resentful. In response, he softened his voice. "Has he paid you back, Mama? Has he returned your earrings or your brooch or your bracelet? Has he even offered you an apology? Or has he pretended it never happened?"

"It was a long time ago."

"A long time ago?" he repeated, his voice touched with incredulity. "So long that he's forgotten he stole from the woman who treated him like a son?"

"He obviously needed those things or he never would have taken them," she insisted.

"He probably did need the cash he stole from my desk, but your jewelry? Daddy's ring?"

Setting her sherry down untouched, she squeezed her hands tightly together. "It was a long time ago."

Raymond knew that tone, that posture, that look. It meant end of discussion. She'd heard all she intended to listen to. She wasn't going to find fault with Billy Ray for stealing from her, and there was nothing he or anyone else could do about it. Or so she thought.

As they had agreed earlier, Frannie excused herself from the room, and he moved to sit close to his mother. "It's true that I used to resent Billy Ray. You wanted to treat him like a member of the family, and I didn't think he belonged. I still don't, but that's beside the point."

"And what is the point, Raymond?"

"The money he stole from me doesn't matter. I would've given it to him if he'd only asked. But the other things—the earrings your parents gave you when you and Daddy got married, the brooch that had been in the family for nearly two hundred years, Daddy's ring . . . those things mattered. Knowing they were invaluable to us, he took them and probably hocked them for a few bucks. We'll never get them back."

Miss Rose's rigid stance slowly relaxed, and she patted his hand. "You were right before, Raymond, when you called them 'things.' That's all they were. Things. Yes, they held a great deal of sentimental value, to say nothing of their monetary value, but in the long run, they're still just things. Possessions. Metal and stones. What counts in life is people. You say you would have given Will the money if he had asked you for it. *I* would have given him the jewelry. If it helped him at a time when he needed help . . . what more could I want?"

His frustration was almost savage in its strength. Pulling away and leaving the sofa, he paced the room, the faded Persian rug underfoot muting his steps. What had ever made him think he could talk calmly and rationally to his mother about Billy Ray? She was absolutely blind to his faults, substantial as they were. She believed he had fathered that Robinson boy and run away to avoid his responsibilities toward him, but she didn't care. She believed he had stolen precious family heirlooms, and she didn't care about that, either. Even the knowledge of what he might do to her dear friend Celine didn't bother her. But what Raymond was about to tell her would.

Stopping in front of the mantel where Frannie's collection of fragile antique crystal was displayed, he sighed softly. "I'm glad you can look at it that way. I just hope those old ladies in Alabama can be as forgiving."

The silence in the room was palpable. He picked up a crystal bell used by one of Frannie's illustrious forebears to summon servants and shook it. Its ring was sweet and clear. Returning it to its place, he faced his mother. It was clear from her expression that, even though she had hired someone to track Billy Ray down, she hadn't known what he was up to when she'd found him. Naturally, Billy Ray hadn't seen fit to tell her.

"What are you talking about, Raymond?"

"The letter you sent asking him to come home had to be forwarded to him at the county jail. It seems he learned some valuable lessons while he was living with you. He learned how to befriend, then rob generous, trusting old ladies— widows who had no man around to protect them, who let him into their homes, who treated him fairly."

"Where did you hear this?"

"Sheriff Franklin told me. He thought it prudent to check into Billy Ray's background."

"And this is what he found."

"Among other things." Raymond returned to the sofa. "Billy Ray has been in jail in virtually every state in the South. These charges in Alabama were dropped because the case wasn't airtight and because when he got out, he was leaving not only the town but the entire state to come back here. But he has convictions, Mama. He's been found guilty of a whole string of charges. He's done time."

Looking at her, for a moment he regretted telling her. Her expression spoke of disappointment. Just as he'd known she would never hold Beaumont responsible for stealing from *them*, he had also known she wouldn't tolerate his stealing from others. But he hadn't expected her to look so disillusioned. He hadn't expected her to suddenly look so *old*.

Moving cautiously, as if each motion caused her pain, she

scooted to the edge of the sofa and stood up. "I think I'd like to go home now."

"I'll take you."

She remained that way, quiet and weary, all the way home. There, when he opened the car door for her and helped her out, he quietly said, "I'm sorry, Mama." And he meant it. He really was sorry. But he would do it again if he had to. He would do whatever it took to get Billy Ray Beaumont out of their lives once and for all.

The bicycle tires made a rhythmic whisking sound as Jared Robinson rode along the pavement. The bicycle was his normal mode of transportation, at least until he got his driver's license next year, but the summer heat took much of the pleasure from it. Tonight it wasn't so bad—sticky, but a little cooler now that the sun had gone down.

He had told his grandparents that he was going over to his friend Joey's house. His grandmother had objected to his riding his bike at night, especially when Joey lived only three blocks away, but his grandfather had said it was all right. After all, Joey did live only three blocks away. How much traffic was he going to run into in three blocks?

So as not to make a liar of himself, he truly had gone to Joey's house. His friend's folks were gone tonight. They attended the Pentecostal church on the west side of town, and services there could go on forever, depending on how the spirit moved them. Joey had asked to tag along with him, but when Jared refused, he had agreed to cover for him until his parents got home. That would be long enough.

He passed the last of the houses before the paved street turned to dirt. He coasted a few yards, then steered the bike onto the grassy shoulder, climbed off, and half pushed, half carried it into the weeds. They were tall enough to hide it lying on its side, not that there was liable to be any traffic. Miss Rose hadn't come to church tonight, and Miss Celine rarely attended on Sunday evenings. No one else lived along this stretch of road, not until it ran into the highway four or five miles up.

It was dark out here away from the streetlamps, but he'd come prepared for that. Not knowing how much moonlight, weak as it was, could penetrate those woods behind Miss Rose's house, he had brought a flashlight along to light his way.

He wasn't sure why he had come out here. He wasn't likely to see anything. Miss Rose kept her house closed up, so unless he came outside . . .

He.

Will Beaumont.

Billy Ray Beaumont.

Jared's mother thought that was a fine name, kind of wild and good-time-sounding and, honey, she used to say, it absolutely suited him to a T. She had talked about him often when Jared was little, too little to remember much of it beyond the name; but when he'd gotten older and more interested, she had refused to tell him anything much at all.

Of course, by the time he'd gotten old enough to be interested in anything, his mother had already lost interest in *him*. She had already dumped him on her parents, claiming that she would be back to get him soon, even coming sometimes, but never with the intention of taking him away. It hadn't been so bad living here. His grandparents loved him, and he had some good friends like Joey, and every August he spent two weeks at his great-uncle's farm on the other side of the river. It hadn't been bad at all. Until Will Beaumont had come back.

Some of the kids at the video arcade downtown had made fun of him, laughing and calling him Jared Beaumont. They referred to Billy Ray as his daddy, asked him if Daddy had finally come home to see him, and gee, wasn't he a little late? Even Joey, his best friend, thought it must be awful to have the father you've never known come home and not even want to see you.

Was it asking so much to want to meet him? To want to be noticed by your own father? To want to ask him why the hell he's ignored you all your life?

Jared didn't think so. His grandfather, though, said that if Beaumont came within a mile of his grandson, he would kill him. His grandmother said she would get a court order to keep him away. They were both wasting their breath. Will Beaumont had no intention of coming within a mile of him.

It wouldn't surprise Jared any if he had forgotten that he even had a son.

He moved slowly through the woods, watching his step, being careful not to make any more noise than necessary. After a steady fifteen minutes, he reached the edge of the clearing behind the Kendall place. Miss Rose's house was dark. There were lights on in Miss Celine's, but the curtains were closed.

There was a light on in the old place they called a guesthouse. It had been built at the same time as the main house, Miss Celine had told him once, and had done double duty back then, acting as a chapel for the Kendall family and as a schoolhouse for their children.

Now it was home to Will Beaumont.

He could hear the sound of a radio, tuned to a distant station. The music was zydeco, all accordion and fiddle, the words probably French. He heard it often when he visited his great-uncle, who lived over on the Bayou Teche. It filtered through the open windows, sounding tinny in the humid night air.

Inside the guesthouse he could see the flickering shadows created by a ceiling fan. The place had to be miserably hot in summer, but apparently Beaumont didn't mind. Jared's grandmother said people like him might as well get used to the heat since they were going to spend eternity burning in hell.

Finding a comfortable place beside a pine tree, Jared settled in to watch. For a long time he saw nothing more; then the light in the corner went off—the bathroom, he supposed—and Will Beaumont walked into the larger room. He wore jeans, his hair was wet, and he had a towel over his shoulders. He seemed restless, pacing the room, passing in front of one window, then the next and the next. A lot of times he moved to the front windows, standing at one or another and staring out.

The only thing to stare at up front was Miss Celine's house. Did Will Beaumont have it bad for her?

Jared found the idea repulsive. Next to his grandparents, Miss Celine was his favorite person in town. She always made time for him at the library, always encouraged him to learn everything he could, to ask questions and to study, yet to have fun, too. She understood him better than most adults did. She was pretty, almost as pretty as his mother had once been, and nice, and he liked her, damn it, too much for her to get screwed up with Beaumont. With his father.

He could almost hear Joey, goofy Joey who was constantly sticking his foot in his mouth over one thing or another. *Miss Hunter and your father? Hey, if they got married, that would make her your stepmother, wouldn't it? That would be great!*

Will Beaumont could marry a thousand women, and none of them would ever be Jared's stepmother for the simple reason that, even if Will did decide to acknowledge his son, Jared would never accept him as his father. Never.

The lights in the guesthouse began going off until only a dim glow came from the closest windows. It was still enough to see by. It was enough to tell that Beaumont was undressing. Then that light went out, too. Bedtime?

Jared stayed there a few minutes longer, his legs cramping, wondering what time it was and whether it was safe to turn on the flashlight and check his watch. Finally he twisted around to face the woods, sheltering the flashlight against his body and shining it on his watch. It was time to head home. There was nothing left to see here, and he didn't want to risk upsetting his grandparents. Will Beaumont had done a good enough job of that on his own.

Will knocked at Miss Rose's back door late Monday afternoon, then opened the door and stepped just inside, as he usually did, to call her name. When she didn't answer right away, he moved further into the kitchen, down the hall, listening for a sound from her. Ordinarily he would assume she was busy or napping and would leave her alone, but he couldn't forget how tired she had looked last night, how fragile. She had fixed him a plate at dinnertime and asked him to take it back to the guesthouse, as she didn't feel up to company. When he'd brought the dishes back an hour later, she had already been asleep, even though it wasn't even eight o'clock.

"I'm in here."

He went into the small sunroom on the east side of the

house. It had been his favorite place when he was a kid, the only room in the house that wasn't furnished with valuable antiques, the only room where everything was light and bright and warm. It was filled with plants and comfortable old furniture made for sprawling and held the only television, a tiny black-and-white, that Miss Rose had ever allowed in the house.

She was watering the plants on one of three tall brass racks when he came in. When she finished, she set the can aside and sat down in the nearest chair. "Have a seat, Will."

"Thanks, but I'm on my way into town. I thought I'd see if you needed anything before I left."

"Please sit down."

Feeling like a ten-year-old boy again, he obeyed.

She sat stiffly across from him, not relaxing in the chair, not easing that stern look on her face. "You know I had dinner yesterday with Raymond."

He nodded.

"He told me some things that I found very disturbing. Naturally I didn't want to believe them, but I spoke to Sheriff Franklin this morning, and he confirmed them."

The mention of the sheriff's name made his muscles tighten and set off a sick, achy feeling deep inside.

"You were in jail when you got my letter asking you to come home, weren't you?"

He swallowed hard and felt his hands grow clammy. He should have told her that the day he got the letter. He should have called her from Alabama and warned her that he wasn't the same boy she had raised. He should have told her everything about the life he'd made for himself—about the times he'd taken money from women, about the things he'd done without getting caught, about the times he had gotten caught, about every arrest. He remembered the details—the dates, the places, the charges—of each one. Together they made up his biggest shame.

But he hadn't called her. He hadn't warned her. He hadn't confessed to her because he had wanted to come home. He had wanted to see her again. He hadn't wanted to know that she didn't believe him, that she didn't have faith in him, that she didn't want him. Because he hadn't trusted her to trust him.

"Yes, ma'am," he said grimly. "I was."

"You were suspected of stealing from the elderly women you worked for."

"Yes, ma'am."

"And it wasn't the first time you'd been arrested."

"No, ma'am."

He waited, waited with his jaw clenched, with his muscles so taut that they were almost in spasm, waited for her to ask him that one important question. *Did you do it?* He waited for that one show of faith, that one bit of trust that no one had shown him in more than sixteen years. *Are you guilty?*

A minute passed, then two, then three, and still she sat there, her head bowed, silent. Damnably silent.

The tension inside him gave way to trembling. She wasn't going to ask. She believed he was guilty. Without even a word from him, she had already judged and condemned him. The last person in the world who had ever believed in him had stopped.

He stood up, his movements jerky. "Give me fifteen minutes and I'll be out of here."

She looked up then, her blue eyes old and faded. "I don't want you to leave."

But there was no reason to stay, not now. Not when he'd let down the only person who still cared for him. Not when he would be reminded every time she looked at him that she believed he had robbed those old ladies. Not when he would have to face her disappointment, her blame, and her condemnation every day.

Not when soon Celine would be looking at him that way, too.

"I've still got plans for you, Will," she said softly. "Please don't go."

"I'm sorry, Miss Rose." Then he turned and walked out. He closed the back door very quietly behind him, then went to the guesthouse.

In the ten days he had been here, he had cleaned and dusted, mopped and rearranged. He had unpacked everything he'd brought with him, placing it all in the mirror-fronted armoire that stood near the bed. Now he took his suitcase from the corner, laid it on the bed, and began removing his things from the armoire.

There wasn't much. He didn't own anything, he'd told Celine, that he couldn't put in a bag and take with him when he moved on, and that was true. Jeans, some shirts—mostly T-shirts—an extra pair of tennis shoes, and a leather jacket for winter. He put all that into the bag, then added an old cheap Bible and an older, cheaper pocket watch that had belonged to his father, a creased manila envelope filled with photographs from when he was a kid, and the expensive gold watch Miss Rose had given him for his eighteenth birthday, broken now and too costly to fix but too important to throw away.

Then he shoved the suitcase aside and sat down on the bed, leaning his head back against the brass headboard. Just like the last time he'd left Harmony, his eyes stung and his throat was tight. He had cried then. Eighteen years old and holed up in a cheap motel off the interstate, he had cried over his leaving. The next morning he had headed for New Orleans, walking hitching rides. He'd been in the city about six hours when he'd realized that the money Raymond had given him wasn't going to last long. Until he got a job, there would be no more motels at night, no more expensive restaurant meals.

That money from Raymond had been part of their agreement, the one that made Celine so curious. One afternoon when things were getting ugly, when Jock Robinson was threatening to have the sheriff haul his ass into jail for messing with his sixteen-year-old daughter, Raymond had come out here to see Will. He had timed it so that Miss Rose was gone and had warned Will not to discuss his visit with her.

He'd never made a secret of his dislike for Will, had never tried to hide how much he wanted to see him gone from Harmony and Miss Rose's life. Finally he had seen the opportunity to achieve that. If Will stayed in town, he had one of only two things to look forward to: marrying Melanie Robinson, accepting responsibility for her and her kid, or getting thrown in jail for a long, long time. The sheriff was a good friend of Jock's, who would do that and a whole lot more for him; so was the judge.

But in exchange for his leaving—and a promise that he would never return—Raymond had offered him five hundred dollars. It was more money than Will had ever seen at one time. It was enough to take him far away, enough to live on for a long time, or so it seemed. And once it had become clear that even Miss Rose didn't believe him, he hadn't had any real reason to stay. So he had gone to Raymond's house one spring evening, as the man had insisted, and he had taken the money and given his promise.

The money had run out within a few months, but by then he'd gotten used to sleeping on the ground, to stealing a meal or two from some rural family's garden, to working whatever jobs a strong eighteen-year-old kid could get. He'd gotten used to living hand to mouth, to being dirty and hungry most of the time. By then he'd lost whatever pride he'd ever had. Pride was a luxury a hungry kid couldn't afford. It was something a man like him had trouble hanging on to.

Leaning forward, he closed the suitcase and fastened the rusted clasps. He had just finished that when a knock sounded at the door. Through the screen he could see Celine, looking hot and sweaty and too damned appealing. Annoyed by the involuntary tightening of his muscles caused by simply seeing her, he ordered her away in a nasty voice.

Of course she didn't leave. Why should anything go right for him today?

Opening the screen door, she stepped inside. "This will take only a minute. I brought you some books—" Her gaze shifted from him to the suitcase, and the canvas bag she was carrying slid to the floor with a dull clunk. "Going somewhere?" she asked coolly.

He glanced at the bag, then at the open armoire, its shelves and drawers empty, as he rose from the bed. "That's what it looks like."

"Why?"

"I get restless after being in the same place for long."

"What about Miss Rose?"

"What about her?"

"Does she know?"

He shrugged.

"What about the job she offered you?"

"You and I both know she created that job to give me something to do. Work on the house will go just fine without me."

She stared at him, momentarily at a loss for words. If he'd been in the mood to be flattered, he thought he might have been. Her reaction went beyond surprised to stunned. She wasn't thrilled by the idea of being rid of him, by the prospect of peace returning to her precious little town once more.

"Did she tell you what she wanted? Is that why you're leaving?"

He didn't reply.

"Yesterday you said you owed her something. Today you've changed your mind?" Her voice was quickly taking on an angry, dismayed edge. "How does that work, Will? You only feel obligated to people when it suits you, when they're not asking anything of you?" She gave him a chance to respond, but when he didn't, she continued. "You came back home when she asked you to. You let her believe that you were going to stay awhile. You told her you would oversee the restoration of her house. You made a commitment to her, and today you're backing out. You're leaving again. You're running away again, just like before."

"You don't know what you're talking about," he muttered as he approached her, the suitcase in hand.

"Why did you change your mind?"

"It's none of your business."

"Are you in trouble?"

His smile was thin and bitter. Naturally she would reach that conclusion. Problems with the law were expected of him. "Honey, I've always got trouble of one sort or another."

"Is it something to do with the Robinsons?"

He stopped right in front of her, menacingly close. "I told you Saturday: nothing in my life is any of your business. Including this."

Celine exhaled softly to ease the tightness in her chest. All the way home, carrying the heavy load of books, she had looked forward to seeing Will. She had considered inviting him out to dinner, had even considered making a serious attempt to seduce the man. She hadn't imagined that she would be lucky to catch him in time to say good-bye. She hadn't considered a future—not the next few weeks, at least, or maybe even the next few months—without him. Sure, he would leave eventually, but not like this. Not without saying good-bye. Not without . . . *something*.

"So you're running away from whatever's wrong. That was an understandable response from an eighteen-year-old boy, but for God's sake, Will, you're thirty-four now. When are you going to grow up? When are you going to handle your problems like a man? When are you going to quit running and face life head-on?"

"You don't know what you're talking about," he repeated with a fierce scowl.

She sighed again. He was right. She had no idea what kind of trouble he was in or what kind of force was driving him.

All she knew was that she didn't want him to go. And that she wanted to go with him. And that, even if he would let her, she didn't have the courage.

He was right. She really *didn't* know what she was talking about.

"Well . . ." Straightening, she moved away from the door. "Life won't be the same around here without you."

He had no response. He just continued to give her that cold, hard, stony look.

"There's one thing I want to do before you go." Quickly, before he could guess her intentions, before she could lose her nerve, she closed the distance between them, cupped her palms to his cheeks, and kissed him.

It wasn't the greatest kiss in the world. She was awkward, and he was stiff. But it was enough to make her quiver. It was enough to warm her blood. It was enough to hint at the heat and sinful pleasure he could give her if he was willing. It was enough to say good-bye.

Just as swiftly as it had started, it ended. She dropped her hands, took a step back, then spun around and left the guesthouse. Every step across the yard, she could feel his brooding gaze following her.

Inside she turned the air-conditioning on, then went into

the bathroom to splash cool water on her face. Only then did she look into the mirror. When she could pretend that the water was the cause of the brightness in her eyes. When she could blame it for the unshed tears caught in her lashes.

It was stupid to feel this way. She scarcely knew Will. So what if the sexual chemistry between them was explosive? Any man as wickedly sexy and as frankly suggestive as he was could generate the same chemistry, especially in a woman who had been alone as long as she had.

But berating herself did no good. She didn't want him to go. She was going to miss him. And the simple truth was she'd never met another man as sexy.

She kept the drapes and blinds closed, her view of the guesthouse, the lawn, and the road outside shuttered. She fixed her dinner and ate it at the small kitchen table, then cleaned the kitchen and watched TV. After her shower, dressed in a thin cotton nightgown, she finally raised the blinds on the window beside her bed.

The sun had set, and the stars were faintly visible in the sky. The guesthouse was dark and still. Even from here she could see that the front door was closed. Where would he go? she wondered. Did he ever have a destination in mind when he set out, or did he just travel until he saw a place he liked, a place that felt familiar, that looked as if it might offer him something?

And what exactly was he looking for? What offerings might make him stay awhile? A job? A place to stay? A few days or a few weeks without suspicion? Or maybe a beautiful woman.

Celine had long ago resigned herself to being pretty enough—that was the way people always phrased it. *That younger Hunter girl is pretty enough, but have you seen her sister? Celine is pretty enough, but Vickie* . . . She had never been as pretty as Vickie, as vivacious and outgoing, as charming and popular as Vickie. Her sister had gone from a pretty little girl to a lovely young lady to a beautiful woman, while the awkward stages of growing up had lasted forever for Celine. She had stayed tall and skinny, graceless and curveless and flat for so long that she'd feared she was destined to be that way forever.

She had eventually grown into her body, but she had never caught up with Vickie. She had never quite stopped wishing she could be her sister for a while. She had never forgotten her father's frequent reminders that *she* was the brainy one, while Vickie was the pretty one. Richard thought she was the nice one, while Vickie was the sexy, alluring one.

And now Will thought she was the prissy one, the naive and innocent one, interesting enough to play with but not to go to bed with. But he would find a woman now that he'd left here. A beautiful woman. A sexy one. One who had nothing in common with Celine.

A streak of lightning lit the sky to the east, followed a moment later by a rumble of thunder. For an instant, all was silent, even the tree frogs and whippoorwills stopping their night calls; then the wind picked up, and the sounds resumed.

She turned away from the window, took a brush and a shimmery gold band from the bathroom counter, and went outside to the porch. As a little girl she had been fascinated by storms. Her father, ever the scientist, had tried to explain the technical creation of thunder and lightning, but she had never listened. Like the special effects wizardry in her favorite movies, she preferred the mystery of nature's magic over the facts of science.

Sitting sideways on a low cypress bench, she parted her hair, then began brushing one section at a time, combing out tangles, drawing the soft bristles through in long, smooth strokes. When that half was done, she turned to the other, giving it the same treatment, and then she gathered it all together, intending to fasten it off her shoulders in a ponytail.

"Leave it down."

Startled, she looked for the source of the softly uttered command and found Will, shadowy and unmoving, in the corner. She was glad, indescribably glad that he hadn't left after all, but she didn't show it. She simply turned back to gaze across the lawn and slipped the rubber band in place. "It's hot."

He came out of the shadows, straddling the bench behind her, removing the rubber band so carefully that it didn't even tug. "It makes *me* hot," he murmured, gathering her hair in his hands, burying his face in it.

She stared straight ahead, her breaths shallow, afraid to move. "So you decided not to go," she said, attempting to sound normal but managing only strained. Grateful. Aroused.

He raised his head but didn't release her hair. He combed his fingers through it, testing its weight in his palms, letting it fall and catching it again. "And let that prissy little Hunter girl accuse me of running away again?" he teased.

A shiver of relief swept through her. A Will who could tease, who was obnoxious and arrogant, she could deal with. No matter how merciless he was, she preferred him over the grim, bleak man she'd seen earlier.

He moved to sit in front of her, his legs spread wide, his knees pressing against hers. "Let's take our clothes off, Celie," he suggested as another flash of lightning touched the sky. "You wrap your legs around me, and we'll set the night on fire."

She gave him a long, steady look. "What is it you want from me, Will?"

He replied without hesitation, without thought. "Just your body. That's all. Nothing more."

Nothing more. Not her heart. Not her undying love. Nor commitment. Just her body.

She could learn to handle that.

"All right." Without waiting for a response from him, she began unbuttoning her gown. There was one row of buttons, tiny pink buttons, from neck to hem that she rarely bothered with. She usually just pulled it over her head instead, but tonight she couldn't just all in an instant bare herself to him. Tonight she forced each tiny button free.

She had reached her waist when Will grasped her hands tightly in his. He didn't say anything, and she couldn't see his expression in the shadows, but she knew he wanted her to stop. His suggestion had been flippant, a tease, meant to draw a response—a *different* response—from her.

But she wanted to take her clothes off, wanted to take his off, too. She wanted to take him inside her and to wrap her legs around him, holding him there. She wanted, just once in her life, to set the night on fire.

Freeing her hands, she scooted back, then drew her feet onto the bench, wrapping her arms around her knees. Her gown fell to her feet, covering her legs. The top was still unbuttoned, but she was adequately covered. "Why were you going to leave?" she asked, then immediately warned, "And don't say because you got restless."

"How about if I say it's none of your business?"

"How about if I kick you someplace where it really hurts?" she countered, wiggling her foot to the side, making contact—very brief contact—high on the inside of his thigh.

He lifted her foot and set it down on his leg, balancing it there with his fingers around her ankle. Uncomfortable, Celine pulled away. When he reached for it again, she gave him a hard look. "Don't play games, Will. Don't start something with me that you have no intention of finishing."

There was a flash of lightning, then an answering growl of thunder that vibrated through the house and the bench and into her body. In that instant of light, she saw the expression on his face, serious and regretful. He *had* changed his mind about leaving, hadn't he? she wondered with an edge of panic. He hadn't simply delayed because of the late hour or the incoming storm, had he?

"Will?"

He glanced at her. She could feel his gaze on her face even if she couldn't see anything. "I'm staying," he replied in response to her unanswered question.

She gave a soft sigh. "Why did you want to leave?"

"Don't you get tired of being told that it's none of your business?"

"No."

"Well, I'm sure as hell tired of saying it."

"So say something else," she invited softly, but he didn't.

They sat silently for a time. The wind blew a gust in their direction, bringing with it a moment's coolness and the sweet, welcome smell of rain. Then it changed direction and left them hot again, hot and sticky and waiting for relief. But rain, cool and refreshing, wasn't the solution for what ailed her, and she doubted that it would do much good for whatever was eating at Will, either.

He shifted positions on the bench, turning to the side, leaning forward to rest his arms on his thighs, and finally he spoke, his voice flat, his tone empty, his words unexpected.

"Sometimes things just don't work out the way you want them to."

Celine sat a little straighter and gave him a wide-eyed-with-wonder look. He had answered a question, had actually told her one of those many things that were none of her business. Of course he had done it in a way that had raised even more questions. What was it that hadn't worked out? What had disappointed him enough to send him on his way? What had he hoped for? "What sort of things?" she asked softly, hoping he wouldn't notice that she was prying.

"Everything. Anything. Nothing at all." He paused. "The rain will be here soon."

She could smell it, could almost, she fancied, hear it blowing their way. The lightning was brighter, the thunder more threatening, the wind picking up until it tousled his hair and stirred the ruffle at the hem of her gown. She wanted to go out onto the grass, where the porch with its screens couldn't shelter her, and let the wind catch her hair, let the rain soak her skin. But the idea of a late-night dance in the rain lost its appeal with the sudden crack of a lightning strike nearby.

"Why did you decide to stay?"

Will rolled his gaze heavenward. Saintly, Miss Rose had called her. More stubborn than any devil could ever be, he swore. "How many different ways can you phrase the same question?" he asked, but before she could answer, he went on. "I have a question of my own, and it's a whole lot more interesting than yours. Why did you kiss me?"

"Why did you back off when I took you up on your suggestion?" she challenged.

He recalled that moment when she had begun unbuttoning her gown and squeezed his eyes shut. The erection that had swelled to life when she'd stepped onto the porch showed no signs of abating soon, especially when he could see her in his mind, her head bowed, her fingers patiently working each snug-fitting button. God, it would have been so easy to go through with it, to not stop her, to let her undo every single one of those buttons, then lift her onto his lap. "Fire" wouldn't even begin to describe the heat that would have engulfed them.

"I can't believe there isn't at least one man in town who

wouldn't be happy to have you in his bed, so why are you hanging around me? Are you going for the shock value? Do you figure that sleeping with me will shake up this dull little town of yours? Are you looking for a new image?''

''I've been to bed with two of the men in this town. Neither one was particularly satisfying.''

He gave her a sideways look. The thought of Celine with another man should make him jealous, and it did. But it also aroused him further. ''And you think I would be?''

From the shadows beside him came a laugh. It was meant to be dry and mocking. Instead it was enticing—soft and gentle and so assured. ''I know you would.''

He wanted to show her that she was right, wanted to give her the best night of her entire life. But he couldn't. He shouldn't. He wouldn't.

''Don't be so impatient, Celie,'' he said, injecting a patronizing note of arrogance into his voice. ''Someday you'll find a nice guy who's not half-bad in bed, and you'll settle down and raise a bunch of prissy little kids, and it won't be long at all before you'll be wishing he would find some other woman to satisfy and leave you alone.''

But if she happened to find this nice guy while *he* was still here, he thought with a scowl, he would kill the bastard, and he would punish her for looking.

Punish with pleasure.

Swallowing hard on a groan, he left the bench and went to stand at the screen door. There he watched as the first drops of rain arrived, big fat ones that plopped on the wooden steps and splashed in the dust and splattered through the thin mesh of the screen to land on his arms, to dampen his shirt.

Each drop seemed to bring two more, until the sound of the rain drowned out everything except the thunder. This was a downpour, hard on the land when everything was dry, running off to fill the creeks and streams before the earth had a chance to soak up any of it. But it cooled the air, and it replaced the usual night scents—the flowers, the earthiness that came from the constant dampness, the acrid chemical odors from the plants upriver—with its own. It was cleansing.

''Where were you going to go?''

He hadn't heard Celine's approach—dangerous, he warned

himself. He could hardly handle her when he knew she was there. He couldn't deal with a surprise appearance.

Risking a glance at her, he saw that her nightgown was still unbuttoned, but held securely together by her arms folded across her chest. He wished she would move her arms. He wished she wore a heavy robe over the thin cotton. He wished he could see all of her, and just as hard he wished that she was covered from neck to foot in something as impenetrable as armor.

Looking away again, he forced his attention back to her question. Where had he intended to go? *Away.* East again, maybe, to one of the little tourist-oriented beach towns on the Atlantic. Jobs were always plentiful in places like that in the summer. Or maybe north this time to cooler climates, or west to the dry heat of the desert. There were a thousand places he could go.

He could even return to that tiny little town in Alabama. He could turn himself in to the sheriff there and get locked away for years to come. That was one sure way to keep himself away from Celine.

"I didn't have any plans," he finally replied. "I never do."

"You just wake up one morning and decide it's time to move on?" she asked, taking a place at the opposite side of the screen door and, like him, intently watching the rain. "And you hitch a ride or walk until you find yourself in another town that looks like a nice place to stay awhile?"

"That's about it." But there weren't many "nice" places to stay, not for someone like him. He chose his towns based on how much work he could find, on how hungry he was, on whether he would have someplace other than the ground to sleep at night.

"Did you ever find someplace where you were tempted to stay?"

"Nope, never have. There were a few, though, that were mighty hard to leave." He gave her a lascivious grin, making it clear exactly what was so hard about leaving those places. But he was deliberately misleading her. There had been a couple of places he'd regretted leaving—that much was true. But it wasn't because of the women he'd been with in each town. It was the comfortable life—the soft bed, the clean sheets and clothes, the baths whenever he wanted, the three meals a day. Living the way he had, those things had been much harder to give up than the women, the sex, and the intimacy.

Changing positions, he also changed the subject. "I saw the books you brought." The canvas bag she'd left on the guesthouse floor had been filled with them—big, heavy volumes on restoring old houses. He had meant to stop by the library when he went into town this afternoon and find just such books, but that was before Miss Rose had dropped her bombshell. That was before he'd found out that she trusted him no more now than she had sixteen years ago.

That was before he'd realized that, when it came to him and this town and the people in it, nothing had changed. *Nothing*.

"I thought you might like to look through them before you start work on the Kendall house."

"You're such an efficient librarian," he teased. "Do they pay you well for anticipating your readers' needs?"

"Enough."

"Enough," he echoed quietly. Turning toward her, he pulled her arms from her chest, then drew her close. He resisted the urge to hold her, to push the pale pink fabric aside and reveal her breasts, to draw the wide straps off her shoulders and leave her naked against him. Instead, carefully, with unsteady fingers, he fastened every button on her gown. "There's not enough money in the world to make anticipating *my* needs worthwhile, Celie," he warned softly, seriously, regretfully. "The only thing you're going to get from me is hurt. Don't forget that."

Then, though the rain hadn't let up one bit, though there was lightning and thunder all around, he left the porch, left her, and dashed across the yard to the guesthouse. There he paused at the door, looking back.

She was still standing there. The way she didn't want to be. The way he needed her to be. The way *he* had always been.

Alone.

Chapter Six

Will spent all of Tuesday and most of Wednesday, late into the afternoon, stretched out in the hammock, one or another of Celine's books open and resting on his stomach. There was a lot to learn about restoration, and he had precious little time to learn it. It was in his favor that he'd done just about every job imaginable on a construction site: driven heavy equipment, mixed and poured concrete, laid brick, poured foundations, framed walls, and roofed.

Of all the jobs he'd done in all the years he'd been gone, construction was his favorite. It allowed him to work outside and to use his hands. It allowed him to build something that would remain long after he had moved on down the road. It gave him something in which to take pride. He might not be worth much himself, but his work was good.

He had spoken to Miss Rose yesterday morning about the job, about the people she had already hired. Supposedly he would be in charge, but a man named Roger Woodson was really the boss. He and his crew did this sort of work all the time. He had experience and was respected as a fair man. When Miss Rose introduced them Monday morning, Will would find out, he guessed, just how fair Woodson really was.

The thought of Miss Rose brought him a sigh that was as

136

heavy and still as the late-afternoon air, and he put the book down to stare up at the leafy canopy above him. Other than their brief conversation yesterday, he'd hardly seen her. He had helped himself to a sandwich for lunch while she was gone into town both yesterday and today, and he had skipped dinner last night. He was afraid that he wasn't going to feel comfortable taking his meals with her anymore. He wasn't going to feel comfortable living here, either, not until he'd started working. Not until he started to feel as if he were earning his keep.

Did you steal from those women?

That one question would have made all the difference in the world to him. If she'd had even the slightest doubt as to his guilt, if somewhere deep inside she had believed that the boy she had helped raise wasn't capable of stealing from old ladies . . . But she'd had no doubts. She had listened to Raymond's and the sheriff's accounts of the incidents, and she had automatically believed Will was guilty.

And something in their relationship had been automatically lost. Irretrievably so? God, he hoped not. Miss Rose was all he had left. And if she didn't have enough faith in him to believe he might be innocent, Celine certainly wouldn't. When she found out, she would look at him the same way Miss Rose had. She would doubt him the same way Miss Rose had.

There wasn't a chance in hell that Celine wouldn't find out. He might have counted on Sheriff Franklin to keep his mouth shut, but Raymond would turn it into common knowledge. He would make sure that no one in town risked trusting Will—not that anyone besides maybe Celine did, anyway.

Speak of the devil!

Raymond's big expensive Lincoln glided to a stop between the two front houses. The windows were up, the air-conditioning no doubt running, and the engine was purring softly. The Town Car was nice, one of the many luxuries Kendall money had bought Raymond. He had never appreciated everything he had, Will thought, as he watched the man get out and start across the grass. The nice home, the big cars, the fancy clothes; he took them all for granted as no more than a man in his position was due. He needed to go hungry for a while.

He needed to have nothing to rely on for transportation but his feet. He needed to know what it was like to have to work for a living, really work, with his hands and his back and his muscles. Then maybe he would have more sympathy for the people who'd made him and all the Kendalls before him rich. Then maybe he would appreciate the luxuries and the privileges birth had given him and better value all that he had.

"Miss Rose isn't here," Will announced before Raymond could speak. Of course Raymond had already figured that out after seeing that his mother's car was gone. In fact, Will would wager he had known it before he'd even left his elegant, air-conditioned office at the bank. Hell, he probably even knew that she was attending a meeting of the ladies' auxiliary at the church and that she was due back after this evening's midweek service.

Will settled more comfortably in the hammock, shifting the library book to the side so its title couldn't be seen. Raymond didn't yet know about his mother's plans to restore the old family home, and Will certainly wasn't going to let it slip. Let him find out when work started, or when gossip began spreading through town, or when Miss Rose chose to tell him.

Raymond removed his coat and loosened the tie around his neck. Naturally, he didn't want to sweat all over his expensive linen suit. Dressed as he was in jeans worn thin and a T-shirt in only slightly better shape, Will wasn't concerned with the heat.

"So you're still here."

"I sure am."

"Did she ask you to leave?"

Will grinned. Of course that had been the goal behind Raymond's tattling to Miss Rose about his arrest record—to get Will out of Harmony and out of Miss Rose's life. His ploy would have succeeded, too, if Celine hadn't interfered. If she hadn't accused him of running away and made him feel guilty and a little bit ashamed, he would have given Raymond exactly what he wanted.

"No, she didn't," he replied, and his grin became wider.

"In fact, when I offered to go, she asked me to stay. She even said please."

"How did you manage that?" Raymond asked. "No one's ever been able to manipulate my mother—*no one* . . . except you. How do you do it?"

"Maybe it's because she feels so fond of me."

"More likely it's because she feels so sorry for you. Hell, even *I* felt sorry for you when your daddy died and your mama ran away and left you behind. The whole town did. But it didn't take long for us to figure out what your mama already knew, that you were a troublesome little bastard not worth a moment of our concern. My mother is just reluctant to admit it." Drawing a handkerchief from his pocket, Raymond dried the perspiration on his forehead, then said, "Tell me, Billy Ray, does it bother you at all that she's still got to look out for you the same way she did when you were ten years old?"

Will's grin slipped, then faded. "She's not 'looking out' for me."

"She's supporting you. She's giving you a bed to sleep in and food to eat. She's giving you money. What do you call that?"

He didn't bother to correct the part about the money. Miss Rose had offered him a wad of cash his first day here, but he had turned her down. He'd had enough left over from his last job to cover whatever expenses he had. "I'll be getting a job soon."

"Not around here, you won't. I guarantee that."

He probably could, too. Everyone in town did their banking at Harmony National, and just about every business needed an occasional loan. Raymond could put enough pressure on most employers to make sure they didn't hire anyone he didn't like.

Good thing Miss Rose never gave under pressure.

"How much will it take to get rid of you?" Raymond's smile was about as pleasant as a fist in the gut. "I realize I bought you cheap last time, but then, last time you didn't hold to your end of the bargain. So how much do you want this time to leave Harmony and stay away?"

"Maybe I don't want to go." The last time he hadn't had anything to lose leaving—other than Miss Rose—and he'd had a lot to gain. Now there was nothing to gain and a hell of a lot to lose. There was Miss Rose. There was the work on the house across the railroad tracks. There was the feeling of home.

And there was Celine.

Almost as if reading his thoughts, Raymond said, "There's nothing for you here, Billy Ray. My mother got along just fine without you, and she'll be even better when you're gone again. No one in town wants you here. The sheriff's just waiting for a reason to lock you up. No one's going to go against my wishes and give you a job. And if you think you're going to get anywhere at all with a woman like Celine Hunter, you're crazy. The novelty's going to wear off soon, and then she won't even give you the time of day."

Will's expression remained bland, but inside he had stiffened. What did Raymond know that had caused him to include Celine in this? Did he know that Will had taken her to dinner or that Miss Rose had deliberately thrown them together last Saturday? Or had he merely noted the obvious—that Celine was a beautiful woman and was living less than thirty feet from Will—and speculated on the rest?

"So what will it take? A couple thousand? I'll give you that if you leave today. That's a lot of money, Billy Ray, more than you've ever seen."

"I don't need a lot of money. Lots of money just makes people like sheriffs and police chiefs look at you funny."

"It'll get you away from here and into a new life."

"I like the life I've got now just fine."

Raymond gave him a long, measuring look, then upped his offer. "Five thousand. I'll give you the cash and drive you into Baton Rouge myself."

"No thanks."

A flash of irritation crossed the older man's face, then disappeared. He was struggling to remain in control, determined not to lose his temper, not to let Will win again. "Seventy-five hundred," he said calmly. "That's my final offer."

"I'm not interested."

"Don't misunderstand me, Billy Ray. Seventy-five hundred dollars is *all* I'm going to offer you. If you turn that down, I'll get rid of you anyway. It'll be a lot harder on you, and you'll wind up with nothing. So you either go now and take my money with you, or leave later without even a penny to your name."

"I've been broke before, Raymond, and I imagine I'll be broke again. My answer is still no."

Accepting that unwillingly, Raymond started to leave, then turned back. "You'll be sorry, Billy Ray. When I'm done with you, you'll be sorrier than hell that you turned me down. Remember that."

Will knew he ought to make some comeback, some arrogant, insulting comment, as he watched Raymond walk away, but he couldn't think of anything. All he could think was that the bastard was probably right. He probably would end up sorry that he'd come back to Harmony, and sorrier than hell that he'd stayed.

He watched until the fancy car was out of sight; then, muttering a curse, he took the library book and went inside the guesthouse. It was nearly four-thirty. Time to change into a clean shirt and walk into town before the library closed. Time to indulge his need to see Celine—though after Raymond's remarks, it would probably be better if he stayed hell and gone away from her.

He took his time washing up, changing from his sweaty white T-shirt to a clean one, walking the mile and a half to the library in downtown Harmony. It was empty but for Celine, sitting at her desk, a hardcover mystery novel open in front of her. She closed it when she saw him, marking her place with a bright orange bookmark, and came to stand in front of him at the counter.

"What are you doing in town?"

"I figured you would read love stories," he said with a nod at the book she'd left on the desk.

"I do. I read everything except men's adventure and technothrillers." She rested her arms on the counter, her hands loosely linked. "So?"

"I came to pick up some things at the store."

"I have to pick up some stuff myself. If you had called, I would have gotten yours, too."

"And saved the good people of this town from having to share the sidewalk with me?"

She frowned at him, the set of her mouth all prim and prissy. Damn, he'd like to make her stop that. It wouldn't be hard—just one kiss. One kiss, and the prim librarian would vanish forever. Hell, after that scene Monday night—her girlish kiss, followed by her bold acceptance of his invitation to remove her clothes—the image of her as prim was slipping fast anyway.

"We'll be closed in ten more minutes."

"I'll wait." He turned away from the desk, away from her, and his gaze swept over the large room. It was just as he remembered from the years when he was in school and had been required to come here once in a while for reports or research. The building was old, the floor covered alternately with industrial-strength carpet and big square vinyl tiles. The shelves were wood and held aging, worn books alongside new ones, and the scarred oak tables and clunky-looking chairs were original furnishings. Somewhere on the underside of one of these tables he had left his mark—an obscenity carved into the wood with his father's old pocket-knife.

"It hasn't changed much in the last twenty years, has it?" Celine moved around the counter to straighten up after the last careless patrons, sliding chairs back into place at one table, stretching to gather books from the center of another.

One thing had certainly changed. He'd never entertained fantasies about laying old lady Russell down on one of those sturdy oak tables and having his way with her. But he didn't mention that.

"Nothing in this town has changed except you."

Holding the books protectively in front of her, Celine smiled brittlely. "Yes, I know. I've grown up." Two nights ago she had wanted to show him just how much, but he hadn't wanted to see. Sometimes she thought he was afraid to see. He offered those sensuous invitations, then backed off before she could accept. He gave her those wicked looks and curiously gentle touches, then turned away. Maybe he *was* afraid. Maybe he really believed that all he could do was hurt her. Maybe he thought she deserved better than he could give. Or maybe he was just playing games. Maybe he was just amusing himself.

She reshelved the books, then, even though it was still a few minutes early, she began shutting off the lights. By five o'clock the library was locked up and they were walking down the street toward the closest grocery store.

"Miss Rose came by the library today before her church meeting," Celine remarked, watching as their shadows, hers long and his longer, advanced before them.

He refused to rise to the bait. "Do you go to church on Wednesday nights, too, Celie?"

"No, I don't. Only Sunday mornings."

He grinned. "There might be a little bit of a sinner in you, after all."

She gave him a steady, dry look in return. "And there might be a little bit of a saint in you, too."

"Afraid not, Miss Celine," he said with a laugh. "I'm bad through and through."

"No one is all good or all bad," she disputed.

"You are. I am." Anticipating her disagreement, he challenged, "Tell me one thing you've done that's sinful."

They reached the grocery store, and Celine paused for a moment in front of the automatic door. "I've lusted after you," she replied, her sweetly innocent smile at odds with her words. "I'd like to do things with you that would make a hooker blush. And you know what, Will?" She moved closer and touched him, nothing intimate, just a brush of her hand across his stomach, and her smile grew sweeter and less innocent. "One of these days, it's going to be a whole lot easier for you to just give in and make me happy than it will be to keep saying no."

With that, she turned and went inside, greeting her mother's next-door neighbor as she got a shopping cart, calling a hello to the minister's wife in the check-out line. She was in the produce section before Will finally joined her, a scowl on his face and an unholy light in his eyes. "One of these days, I just might give in," he agreed. "And if that happens, little girl, you'd better pray that you don't wind up sorry you asked."

She placed a bag of apples in the cart, then met his gaze. "I'm not a little girl, Will," she said quietly. "If you're calling me that to remind me of my inexperience, it's not working. If you're calling me that to remind yourself . . ." She gave him a long, hot look, from his face down to his chest, across his stomach to his noticeable arousal, then back again. "I don't think that's working, either."

Then, after giving him a moment to steam, she offered a friendly, harmless smile and asked, "What was it you wanted to get here?"

If he were the kind of man Will Beaumont was, if he'd lived the kind of life Beaumont had lived, he would be a little more careful out in public, Jared Robinson thought disdainfully. He'd been following him and Celine around the grocery store for the last five minutes, and neither of them had noticed him. If *he* were such a selfish bastard, he would watch his back. He would make sure no one came sneaking up behind him.

But all Beaumont was interested in watching was Miss Celine. He had it bad for her, all right. The way he looked at her was enough to make Jared feel dirty just watching, but he imagined most women would probably enjoy it. Miss Celine seemed not even to notice. Of course, she was too good for Beaumont anyway, and he had to know that.

Finally Jared turned his attention to the shopping list in his hand, seeking out the items and placing them in the plastic basket he carried. So far he'd bypassed everything on it in favor of spying on Beaumont. He would have to hurry and get all of it or his grandfather, outside in the truck, might get tired of waiting and come inside to see what the problem was, and once *he* saw Beaumont, all hell would break loose.

He didn't like the way his grandfather had changed since Beaumont had come back. The fights with his grandmother had stopped, at least, but so had almost everything else. He went to work, he came home, and that was all. He was moody and distant. He stayed up late at night and looked at pictures of Melanie over and over. He didn't take Jared fishing on

Saturdays anymore, and he didn't want to play ball or work on the old '65 Chevy they were fixing up for Jared to drive next year. He just brooded.

Jared turned onto the aisle with the paper towels and came to a sudden stop. There right in front of him were Miss Celine and *him*. He looked at Jared, but didn't recognize him—didn't even *recognize* him! Miss Celine, of course, did, and she automatically started to smile and say hello before she realized how uncomfortable this meeting would be. Her smile disappeared, and she looked from him to Beaumont, then back again, and finally said, "Hello, Jared."

He didn't say anything. Neither did Beaumont, not even when she went on. "Will, this is Jared, Melanie Robinson's son."

Your son, Jared thought fiercely as an angry hot flush crept up his neck. That was what she should have said. But that would have sounded too stupid: Will, this is Jared, your son. Jared, meet your father. Any man who needed an introduction to his own son ought to be shot, his grandfather would say, and Jared agreed.

For a moment they just stared at each other. Jared had always been told that he didn't look one bit like his father, and now, close up, he could see that was true. Beaumont was as dark as Jared was fair, as hard as Jared was soft. His eyes were dark brown and blank, as if this meeting meant no more to him than any other person he'd ever met—maybe even less. And why should it mean anything? Even more than Melanie, Beaumont had never wanted a kid. Jeez, he'd left home to avoid having to acknowledge having one. And sixteen years hadn't changed anything. He wasn't going to acknowledge him now.

After a long time, Beaumont extended his hand and said his name. There was something dismissive about his voice, as if he would forget Jared's name and everything else as soon as he was out of sight.

Jared refused to shake his hand. He refused to speak to him at all. He was going to say something to Miss Celine—he couldn't ignore her just because she had the poor judgment to be with Beaumont—and then he was going to walk away. But before he could think of what to say, Miss Celine moved away from the shopping cart. "I'm going to get something I forgot," she said, her smile false, the cheer in her voice phony. She touched his shoulder as she passed, then disappeared around the corner, leaving him and Beaumont there alone.

Beaumont moved to where Miss Celine had been standing and wrapped his fingers around the cart's handle. He was uncomfortable, Jared realized. He recognized the signs— the shifting back and forth, the clenched hands, the pure awkwardness—because he was experiencing them, too. Funny. He hadn't expected uneasiness from a lying bastard like him.

"You look like your mother," Beaumont finally said.

Meaning he didn't look at all like *him*. Jared was grateful for that. "So you remember what she looked, like?" he asked sarcastically.

"Yes, I remember her. How is she?"

"She's living down in New Orleans selling herself to whoever's got the money to buy." The words were harsh and brutal, but Jared didn't flinch from them. As much as he loved his mother, he could be honest about her. She was little better than a prostitute. The only difference was she didn't find her customers on the streets, and she preferred long-term arrangements—a few weeks, a few months—over an hour in a cheap hotel.

Whatever she was, this man in front of him was somehow responsible.

"Listen, kid, I know you've heard all your life how I got your mother pregnant and refused to marry her and ruined her life, but . . ." Beaumont broke off, looked away, then back again. "It's not true. I'm not your father."

Jared stubbornly stared at him, refusing to hear his words, refusing to let his denial penetrate. "Grandpa said you lied about it then and that you would lie about it now. He said you were worthless trash that didn't know the meaning of truth and responsibility and honor. He said—"

"Look, it's too bad your mother got pregnant so young and too bad you had to grow up without a father, but—"

This time it was Jared who interrupted. "I couldn't care less about having a father. I have my mother and my grandparents. I don't need a father."

Will Beaumont smiled then, the same kind of smile Jared's mother wore when she visited, just before she returned to New Orleans without him. A sad kind of hurtful smile. "Yes, you do. Every kid needs a father."

Jared stared a moment longer, then spun around and walked away. All the way to the front and the check-out line, he could feel the man behind him, although when he risked a glance, he saw that Beaumont hadn't moved. And as he paid for the groceries, then carried them outside to his grandfather's truck, Beaumont's last words kept echoing in his head. *Every kid needs a father.*

He jerked the pickup door open, climbed in and slammed it, then settled the grocery bag between his feet. His grandfather was giving him an odd look, but Jared just stared straight ahead. If he looked at his grandfather, the old man might see that he was upset, might wonder why, might ask questions or go into the store to find out.

"Are you okay, son?"

Son. It was what his grandmother had called him ever since he'd gotten too big for sweetie or honey, what his grandfather had always called him. But he wasn't their son. And the two people who should be calling him that . . . His mother called him sweetie, even though he was too big, and baby when she was drinking, and his father . . .

He drew back from that title, that connection, and bitterly rephrased it. The man who denied being his father called him Jared in that meaningless way and, worse, kid. Jared hated being called kid.

"Son?" his grandfather prodded.

Twisting his head to the side he saw Miss Celine and Will Beaumont through the plate glass windows. They were at the check-out. Soon they would come walking out the door.

Forcing a smile, he turned to his grandfather. "I was just wondering whether I got everything. Let's go, Grandpa. Grandma's waiting for these groceries so she can fix dinner."

"Tell me about Melanie Robinson."

Celine glanced up at Will as they left the store, trading its air-conditioned comfort for the late-afternoon steam bath. Almost instantly, she fancied, she could feel the curl sliding from her hair, could feel damp spots forming on her dress. "She moved away right after you left. When Jared was small, she brought him here for a visit with his grandparents and never came back to get him. She lives in New Orleans now."

"And does what?"

"You mean work?" She lifted her hair, then let it all fall over her left shoulder. "I don't know that she has a regular job. She used to work at a club in the Quarter. One of Vickie's friends ran into her there. Mostly . . . well, the gossip is that mostly the men support her. She's been involved with quite a few of them in the last fifteen years."

"What do you mean 'involved'? Is she a hooker?"

She bent to pick a dandelion growing in a sidewalk crack and twirled it between her palms. She didn't like this conversation—didn't like gossiping about someone she didn't know, didn't like gossiping about someone Will knew all too well. "I mean she trades the only thing she has to give—sex—for whatever it is she needs." After a moment, she quietly added, "The same thing you used to do."

She could feel his hard gaze on her as they waited for an eighteen-wheeler to go rumbling past. Refusing to look at him, she crossed the street when it was clear and walked into the cooling shade of the live oaks on Miss Rose's street.

Switching both grocery bags to his right hand, Will stopped her with his left hand on her arm. "The same thing I used to do?"

Finally she did look up at him, her gaze connecting with his. "You cleaned rich people's swimming pools, parked their cars, and slept with their lonely rich daughters when they needed someone in their beds. When you needed a bed, period," she repeated from their conversation last weekend. "According to rumor, Melanie does more or less the same. Does that make her a prostitute?"

He looked at her for a long time, his eyes dark and intense, his manner wary, his hand hot and sweaty against her skin. Then he released her, looked away, turned away. "I don't know," came his grim reply.

Was he truly undecided? she wondered. Or was he unwilling to condemn Melanie knowing that whatever label he stuck on her would apply to himself as well? "I don't think so," she said softly, firmly. "I think it just makes her someone doing the best she can to survive."

A person did what he, or she, had to to get by, and who was she to judge their choices? Her life had been blessed. She had never gone hungry, had never been forced to sleep on the ground, had never gotten desperate. At the lowest point in her life, her breakup with Richard, she'd still had a place to live, food to eat, people to turn to. She might have been heartbroken, but she'd still had her pride, her self-respect, and her dignity. She'd had hope.

Melanie had lost hope. She was still hanging on, true, but she was a sad woman living a sad life. It seemed that she hadn't known any real happiness since she was fifteen and the prettiest girl in town. She had so much going for her—beauty, parents who loved her, a handsome son who needed her—but she seemed unable to turn her back on the life she'd found herself in. She couldn't give up the men and the alcohol and everything else, not even for her son.

For Will's son? Celine wondered.

Walking out of the shade trees and into the evening sun, off the cracked sidewalk and onto the dirt path, she asked, "How did it go with Jared?"

"He's an angry kid."

"He has a right to be. Did you tell him that you don't believe you're his father?"

He scowled at her. "I'm *not*. And, yes, I told him. The kid's *not* my responsibility. I don't owe him anything."

She sighed softly. Poor Jared. He was the innocent one in this mess, and he'd probably been hurt most of all. How sad for him, if Will really was his father, that he'd been fed such hatred for him over the years. And how sad, if Will was telling the truth, that Jared had hated the wrong man all his life. If Will was telling the truth, the boy might never know even his father's name.

If Will was telling the truth. She still didn't know. She still couldn't quite believe him.

At the bottom of the steps leading to her porch, he stopped and offered her the bag containing her apples and tissues.

She accepted it with an invitation. "Miss Rose won't be home from church for a couple of hours. Want to have dinner with me?"

Will gave it a moment's consideration. He could go on back to the guesthouse, put away the fruit and cans of soup he'd bought, cook his dinner on the hot plate he'd found in one of Miss Rose's boxes, and read up on restoration until bedtime. A boring evening, for sure, but he might learn something.

Or he could stay here and sit across the table from Celine and eat her cooking. He could have the kind of normal evening that men all over the country had. He could talk to Celine or, better still, listen to the sultry Southern tones of her voice. He could indulge his fantasies about her. He wouldn't be bored and he probably wouldn't learn anything, but he would sure as hell feel a thing or two, and feeling beat learning any day.

He accepted her invitation and followed her inside the house. It was dark and dreary inside until she opened the heavy drapes and the blinds. Then she excused herself and went into the bedroom.

The cottage wasn't large. The living room was centered in front, with two doors opening off the back wall, one on the left to the kitchen, on the right to the bedroom. There was a tiny bathroom in the bedroom that shared a small bump-out space with a laundry room. It was more than big enough for a woman who lived alone. For a woman who didn't share her life, much less her space, with anyone.

The living room was square and furnished with the same heavy, dark pieces Miss Rose had lived with fifty years ago. The god-awful ugly upholstery of the chairs—giant cabbage roses—had been covered with slipcovers, and a new-looking quilt in pastels was draped over most of the sofa. The dark wood paneling he remembered had been replaced; the walls were soft pink in here, buttery yellow in the kitchen, mint green in the bedroom.

There were little personal touches all over—photographs, knickknacks, magazines, and books. The pictures were mostly family, the magazines for women with articles on fashion, homemaking, and child rearing. The books were organized alphabetically on the shelves that flanked the marble fireplace, sharing their space with a collection of small gnomelike creatures, wooden nutcracker soldiers, and primitive pottery bowls.

Hearing her return from the bedroom, he asked without turning, "Why does a librarian have so many books at home?"

"Because she loves to read."

"You have thousands of books at your disposal at work every day."

"These are my favorites, the ones I want to keep." She paused in the kitchen doorway. "I have a batch of sauce in the freezer, so we can have spaghetti and salad. Or, if you prefer, I've got a pot of jambalaya left over from last night."

His father had made a wicked jambalaya with chicken, sausage and shrimp, onions and peppers, celery and rice and seasonings by the cup. Served with corn bread and bottled pepper sauce, it was fiery, filling, and delicious. The memory of it made his decision an easy one. "Jambalaya's fine." Finally turning from the shelves, he followed her into the kitchen, where he stopped just inside the door to watch her work.

She still had on the same shapeless blue dress with a white T-shirt underneath that she'd worn to work, but her feet were bare now and her hair had been confined to a braid tumbling down from the crown of her head. She looked young, beautiful, and so damned innocent. No woman that beautiful should look that innocent.

Of course, looks could be deceiving. What had she said to him outside the store this evening? *I'd like to do things with you that would make a hooker blush.* If he ever let himself take her to bed, he just might be surprised. She was beginning to discover her own sensual nature, and she thought she wanted to discover it with him. She had an itch that she wanted him to scratch.

He moved to lean against the doorframe, his arms folded across his chest. "Why aren't you married and cooking for a husband every night, Celie?" he asked, aware that his voice was hoarser than it ought to be, that her answer was more important than it ought to be.

She turned from the pot she'd set on the stove and gave him a long steady look. Will knew that she knew he'd overheard her argument with Vickie Sunday, knew that he'd heard her sister's talk about the man Celine had been engaged to marry. But he hadn't said anything about it, and she hadn't brought it up, either. After all, finding out that her fiancé was sleeping with her sister couldn't be a very good memory for her. It couldn't be anything that she wanted to discuss with him.

She turned her attention back to dinner, stirring the jambalaya, wrapping big squares of corn bread in foil for the oven. "I got as far as picking out my dress and the invitations," she said evenly, as if discussing something totally unimportant. "Then he decided he preferred sleeping with Vickie over me."

"What is he doing now?"

"He's married—not always happily—and raising a family."

He wondered if she found any satisfaction in the "not always happily" part. He doubted it. "Do I know him?"

"No." Having done all she could with dinner, she filled two glasses from the pitcher of tea in the refrigerator, then carried them to the small table pushed against one wall.

Will sat down across from her and accepted one of the glasses. "What about the other guy?"

"The other guy?"

"You said you'd been involved with two men from this town." Actually, she'd said she had been to bed with two men from this town. He was in pretty sorry shape when the mere idea of Celine and sex, even with other men, could make him hot, but he was certainly feeling the heat.

She pulled a paper napkin from the ceramic holder, a monstrous thing in shades of yellow, white, and blue, in the center of the table and folded it, using her thumb to put a crease down the center. "He was a mistake," she said flatly. "I think I wanted to see if the problem was with me or—" She hesitated at naming names. "Or with my ex-fiancé. It was hard to tell."

"If you still don't know, little girl, then you've been picking the wrong men."

She gave him a frankly curious look. "Is that what you think? That you're the wrong man for me?"

His reply was as soft as her question. "I don't think it, Celie. I *know*."

"Why?"

"Because I know you and I know myself."

"What if I don't care?" she asked, then nervously touched her tongue to her upper lip. "What if I still want to—still want you—anyway?"

The desire that was ever present inside him started growing stronger, more painful, more insistent. It would be so easy to give in—as she'd said at the store, a whole lot easier than saying no. He could just take her to bed and to hell with the consequences. He would pay the price tomorrow, but he would have this one night. He would know how it felt to be inside her. He would learn the true meaning of pleasure and passion, of want and need. She would know that her disappointment in sex was rightly blamed on the men involved and not on herself.

But she would learn other things, too, things that he didn't want to be the one to teach her. About being used, about being distrusted. About being looked on with the same disdain that he received just because she associated with him. About being discarded and hurt and left behind. But she would have a good time in the learning.

Why not go to bed with her? She was a grown woman— a little naive for her age, a whole lot innocent—but grown all the same. She knew what she was asking for. She knew what she was risking. Why couldn't he just turn off the oven and the stove, take her in the bedroom and lay her down on the iron bed and answer all her questions? Ease her self-doubts. Show her how good it could be. Make her feel and want and need so much that she would weep when it was over.

Why not? Because she wasn't the kind of woman a man took to bed casually. Because for once in his life he wanted to do the decent thing, the right thing. Because she deserved better than to be dragged down to his level. Because, damn it, she deserved better than *him*.

He offered her a grin so cocky that she would never suspect

it was forced. "What would the saintly members of the First Baptist Church say if they heard such talk coming from you?"

Her answering smile was cool. "Some of them would say I was damned and bound for hell," she acknowledged as she stood up. "Most would think that it wasn't my fault for falling under the spell of a sinner like you."

Then, before crossing the room to the stove, she softly added, "And a few would like to join me for the ride."

Melanie Robinson fluffed her hair, touched up her bright red lipstick, then solemnly studied her image in the mirror. Her reflection was at odds with this room, where she had grown up. The lavender-flowered wallpaper, the white furniture with gold trim, the canopy over the bed, and the shelves of dolls and school mementos were better suited to a teenage girl, to someone who had her whole life stretched out ahead of her, someone who hadn't already learned the hard lessons that *she* had learned.

The room looked exactly as it had when she had left home sixteen years ago. Time had stopped within these four walls. Her cheerleader's uniform still hung on the back of the closet doors, the colors faded now. Her school notebooks were still neatly stacked on the desk under the window. Her sophomore picture was still wedged between the glass and frame on the dresser mirror.

She had loved this room when she was a kid. Now it gave her the creeps. It reminded her of the stories she'd heard about someone dying and the family keeping everything in his room exactly the way he'd left it. Except *she* hadn't died.

Or had she? The face looking back at her in the mirror bore little resemblance to the photograph there, and the spirit inside—weary, worn, and defeated—had nothing in common with the happy, hopeful, and in-love girl she had once been. Maybe that Melanie *was* dead, and she was just a tougher, harder, sorrier replacement.

She combed her hair again, then sprayed perfume heavily over her blouse, her wrists, and her throat. Her clothes were simpler than she would have chosen if she were home in New Orleans: a tight red skirt and a rounded-neck blouse that could be as demure or revealing as she wanted. Her feminine vanity would have preferred something with a little more flash, but she was here on business.

She was going to see Jared's father. She was going to get enough money to last the rest of her life.

She slipped into a pair of red heels, then carefully made her way down the stairs. Her mother was sitting in the living room, the television tuned to some talk show that was going unwatched. Instead her attention—her disapproval—was directed to Melanie.

"Where is Jared?" Melanie asked when she reached the bottom.

"Over at Joey's house."

"Good. I don't know how long this will take, so don't hold dinner for me."

"The least you could do is wait till your father gets home and say hello."

Melanie gave an exaggerated sigh. They had had this conversation already. Her mother didn't want her to go asking for money. She thought it made Melanie look greedy, and she was sure Jock shared her opinion. She was convinced Jock could dissuade her from her purpose. But Melanie didn't care if she looked greedy. A man had an obligation to his child and to that child's mother, and the measly few bucks he had given her when she was pregnant didn't come near fulfilling that obligation. "I'll say hello later, Mama."

Picking up her handbag, she went outside to her car. Even though she'd parked underneath the shade tree, the vinyl seat burned through her clothes. She didn't even have an air conditioner to help ease her discomfort; the thing had given up the ghost months ago. Maybe that was the first thing she would do with the money she got, she thought dreamily. Buy a brand-new, loaded-with-extras car. A Cadillac, maybe, or a Corvette—a fast and flashy 'Vette that could take her clean across this country to a better life.

She'd spent as little time in Harmony as possible in the last sixteen years, coming usually only to see Jared or to borrow some money from her daddy, but she still remembered the way to Miss Rose's house. Billy Ray had taken her there only once, one crucial evening that had sealed his fate and saved Jared's father's ass. It had been after a basketball game at the high school gym. Billy Ray didn't like basketball, but he had sure liked watching her in the skimpy skirt of her cheerleading uniform, with its kicky little pleats and the matching little panties that were meant to be seen.

After the game they'd gotten a burger at the Dairy Queen, and then he'd taken her to the Kendall place, to the guest-house, where he'd intended to sweet-talk her right out of that blue-and-white uniform. There was a bed there for comfort, a candle in a brass holder for light, a tiny transistor radio for music. And he had succeeded in getting her at least partially out of the uniform—from the waist up—when old Miss Rose, seeing the light or hearing the music or just plain old nosy, had come to investigate.

Billy Ray had never known she was there. He hadn't heard the door open, hadn't seen her embarrassed and disapproving look. He hadn't seen her turn and leave again without a word. But Melanie had.

And when her fears of pregnancy had been confirmed six weeks later, she had used that knowledge—had used it against Billy Ray.

She wasn't sure exactly why she was going to see him today. To apologize, maybe. To tell him that she hadn't meant to cause him any problems. Maybe to see if he was still as handsome, still as wild, still as willing, as in the old days.

When she reached the Kendall place, she slowed to a crawl, not sure what to do. There was a car in the cottage driveway— Billy Ray's maybe?—and another, older than the hills, parked at the main house. If Billy Ray was staying at the cottage, so much the better.

But what if he wasn't? What if she knocked at the door expecting to see him and some stranger answered? Better that she should go to the big house . . . where that crotchety old woman would give her one of those steely cold, beneath-her-notice stares. Old Miss Rose had never liked Melanie and had never made any effort to hide it. She'd made it plain to everybody, even while urging Billy Ray to do the right thing by her, that she held Melanie entirely responsible for ruining his life.

She parked on the grassy shoulder on the opposite side of

the road, combed her fingers through her hair, checked her lipstick one last time, then got out. When she reached the yard, she saw a tall, slender woman watering flowers, bright red geraniums in pots beside the cottage side steps. Did Billy Ray have a wife? she wondered, her visions of a pleasant hour's diversion draining away with dismay. But surely her mother would have mentioned a wife. Surely the entire town would have taken notice if Billy Ray Beaumont had brought himself home a wife.

"Can I help you?" the woman asked when Melanie was close enough.

"I'm looking for Billy Ray." She heard the hesitance in her voice, the uncertainty caused by facing this entirely-too-pretty woman. Her hair was long and a gorgeous brown—it had never seen a drop of the bleach Melanie's required now to keep its healthy blond shine—and she was wearing one of those long, flowing, flowery dresses that Melanie adored but couldn't wear because, at only five-foot-two, they made her look dumpy. There was nothing dumpy about this woman.

"He's back there." She gestured toward the guesthouse with a nod that made her hair shimmer in the sun.

Melanie started to walk away, then stopped again. "Do I know you?"

The woman gave her an even look. There was no expression in her eyes, but she didn't approve of her coming here, Melanie thought. She didn't like her. Women could sense that sort of thing. "We haven't met," she said politely. "I'm Celine Hunter, Vickie Hunter's younger sister."

"Celine . . . Oh, yes, the librarian. Jared's always talking about you. Well, this is a relief." When the woman looked at her questioningly, Melanie explained, "Mama told me in one of her letters that Jared had a little crush on the librarian. Since the only librarian I've ever known was old lady Russell, I was a bit worried about what kind of son I had. Now I can see he's got very good taste." She stuck out her hand. "I'm Melanie Robinson."

Celine switched the hose to her other hand, then shook hands with her. Her palm was wet, and Melanie drew hers back damp. The water felt good in the day's heat. "You don't look anything like that sister of yours. I went to school

with her, you know. You're a lot prettier than she ever was."
Then, embarrassed by her bluntness, she excused herself with
an awkward smile and made her way to the guesthouse at
the back. There she patted her hair, tugged at her blouse,
and smoothed her skirt before knocking at the door.

The door was open, the room beyond shadowy. She could
hear the sound of a radio turned low and the steady whir of
a fan, but she couldn't see anything until an instant before
Billy Ray stopped in front of her. She wasn't sure how he
would react, whether he would be as pleased to see her as
she was to see him. Somehow she didn't think so. She waited
in silence for him to speak.

He was handsome, shirtless and, lordy, still sexy as hell.
Watching her, he raised the glass he held and drank deeply
from the clear liquid inside. Water or liquor? she wondered.
Maybe a little vodka to help get him through these devilishly
hot evening hours? She had a particular fondness for vodka.
Just the thought of it made her mouth water.

"This must be the month for homecomings," he said at
last, leaning one shoulder against the doorjamb, keeping the
screen door between them. "How are you doing, Melanie?"

"Getting better every day," she replied with a bright smile,
thinking with all too painful honesty what a lie that was.
"And how the hell are you, Billy Ray?"

"I've been better. I've been worse, too." He drank again,
emptying the glass, then studied it for a moment. "What
brings you up this way?"

"Business."

"Funny. I understood your business was the kind con-
ducted in private in cheap hotels. I wasn't aware Harmony
had any hotels at all."

Melanie flinched away from the unexpected sting of that
remark. Billy Ray had long been regarded, especially by the
parents of easily bewitched daughters, as the devil himself
in human form, but he had never been given to cruelty. Of
course, after what she'd done to him sixteen years ago, he
was entitled to that and much more. She just hadn't expected
it. "Can I come in?"

He showed no inclination to move aside to allow her entry

until he'd followed her gaze to Celine, bending now to pluck weeds from one of the pots. Then he stepped back, opened the door, and invited her in with a sweeping gesture.

Homecomings, he had said. Here she was back again in the place where his troubles had started. Where *she* had started them. The big room was clean and neat, one part obviously set aside for living, the rest for storage. She wondered why he chose to live out here with no air-conditioning, no big comfortable bath, and only a two-burner hot plate for cooking. Had Miss Rose welcomed him back but banished him from the big house? Or had it been his choice to sleep in the place where he supposedly got her pregnant?

"So what business do you have in Harmony?" he asked, disappearing into the bathroom to refill the glass. It was water, she thought, disappointed. She surely could have used a shot or two of vodka.

She thought about lying, about telling him that she'd wanted to visit her son or that she'd driven all the way from New Orleans just to see him. But if anyone deserved her honesty, it was Billy Ray. Next to Jared, he had suffered most from her dishonesty. "I came to ask Jared's father for some money." She smiled tautly. "For a little child support."

He set the glass on the stack of boxes beside him and emptied his jeans pockets, turning them inside out. "Thirty-two dollars and change," he said flatly. "That's all you'll get from me."

Embarrassed, Melanie turned away, going to look out the window beside the bed. "I'm sorry about all this, Billy Ray," she said softly. "I never thought about what it would do to you. I was in trouble, and I needed a way out, and . . . you were it."

The chill was still in his voice, but it wasn't so hostile when he spoke again. "My name is Will."

Turning, she studied him for a moment. Yes, Will fit him. Billy Ray was a fine name for a wild young boy with laughing eyes, a wicked grin and a go-to-the-devil attitude, but Will was better suited to the grown man he had become. "I'm sorry, Will."

"So am I." He sat down on a wooden trunk, the old-fashioned kind with a rounded lid, and braced his bare feet on the sloping sides. "I met your son yesterday."

Her smile came quickly, the way it always did when she thought of Jared. "He's a good boy."

"He thinks I'm his father, and he's not too pleased at the prospect."

"Did you set him straight?"

"Like he'd believe me?"

She looked around for a place to sit, but there was only the bed. Fifteen minutes ago she had thought Billy Ray Beaumont's bed a fine place to be on a terribly hot day. Now it didn't seem so. This wasn't the boy she had known and played with and used. This wasn't the boy she had betrayed with her lies. This was a man who might be polite, who might let her come into his house and hear what she wanted to say, but that was all. He was never going to forgive her. He was never going to make the mistake of trusting her again. He was never going to give her a pleasant hour's diversion.

"Where did you go when you left here?" she asked, looking for some common ground, something they could talk about like friends.

"I started out in New Orleans. I've seen every nothing town in the South since."

She smiled. "I started out in a nothing town in Georgia—with my mama's older sister—and wound up in New Orleans."

Silence fell then, the kind that made her shift uncomfortably from foot to foot. The high heels were starting to pinch her toes, and she was hotter than holy hell with nothing but those ceiling fans overhead to cool the room. She was about to make some excuse and leave when Billy—when Will spoke.

"Who is he, Melanie?"

She didn't need to ask who he meant. There was only one man in her life who could possibly interest him. "I can't tell you."

"I've been blamed for what he did for the last sixteen years. I had to leave my home. Since I came back, I've had to tolerate whispers and curses and pointing fingers. Don't I have a right to know?"

She twisted her hands together. "I wish I could tell you, Will, really, I do. But he made me promise not to. That was part of our deal when he gave me the money before—that I would never tell anyone who he was. It'll be part of our deal this time, too."

"So you're not looking for child support," he said cynically. "You're here to blackmail him."

"Jesus, Will, you've gotten mean," she tried to tease. "First you call me a whore, and now this."

But it was true. She *had* come home with blackmail in mind. She had even rehearsed what she would say. *Billy Ray's come back now, you know, and, jeez, I feel so bad for what I did to him—lying like that. Naturally, he'd be happy to see his name cleared after all these years, to be able to prove to all those small-minded, self-righteous people who judged him that he wasn't guilty after all. Of course, if his word and mine aren't enough to convince everyone, there are new tests now that can prove beyond a doubt who Jared's father really is.*

"Why did you lie about it in the first place? When you found out you were pregnant, why didn't you tell the truth instead of blaming me?"

Why? Because she had been sixteen and afraid. Because the man she loved more than anything in the world had threatened to cut her out of his life if she ever breathed his name to anyone. Because her father was making threats of his own. Because when it came right down to it, she had known that no one around would have believed her over Jared's father. And, like the birth control she had been using, paternity tests that long ago weren't infallible.

And even if she had proved it, what would she have gained? Marriage? Not in this lifetime. Money? He'd given her that anyway. Love?

She sighed softly. It had taken her a long time to discover that the things he felt for her, the things he had called love, weren't. They were simpler, baser, far less pure. They began and ended in her age, her innocence, her willingness, and her trust.

"It was so easy to blame you. Everyone knew we'd gone out a couple of times. They all knew that you went to bed with just about every girl you ever dated.'' She shrugged. ''Naming you satisfied everyone. The other girls' parents could be smug and say that they'd known something like this would happen and thank God it hadn't happened to *their* daughters. My father got to tell my mother that she should have listened to him when he'd said I couldn't go out with you. My mother got to remind me that she'd warned me you were up to no good. And the whole town had a chance to tell Miss Rose that she'd been wrong ever to take you in.''

He stood up from the trunk and walked to the front windows, looking out. ''And you're not going to tell anyone the truth, are you? You're not going to tell Jared that he's wasted all his life hating the wrong man. You're not going to tell your parents that you lied.'' His voice grew harsher, softer. ''You're not going to give up an opportunity to bleed this guy dry, are you?''

Hesitantly Melanie approached him. ''No. I'm sorry, Will, but I'm not. Don't you see I've got a chance here? Now that you're back, he'll be worried. He'll be afraid that I'll feel sorry about what I did and might want to set things straight. He'll be willing to pay some real money to get rid of me this time.''

He continued to stare out. ''You won't even tell one person?''

''I can't tell Miss Rose.'' She knew he loved the old woman like a grandmother, knew that Miss Rose's failure to believe in him all those years ago had hurt him. It was only natural that he'd want her to know the truth, that he would want to say, ''See, I didn't lie to you.'' But Melanie couldn't do that for him. She couldn't even tell Jared the truth. Did Will really think she would tell Rose?

''I am sorry, Will.''

He gave no sign of hearing her apology. She touched his arm, and he gave no sign of noticing that, either. With a sigh, she withdrew her hand. ''I'd better be going.''

Finally he turned and gave her a long, hard look; then he said, ''I'll walk you to your car.''

It was a courtesy she hadn't expected. When they got about even with the cottage, she understood the reason behind it. She saw the look he gave Celine, tending the flowers in the shade on the porch. Had she spoken too quickly there at the window? Was it Miss Rose to whom he wanted to prove his innocence?

Or pretty Celine?

"How long will you be in town?"

"As long as it takes him to make up his mind." She smiled uneasily. "He's got a lot to lose. It shouldn't take long."

"And what are you going to do with this money? Take your son? Raise him? Be a mother to him for once?"

She opened the car door, then leaned on it and looked up at him. "No. I'm going to use it to go far, far away from here. Jared doesn't need me. He's got Mama and Daddy and the rest of the family. He's got friends, a real home. He doesn't need the troubles I'd bring."

"Having all those things doesn't change the fact that he doesn't have you. You're his mother, Melanie."

His quiet statement made her feel unbearably sad. "Yes, I am his mother. I'm also a realist, Will. I have a craving for hard men and rough sex. I like to get high. I like to experiment with booze and drugs and men and, occasionally, with women, too. It's like a hunger. I know it's wrong and perverse, but it's my life, and I can't walk away from it. Believe me, I've tried. And that's no life for a kid, especially one as handsome and sweet and smart as Jared. He's better off here. He's better off without me."

She tossed her purse into the car, then gave him a determined smile. "I probably won't see you again, Will. Do you think it would offend Celine over there if I gave you a kiss good-bye?"

He smiled, too, just a little, and she pulled him down and pressed a kiss to his cheek. Then, wiping the lipstick away with the pad of her thumb, she murmured, "Take care of yourself. Have a good life." She climbed into the car, started the engine, then called out the open window as she drove away.

"I'm going to."

Chapter Seven

Have a good life. I'm going to.

Will watched until Melanie's car was out of sight, until the dust left in her wake had settled once again on the road. As much as he resented her, he felt sorry for her, too. Life had been no easier for her than for him—harder, in fact, with her being so young and having a baby.

Maybe this mysterious man she was going to see would come through for her. Maybe he would give her enough money to get away from here. Enough money to support the life she was looking for. Enough money to drink herself to death? he wondered cynically. Enough money to overdose on?

Someone doing the best she can to survive. That was how Celine had described Melanie. Unfortunately, all too often the best you could do wasn't good enough. Celine hadn't had to learn that lesson yet. He had. Melanie had.

Finally he left the road and started across the yard—though not to his house. He went to Celine, climbing the steps onto the cottage porch and letting the screen door bang behind him. He wanted to see her. He was going to touch her.

She was bent over a half barrel filled with yellow-and-orange flowers on the west side of the porch. The hose, discharging water at little more than a trickle, lay at her feet while she clipped dead blossoms from the stems, collecting them in her cupped palm. He allowed himself a moment to enjoy the curve of her bottom where her skirt, tucked between her legs to keep the full hem out of the water's flow, was pulled taut.

Then he crossed the porch to her, ignoring the puddle of water around his bare feet, and looped his arm around her waist, pulling her upright and tight against him. She didn't protest and push away or cling tighter. She dropped the scissors and the dead flowers, then leaned back against his arm so that they were intimately touching from waist down, and she looked at him in a way that made his body go hard, damn, so hard and so fast that it hurt.

"I wasn't aware Melanie had such an effect on you," she said, her voice low and husky.

"She doesn't." His denial came out harsh, his admission ragged. "But you do. You have, damn it, since the first night I got back."

Her eyes, such pretty green eyes that saw too much and yet not enough, became shadowed. "And what are we supposed to do about it?"

"Nothing. That's the problem, Celie. You and I aren't ever supposed to do anything together."

She touched his chest, tracing over one of the scars that he'd picked up somewhere along the way. It couldn't be called a caress, not the matter-of-fact way she did it. It wasn't intended to entice or arouse, but it did. It made the muscles in his belly clench. It made his jaw hurt. It made him believe he was absolutely out of his mind for doing this.

"You've never been known for doing what you're supposed to," she softly pointed out.

With his free hand, he lifted her chin, forcing her to look at him. "You've always been known for doing exactly what you're supposed to."

"Then maybe it's time for a change."

"It is," he agreed grimly. "Time for me to do what's right. But not without this."

He kissed her then—not a friendly little peck like Melanie had given him or an awkward little taste like Celine had offered Monday night, but a claiming, a taking, of her mouth.

He used his mouth and his tongue, his hands and his body. He filled her mouth, stroking her tongue, and held her tight, flattening her breasts against his chest, cupping her bottom in his hands, pressing his erection hard against her belly.

She moaned, a helpless hungry sound that passed from her into him, making him hotter, making his muscles clench, his balls tighten. He kissed her harder, deeper, stealing the very breath from her. He kissed her as if it would be enough, when he knew in his head that nothing less than everything would ever be enough, when he knew in his heart that he could never have everything.

Aching, tense, about ready to come with no more than this, he ended the kiss and raised his head. For a moment her eyes remained closed, her lips slightly parted. When she finally looked at him, there was a soft, dazed, hungry look in her eyes. He brushed a strand of her hair back, rubbed his thumb across her mouth and wished like hell he could be someone else, someone with the right to kiss her again, someone entitled to carry her inside and make love to her the rest of the night. Someone good enough for her.

Her hands were on his shoulders. He pulled them away, pressed her palms together, then released them and took a step back. That step, the one that took him away from her body, should have been the hardest, but it wasn't. The closer he got to the door, the farther away from her, the harder it was to leave.

Still dazed, now bewildered, Celine asked, "Where are you going, Will?"

He stopped at the screen door, but he didn't turn around. "To Miss Rose's to borrow her car."

"Then where?"

This time he did look at her. "To the trashiest dive in the parish. I'm going to get drunk, and I'm going to find myself a woman, and I'm going to get laid." He waited for those words to sink in, then quietly finished, "I'm going to forget about wanting you, Celie. I'd recommend that you do the same."

Celine stood motionless for a moment, then followed him as far as the screen door. He was crossing the yard to the guesthouse, no doubt to clean up and change clothes before seeing Miss Rose.

Before going out to find himself a woman and get laid.

Merely thinking the words made her teeth hurt, made her ache to slap him so damn hard that he wouldn't be able to think about anything, much less getting laid, for a long, long time.

Son of a bitch!

As he reached the steps leading to the guesthouse, she suddenly called his name. When he unwillingly stopped, his back still to her, she opened the screen door and stepped onto the top step. "Thanks for the advice," she said sweetly. "But you'll have to forgive me if I don't take it."

He stood there a moment, his stance rigid. Finally, with Celine counting the seconds, he opened the screen door and disappeared inside. Ten minutes later, wearing a clean black T-shirt, his hair slicked back from a quick shower, he came out again and went to Miss Rose's house without even a glance in her direction. He spent maybe five minutes there before driving away in her car.

With a sigh, Celine returned to the west side of the porch and the marigolds there. She wondered where Will was going. She wondered if he really would do what he'd said. She wondered if maybe he was meeting Melanie. She wondered if sleeping with another woman really would make him lose interest in *her*.

"The idea behind deadheading flowers is to cut off the blooms past their prime so they don't drain the nutrients away from the new blooms," Miss Rose said in her old-lady fragile voice.

Celine looked at her blankly, then followed her pointing finger to the blossoms that had fallen to the floor—big yellow flowers that had just fully opened, loosely closed buds showing an orangey red fringe around the top that were preparing to open, tight green buds that needed another few days growth before they revealed the flowers inside. With a frustrated sigh, she dropped the scissors in a puddle, picked up the hose, and sank down in the closest chair to water the plants.

"You and Will aren't getting along well, are you?" Miss Rose asked sympathetically.

Celine gave her a dry, almost sarcastic look. "How could you tell?"

Miss Rose drew another chair over and seated herself. She didn't slump comfortably like Celine but sat erect on the edge of the thick cushion. "Will has never had an easy time of life, you know."

"Why did you take him in, Miss Rose?" she asked, watching the water flow in a smooth stream into the sun-baked earth. "You didn't have any family connections. You didn't ordinarily take such a personal interest in your charities. You weren't responsible for him."

"You know, Celine, that's part of the trouble in this world. No one feels any responsibility for anyone else. You see some homeless person on the sidewalk, you don't offer to help. You don't take him home and feed him and help him get a job and get back his self-respect. You step over him in disgust and say, 'It's not *my* problem.' We *are* responsible for each other. If I'm blessed with a nice home and food on the table, I have a God-given responsibility to help those who aren't."

Miss Rose practiced what she preached, Celine thought with a faint smile. But after a lifetime of preaching, she hadn't been able to get the point over to her son. Of all those who had complained about her giving Will a home twenty-four years ago, Raymond's complaints had been loudest and longest. Raymond didn't believe in helping the riffraff. His idea of a worthy charity was himself. What a disappointment he must be—in that respect, at least—to his mother.

"Claude Beaumont was a good man," Miss Rose went on. "He used to do occasional jobs on the side for Wynn and, later, for me. He loved his wife and his son, who, oddly enough, had no fondness at all for each other. Even when Will was a little boy, when he was sick or hurt, he wanted his father, not Paulette. I don't believe the woman had a maternal bone in her body. Claude used to worry over what would become of Will if anything happened to him. He knew he couldn't count on Paulette to take care of the boy."

"So you told him you would."

Miss Rose shrugged. "I had this big place, three houses,

and only me to live here. I had the money and the space"—
she gave Celine a sharp-eyed look—"and the responsibility
to raise him."

"Do you have any regrets?" Celine asked with a smile,
knowing the old lady's answer before she gave it, knowing
she hadn't regretted anything regarding Will.

But Miss Rose surprised her. Her gaze distant, her sigh
troubled, she replied, "Yes, dear. I'll always regret his leaving here."

"But that wasn't your fault. He has no one but himself
and Melanie Robinson to blame for that."

"You know, he's always denied being Jared's father. I'll
never forget the look on his face that night Melanie and Jock
and the sheriff came out here to see us. That was when she
accused him to his face. At first he was so surprised, and
then angry. He swore that he couldn't possibly be her baby's
father, that he had never even been to bed with her."

In sixteen years he hadn't changed his story, Celine
thought. But neither had Melanie. "Why didn't you believe
him?"

Again Miss Rose sighed, a sad, troubled sound. "Because
I saw them. He had taken her to the guesthouse—he lived
in my house then. I thought there was an intruder, and I went
to investigate, and I saw them in that bed." She glanced at
Celine, her expression apologetic and a little abashed. "I
didn't want to embarrass him. He was eighteen, after all, and
I knew he had been . . . intimate with one girl or another for
some time. I'd heard all the rumors."

And she hadn't wanted to get involved, Celine thought,
turning the hose from the barrel and crimping it to stop the
flow of water. Miss Rose had been raised in a different time.
She had probably known when Will had become sexually
active, but she hadn't wanted to involve herself in the issue.
Besides, he had been eighteen—not a boy to be admonished
or punished, but a young man. A young man who was doing
exactly what young men his age were supposed to do.

Why had he lied to her? she wondered, aware of how deep
her disappointment went. Why had he insisted that he'd never
been to bed with Melanie when he had? Why couldn't he

just admit that he had been frightened, that the awesome responsibility of a wife and a child was more than he could handle at that time? Why was he still lying about it?

But he had seemed so sincere. It had seemed so important to him. He had never wavered in his denial in sixteen years. And he understood obligations better than anyone gave him credit for. Hadn't he come back here because he'd felt obligated to Miss Rose? Wouldn't he feel the same sense of obligation to his own son?

But what had once been his word against Melanie's was now his against Melanie's and Miss Rose's. And while both Will and Melanie stood to gain by lying, Miss Rose didn't. She had no reason not to tell the truth.

Unless she had jumped to conclusions. Unless she had seen something that appeared to be more than it actually was and had, based on all those rumors she'd heard, assumed the worst.

She turned to ask the old lady for details—what exactly had she seen? What were they wearing? What were they doing?—but the blush coloring Miss Rose's cheeks stopped her. She was already uncomfortable enough with the subject, so Celine let the topic drop to save her any further discomfort.

Heavens, she was confused. She didn't know what to believe anymore. Maybe, after she asked Will about what Miss Rose had seen, the matter would be clearer. Maybe, based on what he told her then, she would figure out the truth.

"I should have handled the situation differently," Miss Rose went on after a moment. "I shouldn't have let him leave that way. I should have gone after him. But I knew bringing him back would mean jail, and, well, frankly, I was disappointed in him. I thought his father and I had raised him better than that." She sighed softly. "That's the only time he's ever lied to me. The only time."

"Do you really think they would have sent him to jail? Getting a girl pregnant isn't such a terrible thing, and, Melanie's age notwithstanding, she was still a willing participant."

"Under the law back then, a minor didn't necessarily have the right to be willing. And the judge was a good friend of Jock's. Between that mess and the thefts—"

Celine had been watching the sun sink in the western sky. Now her head swiveled around so quickly that a heavy strand of hair slapped against her cheek. "What thefts?"

Miss Rose looked truly uncomfortable. "Oh dear," she murmured, getting to her feet and edging away while her hands fluttered, agitating the heavy air. "One of the disadvantages of getting old, dear—you get to reminiscing and talking about the past and your mouth runs away with you. Now . . . since we've been abandoned by the only male on the place this evening, would you care to have dinner with me, dear?"

"What thefts, Miss Rose?"

She drew herself to her full height and gave Celine a cool and haughty look. "I don't care to discuss the matter any further. Now do you or do you not want to share my dinner?"

"Not unless you're going to answer my question," Celine replied crossly.

"Very well. Good evening."

Celine watched her go. God, why was she always watching people she cared about walking away from her? Then she shut off the hose and went inside the house. There she changed into a thin cotton skirt and a tank top. She put her hair up, slid her feet into a pair of flat sandals, then took her purse and keys from the table and went outside to her car.

There were only three reliable sources that could tell her more about these thefts: Miss Rose, who obviously wasn't going to say anything more than she already had; the sheriff's department, provided reports had been filed; and the old newspapers. Crime was so unusual in Harmony, even these days, that a break-in was front-page news. A crime of any sort committed by Will Beaumont sixteen years ago would have been a hot story.

As librarian, she happened to be the keeper of old newspapers.

She parked in the alley out back. It wasn't likely that anyone, seeing her car on the street, would come inside to find out what she was doing there after hours, but she took the extra precautions anyway. She didn't want to be disturbed.

The newspapers were on microfilm, the boxes neatly stacked on a shelf underneath the counter. Harmony's only

paper was a weekly and, at its wordiest, was never more than
twelve pages. Forty-some years' worth fitted neatly in the
small corner space allotted it.

She fitted the proper spool onto the machine, focused it,
and pressed the button to advance the film. She wasn't sure
exactly when Will had left town, so she started with January,
scanning each page, stopping at last in the third week of
March.

Local Family Robbed.

The details were sketchy, most of them coming secondhand
from the sheriff. The missing items were jewelry, valued at
approximately fifteen thousand dollars, and some five thousand dollars in cash. The victims were Rose Kendall and her
son Raymond. And the suspect was Billy Ray Beaumont.

Celine read the rest of the article, about how Billy Ray
had left town the night of the thefts. It reported that he had
lived with Miss Rose for the last eight years and had access
to her house, which explained why there was no sign of
forced entry. He had been seen leaving Raymond's house
that night, where entry was gained through a French door
with a broken window—a door covered with Will's fingerprints. She read all of it, and then she read it again. And she
didn't believe a single word of it.

Will stealing from Miss Rose? Not in this lifetime. Not
even if he were desperate. He would go to jail first. Hell, he
would have married Melanie first. He might have done a few
less-than-honest things in his life, she had no doubt of that,
but stealing from the only person in the world he loved wasn't
one of them.

So who had robbed the Kendalls? Who had taken their
jewelry and walked off with their cash?

Maybe someone who had known Will was leaving town.
Someone who had seen an opportunity to frame him. Someone who had realized that, after Melanie's accusations, the
townspeople, the sheriff, Raymond, and even Miss Rose
would be willing to declare him guilty of anything and everything. Someone who had gotten off scot-free.

Digging out a dime from the bottom of her purse, she
dropped it into the coin slot and printed out a copy of the
page. She folded it and stuck it deep in her purse, then

rewound the spool and returned it to its box under the counter.
Then she went to the phone on her desk.

It took less than three minutes to arrange a meeting with
Raymond in thirty minutes at the restaurant two blocks down
the street. That would give her time to eat dinner, time to
think about what she had learned, time to separate logic and
reason from emotion. Time to consider what she believed.

"What do you think she wants?"

Raymond gave his wife an impatient look as they entered
his office. "How am I supposed to know? She said she'd
like to talk to me this evening."

"Maybe she's changed her mind about our offer to spy on
Billy Ray."

"Maybe." It didn't seem likely to him, but, hell, who
could tell with a woman? That Sunday Celine had seemed
offended, almost insulted, by his suggestion that she keep
him informed of Billy Ray's actions. This evening she might
be annoyed enough with Beaumont to accept. After all, Melanie Robinson was back in town, and according to gossip, the
first person she had gone to see was Billy Ray. Maybe that
hadn't sat too well with Celine. Maybe she was the jealous
type.

Just to be on the safe side, Raymond removed a few hundred-dollar bills from the middle desk drawer and slid them
into his wallet. If Celine had decided to sell out the bastard,
cold hard cash in hand would help offset any sudden attacks
of conscience.

"I'll be waiting for you," Frannie said as he slipped on
his suit coat. She walked him to the French door, the one
that opened right out onto the gallery near his car, and gave
him a slow, lazy kiss. "Try not to stay out late."

It didn't take him long to reach the restaurant. Hell, this
was Harmony, Louisiana. It didn't take long to get anywhere—except someplace important. He parked in the tiny
lot at the side and walked inside and straight to Celine's table.

"You're looking prettier than ever," he said as he slid
onto the bench across from her. The compliment was intended
purely as flattery, which didn't diminish the fact that it was
true. She really was a beautiful woman—not in that stunning,

exotic, make-you-hard manner of Frannie's, but in a simpler, quieter way. "So what brings you out on a hot June night?"

"Questions." She toyed with the remains of a piecrust on a dessert dish, flaking the pastry into tiny crumbs, then pushed it away and turned her attention to him. "What kind of agreement did you have with Will Beaumont when he left sixteen years ago?"

Raymond smiled. He liked a woman who got straight to the point. He was prone to beating around the bush himself, so he appreciated the direct approach. "What makes you think we had an agreement?"

"I was sitting on my porch the night you went to see him, his first night back in town. I heard you say that you'd had an agreement but you should have known better than to trust a Beaumont."

"Why, Celine." His smile deepened. "You acted so insulted when I suggested you keep an eye on him that day after church, when you were already spying on him."

She didn't say anything. She just sat there with her hands primly folded and waited.

"All right. I did make a deal with Beaumont. He wanted to leave town but didn't have the money. Jock Robinson was determined to see him locked up in jail for ruining his little girl. Of course, there never was any love lost between Billy Ray and me, so I was happy to hear he wanted out. I gave him a couple hundred dollars in exchange for his promise that he would never again come back to Harmony or contact my mother."

"Where did you give him the money?"

"At my house." He paused to order a cup of coffee. Once the waitress had brought it over, he continued. "Of course, that was my first mistake."

"Why was that a mistake?"

"I always keep some cash in my office at home—not a whole lot, a thousand dollars, sometimes more. Frannie likes to carry cash, and she's always forgetting to come by the bank. It's just a convenience. Anyway, Billy Ray must have seen the rest of the money, and later that night he came back. He broke in, and he took it."

"Was anything else missing?"

His expression hardened; so did his voice. "Yes, a ring that belonged to my father. It wasn't worth much—not more than a few hundred dollars—but it held great sentimental value for me. My father died when I was young. That ring was one of the few things belonging to him that I had, and Billy Ray took it." He let a heavy dose of bitterness seep into his voice. "He probably pawned it somewhere for a few dollars."

She didn't ask anything else, and he used the silence to try to read her. Her eyes were dark, her expression stony. He wondered idly if she *was* sleeping with Beaumont, if maybe they'd had a lovers' quarrel. Maybe he had gotten her into bed and then lost interest, which seemed to have been his standard operating procedure back in high school. Raymond had never envied Billy Ray anything except his easy way with women. Lord, all he'd had to do was crook his little finger and girls had come running.

Apparently that hadn't changed. According to Frannie, he was the prime topic of conversation in the beauty salon, those he had slept with lording it over those few he had missed, and in the bank the other day he'd overheard a few vulgar remarks concerning Billy Ray's body and what the two women speaking would like to do with it, alone, together, or in a crowd. Celine's trashy sister had been talking all over town about how he wanted to resume their old relationship. *Relationship*, Raymond thought derisively, as if a couple of dates and a hard screw in someone's backseat constituted a relationship. Even Celine, sweet Celine, who had shown little interest in men since her idiot fiancé had dumped her for her sister, seemed taken with the bastard.

"I heard Miss Rose was missing a few things, too."

Celine's soft voice drew him out of his thoughts. Lord, he'd told this story so often that he didn't even need to pay attention to do it. "A few things? A pair of diamond earrings that were given to her by her parents on her wedding day. A cameo brooch that had been in the Kendall family for two hundred years. An emerald bracelet that was one of a kind. To say nothing of the nearly four thousand dollars stolen from the bureau in her room."

"Why did she have nearly four thousand dollars at home?"

"Habit, I suppose. She lived through the Depression, you know, saw the banks close and leave all their customers with nothing. Even though she was just a child, it left quite an impression on her. I'll bet you she's got a couple thousand there now."

"Why wasn't he arrested? An eighteen-year-old kid on his own for the first time ever? It was only logical that he would go to either Baton Rouge or New Orleans first. Were the police there notified?"

"No. Mama wouldn't allow it. She insisted that he never would have taken those things unless he'd needed them." He sighed heavily. "What can I say? She has a soft spot in her heart for him, though only God knows why. Now . . . it's my turn to ask a question or two. What has he been up to?"

"I don't know what he does with his days, of course, since I'm at work. He spends his evenings alone. He's come into town twice—"

"To see you both times." He laughed at the startled look that appeared briefly in her eyes. "The grapevine in this town is nothing if not efficient. Does he have any company?"

"No." She met his gaze evenly then. "But today Melanie Robinson came to see him."

"That must have been a touching reunion. They're two of a kind, you know? Neither one of them gives a damn about their kid. They're just concerned with themselves, with not being bothered by him. Some people don't deserve to be parents."

That brought a touch of sympathy to her gaze. He and Frannie were childless by choice, of course, but the story around town was that they couldn't have children, that Frannie's one and only pregnancy had ended in miscarriage, that the doctor had said it was impossible to try again. He knew the rumors, and well he should, since he had started them himself. Frannie's pregnancy ten years ago had been unexpected, unplanned for, and unwanted, and so she had, on a shopping trip to Dallas, aborted it. A child would have interfered with the way they lived. There would have been changes, demands and obligations, restrictions and limits that they weren't willing to accept.

Everything would have been fine, but somehow his mother had found out about the pregnancy. Rather than tell her the truth, he had lied. The abortion had become a miscarriage. The follow-up surgery to ensure that such an accident didn't happen again had been changed from a voluntary procedure to safeguard their chosen lifestyles to surgery necessary for his wife's well-being. Instead of anger and bitterness over their selfish behavior, they had received sympathy, not only from Miss Rose but from everyone.

He wondered how far Celine's pity would get him. She was a beautiful woman. In spite of her men, she still possessed a certain innocence. And if she was willing to sleep with Billy Ray Beaumont, she must have a sense of adventure.

He considered the possibilities, then thought of his mother living right across the yard from Celine and of his wife waiting at home for him. Innocence held a certain appeal. But it couldn't begin to compete with all of Frannie's gifts. With all of Frannie's dirty little talents.

Pulling out his wallet, he withdrew one of the hundred-dollar bills, along with a couple of ones. He slid them to the middle of the table, then stood up. "Pay the tab for me, will you, Celine? I need to get on home." With his smoothest, most charming smile, he added, "It's been nice talking to you. We'll do it again sometime. Maybe next week?"

From time to time, usually when he was well on his way to falling-down drunk, Will contemplated exactly what appeal places like this held for him. This little bar, located at the junction of two roads leading to better places, was like every other little bar he'd ever been in. The place stank of sweat, smoke, and booze. The customers were tough, hardworking people who found little pleasure in their lives beyond an evening's drinking here. The beer was cold and cheap, the waitresses minded their own business, and the music on the jukebox was loud.

He belonged in places like this. He was no different from these people. He'd never had it easy. He'd blown whatever chances had come his way. He had worked damned hard for damned little money, and he was never going to get ahead. No matter what he did, no matter what he accomplished, he was always going to be exactly what he was now. Untrustwor thy. Unwelcome. Unwanted. Except by Celine.

He had left her four hours ago fully intending to meet thre of his four goals: find a bar, get drunk, and get laid. Th fourth, forgetting about her, would probably be impossible but he could try. He could pretend.

So far he'd achieved only one: he'd had found a bar. H needed more beer—so far he'd had only four, not enough t make him friendly, much less drunk—and he hadn't yet seer a woman who could make him even think of sex.

God, this was just what he needed, he thought, closing hi eyes and leaning his head back so far that it hit the wall. A case of lust so bad that he couldn't rouse even a semihar attraction to another woman, and all for a woman he couldn' have and, by rights, shouldn't even know.

"Mind if I join you?"

The throaty voice reminded him of Celine, but where he huskiness had to do with arousal and desire, he would be this woman's came from too much booze and too many ciga rettes. She was standing beside the booth, her hand restin on the back of the vinyl seat opposite him. Her fingernail: were long, starting to curve under, and were painted som unnaturally dark tint. They would come in handy fo scratching someone's eyes out, but not much else.

When he nodded, she slid onto the bench. Her hair wa: bleached blond and her makeup heavy. She looked to b anywhere from thirty to fifty—it was hard to say. Howeve many years she had lived, they had been tough ones. They showed on her face and in her voice and in her spirit. She reminded him of Melanie, he realized. Sad. Used. Kind o pitiful.

God, now he was feeling superior to someone else. Maybe the booze *was* starting to get to him, because he sure as hel knew better than that when he was stone cold sober. There wasn't a soul in this world who had sunk lower than him.

The woman signaled to the bartender, lit a cigarette, ther extended her hand. "I'm Eva."

"Will." He shook her hand, then ordered another beer fo himself.

"You visiting someone around here?"

"Over in Harmony."

"This is a quiet night. There's more action in here on weekends." Accepting the glass and the bottle the waitress brought, she tossed off a shot of whiskey in one eye-watering swallow. "You looking for some action?"

He smiled wryly. "I don't know what I'm looking for."

"You've got woman trouble, haven't you?"

"Yes, ma'am, I do."

"Your wife?"

He finished the last swallow in the bottle before exchanging it for the new one the waitress had brought. *Your wife?* The words had an alien feel to them. Back when he was young, he had naturally assumed that one day he would get married because that was what people did; they grew up, got a job, got married, had kids, and died. He had never known anyone who hadn't been married at least once. It was normal. It was expected.

That was one of the expectations he'd given up when he'd left Harmony. Keeping himself alive had been practically more than he could manage. He'd never held a job for long, had never stayed in one place more than a few months, had been in more trouble than he'd thought possible. What could he possibly have offered any woman? Sex? It might sustain a relationship in the beginning, but it wasn't going to keep a wife and kids fed. It wasn't going to pay the rent or the bills. It wasn't going to satisfy a woman who wanted better than a hand-to-mouth existence. And the best sex in the world wasn't going to make him want to setle down and be a husband.

"I'm not married," he said with a grin. "Never found a woman who would have me."

"Then the women where you come from must be stupid. Where is that?"

"Everywhere."

"You move on a lot?" She tapped the ash from her cigarette with one of those dangerously long nails. "Maybe that's the problem. It's hard for a woman to love a man who keeps leaving her behind."

"Where are you from?" he asked, not so much out of interest as because he didn't want to talk about being loved by a woman. *Any* woman.

"New Orleans. Memphis. St. Louis. I've lived all my life on the banks of the Mississippi." After downing another shot of whiskey, she laughed. "I'll probably die there, too. So . . . you got family here?"

He shook his head.

"Me neither. Mine's all over. I went from St. Louis to New Orleans with my first husband; my oldest girl still lives down there. I wound up in Memphis with my second husband and left the younger two kids there. My third husband brought me down here when he was looking for work. He found it, all right, and ran away six months later with the boss's wife." She gave another raspy laugh. "Men are all bastards, you know? Including you. Out here in a cheap honky-tonk drinking with me instead of home patching up things with that woman of yours."

"Some things can't be patched," he replied grimly. His entire life was a good example.

They sat in silence for a while, Eva drinking, Will mostly watching the smoke from her cigarettes curl upward, then flatten out. When he breathed it in, it stung and stank, making him remember why he'd quit smoking years ago, how sick he'd gotten of the smell that had permeated his clothing and even his skin. Everything had started to smell of cigarettes, to taste of them. It had taken weeks, it seemed, to get the stench out of his pores.

"This place will be closing soon," Eva remarked with a glance at the neon clock over the bar. "You got somewhere to go home to?"

"Yeah." Not that he wanted to. He didn't want to face another night in the guesthouse, too hot and sweaty—and too damned horny—to sleep. He didn't want to be that close to Celine. He didn't want to see her or hear her voice. Damn it, he didn't want to even think about her.

Tapping her nails on the Formica-topped table, she quietly said, "You can stay with me if you want."

He'd had such offers from women before. Sometimes he

had accepted them. Usually, if he could afford to, he had turned them down.

Tonight he could afford to.

"Thanks, Eva, but . . ."

"But no thanks." She smiled regretfully. "I'm not your type, am I? Just my luck. I attract men like my ex-husbands. Never the pretty boys like you."

"It's not that at all. I've just got someone else on my mind tonight."

"Ah, your woman. Is she pretty?"

Images of Celine started to form before she even finished asking—serious and even and all too cool, laughing, smiling, dazed and aroused, unbuttoning her gown on a night-dark porch. He forced them away and concentrated on the woman across from him. "I think she is."

Eva smiled, softening the hard lines of her face. "That's all that counts, isn't it? Go home, Will, wash the smell of this place off you, apologize to her, and make things right."

He summoned the waitress, paid his tab and Eva's too, then stood up. "Some things can't be made right."

"Honey, don't I know it," she replied with a rueful laugh. "But it's always worth a try."

"Thank you for your company, Miss Eva." He offered his hand, and she took it with a smile.

"If you ever want to talk again, I'm here most nights," she said. "Next time it'll be my treat."

The air was cleaner outside, heavy with humidity and smelling faintly of the river and the chemical plants that lined its shores. It was a familiar combination, not totally unpleasant. Even though he'd smelled similar smells in Alabama along the Mobile River, or on the Savannah River in Georgia, he had always associated it with this particular place. With Harmony.

Sighing, he walked across the graveled lot to Miss Rose's car, then just leaned against it for a moment. He was okay to drive back to the Kendall place; he just didn't want to do it. He didn't want to go there.

But where else could he go? All his life there had been so few places for him—no relatives to visit, no friends to drop in on. Even when he'd been involved with one woman or another, he had still been as alone as a person could be. Over the years he had convinced himself that that was the way he wanted it. That was the way his life was. He'd had no choice in it, and so he told himself he liked it. Maybe, all those years, he had lied to himself.

Maybe he had never been satisfied, maybe he had never settled down, because none of those dozens of towns where he'd lived had been Harmony. None of them had been home. Maybe he had never let himself care about anyone because deep down inside he had known he didn't belong in any of those places. Maybe he had remained so alone because the people meant to fill his life were back home in Harmony.

Muttering a soft curse, he climbed into the car and drove at a rate well below the speed limit back to Miss Rose's. Her house was dark as he'd known it would be—she had told him to keep the keys until morning—and so was the cottage. But that didn't mean he was safe from Celine, who had an unfortunate habit of sitting on her porch in the dark.

He didn't try to see if she was there tonight. He dismissed the soft creak that came from that direction as a product of his imagination. He pretended that click as he climbed the steps to his door wasn't the sound of her door closing.

But once he was inside he couldn't resist the need that drew him to the window directly across the yard from her bedroom. He stayed back in the shadows, able to see the pale ghostly figure in her window but out of sight himself. He watched for countless minutes until she finally disappeared, gone to bed, he supposed. Alone.

There was some truth, as there often was, to popular sayings. Life really was a bitch.

Bitch.

Melanie Robinson was a greedy, no-class, whoring bitch who actually thought, after all these years, that she could get some more money, that she was *entitled* to it, as if getting pregnant and bearing that brat entitled her to anything.

She had come here this evening, acting all pretty and simpering and young, as if sixteen very hard years hadn't passed since the last time. As if she could possibly appeal to any man now. She was only thirty-two but looked well over forty. She was putting on weight and bleaching her hair to the point that it should be falling out, and all the makeup in the world couldn't hide a lifetime of self-abuse.

Fifty thousand dollars, she had asked for, or she would tell everything—about how she had been seduced and introduced to perversions she hadn't even dreamed of. How she had lied when she had named Billy Ray Beaumont as her baby's father. How she had been paid to leave town before the baby was born, how she had been paid more to stay away.

Fifty thousand dollars. She thought it would buy her a new life, a new start, but she was wrong. With her lifestyle, fifty thousand dollars wouldn't last any time at all. What she didn't drink away or snort up her nose, she would spend on luxuries—a car, clothes, jewelry. She was such a fool. She thought she could buy class, probably even thought she could buy the attention of some new man with lots of money and sexual preferences that were a little on the wild side. But all the fancy clothes in the world couldn't disguise exactly what she was. A whore. A tramp. One who had made a very serious mistake.

Fifty thousand dollars wouldn't be enough for someone like Melanie. She would run through that as if it were water, and then she would be back, wanting more. Another fifty thousand, maybe a hundred, on and on until there wasn't anything left. Or until she was stopped. She had to be stopped.

Go back to New Orleans, she had been told. You'll get your money there as soon as possible, two weeks, maybe more.

She had left her address, a filthy little place in the Quarter, and even her phone number, and she had gone away, just as happy and bubbling as you please, assured that she had succeeded, that any day now her doorbell would ring and her fifty thousand dollars would come strolling in.

Enjoy your good fortune while it lasts, Melanie.

Because there wouldn't be any money.

There wouldn't be any confession.

There wouldn't be any scandal.

And soon, very soon, there wouldn't be any Melanie.

* * *

Saturday afternoon was hot, so hot that even the air seemed to reject the idea of moving. Celine was lying on the sofa, the air conditioner on, the ceiling fan overhead turning, and contemplating a move somewhere up north. Alaska, maybe, or some remote island in the Arctic Ocean. Hadn't she always wanted to take off for places unknown? Hadn't she thought just a few weeks ago that this might be the summer she would do it?

Maybe she was too big a coward to run away. Maybe she couldn't even find the courage to cut off the hair she'd kept long all of her life. But she had summoned up the will to quit being sensible the moment she had laid eyes on Will Beaumont. She, who had never initiated sex even with Richard, had all but thrown herself at him. Too bad he hadn't been interested in catching her.

She could blame her behavior on the heat. It had already been a restless hot summer, and July was still nearly two weeks away. Such relentless heat made living uncomfortable. It seemed to intensify everything. She was more aware of her body, more aware of its needs. If Will had come back in the fall, with its warm pleasant days, or winter, when it was nice and cool, she would still want him, no doubt, just not so intensely.

She was watching the blades on the ceiling fan twirl when a knock sounded at the door. She had few visitors here: Miss Rose sometimes or Vickie, her parents on rare occasions and, even rarer, friends from town. But she knew instinctively who this was. Not Miss Rose or Vickie or any of the others. It was Will.

"Come in," she called, not sitting up, not changing positions at all.

The door swung open, and he walked in. He wore his usual faded jeans that fitted entirely too well and a T-shirt, white and tucked in, the hems of the sleeves turned up a time or two. For pure sex appeal, she thought appreciatively, nothing beat tight jeans and a white T-shirt. And no one wore them as well as Will Beaumont.

"You look hot," she said by way of a greeting, stating the all too obvious. His skin glistened with sweat, and his hair was damp where it fell over his forehead. Just looking at him gave Celine a new appreciation for high temperatures and sweaty bodies.

"You look lazy." He came to stand at the end of the sofa. "You're such a reliable, efficient woman. I wasn't aware that you had a lazy bone in your body."

"This is summer. I like to take it easy in the summer."

"Your taking it easy sure makes it hard for me to do the same." With a long, leisurely look, he encircled her ankle with his fingers. "Get some shoes and let's go for a walk."

She studied his hand—brown, strong with long, lean fingers—and wished he would from time to time touch her elsewhere—her face maybe, definitely her breasts, anyplace underneath her clothes. Then she shifted her gaze to his face and murmured, "The manners Miss Rose taught you didn't take, did they?"

"A lot of Miss Rose's lessons didn't take," he drawled, releasing her ankle and sliding his hands into his hip pockets. "Lucky for you and your spotless reputation that the important ones did. Get your shoes."

"You have a bad habit of issuing commands, Will." Her scowl as she got to her feet was proportionate to his grin. "Just once I'd like to be asked instead."

"I rarely ask."

"I know. Because you rarely need to."

His only response was a broadening of his grin. He knew, damn him, that she was going to come along whether he asked, demanded, or ordered. He was entirely too sure of himself. Entirely too sure of her.

In her bedroom she slipped into a pair of white canvas shoes. She didn't bother changing clothes—shorts would be no more comfortable than the full cotton skirt she wore—but she did put her hair up with a wide gold barrette.

"Where are we going?" she asked as they left the house and the porch.

"Nowhere. Isn't that what lazy hot summer days are best for? Going nowhere and doing nothing?"

His cynicism-shaded words made her smile as she followed him into the woods. Her childhood summers had been like that—long days of doing whatever captured her fancy, fishing from the river side of the levee or riding her bike along seldom-traveled back roads, swimming in old man Applegate's pond or filching berries from someone else's vines.

Her favorite pastime, though, had been exactly what Will had said—doing nothing—and her favorite place to do it had been high in the wide intricately patterned branches of a hundred-year-old live oak in her parents' backyard. She had planned her life up there in that tree, curtained from prying eyes by leaves and delicate Spanish moss, balancing on one limb, swinging from another. Growing up, falling in love, getting married, having kids and growing old—that was what she had looked forward to. She had envisioned at least a dozen kids, and when she died, she had seen herself surrounded by countless grandchildren and great-grandchildren, every one of whom she would have spoiled rotten. Such ordinary plans. Such common dreams. Richard had fitted perfectly into them.

Will didn't fit at all. But he could learn. If he were interested. Which he wasn't.

Even though he walked at her side, she didn't look at him. She kept her attention on the forest floor, where a heavy layer of pine straw muted their footsteps. It was spongy and soft, dusty reddish brown on top, darker underneath where the decaying process was already turning its nutrients into rich, dark earth. Occasionally she gathered armloads of it for Miss Rose's flower beds. There was nothing better, the old lady insisted, although for her own flowers, Celine preferred the commercially packaged convenience of pine bark.

Finally she did look up at Will. "You seem to be in a reasonably good mood. Did you have a nice time Thursday night?"

"Yeah, I did." That damnable grin of his reappeared. "Want to hear all the nasty details?"

Her gaze remained steady, her expression open. "I'd prefer to rely on my imagination. Reality tends to be such a letdown."

He stopped her and trailed one long finger along her arm, from her wrist to her elbow and on up to her shoulder, caressing just inches from her breast. It was a simple touch that left a tickly, shivery sensation in its wake, that made her nipple harden and her breast grow achy with neglect. "Let me assure you, Celie," he softly taunted. "Nothing about *my* reality is a letdown."

Because she couldn't stand still and let him touch her when she knew it was all he would offer, she began walking again, away from his hand and from him. "Esteem may be a problem," she murmured, "but you've never lacked for self-confidence, have you?"

He didn't reply, but gave her a look so hard that she could feel it burning in the middle of her spine.

"I had a nice time Thursday, too," she announced, when the sounds behind her told her that he was near.

"You find something educational on TV?"

His mocking was intended to annoy her. Instead she found it comfortable. Familiar. "No. I had dinner with Raymond Kendall."

This time it was Will who stopped walking. After a moment, she turned and faced him across a clearing of pine needles and cones, of fallen limbs and delicate ferns. What little sunlight filtered through the trees touched him—his hair, one shoulder, the other arm—and left her in the shadows.

For an instant she thought she recognized jealousy in his eyes—served him right—then she saw irritation, annoyance, and some anger. Then it all disappeared as he moved toward her, one slow step at a time, dark and threatening and handsome as sin.

"If you think an old man like Raymond can make you forget about me, Celie, you're badly mistaken," he warned in a shiveringly soft voice.

She didn't back away, didn't give him that satisfaction, didn't deny herself the satisfaction of being close, dangerously close, to him one more time. Keeping her gaze on his face and not on his chest, only an inch or two away, or any other part of the body that was keeping her awake at night, she boldly replied, "Some women like older men."

"Not you."

"No," she agreed softly. "I like *you*."

Will stood there, not quite touching her and not quite willing to move away. His hands were clenched behind him to stop him from reaching for her, but damn it, it was a losing battle, and so slowly, reluctantly, he backed away. "Why did you go out with Raymond?"

"I didn't go out with him. I met him at the restaurant."

When she was out of reach, he repeated an admonishment she had once given him. "You're playing with words, Celie."

That was a mistake, because she came closer and, her voice tantalizing and soft as a whisper, she responded with his own words. "Maybe you'd prefer that I play with you. That could be arranged, Will."

They stared at each other for a moment; then he laughed. It was arrogant and cocky as hell, and he had to force it past the thickness in his throat. "You've got a smart mouth."

"And it's good for a lot of things other than talking," she replied. Slowly, teasingly, she turned and walked away— damn it, *sauntered* away—with her hips swaying seductively and her long, long legs revealed with each step as her skirt swirled around.

It had been a long time since he'd found such pleasure in simply watching a woman—not touching, not holding, not kissing, but just watching. Hell, it had been forever since he'd found much pleasure at all, but he had certainly found it here. He could stand here and watch her and get hard and . . . *Damn.*

Pushing those thoughts to the back of his mind, he caught up with her as she reached the clearing where the railroad tracks cut through the woods. They crossed the gravel bed to the rails, but instead of continuing across and into the woods again, Celine stepped onto one glistening rail, carefully placing one foot in front of the other, balancing with her arms slightly out from her sides.

"What were you doing with Raymond?" he asked, walking alongside her, spacing his steps evenly so that each one landed on a creosote-soaked tie.

"Talking." She wavered unsteadily, and he automatically reached out, holding her arm until she regained her equilibrium.

"About what?"

Her laughter was as free and natural as his own had been

strained earlier. "Only one topic of conversation interests Raymond these days."

And *he* was lucky enough to be it. Looking off down the tracks, he scowled and wished briefly—for the tenth time? the hundredth? the thousandth?—that he was somewhere, anywhere else but Harmony, Louisiana. He didn't belong here. Other than Miss Rose and Celine, nobody wanted him here. He'd caused problems for Jared and Melanie and for himself. Raymond wasn't going to give him any peace, and neither was Celine.

But being bothered by Celine was a world apart from being bothered by Raymond. Being tormented by her was nothing less than pure pleasure.

"He really doesn't like you."

"The feeling is mutual."

Her foot slipped off the rail, landing on his own. Murmuring an apology, she stepped back up, this time resting her hand on his shoulder for balance. "Watch out for him."

He faced her. "Why do you say that?"

She stopped and turned, too. "Because I don't trust him. He's willing to pay to get rid of you."

He remembered his first Sunday back, when she had come to him out in Miss Rose's yard and announced that Raymond had offered her money to keep an eye on him. Not used to being refused something he wanted, Raymond had no doubt repeated his proposition Thursday night. "Did he offer you money again, Celie?"

"Yes. A hundred dollars." She stood there, eye to eye with him, without shame or apology. "And I took it."

He had gone years without being surprised by anything a woman said or did, until he'd met *this* woman. Everything about her was a surprise, from how much he wanted her to how much *she* wanted *him* to how poorly prepared he was for dealing with her. "So are you spying on me now, little girl?" he asked, his gaze narrow and hard, his voice hard, too. "Are you going to repeat everything that goes on to him?"

There was still no hint of apology in her green eyes. "*He* thinks so."

He *thinks* so. Meaning that she wasn't. Meaning that she was playing a damned game with Raymond. Will didn't like that. He didn't like the idea of her even speaking to the bastard, much less fooling around with him. Raymond could be a dangerous man when riled. "What about the money?"

"I had no intention of taking his money. He just gave it to me, as if he could buy me, as if I were some whore waiting to be paid for her services." Although it wasn't necessary, although she was standing still and had both feet on the rail, she braced both hands on his shoulders, and because it felt good, he let her. "I'm going to give the money to Jared," she continued, her voice growing a tone softer, a shade huskier. "He's saving for college. He can use it, and Raymond won't miss it."

"You make a fool of him, Celie, he'll hurt you."

She laughed huskily. "I'm a big girl. I can take care of myself."

"You're reckless," he said with a hard scowl. "Dangerous. Grown-up, beautiful, and innocent as a baby. Look at you. You get a wide-eyed kick out of walking a rail like a ten-year-old. You honestly think you can deal with a man like Raymond?"

"I'd rather deal with a man like you." She gave him one of those wide-eyed looks, and, God help him, he wanted her, right then. Right there.

Then she released his shoulders and started walking again, and he followed her. "You know, Will," she said thoughtfully, "I've been safe all my life. I never went out with anybody who wasn't suitable. I never did anything that wasn't expected of me. I never had a whole lot of fun. Well, I don't want to be safe anymore. I don't want to be reliable, dependable, levelheaded, boring Celine. I want something different in my life. I want to deal with a man like Raymond Kendall. I want to sleep with a man like you. I want . . ."

She sighed heavily, searching for the right word, then smiled provocatively. "*Passion.*"

She was the one balancing on the narrow rail. *He* was the one who almost stumbled and fell. Passion. That was one thing he *could* give her. He knew all about emotion, about desire and craving. About feeling, wanting, needing, hurting, and losing. About love and hatred and anger and betrayal.

Suddenly she stepped down between the rails and, like him, stepped from blackened tie to tie. "Will you tell me something—the truth?"

"About what?"

"Melanie."

Bending to hide his grimace, he picked up a handful of stones. The first one flew into the woods, landing with a soft thump against a tree trunk there. The second bounced off the rail way ahead, and the third he threw as far as he could. He couldn't tell where it landed. "We've already had this discussion," he said flatly.

"I know. But Miss Rose told me something, and . . . I want to know the truth."

What had Miss Rose said? That she didn't believe him? She'd made no secret of that. Celine had known it from the start. That she had changed her mind and did believe him? Not likely. "What could Miss Rose have possibly said at this late date that would make a difference?"

Celine hesitated, looked away, then back at him. "She says she saw you. In bed. With Melanie."

Chapter Eight

The afternoon seemed unusually sharp to Celine. The sunlight was so bright that it created a shimmering, soft-edged haze in both directions along the railroad tracks. The sky was a nondescript blue, streaked with wispy clouds, and the air was so still that she could hear her own breathing, and Will's, and the insistent buzz of a single gnat somewhere around her shoulder. It was a hot day with no relief in sight. A day empty of promise. No cooling breeze. No refreshing rain. No denials from Will.

He bounced the last stone he held in his palm, tossing it up, catching it, tossing it up again. He didn't seem surprised by her announcement, and he hadn't yet bothered to contradict it. Because it was true? Because he had lied to her that night in the restaurant and now he'd been caught? Because he really was the kind of man who could abandon his son the way he had abandoned Jared?

She had begun believing in him, she realized. She had wanted to believe him so badly, and so she had. And now that he knew his lies had been revealed, he didn't even seem embarrassed. Just thoughtful.

"So Jared *is* most likely your son." She heard her disappointment and hated it.

"Nope."

She looked sharply at him. "But you don't deny that Miss Rose did see you with Melanie. In bed."

"No, I don't. I've never lied about what went on between Melanie and me. I *was* in bed with her one night—the night she supposedly got pregnant. But I didn't have sex with her. It didn't go that far." His gaze turned distant, and his voice softened. "So that's why Miss Rose never believed me. She saw what we were doing and assumed . . ."

The worst, Celine thought guiltily. Everyone assumed the worst about Will, it seemed; she'd just done it herself. No one had ever had any faith in him, but Miss Rose's lack of faith had hurt. It had been a contributing factor to his decision to leave Harmony.

"What *were* you doing?" she asked softly.

He gave her a lascivious grin. "All kinds of nasty things." Then, after a moment, he relented. "There had been a basketball game that night, and Melanie was all hot and sweaty . . . like you are now." He touched her as they walked, brushing a bit of her hair back, gliding his fingers along her cheek to her jaw before withdrawing his hand. "We'd been out a couple of times before. We had done everything except the deed itself, and I figured that was my lucky night, so I took her to the guesthouse. There was no place to sit except that old bed—which was where I wanted her anyway. We kissed for a while, and she took her sweater off, and I had my shirt off."

Stepping back onto the rail, Celine kept her gaze locked on it where it stretched out ahead of her. She could see the scene he was describing all too easily. She could feel his desire and Melanie's and her own, and, damn it, how could she be jealous of a sixteen-year-old girl sixteen years later?

"We got into some pretty heavy petting," he admitted.

Petting. She liked that word. It was old-fashioned but so appropriate. She would like to be petted by Will. Even just the thought of it made her all achy and sore inside.

"I was ready and eager to consummate the act"—he gave the last three words a mocking twist—"but Melanie was holding back. We didn't do anything that night that we hadn't done before. I kissed her breasts, and she had her hand around my—"

Celine's foot slipped, and she stumbled. Breaking off, Will wrapped his arm around her waist to grab her, but he reached high, so that instead of settling at her waist, his hand was on her breast. She expected him to immediately release her, to grin that damned grin and make some sarcastic remark about how his talk had upset her balance. But he didn't release her. The grin, quickly in place, faded just as quickly. He didn't say anything at all.

They looked at each other for a long, hot, simmering moment; then slowly, tentatively, his fingers moved over her breast. They grazed her nipple, sending a jolt of sensation through her, left, then came back for a slower, more leisurely caress.

Any second now, she warned herself, he would stop and walk away. He would leave her here, trembling and aroused and burning inside. He would leave her hungrier than she'd ever been. More dissatisfied than she'd ever been.

He steadied her on the rail, then laid both hands over her breasts, and for a long still moment he simply watched as his fingers stroked, caressed, pinched, soothed. She watched, too, his tanned hands dark against the white of her blouse, his fingers long and strong but gentle, her breasts swelling under his care, her nipples growing noticeably hard.

And then he kissed her.

He brushed his mouth across hers, then coaxed hers open. It started as a sweet kiss, not sexy or wicked or knee-weakening—although it seemed all that and more to Celine—but it soon became hotter, harder, hungrier. He pushed his tongue into her mouth and used both hands to pull her snug against his body, her breasts flattening against his chest, his erection pushing into her belly, his thighs hard and muscular against hers.

With one hand, he popped the clasp on her barrette, and it fell, immediately forgotten, to the ground. Her hair tumbled free, covering her shoulders, and he buried his hand in it, wrapping heavy strands round and round and using the gentle grip to tilt her head back as his kisses moved from her mouth to her jaw, down the long line of her neck, to the pulse at the base of her throat. At the same time he reached for her skirt, catching a handful of fabric, gathering it slowly, pulling it higher, the cotton rubbing against her calf, her knee, finally her thigh, and then his leg was between hers, pressing hard against her. He was solid and strong, and she was hot, so hot that, mercy, she just might ignite.

"Damn, Celie." Will's curse was ragged, his voice strained. He didn't know whether he was damning her or himself, and he didn't much care. He'd been damned in one way or another most of his life. For once he was going to enjoy it all he could. He was ready—already so hard that he hurt. Already so needy that his skin prickled with it.

Raising his head, he stared down at her, and she gave him a lazy, sinfully enticing smile. He had never wanted anything as much as he wanted this with her. Respect, trust, the comforts of home and a place where he belonged—he would give up his last chance for all those things in exchange for this time with Celine.

"Do you want to go back to the house?" he asked harshly. There was no denying what they were about to do here, no denying that it would be more comfortable back at her house. Back where they might be interrupted by any of a number of people, where Miss Rose might wander over for an afternoon chat, where Celine might realize that she could do a hell of a lot better than him without even trying. Back where she just might find the good sense to run screaming the other way.

She didn't answer right away. Instead, she gazed off down the tracks, back in the direction they had just come. When she looked at him, she offered him a regretful smile. "I'm not . . . prepared."

He thought back to that morning when he'd gotten dressed. Every night he emptied his pockets onto the nightstand; every morning he picked everything up as a whole and crammed it back in. There hadn't been much that morning: about fifteen dollars in wrinkled fives and ones, another dollar or so in change, the key to the guesthouse and—Thursday evening's contribution—two plastic-wrapped condoms. *I'm going to get drunk, and I'm going to find myself a woman, and I'm going to get laid.*

He hadn't done any of that, but he had been prepared. Damned lucky for him. "I am."

Her smile widened and became infinitely sensual again.
"Just like a Boy Scout, huh?"

He didn't smile back at her. He couldn't stop scowling so
hard. "Not hardly. So do you want to go back?"

Her voice when she replied was little more than a murmur,
smoky and soft and weaving a seductive spell around him.
"We've come too far."

Too far from the house? Or too far to stop? He didn't ask.
He didn't care. He just kissed her again, filled his hands with
her breasts again, gave himself up to the need again.

Finally they moved away from the railroad tracks, across
the gravel bed and into the woods. They found a place there,
over a small rise, down into a shallow depression that would
hide them from view. The ground was covered with pine
needles, a comfortable enough bed for their purposes.

There he unbuttoned her blouse, one slow button at a time,
and she watched him do it. Each button revealed more of
her: the smooth, tanned area at the base of her throat, the
slightly paler skin between her breasts, the flat expanse of
her midriff, her waist where the concealing yards of fabric
from her skirt began. For a moment his fingers hesitated over
the last button, then he slipped it free and pushed the shirt
off her shoulders. It fluttered to the ground forgotten.

She stood there without embarrassment and let him look—
from her mussed hair falling down her back to her graceful
long neck and slender shoulders to her breasts, soft, swollen,
delicately veined, her nipples rosy-colored and still hard from
his caresses—and, oh, God, he was lost.

She was beautiful.

And he surely was damned.

Celine had never stood half-dressed before a man in bright
light, much less outdoors in sunlight, with all her flaws and
shortcomings so easy to see, but she wasn't self-conscious.
The way he was looking at her, how could she be?

She reached for his hand, twining her fingers with his,
holding on tightly for a moment while she gathered her courage; then she lifted it to her breast. She pressed his palm
against her, then arched her back to savor the effect more
fully. Unexpectedly she sucked in her breath. His touch was
searing, a steamy, blistering heat that made the muscles in

her belly clench and stirred to life an ache that hadn't been satisfied since the day he'd come back to town.

Ducking his head, he kissed her nipple, gently bit it, then sucked it hard, and she wondered dazedly if this little bit— these kisses, these caresses—could possibly be enough to make her feel the way she did—so hot and weak, so quivery and throbbing, so *intense*. Nothing in her experience with Richard or her other misadvised affair had even remotely prepared her for these feelings, for this need. As the saying went, the third time must be the charm. But, no, that wasn't it at all.

Will Beaumont was the charm.

He pulled away from her, and she clung—she, who had never clung to a man in her life—but he only wanted to remove his shirt. Then once again he kissed her hard, filling her mouth with his tongue, tasting, exploring. Passion, she had asked for, and he certainly had that. He made her feel intensely alive—and so very close to dying of want, of need, of the fire inside.

"Please," she murmured, his mouth still on hers. "Oh, please, Will . . ."

Her voice was so soft, a sweet, helpless little sound that ripped through Will with pain-laced power. Damn, but if she said his name like that again, he thought with a groan, he was going to come right here, right now, without the pleasure of even being inside her first. Calling on every bit of strength he possessed, he backed away from her, and this time she let him go. He found their discarded shirts and spread them on the ground, then dropped to his knees in front of her. An appropriate position, his cynical nature mocked. He damn well *should* be on his knees in front of her. He should be begging her. But she wouldn't make him do that. Not Celine.

She was gazing down at him, her eyes shadowy and wide, curious and innocent. Unafraid. She watched him as he reached behind her to unfasten the hook on her skirt and tug down the zipper. For once he was grateful for her taste in clothing. Along with their shirts, this skirt would make a fine bed.

She shifted, self-conscious for the first time now that she wore only a pair of ordinary white panties. Then he drew her down, too, urging her onto her back, pressing against her. Gathering a strand of hair, he tickled the sensitive skin around her nipple, watching it pucker, and he became hungry again for the taste of her.

"Last chance, little girl. Another minute, and I'm going to be beyond stopping."

Just like the first time they'd met, her gaze was steady, level, assured. "I don't want you to stop. I won't be sorry."

Her answer for a moment penetrated his arousal. She could have given him a dozen other answers that he wouldn't have thought twice about, but these particular words—*I won't be sorry*—gave him pause. "That's okay," he said with an odd little smile. "I'll be sorry enough for both of us."

Celine wanted to ask him why, but he had already turned his attention to seducing, arousing, teasing, satisfying her. He took such care, caressing her, kissing her breasts, suckling her nipples. There wasn't a place on her body that he ignored with his gentle, tantalizing, nerve-tingling caresses, not an erogenous zone in existence that escaped his slow, hot, open-mouthed kisses. He made her tremble and shudder and whimper. He fed her hunger until she thought she would die from it. He was relentless, merciless, in his seduction, and she loved it.

God help her, she was close to loving *him*.

Her skin was slick with sweat when finally he eased her panties off, hooking his fingers over the elastic band and peeling them away. Then he touched between her legs, sliding his fingers inside her, first one, then two, and his thumb rubbed her lightly, sensuously, making her muscles contract and her lungs tighten, making sweet breaths damn near impossible to take.

"Do you like that?" he asked, his voice an erotic whisper from down around her hip.

"Y-yes."

"Do you want more?"

"I want *you*," she demanded. "I want you inside me."

With a low, husky laugh, he began removing the rest of his clothes. Tennis shoes landed with a thud one atop the other, followed by socks, faded jeans—followed by a brief pause and a rustle of plastic—and cotton briefs. Celine was feeling too aroused to be shy, too bold to be embarrassed. She watched him undress, and she subjected him to the same admiring scrutiny he'd given her.

She had been fantasizing about his body for days. She had seen him without his shirt and in skintight jeans that couldn't conceal much, but she hadn't been quite prepared for this. Long and lean, all flat planes and hard muscles, slender waist, narrow hips and . . .

Mercy.

He didn't give her enough time to thoroughly admire him, to study him from head to toe, to rub his chest or to caress his muscles, knotted with desire, or to stroke his erection. She wanted to touch him, oh, Lord, wanted to touch him everywhere, wanted to kiss him everywhere, but he didn't give her a chance. He dispensed with the small square packet efficiently, then joined her again on their makeshift bed, moving between her legs, nudging her thighs apart, placing his hands beneath her and sliding slowly, painfully slowly, inch by inch, inside her.

He filled her, stretched her, and her body worked to accommodate him. Supporting himself on his elbows above her, he tangled his hands in her hair, and gently, sweetly, he kissed her.

"You still think I can satisfy you, little girl?" he asked, pushing somehow a little deeper still even as she started to reply.

She gave a supremely pleased sigh. "I bet no one ever called you little boy, did they?"

For a moment his look turned hard, and his mouth settled in an all-too-familiar scowl. "No. They called me names like bastard. Trash. Worthless. No-good. They'll call you that, too, if anyone ever finds out about this."

I'll be sorry enough for both of us. That was why. He thought he was destroying her reputation. With another sigh, this one for him rather than herself, Celine wrapped her arms around his neck and pulled him closer, so close that nothing could come between them. "They'll call me lucky," she corrected him; then, her lips brushing his, she whispered, "Teach me how to kiss like you do, Will. Teach me how to make you hot with just my tongue."

Will stared at her a moment longer, then slowly, wryly smiled. "Honey, you don't have to do anything but breathe to make me hot." But he kissed her anyway, and he began moving inside her, slow, deep, sure.

He had always enjoyed sex, had always found it a damned fine way to pass an hour or two. Wicked and wild, hard and fast, lazy and draining—he'd had it every way possible. Except *this* way. Except special.

Maybe it had just been too damned long. He couldn't even remember the last time he'd kissed a woman's breast or felt a warm hand or a hot mouth around his cock. Months ago. Months since he had come inside a woman. Months since he'd been so aroused, so needy, so don't-give-a-damn horny. Maybe that was the reason this time felt different. Hotter. More powerful. More intense.

It was building now, the orgasm that he craved, building into a raw pain that under other circumstances would be uncomfortable, that now he welcomed. He held her tighter, pushed into her deeper and faster, kissed her harder, stealing her breath, feeding her need, coaxing her along with softly muttered words and sounds.

She finished before him, her body trembling, her cry hoarse and helpless, her breath coming in shallow, rapid gasps. When the muscles deep in her belly clenched spasmodically around him, he came, too, with a great shudder and a groan born deep inside, but still the tremors didn't subside. He had to struggle for each breath. He had to work to regain control over quivering muscles. To regain control over unwanted emotions. Over unwelcome feelings.

Finally he lay against her, still inside her, his skin slick, hers sticky. He could feel the unsteady beat of her heart, could hear the uneven tenor of her breathing. Those, along with the hazy, drowsy smile she wore and the tiny convulsions of her body where it still sheltered him, seemed a pretty good indication that, after a lifetime of being dissatisfied, her luck had finally changed. Still, he wanted to hear it in words. He wanted to hear her say that he had done for her what her fiancé, whom she had loved, and the other guy, the one she called a mistake—like *he* wasn't?—couldn't.

He pulled out of her, dealt with the condom, then shifted

onto his side, leaning on one arm, and stroked her with his free hand. Her breasts were softer now, less swollen, and her nipples were flattening against them. It was tempting to arouse them again, to coax them once more into rigid peaks, but he resisted the urge now. Maybe later. Maybe never.

"Well, little girl?"

He drew the words out, long and tantalizing and, oh, so smug. Like him, Celine thought, with a little smugness of her own. He was long and hard, tantalizing as hell, handsome as sin, and twice as much fun.

Mimicking him, she rolled onto her side and supported her head on one hand. "Thank you."

He didn't expect that. It made him wary. "For what?"

"The best time of my life."

He grinned then, the broadest, cockiest son-of-a-bitch grin she'd ever seen. "I take it you weren't disappointed."

"Only that it had to end. Only that we'd waited this long." She gave his body a long, leisurely look, then softly added, "Only that I didn't get to do anything for you."

He wanted to laugh, to treat it lightly—she saw that—but he couldn't. Instead he swallowed kind of hard and, in a throatier voice than normal, asked, "What is it you wanted to do for me?"

"Maybe I phrased that wrong. I want to do it *to* you. I want to do it *for* me." She smiled tautly, then raised her hand. "Can I touch you?"

"You do, and you're just going to make me hard again," he warned.

"Again?" She looked and smiled again. "You haven't gotten soft yet. Can I?"

He looked uneasy. Because he didn't enjoy being touched? Or because he might enjoy it too much? "You won't have to do anything," she coaxed. "I just want to touch you."

After a moment, he shrugged, and she leaned forward to kiss him. When she gently pushed, he lay down on his back and she leaned over him. His skin was hot, soft, a nice brown all over, slightly darker on his chest and arms than below. As lean as he was, he was finely muscled, thanks to years of hard physical labor—and play. The hair that curled over his chest before tapering down across his belly was black, wiry, an enticing tangle for her fingers. It was thick, but not enough to cover his nipples, brown and flat but growing erect, or to hide the thin scars across his ribs. "How did you get these?"

He shrugged again. She felt the tensing and relaxing of his muscles, the rippling of his skin. "A barroom brawl. A jealous woman. I don't remember."

"Did you give her a reason to be jealous?"

"Probably."

She swallowed hard. With Richard her sister had taught her a difficult lesson in jealousy. With Will, she suspected, she could—probably would—learn more. She wasn't foolish enough, hopeful enough, to think this changed anything, that it in any way bound him to her. He wasn't going to lose interest in other women. He wasn't going to commit himself to her. Hell, he wasn't even going to stay in town once Miss Rose's request had been fulfilled, and there was no guarantee—heavens, not even a reason to hope—that he would spend his nights until then in her bed.

There was no guarantee that he wasn't going to break her heart. Because she *was* foolish enough to know that this changed things for her. Foolish enough to know that it would be awfully hard now to want any other man, foolish enough to make a commitment even when it was painfully one-sided.

"Do you get involved in a lot of barroom brawls?" she asked. She had reached his stomach now, flat and hard and leading her to her goal. She pressed a kiss there and tasted salt. Tears tasted salty, too. The only tears she had cried in months—in years—had been recent ones. Over Will.

"Not anymore. I'm too old for that."

"Too old?" she scoffed, trailing her fingers down his hip to his groin. As he had warned—she preferred to think promised—he was hard, stiff and impressive. Definitely impressive. "You're only thirty-four."

"The life I've lived has made me much older."

"And much more cynical. Much less trusting. And much less deserving?" Not waiting for an answer, she moved to kneel between his legs, bent and took him in her mouth in a sweet kiss. He tasted dark and musky and forbidden. She had never done this before—how uneventful her sex life had been before Will—and she found it awkward but one hell of a turn-on. Even the mere idea of kissing him so intimately made her hot, and that paled beside actually doing it.

With a bone-deep groan, he laced his fingers through her hair, pulling her closer, silently urging her to take him deeper. His erection grew harder, thicker, and she could just taste his flavor anew when he pushed her away. After a moment's fumbling—damn being cautious, she thought wryly—with those muscles she'd admired earlier, he lifted her up his body and settled her on his hips. She wriggled into place, sheathing him in one lazy, slow stroke, then leaned forward to kiss him. "I wanted you to come," she protested, brushing her mouth back and forth over his.

"Oh, I'll come, Celie," he said harshly, then gritted his teeth as she moved against him. "I'll fill you so full . . ."

He kissed her and stroked her breasts and slid one hand between their bodies to rub her, making her whimper and tremble. This time it was quick, a sudden overload, a sudden release. He came only seconds after she did, pumping, throbbing, emptying again.

After a moment, he withdrew his hand, damp from their joining, and held her for a while in his arms. She didn't think he indulged in many quiet embraces, so she rested her head on his shoulder, laid her arm across his stomach, and savored this one.

In the distance the sound of a train whistle sounded. "The 3:18 freight," Will remarked.

She started to sit up, but he pulled her back. "We're safe here. We can't be seen." Stroking her hair, he went on. "When my father died, I used to make elaborate plans to hop a freight to someplace new, someplace away from Paulette. She had never made any secret of how much she hated me, and I figured out real quick that, with my father gone, she wasn't going to keep me around long. I thought I'd be better off on my own than wherever she decided to dump me. I even went to the tracks right outside town a couple of times—the trains slow down through there, sometimes even stop—but I never got up the nerve."

Celine opened her mouth, but instead of saying anything, she kissed his chest. She couldn't tell him that he was wrong, that his mother hadn't hated him. She'd never met Paulette Beaumont, but she knew what everyone else knew: that Paulette had gone off and left her ten-year-old son completely on his own. That the woman had shown less concern for her own little boy than she would have for a pet.

"But I lucked out. I didn't have to leave, after all, because Paulette did."

"Then your luck ran out with Melanie."

He looked down at her and grinned. "It surely did. If I had known the kind of trouble she was going to cause me, I would have stayed a virgin until I was at least twenty-five."

"What a loss for all those lucky women you knew before you were twenty-five."

His amusement faded, leaving him touchingly serious. "There weren't as many as you think—too many, I admit, but I did use some discretion. And Thursday night? I just had a few beers. I didn't . . ." He broke off and shrugged.

Celine pressed her cheek to his chest. Maybe what had happened here did mean something to him. He certainly hadn't been under any obligation to tell her that. But she wouldn't hope.

She heard the train's whistle once more as it crossed the dirt road that ran by Miss Rose's, and she felt its approach in the slight tremors of the earth. A few minutes later it was passing them, rumbling by, the rails creaking under the immense weight. She knew from past experience that the wheels were throwing off occasional sparks as they struck the rails, that if she moved closer she could smell that faint peculiar scent that she always associated with trains, that when it was gone the stillness would return, like a fog that had been parted, then seeped back together.

It was far to the south when its whistle sounded again. Mournful, people called it. She didn't think so. Like most children, she had once loved trains, had made up stories about where they were coming from and where they were going. Will didn't find them sad, either. He had viewed them as a promise, a path to a better future. A future he hadn't yet found.

After a time he set her aside and sat up, then got to his feet. He located his briefs and jeans and shook them to dislodge any curious insects. He didn't turn away from her when he stepped into the briefs. He knew she was watching appreciatively, Celine thought with a sly smile, and so he let her. "For once Vickie was right."

He gave her a sidelong glance. "Vickie?"

"She said your—well, that you were impressive. I agree. I certainly was impressed."

He gave her a wry look, then said, "Whatever Vickie knows about my"—he imitated the embarrassed little shrug she had given—"comes from someone else, because, honey, I guarantee, *she's* never seen it."

"You mean you never slept with her?"

"I told you, Celie, there haven't been as many women as you think." His voice grew sharp with tightly controlled frustration. "Jeez, what does it take to make you believe me?"

She got to her feet and moved close to him, not minding that he had his jeans on now and she was completely naked. "I believe you about Melanie," she said quietly. "I believe you're not Jared's father."

For one still moment he just looked at her, his gaze searching her face as if he could find proof there; then abruptly he stabbed his fingers into her hair, holding her head still, and kissed her with a craving that was all new. As if they hadn't just fulfilled all their wants and satisfied all their passions right there on the ground.

Then, just as suddenly, he released her and turned to pick up her clothes, handing them to her. She put her skirt on first, then her blouse, finally wiggling into her underwear with a modicum of privacy. She buttoned her blouse crooked, did it again, then combed her fingers through her hair.

"Do you want me to find your hair clamp?" he asked as he tied his shoe.

"Yes, please." She sat down on a pile of pine straw, brushed off her feet and slipped them into her shoes, then stood up again to tuck her blouse in. She was hot, flushed, sweaty, and sticky. If anyone saw her looking this way, they would probably guess immediately what she and Will had been up to on their walk. Of course, her enormously satisfied, ear-to-ear grin would make it an awfully easy guess.

He went down to the tracks, then met her halfway back with her barrette. After wiping it clean on his T-shirt, he watched while she gathered her hair together and secured it with the clamp. "One day soon I'm going to get all my hair cut off," she announced.

"Don't. Your hair is beautiful." He drew his hand over it from the crown of her head to the very tips, and Celine knew then that she wouldn't cut it.

At least, not until he left.

They walked in silence along the tracks back to the cutoff that led to Miss Rose's house on the left, to the Kendall mansion on the right. When they had come this way last weekend, she hadn't been able to see any sign of a trail. She had simply trusted in Will's judgment. But now she thought she could tell that the weeds were a little beaten down there, that the bushes didn't grow quite so close, that the ground was a little more traveled.

They remained silent until they were practically home. Then Will stopped her, his manner awkward, his expression serious. An empty place appeared inside her and began growing. This was where he told her that it was nice, but, hey, it didn't mean anything. That he had a life of his own to live. That there was no place for her in it. That she shouldn't expect anything from him.

She was right.

"We can't do that again, Celie."

"Why not?" She shoved her hands into her pockets so she could double them into fists. "I thought you enjoyed it."

"Enjoyment has nothing to do with it," he said sharply. "I enjoy a lot of things that aren't good for me, like smoking and fighting and getting stinking drunk, but I don't do them."

"Are you saying I'm not good for you?" She kept her voice even, interested, but not intense. Not uneasy. Not too damn ready to cry.

"No," he said harshly, the lines of his face hard and unyielding. "I'm saying *I'm* not good for *you*." He turned and started away, leaving her there, not looking to see if she was following.

She wasn't. She stood still between the tall pines where she had first stopped, unable to force herself to take even one step. "What are you worried about?" she called after him, satisfied when he stopped, disappointed that he didn't turn around and face her. "I'm not your responsibility, Will. I'm a grown woman. I support myself, I pay taxes, and I vote in every election. I'm capable of making my own decisions. I'm old enough to decide for myself what I want."

Then he did turn, and she wished he hadn't. This wasn't the man she had just made love with. This was an angry man, a man with a mean streak a mile wide. "And what do you want, Celine? A little excitement in your boring life? A little passion? Am I supposed to provide that for you? Is an affair with the Beaumont bastard supposed to liven up your lazy, hot summer?" His grin was cruel. "I can do that for you. I've done it before. You pay me, honey, and I can do anything you want. You pay me enough, and I can even pretend I give a damn about you."

Stubbornly she hid the pain his words created, kept all hint of it from her expression. She just stood there and looked at him.

He turned away, then, swearing, swung back around. "Don't make me hurt you, Celie."

"I don't want anything else from you," she lied. "Nothing more than what we've already shared. I don't want promises or vows or a commitment. I just want to be friends."

"Friends?" he echoed with a sneer. "You fuck with your friends like that, honey, it's no wonder you're such a popular woman."

She finally found the strength to move then, walking to him, pausing only inches away. "What's your problem, Will?" she asked, her voice dangerously soft. "Do you dislike yourself so much that you can't let anyone else like you?"

He scowled down at her for a moment, then walked away. This time she didn't call after him. This time he didn't stop. He kept walking until he was out of sight. If she was lucky, he would stop when he reached the guesthouse. If she wasn't, he would keep on going.

The pleasure she'd found in the afternoon was gone. Instead of feeling wondrously satisfied and smug, she was suddenly just hot and tired, her clothes damp, her skin clammy, her body uncomfortably sticky in places she'd rather not think about. She needed a cool shower. Rest. Distance.

She needed a fresh perspective.

She needed a new life.

Jared shifted positions on the log, then slapped a mosquito that had landed on his neck. He'd been out here in the trees behind Miss Rose's guesthouse for the last twenty minutes, but little had happened. Will Beaumont was inside, all right. The windows were open, the lights on, the radio playing. A couple of times he'd gotten up and walked to the front windows, looking out at Miss Celine's place. It pleased Jared immensely that she wasn't home, that it was coming up on eleven-thirty and she still hadn't come back from wherever she'd gone.

It pleased him most because, apparently, it annoyed the hell out of ol' Billy Ray.

He hadn't told anyone, not even his mother, about his meeting last week with Miss Celine and Will. His grandmother would have started crying all over again, and his grandfather would have probably come out here and tried to kill Beaumont. His mother . . . He sighed. Melanie would have gone on about how heartbreakingly handsome he was, would have asked if he'd mentioned her, would have wondered if someday he might want to see her again. It seemed she just couldn't get beyond that selfishness of hers. He didn't even know if she tried anymore.

Swatting another mosquito, he considered the meeting dispassionately. That was all he'd been doing for three days now, replaying those few minutes in the grocery store, and he still wasn't sure how he felt about it. He wondered why Miss Celine had been with Beaumont, if she liked him, if she was sleeping with him.

Jared liked Miss Celine a lot. Of course, he knew nothing would ever come of it. She was nearly twice his age. What use would she have for a kid like him? Especially a kid who still hadn't done more than kiss a girl once, even though Ryan McNair two streets over had been having sex with his girlfriend ever since he was fourteen and a half, and Trey

Valdez had started right after he turned fifteen. Jared just liked looking at Miss Celine, talking to her, being with her. He didn't want it to go any farther than that. He would lose respect for her if she showed interest in anything more than friendship.

She was probably a lot more than friends with Will Beaumont. She was probably sleeping with him. Jared had heard his grandmother say so to Mrs. Crawford from next door. Mrs. Crawford had said that practically every young woman in town wanted to sleep with Billy Ray Beaumont and she would believe it of that older Hunter girl, but not Celine. Why, she was entirely too reliable to fall for a man like Billy Ray.

Jared suppressed a disgusted snort. Did Mrs. Crawford think reliable women didn't get hot and bothered? He had seen Beaumont looking at Miss Celine, and she certainly hadn't seemed to mind. She probably *was* sleeping with him. The idea of her having an affair didn't bother Jared. He just wished she had picked someone better.

Beaumont left the bed and went to the front windows again. He was anxious for Miss Celine to come home. Maybe they'd had a fight. Maybe she was just using him for sex and had gone out on a proper date with a proper man tonight. Maybe she was making him jealous. Jared hoped so.

Sliding from the log, he made himself comfortable against it. It had been a quiet hot day today. His mother had gone back to New Orleans only a day after she'd arrived, all happy and pleased. He loved her best when she was like that, when it seemed that nothing in the world could affect her good mood. But it never lasted long. Something always happened. She got drunk; her current boyfriend dumped her; she lost her job if she had one; and she got depressed and morose, crying over everything. Then he could hardly stand to be around her.

Still, it had been nice to see her, except he wished her visit had lasted longer. He wished she had spent more time with him. He wished his grandparents hadn't been so upset by her coming and then leaving. He wished she had wanted to take him back with her.

He wouldn't have gone. Harmony was his home. His friends were here. He liked it here. But it would have been nice, he thought wistfully, just to be wanted. It would have been something special if just once his mother had *wanted* him to be with her.

How would their lives have been different if Will Beaumont had been man enough to accept his responsibility all those years ago? What would it have been like to grow up with parents, with a father to teach him things instead of a grandfather? With a mother who maybe worked but did the motherly things—cooking and cleaning and taking care of him when he was sick, the way his grandmother did? Would his mother still be a drunk? Would she still use the drugs that she preached to him against? Would she still like living on the edge, overdoing the booze and the men, taking too many risks?

He doubted their getting married would have changed much, other than making him legitimate. The marriage never would have lasted, and Melanie still would have indulged herself in every pleasure she could find. Beaumont wouldn't have hung around just because he had a kid to support; he still would have taken off, and Jared still would have been raised by his grandparents. Without a father.

Every kid needs a father. That was what Beaumont had told him last week. His own father had died when he was a kid—Jared had heard the story—but that didn't mean he knew what he was talking about. After all, Beaumont had lived with his father until he died. Jared had never lived with his, had never even known his until now. How could he need something he'd never had?

Picking up a handful of pine needles, he began weaving them together in a loose braid, letting them fall free, then doing it again. He had finished for the third time when suddenly a shadow fell over him. Before he had a chance to react, before he could even think to curse the preoccupation that had kept him from noticing that his protective cover had been chased away by moonlight, the figure bent, grabbed a handful of his shirt, and hauled him off the ground.

"What the hell are you doing out here?" Will Beaumont

growled, holding Jared in one hand so that his toes barely touched the ground. "Are you spying on me?"

His heart was thudding irregularly, and his throat had gone so dry that he could barely swallow. He was more afraid than he'd ever been, but he bluffed it out. "What if I am? You wanna' make something of it?"

Beaumont slowly eased his hold enough that Jared could stand flat-footed. "I ought to call the sheriff and tell him I caught myself a prowler out here. You know what would happen then? They'd call your grandpa and get him out of bed to come pick you up. I don't imagine he'd be too happy about that, would he?"

"Nope. He'd probably come out here and shoot you," Jared said brazenly. And maybe he would—*after* he locked Jared in his room for the next three years. After he ranted and raved and told him how disappointed he was in him.

Beaumont released him, and the pressure of his shirt pulling under his arms disappeared. Jared tugged the shirt back down, carelessly tucking it back into his jeans. For a moment they just looked at each other, but Beaumont had the unfair advantage of having his face in shadow while the moonlight shone almost bright as day on his own.

"Are you working for Raymond?" Beaumont moved out of the shadows, leaning back against a tree that was wrapped around the trunk and up into the branches with wisteria vines, some as thick as Jared's arm. Early in the spring they would be weighted down with heavy lavender blooms, but the rest of the year they looked like ropes, grown dirty and dark with time.

He looked relaxed standing there, one knee bent, his foot braced against the lower trunk, as if having a conversation in the woods with a prowler was nothing unusual for him. Of course, if the rumors were all true, more often than not, he *was* the prowler in the dark.

"I'm too young to work at the bank," Jared replied sarcastically, then remembered Will's second question. *Are you spying on me?* He hoped his grin looked more natural than it felt. "I don't imagine Mr. Kendall is too happy about you being back here."

"No, he's not. You want to earn a little money for that college fund of yours, you go see him. He'll probably pay you well for hiding out in the woods here." He folded his arms over his chest. "So . . . what *are* you doing if Raymond didn't send you?"

Jared shifted his weight from foot to foot and avoided answering.

"Oh, I get it. You're checking out your old man, huh?" His tone was derisive and mocking and made Jared want to punch him. "I told you, kid, I'm not your father. You're not my son."

"Yeah, right," Jared muttered. "Why would my mother lie about it?"

"You tell me. You know her better than I do. I only went out with her a couple of times." Beaumont pushed away from the tree, and for a moment Jared tensed, ready to back away, to run away, all the way home if necessary. But Will didn't make a move toward him. He just stretched, then started toward the guesthouse. He'd gone only a few feet when he glanced back. "Want something to drink?"

Jared just stood there without saying anything, and with a shrug, Will walked away. The woods became quiet again after his passing, then the tree frogs picked up their interrupted song.

I'm not your father. You're not my son.
Why would my mother lie?
You tell me.

His mother did lie, Jared admitted. She lied if she didn't feel good or if she was angry or if she was feeling guilty. She lied when she'd done something she shouldn't and when she hadn't done something she should. She lied about her drinking, her drugs, and her men. She lied to his grandparents about work and money for sex and settling down. She lied to the landlord when the rent was late and to her boss when she didn't want to go to work and to her boyfriend when she'd been with another man. She lied to keep herself out of trouble, and she lied to get herself into trouble.

She lied with good reason and with no reason at all. *Why would my mother lie?* Melanie lied because that was what

Melanie did. But had she lied about this? Had she lied to him for fifteen years about his father?

He didn't want to believe it. He wanted to make Will admit that he *was* his father just so he could prove to himself that this time his mother had told the truth. Not so he could prove it to anyone else. Everyone else already believed her. So he could prove it to *himself*.

His feet began moving almost without his realizing it, and they carried him not back through the woods but toward the guesthouse. Toward Will Beaumont.

The door was open, the screen door unlatched. Beaumont was sitting on the bed, pillows propped behind his back, a can in his hand. A galvanized bucket on the floor nearby held melting ice and another couple of cans. Beer? The drink he'd offered a fifteen-year-old kid was beer?

But when he looked closer, Jared saw that it wasn't beer. It was Coke. What kind of hotshot, good-for-nothing-but-trouble ladies' man stayed home by himself drinking Coke on a Saturday night?

"Come on in."

Hesitantly Jared opened the screen door and stepped inside. It was about as hot in here as it was outside, at least until he moved closer and could feel the breeze from the ceiling fans. Beaumont offered him a Coke, and he took one from the bucket before settling against a tall stack of boxes. The soda wasn't very cold, but it tasted good anyway.

"Has your mother gone back to New Orleans?"

"She left Friday."

"Did she get what she wanted?"

"You tell me."

Will—no, Beaumont, Jared mentally corrected. He kept slipping, but he wasn't going to start calling him by his first name. He didn't want to get that close.

Beaumont chuckled. "You don't give up easily, do you? But I guess when you've believed the same lie all your life, it's not easy to give it up."

"How do you know about my college fund?"

"Celine told me. She says you're a bright kid."

Jared glanced over his shoulder. Through the tall windows

in front, he could see the entire back and the east side of Miss Celine's house. It was still dark. "She's not home tonight."

Beaumont didn't say anything.

"Looks like she's not coming home tonight," he said with a sly grin. When he looked back, he saw the jealousy and anger in Beaumont's eyes, saw the stiffness in his muscles. So he suspected that Miss Celine was out with another guy, too, and he didn't like the idea, not one bit.

"Where are you planning to go to college?"

Jared considered not answering. It wasn't like the guy had a right to know anything about him, but the manners his grandparents had taught him were too deeply ingrained. Respect your elders when you could, and pretend you did when you couldn't. Of course, under the circumstances, both his grandparents would probably say manners didn't apply, not in dealing with Will Beaumont. Still, warily he replied, "The University of Texas."

"Why there?"

"Because it's not here."

Beaumont smiled cynically at that, giving Jared the uncomfortable feeling that he knew exactly what Jared meant by that. He didn't like the notion, didn't like the idea that, on one matter, Will Beaumont understood him better almost than he understood himself.

"What are you going to major in?"

"Business. I'll probably go into law." He paused, then, his voice becoming sharper, slyer, remarked, "You never finished high school, did you?"

"No, thanks to your mother and your grandfather, I didn't." He drained the last of the Coke, then crumpled the can. "But a high school diploma wouldn't have made much difference in my life. Even if I had finished, I still would have been better off at jobs using my back instead of my brain."

Silence fell over the room then, heavy and uncomfortable. Jared looked around at the stacks of boxes and trunks and at the meager furnishings—bed, armoire, rickety card table with a hot plate. It was as clean and neat as his grandmother's house, but still kind of shabby. Kind of poor. It wasn't nearly as nice as what Will had once had in Miss Rose's house, but, if the stories Jared had been hearing were true, it was a lot nicer than what he was used to.

Finishing his Coke, he tossed the can into the small box that served as a trash can, then started sidling toward the door. "I've got to get home."

Will stood up from the bed. "I'll give you a ride."

"*No.*" If his grandparents saw or heard him getting out of a car, there would be hell to pay.

"It's after midnight."

"I don't want a ride. I don't need it." He was close to the door now. Without giving Beaumont a chance to say anything else, he bolted outside, letting the screen bang, cutting across the grass for the road at a jog.

He didn't look back and he didn't slow down until he was two houses from his own. There he slowed to a walk, catching his breath, concentrating on his body's weariness from the more-than-a-mile run, refusing to think about his visit to the guesthouse.

Once he reached the house, instead of trying to sneak inside, he went around back and stretched out on a chaise. He was hot and sweaty, and he couldn't take a shower at this hour without waking one of his grandparents. They would be full of questions, and right now he didn't have any answers. Not one.

Celine was sitting on the glider on her mother's porch, gently swaying back and forth, when the front door opened. Preparing herself for the noise of her nephews or the whiny demands of her niece or—worse—Vickie, she forced a smile of greeting only to discover that it was her brother-in-law who was joining her.

Richard sat down beside her and positioned his foot so the glider wouldn't move. "You weren't in church today."

She had told her parents when she arrived for Sunday dinner that she had been running late this morning, that she had sat in the back row. Because she had done that before, and because she had rarely, if ever, lied to them, they had believed her. Vickie had believed her. But apparently Richard had known she was lying. But she didn't care. She wasn't embarrassed at getting caught.

"I had to take Amy out near the end of the service," he explained. "I saw you drive by."

She still didn't say anything.

"Is everything all right, Celine? It's not like you to miss church. It's not like you to lie."

With a sigh she smoothed the wrinkles from the dress she'd changed into to fool her parents. "I didn't feel like being a saint this morning, Richard, all right?"

He chuckled. "That's how they talk about you, isn't it? Sweet, saintly Celine. So you didn't want to be a saint this morning. Does that mean you were a sinner last night?"

She gave him a chastising look before pushing his foot away and setting the glider in motion again. It was none of his business that she'd done her sinning yesterday afternoon. Last night she had sat alone in a motel room in Baton Rouge, feeling angry and hurt and most of all sorry for herself. She had fallen asleep moping over Will and had gotten up this morning wondering if he'd even noticed she was gone.

"I need to talk to you, Celine."

At the serious tone of his voice, she turned to look at him—*really* look at him. When he had broken up with her and married Vickie instead, she had stopped paying him much attention. At first it had hurt too much to see the man she loved with his arm around her sister, wearing the wedding ring her sister had given him. Later it had just become habit to give him a quick look without really seeing. He had become just Richard. Just her sister's husband.

He was still an attractive man—blond hair, blue eyes, a nice smile—even if he had gotten soft around the middle. He worked hard and earned decent money, which Vickie went through as quickly as he made it. On Saturdays he played golf, and in the spring he coached Matt's Little League team, and he usually treated Vickie to a romantic weekend in New Orleans for their anniversary. Even though he and Vickie had had some problems, Celine imagined that he was probably a good husband, definitely a better husband than Vickie was a wife.

He would have bored Celine silly.

"What's up, Richard?" she asked, even though she didn't want to hear his problems. She had enough of her own to think about now.

He loosened his tie, then shifted uncomfortably. "What do you think of your new neighbor out there?"

The muscles in her neck began tightening. "He's quiet. He keeps to himself. And having him back here makes Miss Rose happy."

"Does he have many visitors?"

"Not that I'm aware of."

"I understand Jock Robinson's daughter came back to see him, to ask for some money from him. As if he would have any to give."

"She went to see him," Celine admitted carefully. "I don't know why." She had never asked Will what Melanie had wanted. There had been time for little other than that kiss before he left Thursday, and yesterday Melanie's schemes hadn't been on her mind.

"Has anyone else been to see him?"

She reviewed the visitors she knew about in her mind. It was a short list: Raymond, Sheriff Franklin, and Melanie. Will had spent more of his life in Harmony than away, but only three people—five, of course, counting herself and Miss Rose—cared enough about his return to visit him. "Not that I know of," she lied. "Why are you so curious?"

Richard had trouble meeting her gaze, and he couldn't find the proper words to start. Finally he just blurted it out. "I think Vickie's having an affair with Billy Ray Beaumont."

Once it was out, he looked so relieved, as if saying it aloud made it easier. Once fears were voiced aloud, they could be proven to be irrational and unfounded. Celine knew that was what he wanted her to tell him—that he was wrong. He wanted her reassurance that Vickie wasn't having an affair, that she loved him too much to do that to him, that their marriage was too important to her to risk on a fling with Will.

But giving him those assurances would mean lying—again. Oh, she believed Will when he'd said that he had never been to bed with Vickie, not sixteen years ago and not now. She was as sure of that as she was of her own name. She was almost as sure that Vickie wasn't having an affair, but it had nothing to do with love for Richard or respect for her marriage. Her sister thought she was playing hard to get. She thought Will was eventually going to come sniffing around. She thought that sooner or later he would get tired of doing without a woman in his bed and that *she* would be the obvious choice, his only choice.

Wrong, sister dear, Celine thought with a hint of malicious satisfaction.

"Have you heard anything? Has she told you anything?"

She forced a smile. "Richard, I assure you, Vickie's not having an affair with Will."

"How can you be so sure? She's been acting strange ever since he came back—all secretive, you know? She's getting her hair done and leaving the kids with your mother while I'm at work and buying new clothes."

"Maybe she's getting her hair done and buying new clothes for you."

"But leaving the kids during the day? Where is she going then?"

"I don't know. Have you asked her?"

His expression turned gloomy. "I can't. What if she says she's seeing him?"

"What if she says she's going to one of her meetings or having lunch at the country club?" Celine countered. Richard's income and his active role in the community placed the Jourdans among the social elite in Harmony, and that placed Vickie on various committees around the parish and gave her a membership to play with at the local country club.

"I don't know," he said with a sigh.

"Look, Richard, I don't know what's going on, but I promise you, she isn't having an affair with Will. Not with Miss Rose out there all day. You know how she feels about Vickie."

Finally he chuckled again. "The old biddy never has liked her, has she? It's because of you, you know. Miss Rose thinks the sun rises and sets on you. She's never forgiven Vickie and me for hurting you."

He'd forgiven himself, Celine thought. The easy way he

referred to it was proof of that. "What you and Vickie did worked out best in the long run—for me, at least. Because you know what, Richard?" Leaving the glider, she walked to the door, then stopped and gave her brother-in-law a pleasant smile. "*I* would've divorced you years ago."

Chapter Nine

"Mr. Kendall?"

Raymond looked up to find one of the new accounts representatives standing in the door. His secretary was away from her desk again, but he didn't really mind. He encouraged an open-door policy between the officers and the others in the bank. He had discovered early on that employees liked the personal touch, and so he knew every name, every spouse's name, most of the backgrounds, and most of the families of every person who worked for him. This one was Marianne White, a divorced mother of two who was having an affair with her neighbor's husband. One of these days they were going to be indiscreet, and Laura Valdez, built like a fireplug, was going to kill one or the other for it. Privately Raymond hoped it was her husband. Marianne was a good employee, nothing to look at but dedicated to her job. He would hate to lose her.

"Come in, Marianne. What can I do for you?"

"Your mother was just here, Mr. Kendall. She opened a new checking account."

"But she already has a checking account with us."

"Yes, sir. This one's a business account."

He frowned. "My mother doesn't have any business per se. Are you sure?"

She leaned across the desk, offering him a couple of small signature cards. "Here are the authorized signatures. She said they would be in later to sign them."

The name on the first card was vaguely familiar. Roger Woodson was a contractor who, when the housing boom went bust a few years back, had turned to specializing in the restoration of expensive old houses, with expensive fees to match. He'd made quite a name for himself in Louisiana and was the man of choice for many such big-ticket projects.

Expensive old houses. Raymond tapped the cards on the desktop, houses like the old Kendall place down the road from his mother's house. Surely that was just coincidence. His mother couldn't be intending to waste the hundreds of thousands of dollars necessary to fix up that old place. Even she had better sense than that.

"How much did she deposit into this account?"

Marianne handed him a copy of the deposit slip. The sum was substantial, causing him to wonder briefly where it had come from. Doubtless from one of her numerous investments that she'd told him nothing about.

Then he remembered the second signature card and looked at it. The name leapt out at him, right there in black-and-white. William R. Beaumont. No wonder he hadn't taken the seventy-five hundred bucks Raymond had offered him last week. He'd known that in a few days he would have access to much, much more.

Son of a bitch!

"How long ago did my mother leave?"

"Just a few minutes. I came up as soon as she was out of the bank."

"Thank you, Marianne." He got up from his desk and shrugged into his jacket.

"Is there a problem? Should I—"

A hell of a problem, he thought privately, and just what he needed to start his week out right. Damn it all. "If Roger Woodson and Billy Ray come in while I'm out, go ahead and have them sign the cards. Oh, and tell Virginia that I've gone out." He hurried out of the office, down the stairs, and out the double glass doors, nearly bowling his mother over where she stood waiting for him.

Waiting for him. She had known Marianne would go straight to him, and, damn it, she had known *he* would come straight to *her*. And here she was, just as smug and superior and so damned sure she was right as always.

"Hello, son. I've been expecting you."

He ignored her greeting. "What the hell's going on, Mama?"

Anger flashed in her eyes, reminding him that she might be over seventy but she hadn't lost any of her sharpness, any of her competence, her control, or her temper. "Don't use that language around me, Raymond. It shows a lack of class."

Reining in his own temper, he breathed deeply and counted to ten before calmly asking, "What's going on, Mother?"

" 'Mother.' I guess I'm in trouble, aren't I?" Moving back out of the morning sun, she seated herself on the bench in the alcove there. "I knew that White girl would go running to you. Do you pay her extra for being a tattletale?"

"Marianne was just doing her job. Do you want to explain to me what you're doing? Why you've apparently hired Roger Woodson? Why you've given Billy Ray Beaumont access to more than $75,000 of Kendall money?"

"Certainly. I've hired Mr. Woodson to return the Kendall mansion to its original state, the way it was before your fool of a great-grandfather set fire to it. Work began this morning. As for Will, he's overseeing the project. He'll be working closely with Mr. Woodson. Naturally, he needs to be able to pay bills."

"And does he need to be able to sneak off with your money?"

She gave him a withering look. "Will's not leaving Harmony. He's got ties here just as you do. Maybe even stronger than yours."

Raymond scoffed at that. "Kendalls have always been important to Harmony. Without our family, the town would have died years ago. What have the Beaumonts ever done? What have they ever amounted to?"

"I've known three generations of Beaumonts. They've been good people, hard workers with a respect for the land, for this place and its history that you've always been missing. Will Beaumont belongs here, Raymond, as much as you do.

Maybe more." She sat primly on the bench, back erect, hands folded over her purse, ankles crossed. "Is that all? Because I do want to get out to the house and see how the first day of work is going."

"Do you have any idea what you're getting into? Do you know how much it's going to cost to save that old place? And for what? You're not going to live there. *I'm* certainly not going to live there. Are you going to open it up to the public and have tourists come tramping all over our property?"

"*My* property," she corrected him. "Until I die, it's mine. And, yes, I know exactly what I'm getting into. I know this is a big project with a big price tag. Mr. Woodson gave me quite a detailed list of expenses and cost." Then, with a thoughtful sigh, she went on. "I haven't decided yet what I'm going to do with it. Frankly, though, Raymond, I don't see that it's any of your concern."

He simply stared at her for a moment, his mouth agape. Then, silently muttering all the curses he couldn't say aloud, he drew in a deep breath. "None of my concern? You're spending Kendall money to save an old house that should have been torn down a hundred years ago, and you say it's none of my concern?"

Rose got to her feet. "It's my money, my house, and my business. Now . . . is there anything other than Will and the house that you want to talk to me about?"

"He's going to make a fool of you again, Mama. You trusted him last time, and look what he did. Now you're making it even easier for him. He's going to clean you out and walk away laughing."

She gave him a stony hard look. "I said anything *other* than Will."

At his sides, Raymond's hands clenched into fists. He wasn't reaching her. She was so damn stubborn and so damn blind where Billy Ray was concerned. He needed time to calm down, to think this over and look for other ways to proceed. Other ways to stop work—and Billy Ray—without going through Rose.

His sigh sounded of defeat. "This isn't over, Mama," he warned.

She adjusted the hat she wore, then gave him a sad look. "Your fussing will never be over, Raymond. Not until I'm dead and buried in my grave. Give my best to Frannie."

Swearing under his breath, he watched her leave, driving away in that big old car of hers. When she was gone from sight, he started to turn and go inside. On second thought, though, he crossed the street to John Stuart's office.

The lawyer was no help. There was nothing Raymond could do to stop her. Rose was of sound mind, and she had more money than one person could ever need. If she chose to spend hundreds of thousands of dollars on a house that had sat empty for nearly a hundred years, that was her prerogative. And when Raymond asked about having her declared incompetent, Stuart laughed at the suggestion. *Laughed.* "Raymond, I've known your mama all my life," he said, "and I have never met anyone who was *less* incompetent. Her mind's sharper at seventy-one than most folks' are at thirty-one."

"What about Billy Ray?"

"What about him?"

"Can't we say he's exerting undue influence? Can't we find some way to get him out of her life? He's a damn crook, for God's sake. Can't we do something?"

The lawyer just shook his head. "He's here at your mother's invitation. He hasn't done anything wrong—"

"That we've found out about," Raymond interjected.

"He's not taking anything from her. She hasn't given him any great sums of money. All she's done is offer him a place to live for a while, and he's accepted. There's no crime in that." Stuart shrugged. "What are you concerned about, Raymond? Even after restoring that old monstrosity, your mother will still have plenty of money to pass on to you when she dies."

Raymond ignored that last part. "Billy Ray must be behind this. Somehow he talked her into doing this and putting him in charge so he could get to her money. Hell, she'd never shown even the slightest interest in that old house until he came back."

"It doesn't matter, Raymond," Stuart said firmly. "Even if this restoration was his idea, your mother agreed to it.

She's willingly putting up the money for it. She chose of her own free will to put him in charge of it. She hasn't been coerced.''

"How do you know?" Raymond asked, then immediately gave a disgusted shake of his head. Of course she hadn't been coerced. There wasn't a man alive who could force Rose to do something she didn't want to. She'd made up her mind about this project, and no one could talk her out of it.

Unless it turned out to be more of an investment than she'd expected. Unless there were problems she hadn't foreseen. Unless Billy Ray turned out to be more trouble than she could forgive.

He said his good-byes to the lawyer, then returned to the bank. It was funny, he thought, how often the mention of wrongdoing came into a conversation about Billy Ray. Everyone just expected the worst of him. Everyone—except Rose—believed he was capable of just about anything.

So maybe that was the way to go. If Raymond couldn't get his mother to kick Billy Ray out of her home and if the bastard wouldn't leave voluntarily, then maybe the courts could get rid of him. A trumped-up charge, an easy conviction, a few years up in Angola . . . God, that sounded sweet. Only a trumped-up charge of what?

He closed his office door behind him, then sat down behind his desk. Breaking and entering and burglary seemed to be Billy Ray's crimes of choice, but they didn't apply to this situation. Rose had put his name on the damn bank account, and he, more than anyone else, would have access to the mansion while work was proceeding.

But a construction site supplied plenty of opportunities for theft, from replacing quality materials with shoddy ones and pocketing the price difference to making deals with suppliers to falsify invoices and split the profits to outright stealing of supplies and equipment. Would anyone in town be suprised if Billy Ray were accused of stealing money from Rose's business account? If he bought inferior materials to hide the thefts? If he sabotaged the work on the house to prolong the job and his free access to Rose's money? Would anyone doubt his guilt if his careless and questionable business practices caused injury to one of the crew?

No one would. No one would be willing to give him the benefit of the doubt. No one would believe his innocence. No one, Raymond thought with sublime satisfaction, would protest sending him to Angola for a long, brutal time. Not even Rose.

Celine sat at her desk, catalogues spread out in front of her. She was supposed to be choosing new books for the library and searching for the absolute best deal she could get on them, thanks to the shrinking acquisitions budget, but it was hard to concentrate. She felt like a schoolgirl, day-dreaming through the middle of a warm Friday about the plans she had for the weekend.

Except that she had no plans for the weekend. She would probably spend it the way she'd spent this last week—mop-ing, hot, and cranky. Suffering from the weather and her own restlessness, driven to distraction by the persistent demands of her body that she couldn't fulfill, wondering why her luck with men was so consistently rotten.

She put down her pen and gathered her hair in both hands, lifting it off her neck. The cooling system was working hard today, but it couldn't combat the mugginess that came from hundred-degree temperatures and near-one-hundred-percent humidity. She didn't think the unit had shut off even once since she'd come in this morning, and here it was lunchtime. Every day she hoped for a cooling breeze or rain, and every afternoon the skies grew dark, thunder rumbled, and lightning split the air. The promise of rain was so strong that she could smell it, but soon the clouds moved on and the sun came out again, stronger and hotter, it seemed, than ever. False promises. Cruel taunts. Frustrating disappointments.

Those words could describe Will as easily as the weather. He had delivered on his promises of passion and pleasure, only later to deny her even a moment of his attention. He had taunted her with how good making love could be and then had told her that she couldn't experience it again. He had stirred a need in her that was as relentless as the summer heat but had left her with no means of satisfying it.

He was working on the Kendall mansion now. He left every morning while she was still dressing, and he came home every evening after she'd had her supper. In spite of such long hours, he'd found the energy to go out two of the last four nights. She had lain in bed wondering where he was going, whom he was seeing, what they were doing. She wondered why he couldn't spend a little of his time with her. She wondered why he had to have so damned much pride and so little self-esteem—and enough principle to care.

She sighed, and it sounded forlorn in the big, empty room. There hadn't been more than a half dozen visitors to the library this morning. Even the kids who usually sought out its cooler temperatures were staying away. Too bad she couldn't turn out the lights, lock the locks, and hang a sign on the door: closed due to heat. *And restlessness*.

One of the double doors opened, sucking out a breath of the cool air, and Millie Andrews came in. She was Celine's only help in the summer, working weekday lunches and half days on Saturday. Awkwardly tall and sort of pretty, but painfully shy and burdened with what she considered an old-lady name, she was comfortable with the books and the mundane tasks of filing, cataloguing, and reshelving. Attending to patrons was harder for her—especially when that patron happened to be Jared Robinson, Celine had noticed—but she was making an effort. She was trying.

And right behind Millie came Miss Rose. She was dressed as she always was for trips into town: a Sunday dress, sensible shoes, an inconspicuous handbag, and a broad-brimmed straw hat tastefully decorated with satin ribbon and tiny rosettes. It was important for a lady to shield her skin from the sun, she preached, especially when Celine was working in the yard in shorts and a T-shirt.

Celine greeted Millie, then met Miss Rose at the counter. "Come and have lunch with me," the old lady invited.

"The special at the restaurant today is chicken and dumplings, and Mary Jane's dumplings are always tough," she politely declined.

"I'm not going to the restaurant," Miss Rose said, "and I promise you, young lady, *this* meal will be well worth your time."

Thoughts of her favorite restaurants—across Sunshine Bridge, up in Baton Rouge, down in New Orleans—filled

Celine's mind and made her stomach rumble impolitely. "And where are we going to find this meal well worth my time?"

Miss Rose came around the counter and took her by the arm. "Millie, Miss Celine is going to lunch now," she called out. They were halfway to the door before she answered Celine's question. "At the Kendall house. We're celebrating the completion of the first week's work. I'm having lunch catered in from Baton Rouge."

Celine started dragging her heels at the mention of the Kendall house. That meant the crew would be there, which meant Will would be there. She hadn't seen him in nearly a week now. Of course, she had caught tantalizing glimpses of him coming and going, but she hadn't spoken to him. He hadn't come out of the guesthouse when she was sitting on her porch. He hadn't asked her to join him on his nightly visits to wherever. He certainly hadn't asked her to take any more walks with him.

"That sounds nice," she said, searching for a believable excuse even as she spoke. "But I've got some things to take care of in town and . . ."

"Nonsense. You can run your errands tomorrow. Right now you can come and have the best meal to be found in DeVilliers Parish today. Come along now. The tables will be set up by the time we get there, and the men will be hungry."

Trying to stop Miss Rose was like trying to turn the tides, Celine thought with a scowl as the old lady led her toward her car. She let go once they were there, as if she knew Celine would get in the car like a good little girl, as she was supposed to, instead of bolting and running, the way she wanted to.

Of course, she was right. Celine did obediently climb into the car, and she politely took part in Miss Rose's conversation until they reached the Kendall mansion.

It seemed that the quiet of the ghostly place had been shattered forever. What had, a hundred years ago, been a beautifully manicured lawn was now a parking lot for trucks and an occasional van, including the caterer's. There were stacks of lumber, bins of tools, ladders and scaffolding, plenty of people and more noise—saws, hammers, voices, and occasional curses—until it was pointed out that there were ladies present.

Celine tried not to look for Will as she followed Miss Rose and Roger Woodson across the grounds to the house. He detailed the work done so far: the doors and broken windows replaced to secure the interior of the house against any further damage in the form of rain, rodents, or vandals; the burned portions of the upstairs balcony and wall ripped out and rebuilt; the damaged columns shored up for repair.

She trailed behind, hearing their voices but letting the words fade without registering. She and Will had discussed Miss Rose's possible motives for sinking so much money into this place, but she had never asked the old lady herself why she was doing it. Maybe because she respected history and the people whose lives had begun and ended in this place. Or maybe she wanted to leave her mark on this world. She couldn't live forever—although she gave every indication of trying—but this house could.

What kind of mark would Celine leave behind? The way her luck was running, her epitaph would be simple: Reliable, dependable, and an efficient librarian. At this rate there would be no loving husband, no grieving children, no accomplishments of any significance. What a depressing thought that the labels she'd hated all her life would stay with her throughout eternity.

The tour led them inside through newly installed, unpainted doors. The original stain would be matched through chemical analysis, Mr. Woodson explained, and the new doors and window frames would be painted to match. Paint and wall-covering samples from the rooms would also be matched as closely as possible, molding and plaster medallions would be duplicated, and the stenciling that decorated practically every room would be copied exactly.

This kind of work required not so much the talents of a builder but the skill of an artist and the patience of a surgeon, Celine thought. Once the major jobs—the actual repairing and replacing—were done, the rest would be painstaking detail work. How much patience did Will have for that sort of work?

Mr. Woodson and Miss Rose were starting up the stairs when the protesting creak of wood being pried away caught Celine's attention. Instead of tagging along upstairs, she wandered into what had probably been the gentlemen's parlor. It had been done in colors appropriate for a man's room: dark paneling on three walls, watered silk in hunter green on the fourth, the fireplace black marble with veins of dark green. The rug in here would have been richly detailed in maroons, blacks, navies, and browns, and the furniture would have been heavy wooden pieces upholstered in intricately worked petit point. All in all, the effect would have been overwhelming.

As it was, stripped of everything but its warped and decaying paneling and its stained, ruined wall covering, it still had a pretty overwhelming effect on Celine, because the man working a piece of warped paneling from the wall was Will.

She stopped just inside the doorway and watched him work. He was wearing jeans and sneakers, and his T-shirt hung from an elaborate hook beside one window that had been meant to hold back draperies that had long since been removed. He was careful with the board, prying it loose from the opposite side, working it free so that the section came off without further damage. When he turned to set it down, he saw her and became still.

For a moment she just watched him. She wanted to go over and touch him, but common sense told her he wouldn't welcome that. She wanted to pretend that nothing had changed between them.

She moved farther into the room, running her fingers along the paneling, feeling each seam. "Pretty wood," she remarked. "Can any of it be saved?"

He was silent for so long that she thought he wasn't going to answer. Then, laying the panel he held on the tile hearth, he replied brusquely, "No, it can't."

She reached the area where he had been working, where the skeleton of the outer wall now showed. As she circled the room, he moved, too, in a smaller, less defined circle, keeping always away from her. Celine disguised her hurt with a glittery smile. "So what will you do in here?"

"There's a guy down in New Orleans who salvages materials from old buildings that are being torn down. He'll try to find something similar for us.'' He picked up his shirt, dried the sweat from his face, then tugged it over his head. ''What are you doing here?'' he asked as he smoothed the hem down.

''Miss Rose invited me to lunch. I tried to say no, but you know how she is.''

He responded to that with a slight nod. ''What do you think of the house?'' He sounded wary, unwilling to engage her in conversation, but unable to stop himself.

''It's going to be much more of a job than I realized. It'll take a long time, won't it?''

''A while.''

She wanted to ask how long that was. A few months, a year, maybe longer? Would he be here to see it through? But maybe it was better not to know.

Completing her circuit of the room, she stopped at the door once more. Outside she heard a voice call, ''The food's ready,'' and she smiled uneasily. ''I guess it's lunchtime.''

Will considered telling her that he wasn't hungry, then making himself scarce until she and Miss Rose were gone; but he'd been up since six this morning with nothing to eat but a doughnut, and the dishes the caterer had unloaded from his van smelled too good to pass up.

Slowly he crossed the room toward her. She looked so damned beautiful in her fussy, frilly summer dress with its fluttery little sleeves and a big lace-edged collar that ended in points right above her breasts. He wanted to make himself scarce, all right, and take her with him, to find a private corner somewhere and slide that skirt up just enough so he could get inside her and make love to her until they couldn't stand any more. God, he wanted her so badly that he hurt.

He told himself to keep walking, to go past her without slowing, without looking at her, without giving himself a chance to indulge in her nearness. But when he drew level with her right at the door, he stopped, and he turned to face her. He could faintly smell the fragrance of her perfume, mingling with the scents of old wood and decay, of mustiness and his own sweat. She smelled clean and soft and feminine, and she tasted, damn it, the same way. He wanted to kiss her, wanted to crawl between her thighs, inside her, so deep inside her. He wanted to feel her mouth on him, kissing him, sucking him, and he wanted to fill her over and over.

Last Saturday should have taken the edge off this need. He'd ended a long period of doing without, and he'd gotten off not once but twice. He had been more satisfied physically than at any other time in his life. But not emotionally.

God, when was the last time his emotions had entered into a sexual relationship? It had been years. A million women ago. Maybe never.

He stood close to her, so close that his erection was almost touching her, and he looked at her. She was looking back, her lips parted, her breathing unsteady, her green eyes soft with desire and shadowed with uncertainty. She wanted a kiss—he knew that instinctively—but he also knew that it wouldn't stop with that. It wouldn't stop until their clothes were off and his cock was inside her and he was lost again. And if he kept getting lost, someday he would never find his way back.

He raised his hand and almost touched her face. Almost, but not quite. He was dirty from a half day's labor, and two of his fingers, where one of the crew had pinched them in a door, were crusted with dried blood. But he almost touched her, and he did, with one fingertip, brush back a wisp of hair from her forehead.

"So there you are," Miss Rose said, her voice pitched louder than usual, giving them warning that their privacy was about to be invaded. "I thought we had lost you, Celine."

Will stepped back and turned away as the old lady and Roger came into the room. He was grateful for their interruption, he told himself, even if what he was feeling seemed a lot more like frustration than gratitude.

"It's going to be a grand place when it's finished, isn't it?" Miss Rose asked of no one in particular.

"What do you intend to do with it?" Roger asked.

"Oh, I don't know," she replied airily as she turned in a complete circle, taking in the damage to the room and the spot overhead where a chandelier used to hang in the center of a now badly flaking medallion. "Maybe open it up for tours or deed it to the state or maybe even put it up for sale."

"For sale?" Celine echoed even as Will thought the words.

"But, Miss Rose, this land has been in the Kendall family for *years*."

"Yes, and after me, there won't be a single member of the Kendall family who cares. Meredith is never coming back here to live, and Raymond would sooner see the place torn down. It deserves an owner who will care for it, an owner willing and able to keep it up." She smiled brightly at them, then said, "I believe they're holding the meal for us. Shall we go?"

She left first, accepting Roger's offer of an escort, her small thin hand resting on his muscled arm. After a slight hesitation, Celine followed them, and Will reluctantly brought up the rear.

The sight awaiting them outside was a spectacle. The caterer had set up tables in front on the only portion of the gallery that was shaded and free of clutter, and those tables, receiving curious looks from the crew, were covered with white linen cloths and napkins, with china plates and settings of silver, with small centerpieces of pink carnations. Leave it to Miss Rose, he thought with a grin, to do the meal up properly, whether her guests were the cream of Louisiana society or a sweaty, hardworking construction crew.

He washed up, then went to join the crew at the last table. Instead he was directed to the small table at the opposite end, where there were only four seats. Miss Rose and Roger occupied two of them. Celine sat in the third one.

He sat down across from her and concentrated on ignoring her, just as she ignored him. She kept her gaze down, ate little, and spoke only when spoken to. Her manner made her appear shy and demure and every inch a lady. He couldn't help comparing that image to one from last Saturday—naked, her skin slick with sweat, her hair wild and unkempt, her breasts swaying sensuously as she rocked back and forth astride his hips.

Suddenly realizing that Miss Rose had spoken his name, he shifted his attention and a blank gaze to her. "Did you say something?"

"Your mind must be wandering. I asked why you hadn't gone to the bank yet to sign the signature card for the business account."

Perversely, now that Celine's attention was on him, he could push her to the back of his mind. "I haven't had time," he lied. "What's the rush? Until I get around to it, Roger can sign any checks that have to be written."

"The bank needs your signature on file," she replied calmly, with just a hint of steel in her voice.

He could be just as stubborn. Whether his signature was on file didn't matter, because he wasn't going to sign any checks. He had decided that Monday morning when she'd told him and Roger to complete the paperwork for the account. In spite of this gesture, he knew she still didn't have much faith in him—not if she could believe he was guilty of robbing those old ladies in Alabama. Knowing that, there was no way in hell he was going to accept responsibility for spending one penny of her money.

"I'll take care of it."

"When?" she asked.

"Next time I'm in town."

"And when will that be?"

"I don't know. Maybe Monday."

"How about this afternoon?" she countered. "You can ride into town with me when I return Celine to the library, take care of business, then drop me off at home before you come back here."

Great. Drawing out this time with Celine. That was just what he needed to make a miserable afternoon unbearable.

He gave in ungraciously, then excused himself from the table on the pretext of work and went around back. He was sitting on the steps there, peeling bark from a small twig, when someone came looking for him. Of course it was Celine, he thought with a scowl when she sat down at the opposite end of the step. Go find Will and tell him we're ready to go, Miss Rose had most probably said, and like a good obedient child, Celine had complied.

She just sat there for a moment, her arms crossed, her hands clasped tightly to her elbows. She looked cold; he even thought he saw her shiver when he glanced at her. She was cold, and he was so damned hot he was ready to burst into flames.

"Will, I'm sorry," she said at last. "But I can't just disappear off the face of the earth."

He stood up and gave her a long, hard look. "*I* can." He'd done it before. He would do it again.

She seemed distressed as she got up, too, and followed him down the steps and toward the corner of the house. "Don't say that. You can't leave Harmony. You gave Miss Rose your word."

"Billy Ray Beaumont's word isn't worth shit, darlin'," he shot back over his shoulder. "Don't you know that by now?"

"Just ignore me," she suggested. "Pretend I'm not here."

He spun around so quickly that she barely managed to stop without running into him, and he caught her hand, pressing it hard against his groin, against his hardening sex. "Kind of hard to ignore, isn't it?"

She flexed her fingers over him, such a tender touch to cause such exquisite pain, and she hesitantly smiled. "Want to slip off into the woods? I know a place . . ."

He scowled down at her so long that her smile faded, her fingers withdrew, and confusion and hurt appeared in her eyes. Slowly he took a step toward her, and she backed up. He advanced until a faded white column was behind her back, until the dusty red bricks of the gallery were pressing against her legs. Resting his hands on either side of her head, he moved closer, so close that he could feel the heat where her hips cradled his, that he could feel the soft warm puffs of her breath against his chin. "You're not too smart, little girl, are you?" he asked, his voice tauntingly low. "You keep playing with fire, you're going to get burned."

She didn't back down. "Maybe I like living dangerously."

"You don't know shit about danger, honey."

"I know you," she retorted. "You seem to think that you're dangerous."

"I don't think. I *know*."

"I think you're all talk. I think your reputation as the big bad boy is all bluff and no substance. I think—"

Interrupting, he covered her mouth with his, biting her lower lip, pushing his tongue halfway down her throat. She made a startled, choked sound that quickly turned to a soft moan, vibrating through her and into him. He felt it all the way through, and it made him throb.

He shouldn't have kissed her, he acknowledged when he pulled his mouth from hers. It made him hard, made him restless and reckless and horny as hell. It made him wonder if maybe it would be all right to have her just one more time. It made his body turn to stone and his brain to mush.

Celine touched her lips, and he swallowed hard and looked away. She cleared her throat, gave a little cough, then said in a funny little voice, "Tonight is Miss Rose's evening with Sophy Michaud."

He wondered what she was leading up to. Something as simple as dinner or a whole lot more? It didn't matter. He wasn't fool enough to spend any more time alone with her.

"If you would like to come over for dinner . . ."

"I have a date," he said flatly, and she swallowed hard and turned away. He watched her walk as far as the corner, where she paused.

"Miss Rose is ready to go. Are you coming?"

"Tell her I'll borrow one of Roger's trucks and go in later."

Without looking at him, she nodded and walked away. She looked insubstantial, pale, wounded.

He felt like a bastard.

It was for her own good, he told himself as he returned to the gentlemen's parlor, and for his own, too. He knew better than to be wanting things he couldn't have. He knew all too well to stick to his own kind, to people like Eva over at the bar, people with experience, who knew that life was hard, people who knew what it was like to be kicked down as low as a person could go and to have no hope of ever getting back up again.

He wasn't the first man to get an itch for a woman like Celine, and it wasn't going to kill him—although it sometimes felt like it. It wasn't going to kill her, either. She was just curious, that was all, like the women in town. Soon she would meet some decent, respectable guy and marry him and forget all about last Saturday. And if wanting her wouldn't kill him, that, he thought bleakly, that just might.

"A beautiful woman can be hell on a man's nerves."

Roger Woodson walked into the parlor as if there was nothing unusual in finding Will sitting on the floor, arms on his knees, his head hung low. Will slowly raised his head and looked at the older man. "Five minutes with her, and I don't have any nerves left," he admitted drily.

"She didn't seem any too steady herself. So what's the problem?"

"The last thirty-four years, for starters." How old had he been when things had started going wrong? His father had died when he was ten. He'd gotten suspended from school for the first time when he was twelve. He'd had his first taste of sex—heavy kissing and a hand job from a girl three years older—when he was thirteen. And from the time Miss Rose had invited him into her life, he'd been told he didn't belong there, that he wasn't good enough to be there.

If he had known that one day he was going to fall so hard for a prim and proper librarian, for the closest thing to a saint this town had, would it have changed the way he'd lived?

Damn straight. He would have allowed Miss Rose more success in her efforts to mold him into something respectable. He would have believed her old sayings that a person's good reputation was something to be guarded, that a man's name was his honor. He would have kept his pants zipped and his mouth shut, would have settled down and quit trying so successfully to antagonize the holier-than-thou folks in town. He would have grown up to be someone else. But he hadn't known, and he hadn't changed, and now it was too late to ever become what Celine needed.

"I never should have come back here," he muttered. "I hate this town, and I hate the people in it."

"You can always leave again." Roger rubbed his hand over one section of paneling. "Look at the grain of this wood. It's a shame to have to throw it all away. Whoever let the house get in this condition should be strung up from that live oak out front."

After a moment, he returned to the original conversation. Will had the feeling that his attention had never left it. "People underrate the value of flight as a method of problem solving. Running away isn't always cowardly. Sometimes it's best for everyone involved."

Maybe, Will thought. If you could avoid thinking of yourself as a coward. If other people didn't think of you that way, too. If you could somehow put together a new life for yourself to go with your new location. If you could accomplish something, *anything*, other than arousing suspicion and getting arrested.

"You ever regret leaving the way you did?"

Will wondered briefly how Roger knew he'd left and why he expected regret. Miss Rose must have told him, or maybe he'd heard rumors. He and most of his crew were staying at the motel out near the interstate, but they ate their meals and did their shopping in town. What else had he learned?

He got to his feet and picked up the crowbar he'd been using before lunch. "I've regretted just about everything I ever did—and everything I didn't do, too."

"And when you leave here, are you going to regret Celine, too?" Roger asked quietly.

Will gave him a sharp look before wedging the bar behind the next piece of paneling. No one but Miss Rose had ever gotten away with asking him such personal questions. No one but Miss Rose had ever been interested, and he had never liked anyone enough to make them feel it was all right to pry.

But he liked Roger. Maybe it was because the man was fair in his business dealings. He seemed to judge a man on himself and not things like rumors and reputations. He worked as hard as his crew; he knew his business and took pride in his work.

Maybe it was because he reminded Will in some way of his father. Claude Beaumont had been quiet, too, and fair and hardworking and proud. He had been eternally optimistic, believing that life was good and should be celebrated every day. The only thing he could have asked for was a better relationship between Will and Paulette. He had loved them both so much and had never understood why they hadn't been able to love each other. They'd been an unnatural mother and son, but Claude had accepted that and made the best of it. Will had learned part of that lesson from his father. He had learned how to accept, but he had never learned how to make the best of what he had.

"I already regret Celine," he replied at last.

"You could stay."

He grinned wryly. "Yeah, right. That would probably cause the honorable folks in town to form a lynch mob and hang *me* from that live oak out front." He got a start on the board and began working it out. "I don't stay where I'm not wanted."

"Have you ever found someplace where you were wanted?"

"Nope. Never have." But that was a lie. Miss Rose and Celine wanted him to stay. They made him feel welcome. But he couldn't spend the rest of his life in that isolated little world. He couldn't pretend that Harmony and Raymond and Celine's family and friends didn't exist. He couldn't ignore the trouble he was causing them simply by being in their lives.

He hadn't been kidding Celine last weekend about the way people would talk about her if they found out what she'd done with him. A woman in her position, in frequent contact with the town kids, and with her saintly reputation to live up to, shacked up with Billy Ray Beaumont? The whole town would be scandalized. Celine was their darling, their angel. Everyone, with the exception of her sister, adored her, from small children and impressionable teenagers to parents who wished that their own daughters were so polite, so well mannered, so responsible and mature, to elderly folks like Miss Rose.

They might forgive her poor judgment in getting involved with him—although they would never forget it. And they would never forgive *him* anything. Instead of being the wild kid who abandoned the frightened little mother-to-be of his child, he would become the devil himself who had led dear Celine, sweet Saint Celine, right into the sinful fires of hell.

He couldn't do that to her. He couldn't subject her to the gossip, the nasty rumors, the whispers behind her back, the pointing fingers, that followed him wherever he went. Not even if she thought the sinful fires of hell were a fine place to spend this wickedly hot summer, not even if she truly believed that was what she wanted, not even if he *knew* it was what he wanted.

* * *

Vickie stretched out in one of Celine's porch chairs, fanning herself with a painted paper fan that folded into its own case, and watched the guesthouse out back. Celine let her look a while before finally volunteering, "If you're hoping to catch a glimpse of him, you might as well forget it. He isn't home."

Her sister gave her a sharp look. "Where is he?"

"I don't know. I imagine that he's out with a woman," she said sarcastically.

"That's impossible. If he was seeing anyone around here, we would all know." She offered a preening smile. "If he was seeing someone around here, it would be *me*."

Celine gritted her teeth and sighed. If her parents had been so enamored of names beginning with V—Vickie's full name was Victoria Viola, after some distant relative—they should have chosen something more appropriate. Vanity had a nice, suitable ring to it. "Better watch it, sister," she remarked, hearing the catty note that slipped into her voice and making no effort to control it. "Richard thinks you're having an affair."

"Pretty soon now he'll be right." She laughed throatily. "He shouldn't complain. I get so excited thinking about Billy Ray that I just can't wait. Richard's had the best sex of his life since Billy Ray came back to town. So, seriously, Celine, where is he?"

"Seriously, probably with a woman. He had a date last night. I imagine he's got one again tonight." She had come home from work last night in time to see him leave with Miss Rose. He'd taken her over to the Michaud house for her evening out, and then he'd gone on to . . . Well, she didn't know where. Or with whom. But she would bet she knew what they'd done. She hated him for it, hated this unknown woman, too.

She had seen him coming home, too, well after midnight. She had been standing at her bedroom window, gazing out at the guesthouse, when he'd come sauntering across the grass. He'd looked entirely too relaxed, damn him. Entirely too satisfied.

And now he was gone again. Out doing unspeakable things with unsuitable women. And she was stuck here waiting for him with her sister.

Curiously she studied Vickie's shadowy figure across from her. It was hard sometimes to believe they were sisters. They had nothing in common. Vickie took after their mother's side of the family while Celine resembled the Hunters. Their personalities, their values, and apparently even their morals, were totally different. Vickie had no interest in books or culture or learning. She had quit her job the day Richard proposed and had sworn she would never go back to work. She couldn't imagine a better place to live than Harmony, couldn't imagine a better way to spend the day than getting her hair and nails done and buying a new outfit, then having lunch at the country club to show it all off. Her biggest worries were lines around her eyes, putting on a few pounds, or perfectly matching the coppery red shade of her hair each time it was colored.

They had absolutely nothing to talk about except family: their parents, Richard, and her kids. There was rarely much worth discussing about their parents, Richard wasn't a favorite topic of conversation, and while Celine loved her nephews and niece, they were just like their mother: selfish, silly, and whiny, bearable only in small doses.

And then there was Will.

What would Vickie say if Celine told her about last weekend? If she offered the intimate details of their passionate lovemaking in the woods? If she described for her just exactly how impressive Will was? What would she say if Celine confronted her with the knowledge that Vickie had no first-hand knowledge, as she had deliberately—and maliciously—implied, of Will as a lover?

Vickie wouldn't back down. No, sir, when she told a lie, she stuck by it, no matter what proof was offered against her, no matter how reliable the evidence. Celine could remember battles royal years ago between Vickie and their parents when she was caught red-handed, when the evidence was indisputable—chocolate frosting from the cake for company smeared around her mouth, the ring Annalise was missing on her finger, the broken china in her hands and no one else around. Not once in Celine's memory had she ever admitted her guilt. Not once had she offered an apology.

No, if Celine confronted her, she would insist that Will had lied—after all, he had lied about Melanie, hadn't he? And if Celine confessed her own liaison with him, Vickie would refuse to believe it. She would accuse Celine of lying to hurt her, of wanting Will only because she did, of trying to dissuade her from having an affair with him—an affair that was, in her simple way of thinking, inevitable. Somehow she would turn around Celine's afternoon with Will until it all revolved around *her*.

No wonder they had no real conversations, Celine thought with a cynical smile. Vickie was so predictable that conversation wasn't necessary. Celine already knew her responses to everything.

"Are you planning to stay here until he gets home?" she asked.

Vickie didn't hear the irony in her voice. She somehow missed the derision. "What time will that be?"

"I don't know. I don't usually wait up for him."

Speaking of lies, she was getting pretty good with her own. In the last few weeks, she had lied more than she had in the preceding five years. White lies didn't count. White lies were polite, tactful, a harmless evasion to save someone unnecessary pain or embarrassment. But lately she'd told serious lies. She had lied about Will. She had lied *to* him. She had lied to her mother, her sister, Raymond, and even Miss Rose. She kind of enjoyed lying. She liked knowing what she knew and not having to tell anyone else, deciding who got to share her knowledge. She liked not feeling obligated to answer everyone's nosy questions.

She hadn't lied to herself, though. She was being brutally honest there. Before this hot summer ended, she was most likely going to find herself hopelessly in love with Will Beaumont, and he was going to break her heart. She was no different, no more important, no more special to him than any of the countless women in his past; and he was going to walk away from her the same way he'd walked away from them, without a second thought, without a backward glance, without even a fond memory.

"If you want to get to bed, go ahead," Vickie invited. "I don't need your company out here."

Of course not, Celine thought bitterly. She didn't want any unnecessary distractions to draw Will's attention away from *her*.

"Or, better yet, I can go over to the guesthouse to wait."

She was rising from her chair when Celine stopped her. "You aren't going to invite yourself into a man's home when he's not there to stop you."

Vickie's little laugh reminded her of three-year-old Amy's silly giggle. "Don't be ridiculous, Celine. I assure you, Billy Ray would *not* be displeased to come home and find me waiting for him."

Waiting naked in bed, if Celine knew her sister. Just the thought made her want to shake Vickie. "I assure you, if he brings a friend home with him tonight and finds you waiting there for him, he's going to be a hell of a lot more than displeased."

Vickie sank down again. "Oh, he wouldn't bring some tramp here, not with that old woman just across the yard." Then she caught her breath. "But he *did* bring that Melanie Robinson here. That's where they did it. That's where he got her pregnant—right back there in that guesthouse."

Celine wearily rolled her head to one side, then the other. "Go home, Vickie," she said flatly. "Go home to your husband and kids."

Go home where you're wanted.

Sunday morning was the most pleasantly cool day Will had experienced in a long while. When he settled in the hammock around ten o'clock, after the ladies had left for church, the thermometer tacked to the side of Miss Rose's storage shed wasn't a bit over eighty-five, and the breeze blowing in from the west seemed to lower that by a few degrees or so. It was a nice day for doing a lot of nothing while Miss Rose and Celine attended church and visited with their families.

He was, even after a sound night's sleep, close to dozing off when he realized someone had approached him. It wasn't a sound that had alerted him—whoever it was had been quiet—but just a feeling that he was no longer alone, that he was being watched. After sixteen years of being a drifter, of always being the new man in town, he knew all too well what it felt like to be watched.

It was Celine he saw when he warily opened his eyes, leaning against the tree trunk, wearing a loose, sleeveless dress that made her look thin and waifish and not at all ready for Harmony's First Baptist Church. Frowning, he said, "I thought you'd left for church."

"That was Miss Rose. I decided not to go."

"No sins to repent today, huh?"

"Plenty of them. I just don't feel too penitent." She moved away from the tree and dragged an old wicker chaise from behind the shed to a shady spot nearby.

Will gazed up at the leafy canopy overhead and wondered exactly how strong he was, how long he could lie here and talk to her as if nothing more intimate had ever happened between them. As if he wasn't indecently familiar with the body she was hiding underneath that tent of a dress. As if he wasn't needy enough to reacquaint himself with it. "You're the resident saint of Harmony, Louisiana. What could you possibly have done to feel penitent for?"

She crossed her legs at the ankle, and her skirt where it buttoned down the front fell open almost to her knees. "They say lust is a sin. And evil thoughts. Jealousy. And greed."

He shifted uncomfortably. He knew the lust was directed toward him—she'd made no secret of that—and the rest probably was, too. She had probably damned him a hundred times, even though she still wanted him, God, the way he wanted her.

"You owe me a thank-you," she announced.

He tilted his head just enough to see a blur of her. "For what?"

"Vickie was here last night. She wanted to wait at the guesthouse for you to get back, but I sent her home."

It was a good thing she had. He'd come home frustrated enough that he might have figured one Hunter girl was a

resonable substitute for the other. He might have given Vickie
everything she wanted and more *if* they'd done it in the dark.
If she'd kept her mouth shut. If he'd closed his eyes and
pretended.

"Your sister has no morals."

"No," Celine somberly agreed. "She doesn't."

He twisted around in the hammock, settling at the opposite
end so he could see her more clearly. "Who was this man
she took, this man you wanted to marry?"

"His name was Richard," she answered very matter-of-
factly. "Richard Jourdan."

Richard Jourdan. He'd seen or heard that name before,
sometime recently. . . . Then he remembered. The insurance
agent who was underwriting the coverage on the mansion
while it was being restored was named Richard Jourdan. His
office was two doors down from the bank. "So you still see
him around."

"Every Sunday."

"At church?"

"There, and at my parents' house." She smiled coolly.
"I guess we didn't say enough for you to figure that part out
when you were eavesdropping, did we? I found out about
Vickie's affair with Richard when he told me that he was
marrying her instead of me because she was pregnant."

Her manner was so casual, so accepting, that she might
have been discussing anything from the weather to business
at the library. Was that how she really felt? Will wondered.
Or was she merely covering her hurt?

"What did your parents say when they found out?"

Tilting her head back, she calmly recited, " 'It's really for
the best. You're the smart one, Celine. You can take care of
yourself. You don't need Richard the way Vickie does.' "

Growing up, he'd heard stories about the Hunters, about
how weird they were, how forgetful and eccentric and unrelia-
ble; but he hadn't heard that they were stupid. He hadn't
imagined they could callously brush off their younger daughter's broken heart. He hadn't realized they were as much
complete fools as their other daughter was.

"Even though Vickie was more than three months pregnant
when they got married, they had a big wedding—church

ceremony, white gown, lots of attendants. They all thought I was selfish because I wouldn't be Vickie's maid of honor. They wanted me to stand beside her and be happy while she married *my* fiancé.''

He offered her a grin he didn't feel. ''Are you sure they didn't find you under a cabbage leaf somewhere? You don't seem to fit in with the rest of the family.''

She sighed softly. ''No. Most times I never seem to fit in anywhere.'' Then she smiled. ''Except here with Miss Rose.''

They fell silent for a time, then Celine spoke again, the softness of her voice emphasizing its Southernness. ''Will? Will you tell me something? Truthfully?''

With one foot on the ground, he set the hammock in motion and grimaced at the sky rocking overhead. The last time she asked him for the truth about something, they had wound up naked on the forest floor. This hammock was an inviting place to repeat the experience. ''Tell me what it is you want to know, and I'll tell you whether I'll be truthful about it.''

She hesitated, then leaned forward. ''The robberies. I want to know about them.''

He became so still so quickly that he could hear his own heart thudding in his ears. *The robberies.* Who had told her? It had to be Raymond—unless it was common gossip now, which would also be thanks to him. The son of a bitch couldn't quit. He couldn't leave Will one shred of dignity. Telling Miss Rose hadn't done enough damage to suit the bastard, and so he'd told Celine. Damn him to hell!

''The newspaper said—''

''What newspaper?'' he interrupted sharply.

''At the library. On microfilm.''

Her brief answers didn't clarify anything for him, except that she was talking about old papers. There weren't any old robberies, at least none that would be of interest to the folks here in Harmony. In his years away, he had never stolen anything he hadn't needed—like food—and he had rarely taken enough for his unfortunate victim to bother reporting it to the authorities, much less to a newspaper.

Forcing himself to relax, he said, ''You'll have to be more specific than that, Celie. I don't read old newspapers, so I have no idea what you're talking about.''

"I'm talking about the night you left Harmony. About the money and the jewelry."

Feeling that she was somehow testing him, he shook his head blankly.

"All right, then let's talk about your agreement with Raymond."

He grinned. "That again? I told you—"

"How much money did he give you to leave town?"

His smile faded. He'd almost forgotten about her dinner with Raymond the week before last. Obviously they'd done a lot more than eat. "What did he tell you?"

"He implied that you asked him for money to get out of town; in exchange, you promised you wouldn't return. I don't doubt that second part, although I think it was probably his idea, that *he* approached *you*."

"And what makes you think that?"

"The way you feel about him. I don't think you would ask Raymond for water if you were on fire." Celine sat back and watched him grin again, that smart-ass grin.

"Honey, I've been on fire since the first night you stood in front of that window half-dressed, and, believe me, Raymond Kendall doesn't have what it takes to put it out."

"Don't do that, Will," she warned as she had done once before. "Don't stir up something you're not going to take care of."

He studied her for a long time. She sat without flinching, letting him see whatever it was he wanted in her face. Then abruptly he rose from the hammock and motioned for her to move her feet so he could sit on the chaise in front of her, astride the weather-stained cushion. "All right. You're right. Raymond did make me an offer back then. Get out of town, escape the trouble with Melanie, and never come back—*never*. Not for any reason. And for leaving, he paid me five hundred bucks, in crisp new tens and twenties, fresh out of the vault at the bank. I'm no fool, Celie. They were going to send me to jail. Back then, nasty things happened in jail to kids like me. So I gave Raymond my word. I took his money, and I ran far, far away."

"And his money was all you took, wasn't it?"

He wore a puzzled look. "I packed whatever clothes would

fit in the bag, along with my dad's Bible and a couple of other things.''

"But there wasn't room in that bag for more money, was there?"

He laughed. "Believe me, if I'd had more money, I would have made room for it, but I didn't. Miss Rose wouldn't let me work during the school year. She gave me an allowance, and it didn't stretch far."

"No room for a pair of earrings. Or a brooch or a bracelet or a ring."

The bewildered look deepened, confirming what she had believed all along. He wasn't faking. Will hadn't stolen anything from Raymond or Miss Rose. He had only taken what was given him. Someone else had taken the rest. If it had been taken at all.

"What are you getting at, Celine?" he asked, his tone part defensive, part accusing. "Why all the questions?"

"How badly did Raymond want to get rid of you?"

He shrugged. "Badly enough to pay."

She accepted that with a nod. "Badly enough to frame you?"

Will simply looked at her.

"Badly enough to steal from himself?" Her voice had dropped a few tones and, with her next question, it softened even more, as if she were reluctant to voice out loud the thought that had only moments ago popped into her mind.

"Did he want it badly enough," she nearly whispered, "to steal from his own mother?"

Chapter Ten

*H*is eyes intense and darker than ever, Will leaned forward threateningly. "What the hell are you talking about, Celie?" he demanded in a low voice. "Who stole from Miss Rose?"

But Celine wasn't intimidated. She didn't shrink away. "According to the newspaper and to Raymond, *you* did." She repeated the sketchy details in the newspaper article and filled in with the bits of information Raymond had given her at the restaurant.

When she finished, his shoulders seemed to slump a bit, and the passion was gone from his eyes. He stood up and walked to the closest tree, resting his hands on a branch above his head, letting his head fall forward. "Son of a bitch," she heard him whisper.

"Who knew you were leaving town that night?"

"Nobody."

"Just you and Raymond."

For a long time he didn't respond. Was he thinking about the implications of that? Raymond, heir to the illustrious Kendall name and fortune, bank president and pillar of the community, had faked one crime and committed another against his own mother. Raymond's dislike for him went beyond animosity and class consciousness, went far beyond his smug insistence that a worthless Beaumont didn't belong

249

in his superior family. Raymond hadn't merely wanted Will out of town and out of the way, but had been willing to see him imprisoned for his own crimes.

Finally Will raised his head and looked at her. "Why would he go to all that trouble? I was *leaving*. I wasn't coming back."

"Maybe he knew Miss Rose would try to find you and bring you back."

"Did she?"

Celine shook her head. "She was afraid that, with these break-ins coming on top of the mess with Melanie, there was no way you could avoid jail."

"So she believes I'm guilty of that, too," he said with a smile that was hurtful in its bitterness. "I was eighteen then. I'd lived nearly half my life with her, and she didn't know the first thing about me. She still doesn't."

Celine didn't say anything. There weren't any words to make him feel better about Miss Rose's lack of faith, and no reason to believe he cared about her own faith in him. Volunteering the information would make her look as if she were currying his favor.

After another silence, he said, "Raymond came over here one day after school when Miss Rose was gone to one or another of her meetings. He asked why I didn't admit the truth about Melanie. He said there was no way I could avoid going to jail, not with Jock being such good friends with the sheriff and the judge. I was scared. When not even Miss Rose believed me, I was damned scared. So when he offered me money to leave town, I accepted."

He had been eighteen, Celine thought, old enough to be considered a man, old enough to vote, make babies, and go to war. But eighteen wasn't a man, certainly not now but not back then, either. He'd still been in school, still a kid, a kid whose life hadn't been the most secure. He'd been abandoned, in different ways, by all the people who should have loved him—his father, his mother, and Miss Rose. It said something for the man he had become that he still loved Miss Rose even though she had failed him.

"Raymond told me to be ready to leave the next evening, to go to his house at seven o'clock that night to get the money.

He told me not to tell anyone because it would get back to Jock or the sheriff, and they would stop me. I had already figured that out; I wasn't talking to anyone.''

He broke off again, staring off into the distance before continuing in that same flat, emotionless voice. ''On Friday night I went to his house, to the side door that opens into his office like he told me. He gave me five hundred dollars; I promised I would never come back and would never tell anyone about our deal, and I left.''

''Raymond told me that he gave you a couple hundred dollars, that you had seen the rest of the money in his desk, that you had come back later that evening, had broken the glass in the door and taken the money, along with a ring that belonged to his father.''

Will didn't bother denying it. Maybe he didn't see any sense in it. Maybe he didn't expect her to believe him. She didn't need his denial.

''Do you think he might have stolen those things himself?''

He gave her a distant look. ''It doesn't make sense. He was getting what he wanted. He was getting rid of me.''

''But he had no guarantee that you were gone for good. You might have changed your mind. You might have gone away and discovered how hard life was on your own. You might have come back here once the money ran out. By then, maybe Melanie would have already had the baby, and maybe Jock would have calmed down. Maybe he would have been willing to accept support for Melanie and Jared from you instead of demanding marriage. Maybe that problem would have been solved, but you still would have gone to jail. The sheriff would have been waiting to arrest you for those break-ins.''

He stared at her for a moment, then shook his head. ''We're talking about Raymond Kendall. I know he doesn't like me, but to commit two crimes just to set me up? That's not logical, Celie. It's not rational.''

Leaving the chair, she approached him, stopping just out of touching range. ''He doesn't simply dislike you, Will. He hates you. And there's rarely anything logical or rational about hatred.''

The conversation obviously disturbed him, and she wasn't

feeling any too comfortable herself. There was something wrong about standing here on Kendall property, where they had both been invited to live, and talking about the respectable Kendall son's capacity for crime.

"He lied to me, Will," she said softly. "He told me he had given you only a couple hundred dollars. A *couple*. Raymond works with money every day. He's the greediest soul I know. He's too precise to say a couple when he means five. And he wanted me to believe that it was your idea, that you asked him for the money."

Finally he released his grip on the tree limb, shoved his hands into his hip pockets, and leaned back against the trunk. "How long have you known this?"

"I found out the night Melanie came to see you."

"So you knew before . . ."

Before they had made love. She nodded.

"Why didn't you tell me sooner?"

"I had other things on my mind last Saturday," she reminded him with a chastening look. "Since then you haven't been particularly easy to talk to."

He had no response to that. "Why are you telling me now?"

"I thought you would like to know all the sins you're being damned for."

"It doesn't matter," he said grimly. "As soon as Miss Rose is finished with me, I'm leaving this town, Celie. And this time . . . I'm never coming back."

Sixteen years ago he had made that promise to Raymond, and eventually he had broken it. But this time he meant it. He wouldn't come back. Celine believed him. She believed him with all her aching heart.

Tuesday afternoon it rained—not a sudden summer downpour that ran off before it did any good, but a steady, gentle rain with the sun occasionally breaking through, glistening on the wetness. Will was on a break, drinking a cold soda and studying the house in front of him. It was a jumble of original, weathered work and new repairs.

Today he had been working on the gallery, chiseling out soft, crumbled brick, cleaning the space, aligning the new brick in place and packing it there. Only those around the edges were held with mortar; the rest were set in sand—swept into the cracks, wet with water, packed down, and filled again.

Roger had sent him yesterday with a sample brick to a site across the river where a ninety-year-old factory was being demolished, and he'd found enough good brick of the same dusty rose so that the patched areas didn't look patched. It was slow, precise work—chipping out hardened sand, removing each old brick carefully so as not to damage its neighbors and fitting the replacement just right so the herringbone pattern wouldn't be thrown off kilter. It left him with a backache and sore knees and far too much time to think.

Celine's little bombshell Sunday had nagged at him until finally he'd admitted that there was nothing he could do about it. Everyone believed he was guilty, and denying it now wouldn't change anyone's mind, especially not the only one who counted, Miss Rose. If Celine was right, if Raymond had set him up, there was no way to prove it. Besides, how much more would it hurt Miss Rose to believe her son was a thief than to believe Will was? Still, it bothered him. It made him feel helpless and frustrated, and God help him, he wasn't sure he could deal with much more frustration.

But not *everyone* believed he was guilty. Celine didn't. She had no reason to trust him, no reason to believe in him when no one else did. But she did. She had the innocent faith of a child . . . and all the charms of a woman.

He had just finished his Coke and was getting to his feet when one of the men called, ''Hey, Will, you have a visitor.'' Standing beside the guy, water dripping from his hair and his clothes, was Jared Robinson.

''What brings you out this way?''

''I heard about the work on the house. I wanted to see how it's going.''

Truth? Or an excuse to come around because Jared still believed he was his father? Will wasn't sure it mattered. ''I'm working around back. Come on.'' As he led the way, he glanced back at Jared. Scrawny as he was, he looked like a drowned rat—his hair slicked back, his clothes dripping,

Melanie's big blue eyes dominating his thin face. "You ever seen the house before?"

"Lots of times. Joey and I used to ride our bikes out here when we were kids and play."

When they were kids. Will wasn't even tempted to grin at the absurdity of such a statement coming from a fifteen-year-old boy. Don't be so eager to grow up, he wanted to tell him. Don't be so willing to give up the innocence and freedom of youth.

But all he said was, "Most people had forgotten this place was even here. How did you know?"

"My mother told me. She always wanted to live in a place like this. She used to say that she should have been born back when the South was the Grand Old South and lived in a house like this and worn velvet and silk and had servants to wait on her and spent her life going to parties and barbecues and balls." Jared leaned against the nearest pillar and watched as Will began working on yet another broken brick. "I told her when she called Sunday that Miss Rose was having the place fixed up. She said next time she's here, she would like to come by and see it."

Will freed the larger section of the brick he was working on, then began removing the rest of it. "What do you do all summer long?"

"Hang out with Joey. Go to the library. Read a lot of books. Every August I spend two weeks at Grandpa's brother's farm across the river." He paused and frowned. "I used to go to the video arcade some, but not lately."

"You have problems there?"

Jared didn't answer.

Will sat back on his heels and looked at him. The boy's cheeks were flushed, and suddenly he found the pattern of the bricks underfoot most interesting. "Because of me?"

He still didn't speak.

"I'm sorry. If I could change things, Jared, I would. But I'm not going to lie. I'm not going to admit to something that I didn't do."

Slowly Jared slid to the ground, still resting his back against the pillar. "Why did you come back?"

Will's grin was rueful. "I've been asking myself that every day since I got here."

"When I leave, I'm never coming back."

"When you leave, you'll make a new life for yourself. That's something I never managed to do."

"Why not?"

He scored the replacement brick he was working with, then cut off the excess length with one sharp blow. After checking the size again, he looked up at the boy. "I don't know. Maybe because I was alone. I didn't belong anywhere. Or maybe I didn't let myself belong. I didn't trust anyone."

"Grandpa says you got arrested a lot."

He grinned. "I figured trouble would eventually find me, so sometimes I went looking for it."

Jared fell silent, and Will continued working, waiting for the boy to speak again. When he did, it was on a subject Will preferred to avoid. "Miss Celine gave me some money for my college fund."

Now it was Will's turn to remain silent.

"She said it was from someone who thought I could put it to good use."

Still nothing.

"Was it from you?"

"No." He said it simply, flatly, not too vehement but not too casual, either.

"Do you know who it was from?"

"Did you ask Celine?"

"She wouldn't say." Jared scowled. "You're not going to, either, are you?"

"I have nothing to do with that money, and if I knew where she got it—"

"You know. If you didn't, you would have just said so instead of asking if I'd asked her."

"I still wouldn't tell you," Will finished. "It's none of my business."

"You like Miss Celine, don't you?"

Looking up, he grinned. "I thought it was a sin against nature in this town to *not* like Miss Celine."

Again Jared scowled. The kid really didn't like being

teased. "I mean seriously. Man to woman. You know. The sex stuff."

Will positioned the brick, made sure it was level, then held it in place with one hand while gesturing to the bucket between him and Jared with the other. "Pour a couple of scoops of sand over this," he directed. Sitting back out of the way, he repeated, "The sex stuff, huh? Along with reading lots of books and going to college and getting away from this town, you *are* interested in the sex stuff, too, aren't you?"

Jared was torn between behaving like the mature young man he wanted to be and the inexperienced kid he really was. The kid won out as a blush stole across his face.

"Anyone in particular you're interested in?" Picking up a whisk broom, Will swept the sand into all four seams, poured a can of water over it, then brushed more sand in.

"Nah," Jared replied, too carelessly to be believed. "So what about you and Miss Celine?"

"She's my neighbor."

"And?"

"And that's all."

"Yeah, right."

"Look, I like Celine. She's a pretty lady. But she can do a hell of a lot better than me."

That still didn't answer his question, Jared thought. So Miss Celine *could* do better than Will Beaumont. That didn't mean he didn't want her anyway. It didn't mean she *wanted* to do better.

"How long are you staying here?" he asked, watching as Will prepared another brick.

"I don't know. It depends on Miss Rose."

"She's a nice old lady. But she sure doesn't like my mom—or Miss Vickie. She says Miss Vickie is like a balloon—all pretty on the outside and absolutely empty inside, except you can let a balloon float away and be rid of it, and you can never get rid of Miss Vickie." He paused, then asked, "She was one of your girlfriends, too, wasn't she?"

"I went out with her a couple of times back in high school. Just before I went out with your mom."

"And didn't get her pregnant," Jared added drily.

Will gave him a hard look. "You know, Jared, whether you believe me doesn't change anything. I'm still not your father."

He moved farther along the gallery, and Jared followed, settling against the next pillar. "I don't know what I believe," he admitted aloud. "But if it isn't you, then who? She wasn't seeing anybody else then."

"She was doing something with someone else then," Will corrected, "because it sure wasn't me. Have you asked her?"

"No."

"Why not?"

Jared weighed his loyalty to his mother against his interest in discovering the truth. For the moment, at least, truth won. "Because I have no way of knowing if she's lying to me."

There was sympathy in Will's eyes, sympathy that Jared didn't want to see. It made him feel uncomfortable, pitiable. Fortunately, Will didn't say anything for a while. He didn't ask if Melanie lied a lot. He just continued working for a while, and when he did finally break his silence, he approached the subject from an angle.

"I don't believe I ever heard my mother lie except for the time she lost her temper and hit me—gave me a black eye. She told my father when he came home from work that I had walked into a door. But she was very plainspoken the rest of the time. She wished she'd never had a son. She'd never wanted me, never loved me, and was counting the days until she could get rid of me." He smiled faintly as he worked. "The last time I saw her was right after my father died. She told me that she was leaving, that she wasn't taking me with her, and that I would never see her again. She was glad to leave, and I was glad to see her go."

Jared stared out over the yard, watching rain splash in the puddles. There were degrees of good and bad. His mother might not rate as much of a mother compared to someone like Miss Celine or his grandmother, but she wasn't so bad compared to Mrs. Beaumont. She had never hit him, had never been mean to him, had never neglected him. Even when she couldn't—or wouldn't—let him live with her, she had still loved him the best she could, and when she had left him, she'd left him with her parents who loved him, too, instead of all by himself with no one to care. But she still lied a lot.

He got to his feet and brushed his clothes off. "I've got to go. Grandpa will be home soon."

"I take it he wouldn't like knowing you'd been out here." Jared gave him a reproving look.

"If you want to put your bike in the back of one of the trucks, I can give you a ride part of the way."

"No thanks." He started to walk off, then stopped. "Can I come back sometime?"

"Anytime. Maybe we can put you to work."

Jared liked the idea of having a job—a real job—to earn money for college, but even if Will wasn't teasing, his grandfather would have a fit. "Well . . . see ya." He walked around to the front, bypassing the steps in favor of jumping from the gallery into the middle of a big puddle. He was already on his way to his bike, parked beneath the giant oak, before the drops even settled.

From the corner of the gallery, Will watched until Jared was out of sight. When he turned to go back to work, he ran into Roger Woodson. "Who's the kid?" the older man asked.

"Everyone thinks he's my son."

"Is he?"

"No."

Roger gave him an intense look. "You sound almost regretful."

Will's smile felt sad. "I almost am."

Roger followed him back around to where he was working. "Some of the materials we ordered are supposed to be in Thursday. Want to run down to New Orleans and get them?"

"Sure."

"You should be able to squeeze in time for lunch in the Quarter. I know some great places to take a pretty librarian," he teased, giving Will a tap on the shoulder as he passed.

So did he, Will thought somberly. And restaurants, or any other public places, ranked pretty low on his list.

Fifty thousand dollars fitted nicely into a briefcase. With the lid closed and the locks secured, it didn't look like much.

It certainly didn't look like the bright new future Melanie Robinson was expecting, but it sure as hell was the solution for its owner.

The drive to New Orleans was easy, a straight shot down the interstate. The Quarter was no more crowded than usual for a hot summer day. Damn fool tourists. In a record-breaking summer like this, why didn't they go someplace cool like Maine? Yes, Maine would be nice—Bar Harbor or Kennebunk Beach. Nice places to spend sweltering long summers.

The Quarter at its best was genteelly shabby. The area where Melanie lived was by no means the best or genteel, but it certainly was shabby. It was as run-down and hopeless as the people who inhabited it. It was a place where wandering tourists got mugged, where hapless residents received worse. No one would be surprised to learn that there had been another murder. No one would care. No one would ever guess who had done it.

Melanie's building was located in the middle of a dying block. Once a lovely home built around a gracious courtyard, it had been turned into cheap apartments. The courtyard served as a garbage dump; its central fountain was broken and weeds grew profusely in the cracks. The building should be razed, the entire block, in fact. An empty lot would be more appealing than this filthy eyesore.

The number Melanie had written down—3C—was in back on the third floor. Good. The farther she lived from the street, the better.

The stairs creaked softly, but no one else was around to hear. The tenants of these apartments were mostly day sleepers: hookers, dancers in the sleazier clubs, drug addicts, thieves, and thugs. Like the mythical vampire, they came out only at night to feed their passions and obsessions.

Past Apartments 3A, 3B, finally reaching 3C. There was a window beside the door, the screen torn and rusted. It was open to allow whatever tiny breezes might stir to flutter curtains so faded that their original color was a mystery. They met at the top and gapped wide at the bottom, revealing a glimpse of a kitchen—cramped, cluttered, slightly sour-smelling.

The first knock, perhaps too soft, drew no response. Another—three sharp taps—also went ignored. The third series of raps was answered with a grumble from within.

A moment later Melanie Robinson opened the door, offered an invitation to enter without even looking, then shuffled away. No question what Miss Melanie had done last night. She looked all partied out and hung over. She was wearing a cheap nightgown in royal blue with gaudy black lace trim. The lace revealed her breasts—heavy, droopy, and white— so white.

She walked over to the dining table that separated the living room and kitchen, paying no attention to the closing of the door, the twisting of the lock, or the footsteps that followed her. She was rummaging through the mess on the table, knocking movie and tabloid romance magazines to the floor, swearing to herself.

"Sorry," she said aloud, her voice throaty and raw. "I've got a bitch of a headache. I need a little something to get me started this morning."

With a relieved sigh, she found what she wanted. Cigarettes in one hand, a bottle of cheap booze in the other, she finally turned around for the first time.

There was a moment of utter blankness on her face—stupid girl—then she lit a cigarette, took a long drag, and chased it with a swig of vodka. "I wasn't expecting you," she said sullenly.

"You would prefer I return home and call to set up an appointment?"

"No." She spoke too quickly, too greedily. Leaning back against the table, she drew on the cigarette, exhaled, then flicked the gathering ash to the floor.

Her position drew the nightgown taut across her breasts, her belly, her thighs. She had soft ugly flesh, the cheesy dimpling visible through the well-worn nylon. Once she had been a truly beautiful girl, enough to arouse anyone's passion, but now she looked ghastly. Overused. Slatternly. Beauty gone bad.

Her gaze shifted to the briefcase, locking on it. The bitch could probably smell the money inside. She was so greedy, and she made no effort to hide it. Her mouth was watering for it, her entire self craving it, the way she craved the booze, the cocaine, the countless men. So much booze and drugs, so many men. She was probably a walking repository of disease. The damage the drugs had done to her organs, the sexually transmitted diseases, the dirty needles, and all the unsafe sex. It was a wonder she was still alive.

"Is that it?" she asked, gesturing toward the attaché with her cigarette, more ash falling to the floor.

Don't give it to her yet. Take your time.

Enjoy.

"You'll keep your end of the bargain."

Melanie raised her right hand, palm flat. "Absolutely." As if the word of a whore meant anything.

"You won't come back asking for more?"

"I swear I won't. This is all I need. I'm heading out of here—out West. I'm starting all over again."

A long stare, a hard silence, then softly, "You swore last time, too, but you didn't keep your word. You came back. You wanted more money."

She wet her lips. "Things have been tough, you know? But I won't need any more after this. Fifty grand. That is *it*."

The slut was lying, and, damn, she was good at it. She sounded so convincing, so *sincere*. But fifty thousand dollars wouldn't last her long, and as soon as it was gone, she would be back, grimy little hand out for more, making promises that she wouldn't keep and threats that she would.

Liar.

"Can I see it?" she asked.

When the attaché was offered, she took it and shoved everything but the vodka from the table to the floor. Her back turned, she set the case on the table and tried to open it. "What's the combination?"

"911. Both locks."

"Funny. Like a call for help."

Yes. But there wouldn't be any help for her today.

She opened the case and drew her hands across the stacks of money, actually caressing each crisp, new twenty- and fifty-dollar bill on top. Damned if she probably wasn't about to come at the sight of so much money and the visions of what she could buy herself with it.

Beside the table was a television, and on top of it was a crystal. It was just like empty-headed Melanie to believe bits of stone and glass could change her life.

Well, guess what, Melanie? This time you're right.

This particular crystal was big, about six inches tall with jagged edges. It felt good in the hand. Solid. Strong. Yes, indeed, it did have some power.

Melanie removed one of the stacks of money from the briefcase and gave a dismayed cry. "Hey, what are you—"

A quick move, and a sudden strong arc brought the rock into contact with her head. She cried out only once, sharp and stunned, surprised almost, then fell in an ugly heap to the floor. Blood flowed freely, warm, matting her hair, soaking into the threadbare carpeting, pooling beneath her.

God, what a powerful feeling! A rush, almost sexual in nature. Who was about to come now?

With a hard nudge, the body rolled over. Interesting how quickly she went from being Melanie Robinson, daughter, mother, slut, betrayer, and pathetic whore, to *the body*. As life ceased, so did identity. She was no longer a person but a thing. The body.

Her eyes were open, her lips apart. Not an attractive sight, but then, she had stopped being attractive years ago. Her greed, her compulsion to have it all—all the pleasure, all the decadence—had robbed her of youthful beauty. Now she was just ugly and fat, staring but seeing nothing.

One hand on her plump throat revealed no pulse, but just to be on the safe side, another blow, square on her forehead, crushing bone and tissue, splattering more blood, disfiguring her poor dead face.

Time to finish. A plastic bag from the pocket for the crystal; it went into the attaché along with the bundle Melanie had been holding when she fell—when she died. Rectangles of plain white bond topped with a few fifty-dollar bills.

Now to ransack the place, make it look as if a struggle had occurred. But the apartment already had that ransacked look: dirty dishes, dirty clothes, empty liquor bottles, three dirty syringes. Leftover bits of food, newspapers and more magazines, photographs, shoes, makeup. A table knocked over, a spilled beer can, the pile Melanie had shoved to the floor herself.

And something to steal. In a city like New Orleans, people were robbed, homes burgled, every day. Too bad poor Melanie had interrupted her thief. Too bad he had crushed her skull. Why, she might even have known him, might even have opened her door to him. What was this world coming to when a woman wasn't safe in her own home?

A thorough search of this room and the next revealed little worth taking. Fifty dollars cash in a bedroom drawer. A pair of decent-quality fake diamond earrings. A ceramic Mardi Gras mask rimmed in gold—not one of the six-dollar jobs from the market but an expensive version, an impulse buy from one of the specialty shops. A Walkman, top of the line, a tape of the blues inside.

Melanie wouldn't be singing the blues anymore. She was out of her misery. Out of everyone's misery. Forever.

It was a quick walk, briefcase in hand, back along the balcony, down the stairs, and through the courtyard to the street. The sun was shining bright out here, the air smelled a little cleaner, and the world seemed a hell of a lot lighter.

They claimed there was no such thing as the perfect crime, but they were wrong. Melanie's death would be considered exactly what it seemed—robbery gone sour. Bad luck. Just one more vicious crime in a city that had too many.

Into the car, parked a block away. The engine started right up, but the car didn't move. Just one minute, one hand between the thighs, an image again of Melanie's skull giving beneath the blow, feeling her warm blood. A shudder, a groan, and release—quick, sharp, hard.

Behind the car an engine revved. The driver was impatient, waiting for the parking space, drumming his hands on the steering wheel. One glance in the rearview mirror, and the perfect crime collapsed.

The driver of the truck was Billy Ray Beaumont. And he could see as easily as he was being seen. He could recognize as he had been recognized.

The problem of Melanie Robinson had been easily resolved, so easily that it was almost laughable. But now it had been replaced with another.

What to do about Billy Ray?

Will watched the German import glide out of the parking space and down the street, then pulled to the curb and shut off the engine. Sixteen years ago, when he had lived for a brief time in this area, an expensive car like that would have stood out like a sore thumb. Now, with all the money from the drug trade that flourished in New Orleans, no one would give a shiny silver Mercedes a second glance.

Climbing out of the truck, he crossed the street and started down the block. The supplies Roger had sent him to pick up wouldn't be ready for another couple of hours; they were waiting on an overnight shipment from back East. That left him with time enough for lunch and to reacquaint himself with his old neighborhood.

He hadn't been here in so long, but he remembered his way around. The place was somehow even more run-down than before. He wondered if any of the people he'd known back then were still around, if any of them were even still alive. Their lives had been hard, and there'd been a danger to living in the city that was missing from the small towns Will had come to prefer. Here in New Orleans there had been times when he'd thought he would surely be dead before he turned thirty, but he had survived that and then some.

He found the place he was looking for—a hole-in-the-wall diner that smelled of grease and spices, of smoke and onions and too little cleaning. Though the restaurant looked to be only one inspection away from being shut down, it had had years ago a reputation for good food and cheap prices.

The food was still good, plentiful, and cheap. He sat at a table next to the grimy plate glass window and ate red beans and rice, jambalaya, andouille sausage, and sweet corn bread, all washed down with sugary strong tea. Roger had suggested that he bring Celine with him on this trip and treat her to lunch in the Quarter, but somehow he couldn't imagine her sitting across from him in this place. It wasn't that she would be snooty about coming here. He just couldn't face the idea of bringing her. She deserved better than this. Better than him.

He was going to miss her when he left Harmony. Going to? Hell, he already did. It was a struggle every night to stay away from her house, not to invite himself onto her screened porch when she sat there, not to invite himself right inside to her bed. He had thought it would get easier as time went by—seeing her, hearing her soft voice, wanting her—but he'd been wrong. Nothing was easier.

The evenings he spent at the bar, drinking alone or with Eva, didn't help, either. He was accepted there—a stranger, but a stranger who was just like them—no better, maybe only a little worse. But that wasn't where he wanted to be. Eva, sweet as she was, wasn't the woman he wanted to spend his evenings with. Drinking to forget Celine wasn't a habit he wanted to get into.

Making love to her, sitting in the shadows on the porch with her, walking through the woods with her: those were habits he could easily fall into. Those were habits he would welcome and never give up.

He paid for his meal, then stepped outside onto the sidewalk. The stench of summer heat and garbage, once so familiar, greeted him as he passed an alley. In this hot, humid weather the odors of the Quarter could be as overpowering as the sights, the exotica, the erotica. It was a unique place, different from any other he'd ever been, always busy, always vibrant and alive. Although he hadn't liked living here himself, he could understand how people like Melanie were drawn to it. But he couldn't understand how she could need this life more than she needed her son.

She probably lived somewhere around here in one of these apartments. If he checked the phone book or asked around, he could probably find her, but for what? He had no desire to see her. She had made it clear that she wasn't going to clear his name, not as long as Jared's father was willing to pay for her silence, and that—innocence, satisfaction, vindication—was all he wanted from her.

He wandered around, passing the bar, now out of business, where he had once worked as a bouncer, the market where he had indulged in occasional treats of fresh fruit and the site of the abandoned building, long since torn down, where he had lived along with countless other frightened young kids running away from life's problems. And when he realized that being back here was depressing rather than nostalgic, he returned to the truck and headed back to the builders' supply. Better to pass his time surrounded by hardware and wood than bitter memories.

Mitch Franklin had once been a frequent sight in the First Baptist Church, back when his wife was still alive. She had been the believer in the family, the doer, the Sunday school teacher, the ladies' auxiliary vice president, and the youth group volunteer. She had organized fund-raisers and headed church dinners, and whenever anyone had needed a hand, she'd been the first to offer. Mitch hadn't been as certain of the existence of a higher power, but he had attended weekly services and carried out whatever jobs his wife volunteered him for because he had loved her.

But a year ago she had died, killed by cancer, and since her funeral, Franklin hadn't set foot inside the church. In his wife's death, his doubts about a good and loving God had been proved.

Now, like everyone else in the congregation, Raymond watched as Franklin, his sheriff's uniform and gun looking out of place in the sanctuary, talked quietly with the reverend up front. It was a few minutes after ten and past time for the service to start, and everyone wondered and whispered about why it hadn't and why Franklin was here.

After a moment, Reverend Davis left the sheriff and started down the center aisle, and the whispers on either side stopped. When he stopped beside Jock Robinson, three rows behind Raymond, there was absolute silence. As Jock, Sally, and Jared followed the minister and the sheriff through the side door that led to classrooms and offices in back, the murmurs started again.

"What do you suppose has happened?" Frannie asked.

Even though the question wasn't directed to her, Rose answered it anyway. "I imagine that daughter of theirs has gone and gotten herself into trouble again," she said tartly.

"Now, Mama, don't go talking bad about Melanie," Raymond reproached. "You're in church, remember."

"A place where young Melanie's face has been absent for at least sixteen years," Rose responded.

The curious whispers gave way to talk, to the kind of visiting that usually took place before or after the service, about families and vacations, activities and the weather and the eventual return to school of kids run wild. Raymond listened and waited and wondered what trouble Melanie could have gotten into that merited a disruption of the church service.

He didn't have long to wonder. Alone this time, Reverend Davis returned to the sanctuary. He took his place behind the pulpit up front and grimly, solemnly announced that Jock and Sally's daughter Melanie had been found dead in her apartment in New Orleans. Raymond heard Frannie's gasp and his mother's whispered, "Oh, Lord." He bowed his head for the prayer the minister was leading, but he didn't close his eyes. He didn't pretend to take part.

Melanie Robinson dead. He shouldn't be surprised. If he'd ever given it any consideration, he would have expected her to die young; he'd heard all the stories about her lifestyle, but he was surprised anyway. She had once been so beautiful, so bright and greedily alive. She had wanted everything, had been determined to have it all. And now she was dead.

He wondered briefly how it had happened. A drug overdose seemed most likely. According to all the talk, she'd developed quite a taste for cocaine and alcohol, a lethal combination if ever there was one.

He regretted her death for Jock's sake, and Sally's. Melanie had been their only child, the light of their lives. They had loved her far more than she deserved. And he felt sorry for Jared. The boy had lived all his life without a father to love or teach or raise or even acknowledge him, and now he didn't have a mother, either. No matter how much he loved his grandparents, they couldn't replace his parents. But he didn't feel sorry for Melanie herself. He wasn't sorry, for her sake, that she was dead.

For her sake, probably even for the sake of those who mourned her, she was better off dead.

* * *

Celine had skipped church again, her third Sunday in a row, and she wasn't feeling particularly sinful about it, either. She just couldn't face putting on hose, a slip, and a pretty linen dress, curling her hair and applying makeup, wearing heels or dressy white sandals. She couldn't endure the idea of smiling and being sweet, of sitting near her sister or listening to sermons on being good and moral when all she really wanted to be was *bad*. She couldn't respectfully bow her head and join in their prayers when the only thing she wanted to pray for was more time with Will, more wicked loving with Will. She couldn't bear the hypocrisy within herself.

Instead, she had dressed in shorts and a tank top, and she had weeded Miss Rose's flowers and was starting on her own. Miss Rose had gone on to church without her. She hadn't criticized, but she'd given Celine a pursed-lips sort of look before she'd driven away. As for Will, Celine thought he might be in the guesthouse—if he had come home last night. Granted, Miss Rose's car had been back in its place this morning, but that proved only that he'd brought it back. It didn't mean he hadn't left again, or walked away or that the woman he was seeing, damn him, hadn't picked him up.

She was on her knees, hot and sweaty, when a car pulled into Miss Rose's driveway. It was almost new, a midsize car in a nice blue color with nothing to set it apart from a million other cars except the antennas on the trunk. One she recognized from the little curlicue as being a cellular antenna. The other, she assumed, must be for some kind of radio.

Sitting back on her heels, she watched the two men get out. They were strangers, neatly dressed, their sleeves short, their ties loosened, and their jackets left in the car in deference to the weather. They were both serious and grim. Calm. Authoritative. Policemen? she suddenly wondered.

The first one had started up the steps to Miss Rose's house when he saw Celine. He reversed direction, and they came toward her. She got to her feet, not wanting to be at such a disadvantage, and squinted against the morning sun as she faced them.

"We're looking for William Ray Beaumont," the taller of the two men said by way of a greeting. "Does he live here?"

Policemen, she nervously confirmed. Here to question Will? To make accusations of some sort? Maybe, God help her, to take him away? "Will lives in the guesthouse," she replied, gesturing toward it.

"Is he there now?"

"I don't know."

The tall one, his hair black enough to gleam under the sun, thanked her, and they crossed the grass to the guesthouse. One of them remained at the bottom of the steps while the other climbed to the tiny stoop and knocked. Three or four solid knocks brought no response.

She stood and watched, unashamed of her curiosity. Was Will in trouble? But how could he be? He worked long hours at the Kendall mansion every day and spent his evenings—most of them, at least—alone. But those evenings he was gone, when he went out probably for a drink and God knew what else . . . There was no end to the trouble he could get into with the right amount of booze and the wrong women.

The two men returned to her. "Do you know where he is?"

She shook her head.

"Does he have friends around here he might visit?"

"Just Miss Rose and me."

"Miss Rose?"

"Rose Kendall. She owns this place. She lives in that house. She's in church this morning." Celine heard herself, her nervous, short sentences, and winced. Still, being questioned by two strange men when she was all alone out here was more than enough to make her nervous.

"And you are . . . ?"

"Celine Hunter." She looked from one man to the other, then asked, "Who are you?"

Her worst fears were confirmed when they both withdrew small black cases and flipped them open. New Orleans Police Department. She paid no attention to the names, simply noticed the official nature of the credentials and that the photographs matched the two men.

"Any idea when Beaumont will be back?"

She shook her head.

"We'd like to wait for him."

Her mouth dry, she gestured to the comfortable chairs in the shade on the porch. "You can wait there."

She returned to her work, but she couldn't concentrate, couldn't ignore the two men sitting quietly only ten feet away. She was so edgy that when she heard a sound behind her, she gave a start and whirled around to her feet. Will had emerged out of the woods and was coming across the lawn toward her.

"Skipping church again, Celie? What are you trying to do? Climb down off that pedestal the folks in town have put you on?"

"Where have you been?" she asked sharply, ignoring his teasing.

"Over at the house. Looking at the work that's been done."

"There are two policemen here to see you."

The easy, pleasant look faded from his face, and his mouth formed a thin line. To someone who didn't know him—someone who didn't trust him—his reaction might speak of guilt, but Celine knew better. She knew it came from years of always being greeted with suspicion, of always being the stranger in town, the drifter, of always being blamed for whatever went wrong because no one knew him, because no one would stand up for him.

She led the way up the steps and onto the porch. The men both stood up, both showed their credentials once again, both shook hands with him.

"You're Billy Ray Beaumont?" the black-haired one asked.

"Will Beaumont."

"But your friends call you Billy Ray."

"The people who knew me when I was a kid do." He glanced at her, standing to his side and just a little behind. His expression was blank, revealing nothing. "Do you mind, Celie?"

Biting her lip, she looked from him to each of the men, then back again. "I—I'll be inside." She left reluctantly, though. She didn't want to go inside. She didn't want to be left in the dark. She didn't want to imagine the worst when these cops' visit probably wasn't anything at all. After all, Will hadn't been in New Orleans in years. How could he possibly have gotten in trouble there?

She closed the screen door quietly, then the door. Will waited a few seconds longer before turning to the men. "What is this about?"

"Melanie Robinson."

The men sat down again, and Will drew a chair to the corner where he faced both of them. Was Melanie in trouble? Maybe. Probably. But why come to him? Why not see her parents instead? "What about Melanie?"

"You know her?"

"Of course." He wasn't about to lie to the cops, not when there were a few thousand good souls in Harmony who would eagerly tell them the truth. "Is she in trouble?"

"No," the blond detective replied. "She's dead. She was murdered in her apartment sometime last week. And your name keeps coming up in connection to her."

Staring off into the distance, Will thought of Melanie, once so beautiful, still pretty in a tired sort of way, so certain that she was finally going to have the life she'd always wanted. Controlled by the alcohol and the drugs and the sex, ashamed, she was too weak to give them up, too weak to fight. She was just doing the best she could to survive, according to Celine.

Now Melanie knew what Will always had known, what he hoped Celine never would: the best wasn't always enough. Melanie had tried. She had done what she could, had done her best, and now she was dead.

Dead.

God, it sounded so final.

"What is your connection to Melanie?"

Will forced his attention to the man. "We dated in high school. When she got pregnant, she claimed I was the father of her baby."

"And you claimed you weren't."

Claimed. Used like that, the word implied dishonesty, untruthfulness. Will didn't mind using it in reference to Melanie. He didn't like having it used in reference to himself. "I wasn't."

"There are tests to prove that."

He knew that, of course. Now that he was working and getting a regular paycheck, he could afford such a test, provided that Jared would also submit. But what would be the point? Without Melanie here to admit her deceit, there would still be plenty of people in town who would refuse to take the results of a high-tech, impossible-to-understand test as proof. After all, test results could be tampered with, couldn't they? Data could be twisted to prove whatever you wanted proved.

"Melanie came to see you not long ago, didn't she?" It was still the blond one talking. The other one sat there silently and listened.

"Yes."

"Do you remember when?"

To the day—and not because her visit had been so important. Because only two days later he had made love to Celine under the hot June sun. "Two and a half weeks ago. On a Thursday."

"And she asked you for money?"

Who had they already talked to? he wondered. Melanie's parents? Probably. And her friends in New Orleans. Melanie surely had liked to talk. In all her life she had kept only one secret—the identity of her lover, of Jared's father.

"No," he replied stiffly. "She didn't ask for money from me. She came . . . I don't know. To talk. To apologize."

"She told her friends in New Orleans that she was coming up here to see her son's father and to get some money—a lot of money—from him. According to her parents, the only person she saw here was you."

"Her parents are wrong. She saw someone else." He smiled bitterly. "I haven't been back in town long. I was in jail in Alabama before I came here. I don't *have* any money. Even if I were Jared's father, even if she had wanted money from me, she couldn't have gotten it, because I've never had any to give. I wasn't even working when she came. I had maybe thirty, thirty-five dollars to my name."

There was a moment's silence. Will wondered if they suspected him, then decided they didn't. He'd been interviewed by cops who were just asking questions, and he'd been interviewed by cops who believed him guilty of one crime or another. There was a world of difference in the two.

"Did she tell you anything about her plans when she was here?"

"She said she was meeting Jared's father, that she was going to ask him for more money."

"More?"

"She said he had paid her before. I didn't ask when. I assumed she meant when she was pregnant, when she lied and blamed me. She wouldn't tell me his name, though, because she said that had been part of their original deal, and it would be part of it again."

"His money for her silence."

Will nodded.

"And if he gave her the money?"

"She was leaving Louisiana. She was going someplace new where she could live the way she wanted, in the style she wanted."

There was another silence, then the other cop finally spoke. "You must have resented her lying about you all these years, making you leave your home when you were just a kid."

They had listened well to the people they had already talked to. They had already known all about his relationship with Melanie, had probably already known about his being in jail before he came back to Harmony. Did they also already know he'd been in New Orleans last week, probably right down in the area where Melanie lived?

"Yeah, I resented her for a long time. But it's kind of hard to stay resentful toward someone whose luck has turned out to be even worse than your own. In the end, I just mostly felt sorry for her."

After a few more questions, they offered another handshake and said a polite good-bye. Will remained on Celine's porch and watched them leave; then he left and headed for the guesthouse. He didn't want to be the one to break the news to Celine. He didn't want to talk about this or anything else right now. He just wanted to be alone.

* * *

Monday was the Fourth of July, and the town of Harmony always celebrated in a big way. In keeping with the holiday, Celine dressed in a full white skirt and a white blouse with a big sailor collar decorated with red-and-blue braid and embroidered gold stars. Her canvas shoes were white and glittery gold, and the ribbons that tied her hair back were red, white, and blue.

She had never felt less like a celebration, though, with the possible exception of Vickie's wedding. She had heard about Melanie's death first from Vickie, later from her mother and Miss Rose. She had gone to the guesthouse, wanting Will to confirm or deny the details, but he hadn't answered the door. She knew she would hear more today. All the talk at the parade, the picnic, the carnival, and the fireworks would be of Melanie and how she had died. There would be whispers, endless speculations, and morbid fascination. It would all be too ugly, too cold. She wished she could avoid it, wished she could, like Will, shut herself away and not be bothered. She wished she could get the images of Melanie out of her mind. Poor, pretty Melanie with her head bashed in. Poor, pretty Melanie dead. She wished she could run away.

Out front Miss Rose sounded the horn. Celine pushed what she needed—keys, money and tissues—into the deep pockets of her skirt, then hurried out.

"Go ask Will to join us," Miss Rose called from the driver's seat.

Although Celine knew it was pointless, she obeyed. She knocked once at the screen door, then opened it and stepped inside. Will was sitting on the unmade bed, wearing jeans that weren't zipped, and looking as if he'd just awakened from a restless sleep. "I'm delivering Miss Rose's invitation to join us in town for the Fourth celebration."

"They still do it up right, huh?" he asked, his voice husky, his eyes shadowy. "Games and rides, lots of food, entertainment, and fireworks?"

She nodded. "Miss Rose and I are running a couple of booths this morning, but we'll be free the rest of the day. Want to come?"

"Do they still have a kissing booth?"

Her smile came faintly. Trust him to remember something that had been done away with years ago. "No."

"Too bad. I surely would have paid a dollar or two to kiss you in front of all those self-righteous bastards in town."

Her smile grew stronger. "Come with us," she offered, "and I'll let you do it for free."

He shook his head. "After the news about Melanie, the last thing they need is to have me barge in on their celebration."

"No one could possibly blame you for that, Will," she said, aware of the uncertainty in her voice.

"You don't sound too sure of that." He left the bed and approached her. "Do *you* think I had anything to do with Melanie's death?"

"Of course not."

"It was on the radio this morning that she was killed last Thursday. What if I told you that I was in New Orleans last Thursday? That I was in the Quarter right where she lived? Would that change the way you feel?"

She stopped him when he'd come close enough—too close—with her hand on his chest. "You couldn't have killed her, Will. You know it, and I know it." Still, she hesitated. "Was that why those cops were here? Because you were in New Orleans that day?"

He shook his head. "Because my name kept coming up in their interviews. Because everyone knew Melanie was planning to ask Jared's father for some big bucks to keep her mouth shut, and everyone believed I was Jared's father."

"Don't tell anyone you were there," she softly pleaded.

"Why?"

Instead of answering right away, she focused her gaze and her attention on his chest. She stroked the tip of one finger back and forth over his skin, then slowly slid her hand lower toward the unfastened waistband of his jeans. When he stopped her with his own hand, she finally looked up at him. "If certain people in town found out that you were in the city the day Melanie died, that would be all the evidence they needed to deliver justice, lynch mob style."

He smiled crookedly. "You worried about me, Celie?"

"Yes, I am."

He held her gaze for a long moment, then he looked down

and lightly traced his finger along the edge of her collar. "You look pretty in your white dress."

"I look better out of it."

"Don't I know it," he replied with a rueful chuckle. Lifting her hand away, he pressed a kiss to her palm, then released her. "Run along now, little girl. Go dazzle all those fools in town. Leave this one alone."

She let him move away, but she didn't leave, as he'd instructed. She simply stood there. "Will you come in for the fireworks this evening?"

"Maybe."

But she had the impression he'd given that answer just so she would leave. With a murmured good-bye, she did just that.

Miss Rose wasn't surprised to see her come out alone. "That boy is the most stubborn and prideful person I've ever met," she grumbled as they drove away. "Half the people in town couldn't care less if he showed up today."

"But the other half would care," Celine said quietly, "and they would make sure he knew it. There's nothing wrong with being proud, Miss Rose. Sometimes that's all he's had to get by."

Miss Rose gave her a long, hard look. "I'm not going to ask what the two of you do in all that time you spend together. You're both adults. That's your business. I would like to know one thing, though: can I be expecting a wedding anytime soon?"

Mention of a wedding and all it implied—love, a family, a future, forever—set off an ache somewhere deep inside Celine. Once she'd gotten over the pain of Vickie and Richard's betrayal, she had assumed that someday it would be her turn to marry. Someday she would find a nice man, fall in love, get married, and live happily ever after. Somewhere along the way since meeting Will, she'd given up on that particular dream. She couldn't imagine the circumstance dire enough to lead him to marry her. Heavens, she couldn't even get him into bed. Love, church, a commitment—those were just sweet dreams. Impossible dreams.

"No," she said flatly. "No wedding."

"Why not? Do you think you're too good for him?"

"Miss Rose!" Celine admonished with a glower.

The old lady just sighed, unchastened. "I suppose *he* thinks you're too good for him. Are you in love with him?"

Before Celine could scold her again, Miss Rose continued. "I've seen how you look at him, and how you look for him when he's not around. I've seen how he looks at you, too. That is not an unreasonable question, dear." Then she smiled impishly. "Just a nosy one."

"Too nosy," Celine replied. Far too nosy indeed. It was a question she couldn't even let herself examine closely.

But it was a question that nagged at her through the day, through hours of celebration that were dampened by talk about Melanie. It was a question that answered itself all too easily shortly after dusk when she went searching for her nephew's soccer ball in the woods that formed the eastern edge of the city park and found Will waiting there. Was she in love with him? Absolutely. And did that change anything for them?

The answer to that also came all too easily. Did the fact that she had fallen in love with Will Beaumont make a damned bit of difference to anyone besides her? Did it change the fact that eventually he was going to leave Harmony and her behind?

No.

Not in the least.

Chapter Eleven

*W*ill was leaning against a tree, bouncing four-year-old Nick's ball up in the air and catching it in his palm. How long had he been there? Celine wondered. How had he known that she would be the one to respond to Nick's whine of *"Please* get my ball," instead of Vickie or Richard?

She glanced back the way she had come. The shrubbery was dense enough, except for that one small path, that they had complete privacy here. Not that she cared, of course, but Will did. She knew he did.

Shoving her hands into her pockets, she strolled toward him, seeing his arrogant grin, her mouth turning up in a grin to match. "What are you doing here?"

He bounced the ball again. "I told you I might come for the fireworks."

"You can't see them from here."

"Yes, you can." He nodded behind her, and she turned to look. The western sky, where the fireworks would be set off, was visible in patches, some of them quite large, through the trees.

She turned back to him. "You can see them better from my mother's quilt on the other side of those bushes."

"Uh-huh. Like your mother is going to graciously invite me to join them on her quilt."

"My mother *is* gracious."

"Maybe. But your sister isn't, and I bet when it comes to his little girl, your father isn't, either." He bounced the ball one last time, then dropped it into her hand and drew her closer. "I don't want to watch the fireworks with your mother and father, or your sister or the man you thought you wanted to marry or their bratty kids."

He wanted to watch them with *her*. That knowledge made the muscles in Celine's stomach tighten, and she felt a familiar, too-long-unsatisfied tingle deep inside. "There are other empty places out there," she whispered.

"Out there I can't do this." He lowered his head and pressed a kiss, light and teasing, to her lips. When she opened her mouth in a soft sigh, he slid his tongue inside and lazily, greedily tasted her.

He smelled of smoke and tasted of liquor. Was he drunk? she wondered dazedly. Was that why he was here, why he was kissing her instead of pushing her away? Had the alcohol given him courage or dimmed all his objections to why they shouldn't do this?

"Out there I can't do this, either," he whispered, unbuttoning her blouse, opening it to the waist, and sliding his hands inside to fill them with her breasts. His gentle caresses on her bare skin made her breasts swell and her nipples harden. They made her groan, a deep, throaty sound that she caught before it escaped.

On the other side of their cover the voices hushed, and in the near distance there was a low boom, followed by a shower of deep purple light from the sky. The fireworks had begun. Celine was experiencing her own personal fireworks in every place that Will touched her. He was bending in front of her now, sucking hard on her nipple, making her nerves curl and tighten, stealing her breath, when finally she found the strength to stop him.

"Why?" she whispered.

A starburst, this one silvery white, exploded overhead and, for an instant, cast its ghostly light on his face. He looked so heartachingly serious. For a long time he remained silent as his thumb rubbed her nipple, drying the wetness his mouth had left and sending exquisite new shivers through her.

Why? Such a tiny question, Will thought, with such big implications. Why was he doing this? Why was he tormenting himself? Why was he taking such unfair advantage of her? Why, God help him, couldn't he stay away from her? Why couldn't he protect her? Why couldn't he keep her safe from himself?

Because he'd had too much to drink before he'd come here? That was the easy answer. The easy excuse. But he wasn't drunk. He knew exactly what he was doing. He understood perfectly the consequences.

Because he couldn't stay away from her? That was a better answer, more truthful. And more truthful still: because he was going crazy without her. Because he hungered for her. Because only she could ease the need and the raw pain that was eating away at him.

There was still another answer, one more basic, more honest, more truthful, than them all. One that dealt with the emotional and not the physical. One that scared him more than he'd ever been scared. One that he couldn't face—not alone, and sure as hell not here with her.

As another starburst exploded overhead, this one in shades of green and blue, he withdrew his hands from her blouse, kissed her forehead, and turned her around so she could see the fireworks, too. He held her against him, her back to his chest, her bottom to his hips, and rested his cheek against her hair and held her with one arm around her waist, the other inside her blouse, his hand covering her breast.

He didn't answer her at all.

It was torture to stand like that—to smell her perfume and her shampoo. To feel the satiny smooth skin of her breast, heavy in his palm. To press his erection into the soft curve of her bottom. To kiss her ear and hear her responding groan, to feel it vibrating through her. It was sheer torture to be so close and yet not inside her.

But soon. Soon this would be over and they would go home and he would take her then. And tomorrow he would regret it.

They were only ten minutes into the fireworks display when, with a thrashing of bushes accompanied by muttered curses, a figure emerged into the clearing twenty feet away.

In spite of the shadows, Will recognized Vickie. He stiffened and would have pulled away, but Celine grasped his arms with surprising strength and held him in place.

"Celine?" Vickie called, her voice hushed, her tone strident. "What the hell is taking you so—" Seeing them, she drew up short. For a moment, he guessed, she didn't recognize them. She hadn't expected to find Celine with a man—any man, but especially him—and so she needed a moment to process what she was seeing. Then she started toward them, her movements quick and jerky, lacking in grace but filled with anger.

He pulled against Celine and succeeded in freeing his arm from her grip, in withdrawing his hand from her blouse. But he suspected it was too late. Vickie had already seen more than she'd expected to, far more than he'd wanted her to.

She stopped a half dozen feet in front of them, stiff and glowering. With one foot, Celine nudged the soccer ball she'd dropped, and it rolled out between them. "There's Nick's ball," she whispered.

Without warning Vickie charged forward, her hand upraised. If she'd intended to hit him, Will wouldn't have minded so much, but her target was Celine. Shifting her to the side, he grabbed Vickie's wrist, forcing it back, holding her more than arm's length away from her sister.

"You bitch!" she spit out, the softness of her voice in no way lessening the venom. "What is this, Celine? Payback? You never forgave me for taking Richard away from you so you have to take Billy Ray?"

"Will was never yours to take, was he?" Celine taunted. "Your great romance was all a lie, just one more of your fantasies. And as for your taking Richard from me, I don't give a damn about that. You two are perfect for each other. You deserve each other."

For a moment, Vickie shook, enraged with her sister. Then, after a couple of deep breaths, she regained control, pulled free of Will, straightened her shoulders and smoothed her clothes. "Like you two?" she asked snidely. "Won't everyone in town get a kick out of this? Their precious Celine down and dirty in the woods with that worthless Beaumont trash. All these years you've been fooling them, making them think you're sweet and innocent and damn near virginal, and all along it's just been an act. You're no better than anyone else in this town. You're just a common slut, and a desperate one, too, if you're willing to do it with *him*." She gave Will a derisive look. "White trash and no class. Just wait until I tell everyone about this."

Releasing Celine, Will bent and picked up the soccer ball, at the same time catching Vickie's arm again. He dragged her across the clearing to the narrow opening she had overlooked, where he shoved the ball into her arms, then leaned down until he was right in her face. "You say one word about Celie to anyone in this town, and, I swear to God, I'll make you sorry."

She opened her mouth to protest, but nothing came out. Maybe she was just too angry to speak. Or maybe she believed him, believed he would hurt her badly. Whatever her reason, after a moment's wide-eyed stare, she pulled away and hurried off.

Will just stood there for a long moment, so angry he was trembling, so disgusted that he was sick. He should have known better than to come here tonight, where Celine's family and friends and her bitch of a sister were sure to be around. He should have hidden when he saw her come into the trees, should have run like hell the other way when she saw him.

He never should have touched her. He never should have held her. He never should have exposed her to this kind of risk, this kind of scene.

She came to him quietly, laying her hand on his shoulder, startling him. He jerked away and moved deeper into the trees, into the shadows, farther away from all those judgmental bastards, and she followed him.

"Let's go home," she softly suggested.

He didn't say anything. He couldn't.

"I'm sorry, Will."

She was sorry. Everyone had something to apologize for except her. She was the only one in his entire life who had never done anything to him that needed an apology, and yet she offered it so easily, so sincerely.

Turning to gaze down at her, he cupped his hand to her cheek. "She called you a slut."

Celine smiled faintly. "She's jealous. She had convinced herself that if you were going to have an affair with any woman around here, it would be *her*."

"She's your *sister*, Celie, and she called you those names just for being here with me."

"In our case, 'sisters' is hardly synonymous with friends. We don't exactly get along. I don't care what she thinks, Will."

Sighing, he let his hand slide free. "You don't understand," he said grimly, sadly. How could she? She had never been treated with anything but the utmost respect. She had never known disdain or hatred, rejection or scorn. She couldn't understand what it was like to be judged and damned for no reason, never to be given a chance to earn a fair judgment.

"No, *you* don't understand," she disagreed. "I don't care what names Vickie calls me. I don't care what names the entire damn town calls me as long as I can be with you."

"You don't know what you're saying."

"Don't patronize me, Will. I *do* know. I know exactly what I'm saying." She fell silent for a moment, then she touched him again, laying her hand on his arm. "So do you," she whispered. "And it scares you, doesn't it?"

Scared? He closed his eyes, tilted his head back, and smiled bitterly. There had been odd moments ever since he'd met her when he'd been damn near terrified.

Looking down at her again, he said, "I'm trying to protect you, Celie."

"I don't want to be protected. I've been safe all my life, Will. I want something different now. I want you."

"You don't know what it's like to be looked at the way people look at me. You don't know how it feels to walk into a store and know that you're being watched just in case you decide to steal something. You can't imagine how it feels to be suspected in everything that goes wrong—every crime, every threat, every ugly scene. That's not the something different you're looking for."

"No," she softly agreed. "But you are."

In frustration he ran his fingers through his hair, tugging hard enough at it to sting. "Is it the sex, Celie? Is that what you want? Because if it is, I'll take you home and fuck you right now. I'll fuck you every night until I leave here if you'll just . . .''

"Quit wanting more?" she asked. "Quit expecting more? Quit caring more about you than about the people in town and what they think of me?"

"You can't care about me!" he insisted. "You hardly even know me!"

In the dim light he saw her smile, so sweet and serene. "I know the important things. I know you love Miss Rose. I know you treat people fairly. I know you're decent and honest. I know you treated Melanie far better than she deserved. I know you're truly concerned about saving me from myself."

"How about the really important things?" he taunted. His voice turned mean as he leaned close to her as, only moments ago, he had done to Vickie. "How about the fact that I sleep with women for money? How about the fact that I have an arrest record that would make your eyes pop out? How about the fact that I've been in jail in damned near every state I've ever lived in—and never got arrested for half the crimes I committed? How about the fact that I was in jail in Alabama when Miss Rose found me, that if I hadn't agreed to leave the state to come back here, there's a good chance I would have wound up in prison?"

He waited, his breathing shallow, for her to draw back, to step away from him, to show some doubt, some small measure of distrust. Anything would be enough. It would be what he needed to keep himself away from her, to keep himself from destroying her.

"Were you guilty in Alabama?" she asked calmly.

"What the hell difference does that make?"

"It makes all the difference in the world. Were you?"

He was the one who drew away, who backed off. "How many times are you going to believe me when I say I didn't do it? Everyone who's ever been arrested claims he's innocent, and most of the time they're lying. When are you finally going to believe that I'm lying?"

"When are you going to start lying to me?" she countered.

Faith. Trust. It had been a long time since anyone had either in him, but Celine did. She trusted him to tell her the truth, and she had faith that he wouldn't abuse her trust. It was simple psychology in action: treat a man the way you want him to act, and if he's any kind of man, he'll start to act that way. Give him trust, and he'll earn it. Have faith in him, and your faith will be rewarded.

He couldn't be the man she wanted, could never be the man she needed. But in his remaining time in Harmony, he could try. He could pretend. He could dream.

Leaning back against the nearest tree, he looked at her. "You give me credit for being a better man than I am."

Without invitation she moved closer, and his arms automatically opened to hold her. "You don't give yourself enough credit," she argued sweetly.

She believed that, but he knew better. He knew that she trusted him to be decent and honest when, in fact, he was incredibly selfish. Her faith in him was blind, seeing only good, discounting all the bad. She would learn the truth all too soon when he left Harmony again. When he took everything she could give and left her with nothing. When he broke her heart. Then she would see through her fantasies and foolishness to the bastard he really was.

Celine found Miss Rose, seated in a lawn chair beside Raymond and Frannie, and told her that she didn't need a ride home. Miss Rose studied her face, illuminated by fireworks overhead and citronella torches nearby, for a long time, then simply nodded. "I'll see you later."

What had she seen in that look? Celine wondered as she made her way to the park gate where Will was waiting. What could that sharp old lady read in her expression that no one else could see?

She put Miss Rose and everyone else out of her mind when she saw Will leaning against the brick arch at the entrance to the park. His white T-shirt stood out in the dark, much as her own white outfit did. He didn't speak as she approached, just shoved away from the brick and took her hand and walked alongside her.

Something had happened to him there in the woods, something she couldn't quite put her finger on. He seemed . . . defeated? No, not that. Never that. Resigned. He seemed resigned to being with her for however much time they had. He wasn't unwilling—she felt welcome in his arms, and she knew he wanted her. He just believed so seriously that it was wrong, especially wrong for her.

He believed his presence in her life could only hurt her. He believed, as Miss Rose had suggested, that she was too good for him. He believed she would surely suffer for their affair. At least he was right about that last part. If he left her, she surely was going to suffer. But better to have whatever pleasure she could and suffer then, than to let the pain start now.

The streets were pretty much deserted. Everyone was at the park watching the fireworks or late returning from their holiday weekend celebrations fishing or camping or partying in the city. All the way home, they saw only one car.

"Doesn't the heat bother you out there in the guesthouse?" she asked as they came upon the Kendall place.

Beside her Will chuckled. "I figure it can't be too much different from the fires of hell, and, honey, that's where I'm going to burn for what I'm doing to you."

As she unlocked the cottage's front door, she scowled at him, even though he couldn't see it. "You haven't done anything *to* me, Billy Ray," she drawled as she led the way inside. "I've been a willing participant—some might say even eager. Maybe we'll burn there together."

Inside he reached for the light switch, but she stopped him. Dropping her keys on a nearby table, she pushed the door shut with her foot, then went into the bedroom. She was standing by the window when he followed a moment later. He came only as far as the door, though.

"Are you sure about this, Celie?"

The hesitant tone of his voice said he wasn't, not at all. The honorable, noble part of him that he denied existed wanted to flee, to protect her, to save her. Thank heavens for the sensual, physical part that was hard and ready even as they spoke. "I'm sure, Will."

After a moment, he came to her, stopping in front, reaching past to raise the blinds so the moonlight could enter the room. Then he kissed her, just once, just for a moment, just enough to make her breasts hurt and the dampness collect between her thighs.

"You stand at this window a lot," he murmured, turning her so that she looked out, so he could move close to her in back. His erection was hard and hot against her, his entire body hot, matching her own heat, her own desire. "At night I can lie in bed over there and see you standing here, just like this."

His mouth was above her ear, his hands on her arms. Will could feel her shudder with each word. "I watch until you go to bed, and I get hard from wanting you, God, Celie, so damned much. I've never wanted any woman the way I want you. I've never wanted anything . . ." His voice, soft and seductive, trailed away into a kiss, and she groaned softly. Then he was releasing her, pulling away, kneeling behind her. He lifted each of her feet, removing her shoes, tossing them aside, and glided his hands along her legs, underneath her skirt and her thin cotton slip, not stopping until he reached her panties and pulled them away, too.

He stood up again, still behind her, catching her around the middle with one arm while with his free hand he unfastened his jeans. There was the rasp of his zipper, the rustle of clothing, and the soft moan—hers? or was it his own?— as he slid his erection, long, hot, thick enough to stretch her, against her bare buttocks.

"I lie over there, Celie," he whispered, his voice as ragged as her breathing, "and I think about making love with you, about touching you and kissing you and filling you, and sometimes I think I'll go crazy if I can't crawl inside you, deep inside you, like this."

He nudged her legs wider, parted her thighs, gently positioning her to take him, and then, with one long, slow thrust of his hips, he filled her, pressing until she'd taken all she could, gritting his teeth as her body adjusted to him, tightening, drawing him deeper still. She was so hot and wet, so ready for him, that he had to clamp down hard to keep from coming right off.

He hadn't lied to her. There were times when he thought he would go crazy without her. But right now, with his cock buried deep inside her, her bottom snug against his hips, her breasts, heavy and swollen, pressing against his arm, her head on his shoulder, her mouth seeking his, her body welcoming him, clutching around him so hard, he for damn sure was crazy. Crazy from the wanting, the needing. Crazy from the heat.

Crazy from the heart.

He wasn't ever going to make the damn stupid mistake of falling in love, of wanting the kind of life he couldn't have—settling down, raising kids, being respectable and upright. But if he ever got that stupid, if he was ever fool enough to want those things . . .

He stiffened as she moved against him, sliding her body along the length of his erection, then back again. His blood was hot, his muscles taut, his cock throbbing painfully for an instant, and then he emptied into her. He groaned and held her closer, and he felt her own orgasm, her body clenching and releasing him, felt her trembling against and all around him.

As he held her shivering in his arms, he thought once again, if he ever got really crazy stupid, it would surely be over Celine.

He undressed her slowly, carefully loosening each button, sliding her blouse off her shoulders, leaving it on the chair in the corner, coming back for her skirt and slip. Celine didn't show such patience, though, when he gave her the opportunity to remove his own clothes. She yanked his T-shirt over his head and tugged off his shoes and socks and jeans. Finesse arrived, though, when she reached his briefs. She removed them so slowly, with such gentle caresses, that, half groaning, half muttering, he damned her for it.

How many times could they make love, she wondered, before she got sore or he got soft? Three? Four? Not even a dozen would be enough. She had never been greedy in her life, had never craved attention or affection or money or power, but she was greedy now for Will's attention, for his affection, for his lovemaking. She was ready to beg shamelessly for him. Any part of him. All of him.

He closed the blinds and turned on the bedside lamp before

he joined her in the bed. In the entire six years she had lived here, no man had ever been in this bed. Will seemed to fill it, to crowd her. It was the sort of crowding she had been craving all her life.

"Thanks to your sister and me, you missed most of the fireworks."

"Depends on your definition. I certainly saw sparks in Vickie's eyes, and I know I saw shooting stars myself just a minute ago." She touched his jaw, rubbing her fingers over the stubble of beard there. "Besides, the fireworks in town are pretty regular. They come around every year whether you want them to or not."

"Right," he agreed. "You can catch them next time." But he ducked his head so she couldn't see his face. So she couldn't read what she knew he'd left unsaid: *Alone*. He didn't plan on being here next July. Once he left, he didn't plan on ever coming back.

Not even for her.

He slid his fingers into her hair and untied the colored ribbons that held it together in a ponytail. Lying on his stomach, half over her, his thigh between her legs, he played with the ribbons, trailing the dangling edges across her breasts, teasing her nipples, making her tremble. "You have beautiful hair," he murmured.

"Thank you. I'll keep it long just for you."

"Will you now?" He grinned, but it wasn't his usual arrogant smart-ass grin. This one was kind of sad. "And how long would you be willing to let it get?"

"How long would you be willing to stay around?"

His expression grew sadder. "I can't stay."

"Then the day you leave I'm cutting it all off, shorter even than yours." She meant it, too. She had flirted with the idea of cutting it for years, but this time she would do more than talk. She would carry through.

He aligned the ribbons, smoothing them through his fingers, then held them up, the ends tickling her belly. "Nice length," he remarked, the subject of her hair closed. "Perfect for some interesting things."

"Such as?"

He fastened them into a loose loop that he could tighten merely by pulling on the ends, then, grinning again, demanded, ''Give me your hand.''

Celine gave him a long, measuring look. The ribbons were a quarter inch wide and more than eighteen inches long. They were strong enough to restrain someone and to cause more than a little pain.

But this was Will. He would never deliberately hurt her.

She raised her right hand, and he guided it over her head and between two of the bars on the iron headboard. Without waiting for another command, she raised her left hand, stretching it through the next space. He pressed her hands together, then slid the soft loop around her wrists, tightening it only fractionally, only enough for her to know it was there. Then he slid into place above her, kneeling between her legs, spreading them wide apart as he pushed inside her.

He took her hard and fast, at the same time stroking her and sucking greedily at first one breast, then the other. Sensations filled her with swift intensity—arousal, need, the sweet feel of his thrusts, the painfully pleasurable throbbing his fingers were feeding between her thighs, the erotic strangeness of the bonds around her wrists, the stimulating knowledge that, while he was free to do what he wished with her, she couldn't touch him, couldn't pull him closer, couldn't draw him down for a kiss. She was open to him, vulnerable and completely trusting.

He came hard, too, his muscles straining, his eyes squeezed shut, his voice harsh, but he didn't stop, didn't soften. She felt the wet sticky warmth of his semen as he continued to rub her, as he sucked her nipples and pumped harder, deeper, stroking her, pushing her quickly into a helpless, shivering, pleading climax. There were no shooting stars this time, just a rush of pleasure so intense she cried with it, a satisfaction so complete that it dimmed everything else, even Will's hoarse groan as he filled her again.

For a time—seconds? minutes? She had no idea—a cozy, shadowy warmth enveloped her. The room, the night, the world outside—everything—seemed to disappear, leaving her alone and trembling with Will. Then finally her muscles stopped twitching, her heart slowed its pounding, and her breathing came easier. The shadows lifted, and she opened her eyes to find him staring down at her. She couldn't resist giving him a God-that-was-good grin. "Mercy."

Mercy indeed, Will thought. He should be on his knees right now begging for mercy on his wicked soul. "Are you all right?" he asked gruffly.

That grin again. "All right? Honey, I think I'm pretty damned good," she replied.

Avoiding her gaze, he reached above her head for the ribbons. Tying her hands had been done on impulse, an impulse that left him half-ashamed now. But before he could undo the ribbons, she slid her hands free and wrapped her arms around his neck. Just as a tug on the ends tightened the bonds, a tug on the loop loosened them. She could have freed herself at any time. Yet she had chosen not to.

"How does that line go?" she asked, nuzzling his jaw. " 'When she was good, she was very, very good, and when she was bad, she was better'? You are so *bad*, Will Beaumont." She kissed him, then tilted her head back so she could meet his gaze. "You know what was wrong with the other men in my life?"

"Yeah." He pulled her closer until they were both on their sides, facing each other, touching even though their skin was uncomfortably slick with sweat. "They weren't me."

It was amazing what air-conditioning, a woman's soft body, and incredible sexual satisfaction could do for a man's sleep, Will thought early the next morning. He couldn't remember the last time he'd slept so soundly, or the last time he'd spent a summer night in an air-conditioned room. He sure as hell couldn't remember—or maybe didn't want to remember—the last time he spent an entire night with a woman. That last time, whenever it was, he'd probably been paid for it in room and board or actual cash.

This time his payment had been pure soul-stealing pleasure.

It was early, the sun not yet up but the sky starting to lighten. He usually got up around six-thirty, showered and shaved and headed off for the Kendall mansion. He needed to get up early this morning, though, to slip out of Celine's house and back to his own before Miss Rose was awake; but he just couldn't bring himself to move yet.

Celine lay on her back beside him, her hair spread across her pillow and over the edge of the mattress. She was a restful sleeper. The only times she had moved during the night were when he'd told her to, when he had urged her with soft words and softer touches to roll onto her side so he could lie close behind her or when he had shifted to the other side and drawn her with him.

She was so damned beautiful that looking at her made his eyes hurt. If he had any sense, he would get dressed, sneak out of here, and hit the road this morning. He would be miles gone before Celine woke up, and he wouldn't stop until he'd gone far enough to forget her.

But just how far would that be? How many thousands of miles would he have to travel to escape her memory? How many endless days would he have to endure?

Finally he slipped from the bed, locating his clothes where she'd dropped them, quickly dressing. He didn't realize that she was awake and watching him until he bent over the bed to give her one last kiss before leaving.

"Where are you going?" she whispered sleepily.

"To the guesthouse."

"Why? Is it time to get up?"

"No. You have another hour or so."

She unwound the sheet that had wrapped around her and sat up, holding it demurely over her breasts. "Are you sneaking away so Miss Rose won't know you spent the night here?"

"Has it occurred to you that maybe I like a little privacy in my affairs?"

If his choice of words to describe what had happened here between them last night stung, she didn't let it show. "Has it occurred to you that I don't care if Miss Rose and the entire world knows about *this* affair?"

He sat down on the bed beside her, his hip bumping hers. "That's easy enough to say when no one knows, Celie. It's harder to live with when everyone does. When I'm gone, you'll be glad we kept it secret."

She was feeling stubborn today—he could see it in her clear green eyes. "Secrets are for shameful things, Will, and I'm not ashamed of you or myself or the things we do together." Then she smiled slowly, triumphantly. "Besides, someone does know—Vickie. I guarantee, you and I will be *the* hot new topic of conversation in town."

"Vickie won't say a word to anyone."

Celine's laughter was light and airy. "You don't know my sister."

"Not very well. But she knows me. She knows me well enough to know I don't make idle threats. She knows I'll make her regret ever being born if she tells anyone anything about you and me."

Sighing glumly, she drew her knees up and rested her arms, then her chin, on them. "Protection?"

"You need it, little girl."

"It's ironic. You have the reputation for being so wild and reckless, yet your behavior couldn't be any more circumspect."

And sweet, saintly Celine was behaving most wantonly. It *was* ironic. The folks in town would get a real shock out of it. He was having trouble dealing with it himself.

"I've got to go." He made it as far as the bedroom door before she stopped him.

"Hey, Will?" She smiled sweetly. "Ask Miss Rose sometime what she would think about you and me together. The old lady just might surprise you."

Which meant she and Miss Rose had already discussed it and, for some Godforsaken reason, Miss Rose was on her side. He gave her a reproving look. "You're a pain in the ass, Celie."

Her grin came quickly and hit him like a punch in the stomach. "Funny. You give me an ache in my—"

When he gave her a sharp, warning look, she broke off, skipped what she'd been about to say, then continued. "Why don't you come back here and take your clothes off and ease it for me?"

He couldn't help grinning back at her and promising, "Tonight, little girl. I'll get you tonight."

Everything was quiet outside. He was carrying his shoes,

and the grass was damp and cool beneath his feet. He liked early summer mornings in the South, before the heat and humidity became unbearable, before most people were up and about. There was something peaceful, soothing, about these times.

But someone besides him was up and about. Sitting in a huddle on the guesthouse steps, watching him in the dim light, was Jared Robinson.

Guilt swept through Will. He should have left Celine's earlier. He should have taken the time to put on his shoes. He should have taken more care to not get caught.

But if Jared recognized the implications of Will's early-morning barefoot journey from Celine's house to his own, he gave no sign of it. He just sat there, his shoulders slumped, his eyes downcast.

Will sat down beside him. "Hey, Jared. Been waiting long?"

"A couple hours."

"I'm sorry about your mom."

"Yeah."

What else could he say? Will wondered. What was it a fifteen-year-old boy needed to hear when his mother had been brutally murdered? He tried to remember the things people had said to him when his father died: we're sorry, our prayers are with you, he's gone to be with the Lord. None of it had comforted him. The sympathy of people he barely knew hadn't mattered to him, and neither had their prayers. As for the last one, it had only angered him. *He* had needed his father a hell of a lot more than God had. All the words he'd heard back then had been meaningless, and he couldn't think of anything different. So he said nothing. He just sat there and waited.

Finally Jared glanced at him. "The funeral is tomorrow. Will you come?"

Will had to swallow hard to keep from blurting out a refusal. He hadn't been to a funeral since his father's, and he certainly wouldn't be welcome at this one. "I don't think your grandfather would like that," he said cautiously.

"My grandfather probably won't even notice. He's not taking this very well. He had to identify her—her body, and ae hasn't said a word since then. I'm handling everything, and I'd like you to come. She—she liked you. She said you were nice to her when she came out here. Not many people were, you know.''

Nice to her. What had he done? Called her a whore and a liar, accused her of blackmail and criticized her for being a lousy mother. Yeah, he'd really been nice.

"All right, Jared," he agreed softly. "I'll come. But if it upsets your grandfather . . ."

The boy nodded in understanding. "Miss Celine, too—would you ask her? People will come mostly because they know Grandpa and Grandma or out of curiosity, but I'd like Miss Celine to be there, too."

"I'll ask her."

They sat in silence a few minutes longer, then Jared said, "She kept telling me things were going to change. She said she would get a regular job, move out of there, and find a better place to live."

He sighed softly and stared off into the distance. There was more he wanted to say, and Will waited quietly for it.

"She kept saying that as soon as she had the money, she would go someplace better, but she never had the money because she was always spending it on herself, always wasting it on her drugs and her booze and her parties." There was a break in his voice then, followed by another pause and a shaky breath before continuing. "Damn it, Will, I'm sorry she's dead, I am, but I'm mad at her for letting it happen! I'm so mad, I hate her for it, and I know it's wrong, I know it wasn't her fault! But she *promised*, she promised she would stop drinking and quit the drugs and settle down and live right! She was always promising, but she never even tried, and, oh, God, I hate her for it!''

By the time he finished, tears were pouring down his face and Will was wishing he was anywhere in the world but here. He'd never offered much comfort to anyone. He didn't even know how, especially to a boy who was almost a man, but he couldn't just sit there. Acting on instinct, he pulled Jared into his arms and remembered, for the first time in more than twenty years, the one thing no one, not even his mother, had offered him when his father died: a shoulder to cry on.

As they sat there, Jared's tears worsening, then easing, he remembered one other thing he'd forgotten: fifteen was nowhere near manhood. For all his maturity, for all his intelligence and grown-up behavior, Jared was still just a child, a child whose father had never wanted him and whose mother had left him years before she'd died.

The sobs faded slowly, although an occasional hiccough and shiver remained. Soon, even those were gone, and the morning was still again except for the sound of the birds in the tree. "Jared?"

When there was no answer, Will looked down at him. His eyes were closed, his mouth slightly open. He was asleep, probably for the first time since hearing the news.

They were still sitting there when Celine came out of the house. Only a moment later, before she had even crossed the yard to them, Miss Rose came out of her own house and started toward them. Neither of them seemed to see anything at all unusual about him sitting with his arms around a scrawny kid who was almost as tall as he was.

"Is he all right?" Celine asked, kneeling a few steps below them and reaching out to brush a lock of hair from Jared's forehead.

"He's asleep," Will replied.

"Why don't you bring him on over to the house?" Miss Rose suggested. "He looks like he hasn't gotten much sleep since Sunday. I can keep an eye on him while you two are gone to work."

Will started to refuse, to tell her that he would just carry Jared inside the guesthouse, then let Roger know he wouldn't be in until later today. On second thought, though, Miss Rose's idea did sound better. Jared wasn't used to leaning on someone else. What was only natural under the circumstances might make him uncomfortable when he awoke.

As soon as the boy was settled in one of Miss Rose's guest rooms, Will left the house, drawing Celine outside with him. "He wants us to come to Melanie's funeral tomorrow," he said. "He wants someone there besides his grandparents' friends and the gossips."

She agreed without hesitation. Of course she would. She was that kind of person. She would be welcomed there. No one would whisper about her behind her back. No one would search her face and Jared's for some sign of resemblance, no matter how minor, no matter how imagined.

She started to go back inside, but she hesitated on the steps. "Will? Why did he come to you?"

"Do you find that so odd?"

Her smile was faint. "You're certainly the person I would turn to if I needed to be comforted. But I was under the impression in the grocery store that he didn't think much of you."

"Maybe he's changing his mind." But he relented under her steady gaze. "We've been talking. He's come out here and to the mansion. I think he knows I'm not his father, but he doesn't want to admit that Melanie lied to him. He's been disillusioned too many times before."

She opened the screen door leading to Miss Rose's porch, then glanced back at him. "Jared would have been lucky to have you for a father, Will. You would make a good one."

Then she went back inside, leaving him standing there, staring at the empty porch.

"Melanie Robinson's funeral is tomorrow at one o'clock," Frannie remarked over drinks beside the pool. "I suppose we should go."

Raymond didn't bother responding. His wife knew their obligations as well as he did. Jock was a friend and a customer. Out of respect for him, they would attend his daughter's funeral and say all the right things and make all the sympathetic offers. Even if they didn't mourn the dead woman. Even if her dying had probably been best for everyone. Even if it had solved problems for everyone.

"It says here that her apartment was ransacked," Frannie said, her attention focused on the Harmony weekly newspaper. A murder was the biggest news this town had in years, and they had devoted much of the front page to it. "That some money, earrings, a Mardi Gras mask, and other personal belongings were missing." She laid the paper in her lap and gazed at him. "Who in the world would steal a Mardi Gras mask? You can buy them cheap all over the city."

Raymond gave her an annoyed look. "Who would choose

someone like Melanie Robinson to rob? We're not talking
about a real bright mind here. If you were a thief in New
Orleans looking for someplace to rob, would you go to a
trashy apartment in the Quarter, or would you travel a few
miles to the Garden District or some middle-class place in
between?''

"And how do you know Melanie Robinson lived in a trashy
apartment in the Quarter?''

His curse was soft and frustrated. "Everyone in town knew
she lived in the Quarter, and, hell, the woman was about as
trashy as you could get. She certainly wasn't living in some
classy place like this.''

"You're talking about your good friend Jock's only daughter,'' Frannie reminded him sweetly, too sweetly. She didn't
like Jock Robinson and had never cared for Raymond's
friendship with the man.

As much as he loved her, Raymond didn't give a damn
whether she approved or not. It suited him to maintain their
friendship. Jock served his purpose and served it well.

Finishing his drink, he got to his feet. "I have work to
do, darling,'' he said, bending to press a kiss to her forehead.
"When Mae has dinner ready, call me.''

He went inside, welcoming the coolness of the house after
the evening heat. July was not the time to be leisurely sipping
drinks on the terrace, but Frannie didn't seem to mind the
heat. She found something earthy, sensual, about it, and he
usually found something sensual in her enjoyment of it.

But not tonight. He had work to do tonight.

In his office he refilled his glass with bourbon and water,
then sat down at his desk and unlocked his briefcase. The
business checks for his mother's new account had come in
last week, and Marianne White, following his instructions,
had sent them to him instead of notifying Rose or Roger
Woodson over at the motel.

He removed them from his briefcase, along with the signature card Billy Ray had finally signed. His signature was a
scrawl—William R. Beaumont—with only the *W* and the
l's, the *R* and the *B* clearly legible. His writing was sloppy
and undisciplined, awkward looking. Of course, the son of

a bitch was probably out of practice. He probably rarely wrote anything besides his name on an occasional paycheck. He had no one to write letters to and had never held a job that required correspondence. With the life he'd lived, he could be totally illiterate, unable to accomplish even this scrawl, and it wouldn't have made any difference.

Drawing a sheet of paper and a pen from a drawer, Raymond propped the card at an angle in front of him and began copying the name. It wasn't easy to be so sloppy, not when his natural inclination was to form the letters neatly, properly. After a page of tries, he was closer to the original, but far from being satisfied.

When a knock sounded at his office door, he slid the sheet underneath the desk blotter, then called an invitation. It was Mae. "Dinner is ready, Mr. Kendall."

"I'll be there in a moment," he replied, giving her a friendly smile, hiding any hint that she'd interrupted something important.

When she closed the door again, he opened the box of checks. Woodson had preferred the convenience of wallet-style checks, bless his heart, rather than carrying around a book-sized register of business checks. The wallet-style made it so easy to flip through, to remove a blank check here, another there. He chose them from the books at the bottom of the box, aware that it would be weeks, maybe even months, before Woodson would reach those particular books, before the absence of these particular checks would be noticed. By then, it would be too late for Billy Ray.

He returned the books of checks to the box in the proper order, put them back in his briefcase and locked it, then placed the loose checks and the page filled with Billy Ray's name in his safe. Now there was only one thing to do before joining Frannie for dinner.

It had taken him several discreet phone calls to get the name he needed, several calls more to make the arrangements. Now he needed just one more call to set things in motion.

He didn't identify himself when the man answered. In a cautiously quiet voice, he simply said, "Start tonight. Do it the way we planned."

He had just returned the phone to its cradle and withdrawn his hand when Frannie walked in unannounced. "Mae's dinner is getting cold."

"I was just about to come."

She laughed throatily. "Oh, I've heard *that* before." She gave his desk, clean and empty, the onceover. "I thought you had work to do."

"It didn't take long."

"Bank work?"

"What other kind is there?"

She came around the desk and perched on the edge in front of him. "I thought I heard you on the phone."

"Eavesdropping, darling?"

Her smile was sweet and charming and the slightest bit challenging. She knew damned well she'd heard him on the phone, but she was willing to let him lie if he wanted.

Raymond knew better. A man didn't lie to Frannie without risking the consequences. While he wasn't above a little deceit now and then, he saved his lies to his wife for the important things. He didn't waste time or energy on the little ones. "I was taking care of business."

"It sounded rather foreboding. Would it by chance have something to do with Billy Ray?"

He met her gaze openly. "Yes, it would."

When she smiled again, he saw the satisfaction in it—and the arousal. She knew he was using his resources—his power, his money, his connections—to get rid of Billy Ray, and it turned her on. She was interesting that way. She didn't require sweet kisses or heated caresses to get aroused, although those worked, too. A display of power, a threat, anger, or a show of force—those things made her just as hot, maybe even hotter. When they argued, when he lost his temper and slapped her or hurt her, she was instantly wet and ready to beg. When he hurt someone else, that aroused her, too. When he eventually got rid of Billy Ray once and for all, that would make her damn near insatiable.

Some of their best sex had involved pain and anger and loss of control. She liked it that way, liked to be overpowered, to be bound with silk cords that left no mark, to be forced to spread her legs and submit to his greater strength. She liked to be raped and mistreated; and that was fine with him, because he damn sure liked raping her.

He stood up and found himself close to her. "Dinner is ready," he reminded her as she slid her skirt up, then took his hand and guided it between her thighs. She was hot and wet and opened to him immediately.

"Yes, it is." Her eyes had gone dark, her voice husky.

He pushed two fingers inside her, then drew them out and rubbed her own moisture over her, bringing her close to climax but stopping at the edge. "We'd better go. We don't want to offend Mae."

Frannie gave him a long, cool look, then murmured, "Bastard," before she shoved his hand away, pushed her skirt down, and walked out of the room. He knew as he followed that she wasn't really angry. They would sit at the dinner table, him hard, her wet, and they would eat and discuss the usual things—his work, her social affairs, maybe their next vacation—and then they would go upstairs to their room. She would curse him for leaving her hanging like that, and he would slap her—though not her face. That was her only rule: there could be no marks that would show.

No, he would tear her blouse open and slap her breasts. That was how she liked it—the little stinging blows that made her beautiful small breasts swell, that left red prints that were slow to fade, that bruised the tender skin around her long, spiky nipples. He would slap her until she pleaded, and then he would make her suck him, would fill her mouth until she damn near choked on him.

Then he would rape her—anally this time, he thought with a smile as he held her chair for her. She always fought that the hardest, always cried over that the hardest and always came that way the hardest. Afterward, she would be so sated, so incredibly satisfied, that she would probably play a little game of her own, would make him do his own pleading. He liked being the punisher. But he also liked being punished.

He sat down, spread a white damask napkin across his lap, covering his throbbing erection, and smiled across the table at her.

"And how was your day, darling?"

* * *

Celine sat at her desk Wednesday afternoon, staring at the round clock high on the wall, watching the second hand sweep around and around. Will was supposed to meet her any moment now, and they were going to Melanie's funeral together. He really didn't want to go, he'd told her last night, but he couldn't find a way to refuse Jared.

And the man kept insisting he was a no-good bastard, she thought with a tender smile. A person certainly couldn't tell it from the way he treated Jared or the way he treated her. No one had ever been so careful, so gentle, with her. No one had ever worried about her. Even Richard, who had professed to love her, hadn't been more than vaguely apologetic when he'd dumped her for Vickie. Her parents, who also claimed to love her, had always assumed that she would be fine on her own, that she would take care of herself, that she needed no one's concern, that she needed no one else to look out for her. And Vickie, her sister, who by nature should love her, had destroyed her happiness once, and she would do it again if she could.

But Will cared. He worried. He wanted to protect her.

The minute hand on the clock had moved forward one more unit, making him officially late. She wasn't concerned. He'd insisted on going to work this morning, which meant he'd had to take off, go home, shower, and change. She had left him the keys to her car so he could drive into town, but she didn't know if he would. The church was only a few blocks from the library, the cemetery only a few blocks beyond that.

He seemed to be developing a tendency toward being late—at least, where she was concerned. He had come over late last night, long after Miss Rose had turned out the lights and gone to bed; and instead of going inside, he had invited her out to sit on the screened porch in the quiet night. They had gone to the side away from Miss Rose's house, and they had made love there. She had initiated it without really intending to, had moved to sit astride his lap, teasing him, trying to provoke him into laughing. She hadn't realized how quickly he would get aroused, how quickly *she* would. She hadn't given any thought at all to how easy it would be to lift her nightgown and unzip his jeans and take him deep inside herself. No matter how innocent its start, she certainly had enjoyed its completion.

He had slept with her but only for a few hours. Late in the night, when he'd thought she was sleeping soundly, he had slipped from the bed, gotten dressed, and returned to his own bed. Knowing her protests would do no good, she had pretended to sleep and let him go.

Now he was late again.

"Miss Celine?"

Drawing her gaze from the clock, she focused on Millie.

"Will you tell Jared . . . Tell him I'm sorry about his mama, would you?"

"Of course I will."

"Will this change anything? Will he still live here with his grandparents?"

"I'm sure he will, Millie." Celine shrugged. "He doesn't have anyplace else to go now."

Millie looked as if she wanted to say something else, but the opening of the door stopped her. She and Celine both turned to watch Will walk in. His hair was still damp from a shower, slicked back with a few strands falling across his forehead. What caught Celine's attention was his clothing. She had seen him in jeans and T-shirts and stripped naked but nothing else. Today he wore a white dress shirt, the long sleeves rolled up practically to his elbows, dark gray trousers, and new black shoes. While he always looked fine, today he looked like Richard. Like Raymond. Like every other businessman in this town. He didn't look like someone to be watched with suspicion. He certainly didn't look like someone who'd been arrested in practically every state he'd ever been.

Last night he had told her about the arrests: arrests for fighting and getting drunk and having no place to stay. None of them, with the exception of the last one, of the claim that he'd robbed those women in Alabama, had been important. None of them, including that last one, mattered to her. It said something for the man he was that they made such a difference to him. Stubborn and prideful, Miss Rose had called him. Yes, indeed, she thought, smiling as he warily approached her and Millie. He was that.

"Will, this is Millie Andrews. She fills in for me. Millie, this is—"

"I know who he is," the girl interrupted with a scowl.

Celine gave her a surprised look. Millie had never been rude a day in her life, not to people who deserved it and especially not to someone who didn't. Then she remembered the girl's crush on Jared, and her surprise faded. "No, you don't, Millie," she said, her voice gently chiding as she got to her feet. "This is Will Beaumont, Jared's friend." She emphasized the last word, trusting Millie to fill in what she left out. *Friend. Not father.*

Years of her mother's teachings took over, and, without raising her head, Millie murmured by rote, "I'm pleased to meet you, Mr. Beaumont."

Will looked from her to Celine, and she saw the twitch of a grin that he controlled. "Yeah, right," he said drily. "I can see that." That earned him a look from the girl that freed his grin. "We'd better be going, Celie."

She had always liked that nickname. From the first time he'd used it, sitting there on the guesthouse steps that hot Saturday morning, when he'd called her prissy, then laughed and said in that sexy drawl, "I think I'll call you Celie," she had liked it. But she liked it even more now that he'd used it in front of someone else. Now that it was no longer a secret.

She got her purse from her desk drawer. "I don't know how long this will take, Millie."

"I can take care of things."

They were halfway to the door when Millie spoke again. "Miss Celine? You won't forget . . . ?"

Celine smiled gently. "No, I won't forget."

Outside he offered her the keys to her car, parked in the library lot, but she refused them. "Let's walk instead."

"Millie," he remarked as they turned toward the church. "What a name to stick a kid with."

"It's a family name. We're big on that down here. Millie's

named after her grandmother. I'm named after my great-grandmother.''

"I'm named after my grandfather, and my father was named after *his* grandfather.''

"Does that mean if you ever have a son you have to name him Claude?'' Celine asked, trying the name in her mind. All she could do was agree with Will: what a name to stick a kid with.

"I'm not having any kids, Celie. Not ever.'' His voice was quiet, his manner serious. He didn't have to say anything else to get the rest of his message across. *I'm warning you for your own good. Don't expect anything but sex from me. Don't hope for anything else.*

She understood. She just chose to ignore it. "I like your clothes.''

He glanced down at his brand-new clothes, then shrugged awkwardly. "Somehow jeans didn't seem appropriate. So what was it that Millie didn't want you to forget?''

"A message for Jared.''

"She likes him?''

"Yes.''

"Does he like her?''

"I'm not sure he's really even noticed her.''

"That's because he likes *you*. Even though he's not my kid, we have that much in common.'' He gave her a long look that made her feel warm and naked, followed by a lascivious grin. "We surely do like you.''

Chapter Twelve

When they reached the church parking lot, it was full. In spite of the heat, small groups of people stood outside, using the last few minutes before the service started to exchange gossip and news. Celine saw her mother, dressed in dramatic black, and standing alongside her, glowering at them as if she'd just spotted the enemy, was Vickie. Her sister was one of the gossips Will had referred to yesterday. She'd never had a kind thing to say about Melanie while she was alive, but here she'd shown up to mourn her death.

Right.

She also saw Raymond, talking with Richard, John Stuart, and Reverend Davis. Raymond gave Will a look sharp with loathing. It didn't ease by much when he turned it on her, not until she offered him a cool smile and a greeting that he was forced to acknowledge.

He excused himself from his companions and blocked their way on the second step. "What are you doing here?" he demanded in a low voice. "You've got balls, Billy Ray, showing up here like this after everything you did to Melanie. You go on home before the family sees you. They've got enough trouble. They don't need you adding to it."

Celine felt sort of tingly sick inside, her attention shifting from Will to Raymond to the few bystanders who had overheard, including Vickie. It was exactly this sort of reaction that had convinced Will he should stay away from her. She would hate it anytime, but especially today when he was here only because Jared had wanted him. She was about to explain that when Jared himself appeared at Will's side.

"Don't worry about it, Mr. Kendall," he said, his voice dull, his eyes shadowed. "I asked Will and Miss Celine to come."

Raymond's manner changed then, from malevolent to pat-him-on-the-head condescending. "You shouldn't have done that, Jared. You know how your grandparents feel about him. You know they won't want him here."

Jared, looking nothing like the child he was, leveled a stone-cold look on Raymond. "She was nothing to you, Mr. Kendall, but she was *my* mother. I can choose who I want to be at her funeral, and if you don't like it, you can leave."

"Now you listen to me, young man—"

Will moved a step closer, and Celine instinctively slid her arm around Jared's shoulders and pulled him a step away. "No, Raymond, *you* listen to *me*," Will said, his voice so low no one else could hear. "Your argument is with me, not the kid. He's having a tough enough time as it is. Leave him alone or . . ."

"Or what?" Raymond demanded. "Are you threatening me, Billy Ray?"

Will's reply was little more than a whisper, and it was so cold that it made Celine shiver. "I'm promising, Raymond. Leave him alone." He stood there a moment, waiting until he was sure his warning had sunk in; then he gestured for Celine and Jared to go ahead of him up the steps.

"Well, well, so you finally found some fatherly instincts," Raymond taunted as they walked away. "It only took you . . . what? Fifteen years?"

Celine stiffened, and at her side so did Jared. She didn't dare glance back to see the look on Will's face until they were through the doors and the lobby and inside the cool, quiet sanctuary.

"Jared, go on up and sit with your grandparents," he said stiffly, his expression hard and shuttered.

"I'd rather—"

"Go on. We'll talk later."

Jared sighed heavily. "All right. Thanks for coming."

Celine watched him walk away, then looked at Will again. "You go on up and sit with your family, too."

"My family's not seated yet," she said coolly.

"Damn it, Celine—"

"Such language in the house of God," she chided. "We can sit back here." Knowing he wasn't following her and ignoring that knowledge, she walked over to the back pew on the right and sat down with just enough space for him on the end.

A moment later he did join her, still angry. "I don't want to sit with you."

"You just walked down the main street of town with me," she calmly reminded him.

"That was different."

She slid over a bit so she could see him more clearly. "What are you so angry about? You know Raymond's going to get his digs in every chance he gets. You should expect it by now."

"I do expect it," he retorted. "When I'm alone. Not when . . ." He broke off and looked away.

Not when someone else was there to witness it. Not when *she* was there. His damnable pride again, she thought grimly.

The mourners outside began filtering in, making their way to their usual seats. Annalise stopped at the end of the pew, smiling absently at Will, and greeted her daughter. "Mama, you remember Will Beaumont," Celine said politely.

"Will?" Annalise peered at him through her glasses, a perplexed look on her face. "No, I don't believe—"

"She means Billy Ray, Mama," Vickie interrupted sarcastically, glaring at both of them.

"Oh. Oh, yes, Billy Ray. So you go by Will now. I'd heard you were back." She smiled one of her forgetful smiles, then said, "Celine dear, aren't you going to come up front and sit with us?"

"No. I'm sitting back here with Will."

"All right, dear. It's nice meeting you, Will. Come along, Vickie, Richard. Reverend Davis is ready to start."

With another hate-filled look from Vickie, followed by a

similar one from Richard, they made their way to their regular pew near the front.

Celine sighed softly. She thought briefly about pointing out to Will that Annalise hadn't been appalled to see them together, but thought better of it. He just might point out that she had also blithely assumed that, rather than stay with him, Celine would follow them up to the family pew, where she *belonged*.

When she finally looked at him, she found him watching her, a grimly amused look on his face. "I really do think they must have found you somewhere. You can't possibly come from that family."

"I'm a throwback to an earlier generation," she said with a teasing smile.

"To a saner generation," he amended. "So that's Jourdan."

"Yes."

"And you wanted to marry him."

"I thought I did."

"You were in love with him."

There was a strange edge to his voice when he made the last flat statement. She gazed up at him, but he was staring straight ahead so all she could see was his profile. "Do you ever get jealous, Will?" she asked, aware of the wistful quality in her voice.

"Answer my question," he demanded.

She didn't bother to point out that he hadn't actually asked a question. Instead, she quietly replied, "Yes, I thought I loved him. When I got old enough to know better, I knew I hadn't." After a brief pause, she continued. "Now answer mine."

Finally he shifted his gaze to her. "Honey, I get jealous when you even look at another man. If I stayed around here long enough to see you marry someone else, I would probably kill him."

She softly replied, "If you stay around here long enough, Will, you just might have to marry me yourself."

"Why?" His expression turned immeasurably bleak. "Because once I've finished tarnishing your saintly halo, no one else will have you?"

"No," she whispered. "Because after being with you, how could I want anyone else?"

The plot where Melanie was being laid to rest was in the center section of the cemetery, far from the cooling shade of the live oaks, magnolias, and sycamores that dotted the grounds. The mourners—Mourners? Who in this crowd, besides that brat of hers, was actually sorry that the bitch was dead? No, those who had come to pay their respects to her parents, those who had come to gawk, were gathered under the funeral home canopy, talking, waiting for the graveside rites to begin.

It was hot, so damn hot. The flowers that draped the casket and covered the ground in front of it were starting to wilt, starting to smell unpleasant. They should get this last formality underway, should get Melanie in the ground, cover her with dirt, and let everyone get out of the sun. Hell, they should have just tossed her fat, ugly body in the town dump and been done with it.

At last Reverend Davis stepped forward and began his final remarks. The family—Jock, his mealymouthed wife, and the boy—looked appropriately grieved. Everyone else just looked hot and bored.

Except Billy Ray. He was somber—not grieving, but sorry. He was sorry pathetic little Melanie was dead.

Damn him. He ruined what should have been a perfect crime. So far he hadn't said anything, hadn't let on that he knew anything. Maybe he really didn't—but with him, who could tell? He was still a problem. He still had to be dealt with.

He stood there with Celine, far enough away to make it look as if it was just coincidence that they'd wound up side by side. As if everyone hadn't seen them come walking up to the church, and later to the cemetery, together. Everyone had noticed that Celine sat at the back with him instead of joining her family up front. Soon they would leave here together, as everyone expected.

Last night he hadn't been trying to keep her at a distance. No, last night he hadn't been able to get enough of her. Of course, he hadn't known he had an audience then, hadn't suspected that someone with a particular interest in him could be hiding in the woods and watching the Kendall place. Jesus, screwing on the porch like a bitch in heat, right out there in plain sight where anyone who'd come driving down the road could have seen them—that was what he'd brought sweet Celine to.

Maybe he truly didn't know what he'd seen in the Quarter the day Melanie had died. Maybe he simply didn't yet realize what he had seen. Maybe he would remain in the dark. Maybe he would leave Harmony without ever making the connection between what he'd seen—*whom* he'd seen—and Melanie's death.

And maybe all that was merely wishful thinking. If he did make the connection, if he did realize exactly what it was he knew . . .

Then, like Melanie, he would have to die.

As soon as the final prayer was finished with a chorus of amens, Celine left to express her condolences to the Robinsons. Will took advantage of the moment to locate his father's grave. He couldn't remember the last time he'd been here much more than sixteen years ago. Some long-ago Memorial Day—Decoration Day, Miss Rose had preferred to call it—when she had dragged him along with her, loading him down with wreaths for the graves of relatives and friends. He had hated the place, the tradition, and the overpowering sweetness of the flowers, and when he had grown old enough—or was it smart enough?—he had always managed to be elsewhere on that day.

In spite of all those long years passed, he remembered exactly where his father's grave was: in the westernmost section of the cemetery, bordered on the east by the drive, on the north and south by broad curving sidewalks, and on the west by a five-foot-tall brick wall. It was marked with a square marble tombstone, paid for, he thought, by Miss Rose after Paulette had left town without taking care of that one last obligation.

The plot, neatly maintained, gave no hint that this man's last loving relative had neglected it for years. The small rectangle of grass was weeded, and a vase of yellow carnations, drooping now in the midday sun, was in the holder in front. Miss Rose's doing again, he thought, seeing a similar arrangement on Wynn's grave in the next section over.

Claude Michel Beaumont. At some point in Beaumont history, the French blood had been strong, but over the years it had become diluted. As a child, Will had gone to sleep to the tunes of old French lullabies, and he'd grown up knowing a few French phrases, learned from his father, who had learned them from *his* father. Both the songs and the words were long since forgotten. He spoke no language but English, had no customs, followed no traditions. He had no family and never would have one. When he died, this particular line of Beaumonts would cease to exist.

Does that mean if you ever have a son you have to name him Claude?

He stared hard at the grave marker, trying to ignore Celine's soft, dangerous voice in his mind.

If you stay around here long enough, Will, you just might have to marry me yourself.

He couldn't think about that—couldn't even consider the possibility. It *wasn't* a possibility, he reminded himself. He had accepted that years ago. He had lived most of his life alone, and he would live the rest of it, however ungodly long that was, the same way. He would die alone.

Five years ago—hell, five *weeks* ago, that had been acceptable. A fact of the life he'd chosen to live. So why did it hurt so damned much now?

A shadow fell across his father's grave, a long skinny one that hesitated, then came closer. When he looked up, it was Jared who stood there. The boy read the name on the tombstone, then glanced at him. "Is that your dad?"

Will nodded.

"Were you close to him?"

"Yes, I was. He was a good man. He spent a lot of time with me, teaching me, telling me stories. He was always happy. He loved life, loved his family and his friends and his job and his land."

"He sounds neat."

"Yeah, he was. I loved him," he admitted, surprised that

he could, surprised that he wasn't embarrassed by it. "I hated God and the entire world when he died."

"How did it happen?"

"A car wreck. He was on his way home from work, and someone hit him head-on. He was dead before the cops got there." He shoved his hands into his hip pockets, then looked around. Most of the mourners were gone. Celine had gotten waylaid by some white-haired old lady who was holding her by the wrist while they talked.

He shouldn't wait for her. She was perfectly capable of making it back to the library on her own, and he had a job to get back to. He should tell Jared he was sorry, say good-bye, and walk along the winding drive to the gate. He should keep on walking. But he knew he wasn't going to. Not now. Not until he had to.

"Did Celine give you Millie's message?"

"Yeah."

"You two friends?"

"Not really. She's all right, I guess. She's real smart, but kind of plain. Kind of weird."

"She's going to be a real beauty someday."

Jared gave him a disbelieving look. "Millie Andrews? At the library?"

"She reminds me of Celine when she was a kid. She had hair as straight as a board and legs a mile too long, and she was all awkward and graceless. Look how she turned out."

Jared turned to look at her. "She's pretty, all right."

Smiling, Will laid his hand on the boy's shoulder. "Son, she's a whole lot more than pretty. She's downright beautiful." Then he realized what he'd said—*son*—and his smile faltered.

"It's all right," Jared said quietly. "I know you told the truth. I know you're not my father."

"How do you know that?"

He shrugged, shook his head, blew his breath out in a sudden whoosh. "I don't have any proof, but . . . my mother lied. Always. About everything. She was so happy when she left here a couple of weeks ago. She had come to ask for money from my father, and she believed she was going to get it." He subjected Will to a serious appraisal. "You look halfway respectable today, but there's no way you'd have the kind of money she wanted, the kind of money that would make her that happy."

Will lifted his gaze skyward, staring for a moment into the spreading branches of a live oak hung with Spanish moss. For the first time in his life having nothing had stood him in good stead. It might not mean much to anyone else, but it was enough to convince Jared of the truth. That meant two of the only three people he cared about in this town believed him. Two people trusted him, had faith in him. How long had it been since that had happened? *Forever. Never.*

"I'd better go," Jared said, watching as another couple—relatives, Will assumed—led his grandparents to the family car provided by the funeral home. "I'm glad you came."

"Are you going to be okay?"

He didn't answer right away, didn't answer lightly at all. "I guess so. It's not like I have a choice, you know? She's dead, and I'm not." He was thoughtful for a moment, then he shrugged. "I'll be all right."

"If you need anything . . ." Will shrugged. "You can get hold of me through Celine."

Jared nodded and walked away. At the edge of the road, though, he looked back. "Can I come by the Kendall place sometime when you're working?"

"Anytime." Will watched him hurry to the car. He met Celine halfway there and paused long enough for her to hug him, then he disappeared inside the big black limousine with its tinted windows, and the car drove away. Will envied Jared the hug, even though he would get his own in time. In private.

"Claude Michel. Claude would be a tough name for a boy today, but Michel . . . Michael . . . that's nice." Celine bent to straighten a sagging bloom, pushing its stem deeper into the vase. When she stood up, she laughed at his scowl. "Yes, I know. You're never planning to have any children. But unless you also plan to give up sex for the rest of your life, there's always that possibility. You know, nothing's a hundred-percent foolproof."

He stared at her. "Are you hinting . . . ?"

"No. I'm just suggesting that you should be a little more open to possibilities."

He gestured toward the gate. "Are you ready to go back to work?"

They walked to the end of the sidewalk, then along the blacktop road, both pointedly ignoring the work going on at Melanie's grave. They hadn't gone far, maybe a block or so, when a car pulled up alongside. Though there were no markings on the side, the tall antenna in back and the blue light on the dash made it unmistakably a police car.

Sheriff Franklin stopped a few feet ahead, got out and faced them over the roof of the car. "Miss Celine," he said with a respectful nod. "Beaumont. I thought I might find you over this way."

"Is something wrong, Sheriff?" Celine asked, her smile even, her manner friendly in a way that was beyond Will. He knew she had to be wondering how the sheriff's appearance was connected to *him*, knew there could be no doubt in her mind that it *was* connected. This was part of what he'd wanted to protect her from—the suspicion, the distrust, the eagerness to lay blame. This was his life. And she was foolish enough to think she wanted to share it.

"I'm on my way out to the old Kendall place," Franklin replied. "I understand you work there, Beaumont."

"Yes, I do." Three little words, but he had to force them out past the tightness in his throat. What had happened at the house, he wondered, and how were they going to pin it on him?

"I just got a call from Roger Woodson. It seems there's some items missing from the work site. I'm going out to make a report. You might as well come along since I'll be needing to talk to you, too."

Some items missing. All the tools, supplies, and equipment left at the house overnight were securely locked in a sturdy storage shed on the side lawn. He had a key to it. He had unlocked it himself this morning. His fingerprints would be all over everything in there. He felt sick deep inside, so sick that he could taste it. He had lived this scene before, had lived through variations of it over and over. It made sense

that eventually he would become used to it—to the doubtful
looks and the accusing questions, to the suspicion and the
condemnation—but he never had. He couldn't face a cop
any more easily now than he'd been able to the first time
he'd ever been arrested, when he was eighteen and in a brawl.

"Will's got my car, Sheriff Franklin," Celine said, still
just as polite and friendly as you please, as if she didn't even
notice that he was dying inside. "How about if he just meets
you out there?"

Franklin hesitated only a moment before agreeing. Will
started to intervene, to step forward and tell the sheriff he
would go along with him now. It was second nature—going
along quietly, offering no reason to be branded uncooperative, giving them no excuse to use force. But the idea of
getting into the sheriff's car, even in the front seat as a
passenger instead of the backseat as a prisoner, and driving
through downtown Harmony was a shame he couldn't bear.
Someone would surely see and recognize him, and it wouldn't
take long at all for the rumors to fly.

*The sheriff has arrested Billy Ray Beaumont again. We all
knew it was just a matter of time before he was up to his old
tricks again. Wonder what he's done this time?*

*He deserved to get picked up. He's gotten too pushy—
forgotten his place. Why, he was walking down the street
with Celine Hunter when the sheriff arrested him. She's much
too good for him, of course.*

He couldn't stand such gossip, couldn't endure having it
touch Celine. And so he stood there, his face hot, his nerves
taut, and kept his mouth shut. He let Celine talk for him.

"Thanks, Sheriff," she called. "We'll see you around."

Will was staring at the ground, his head lowered, his hands
clenched in his pockets. He heard the car drive away, periph-
erally saw the wheels turn out of sight. Even when it was
gone, when the street was quiet and they had started walking
again, he didn't look up. He didn't relax.

Celine slid her arm through his, but he immediately moved
away, twisting free of her. She knew better than to touch
him like that out here where anyone could see, he thought
with a scowl. She could be forgiven for attending Melanie's
funeral with him since they had both come at Jared's request,

but that was probably the extent of her friends' forgiveness. It would never extend to him.

"Why do you act guilty when you haven't done anything wrong?" she asked quietly. "Is it a conditioned response? You've gotten hassled before when you haven't done anything wrong and so now you expect it?" Her voice grew even softer. "Or are you just ashamed of being caught in public with me?"

He didn't answer. She didn't know what it was like to be afraid of cops, to be scared of drawing their attention because all too often closer scrutiny brought some charge or another, some threat, some distrust. She didn't know what it was like to be arrested, handcuffed and searched, fingerprinted and photographed, to be stripped of your clothing and your dignity and your pride and locked in a cell like a dangerous animal. She didn't know. God, there were so many things he could teach her—so many terrible things. Things that could destroy whatever she thought she felt for him. Things that could destroy her.

They had reached the church and turned toward the library before he spoke. "Do you want to ask if I stole whatever's missing?" His voice was sharp, unsteady. "Because that's what the sheriff wants to ask. He wants to ask me where I was last night, who I was with, what I was doing."

"I don't need to ask. And feel free to tell him where you were and who you were with. But," she finished with a grin, "make him use his imagination about what we were doing."

"Damn it, this isn't a game, Celie!"

Her smile faded. "No, it isn't. It's not anything, Will. You're overreacting. If Sheriff Franklin thought you stole those things, he wouldn't have given you any warning before accusing you. He wouldn't be trusting you to show up at the Kendall place on your own. He certainly wouldn't be letting you walk away now. You've had bad luck with the law in the past and you're leery of it now, but there's no reason to be. Mitch Franklin is a fair man. He's a good sheriff. He's not going to pin this on you just because you were arrested in Alabama. He's probably going to talk to everyone who works out at the mansion, isn't he?"

It sounded so simple and reasonable from her point of

view. It wasn't so cut-and-dried from his. Of course, *his* point of view included intimate knowledge of a jail cell from the inside.

At the library parking lot, where he'd left her car, he stopped and faced her. He was stiff and uneasy, which made being threatening a little difficult. Celine herself made it difficult, because she wasn't afraid of him or of what he could do to her. She was a fool—a beautiful one, and sweet, too, but a fool all the same. "If Franklin or anyone else asks where I was last night, you don't know. Understand?"

She met his gaze evenly and didn't back down one bit. "You don't intimidate me, Will Beaumont, and you can't make me lie to a cop. If Franklin asks me, I'll tell him, and I *won't* make him use his imagination."

"Damn it, Celie—" He sighed heavily, admitting defeat. "What am I going to do with you?"

Her smile was sweet in its innocence, lethal in its promise. "Meet me for dinner this evening, and I'll give you some ideas."

"I have ideas enough of my own," he replied, unwillingly responding to her smile and her knowing green eyes, softening in all the wrong places and growing harder in the right ones. "We can't go out."

"We most certainly can," she disagreed. "But I was thinking of staying in." Hitting him with that smile again, she raised her hand, intending to stroke his jaw. "Come on, Will. . . ."

He took a step back to avoid her touch, then another half dozen for safety. "All right. You win."

But that wasn't exactly true. *He* would be the winner tonight—he would get to spend the entire evening and most of the night with Celine. But the time would soon come when there would be no victory of any kind. When Miss Rose was finished with him and he had to move on. When he and Celine would both lose, and lose big.

Dinner was quiet and lazy—sandwiches, chips, and sweet lemonade on the porch of the cottage. Will had little to say, and Celine wasn't feeling too talkative herself, maybe because the obvious topic of conversation was the theft from the Kendall mansion. Naturally, she was curious about it, but Will could be so touchy on issues of trust. She didn't want him to misread her curiosity as suspicion.

There were already rumors going around town, covert whispers that mentioned Will and words like *stole* and *broke into* in the same sentence. She'd heard them in the library and in the grocery store after work, and she'd gotten angry, but there was nothing she could do. Some people would always judge Will harshly. That was a fact of life. For herself she didn't care. She wasn't afraid that he would somehow tarnish her, as he'd suggested in church this afternoon. She just hated to see him hurt. But she'd been silent too long. The matter seemed to hang between them, and she wanted it out of the way. "What happened at work today?"

In the dim light she saw him look at her. He was so wickedly handsome, she realized all over again. Laughing, smiling, staring blankly or brooding, as he was now, he was absolutely the handsomest man she'd ever seen. Just looking at him made her weak.

After a moment he replied, "Someone broke into the shed and stole some equipment—some power tools."

"When did it happen?"

"Between quitting time yesterday and starting time today. It wasn't even noticed until after lunch, when someone needed one of the tools and couldn't find it."

"How did the guy get in?"

"Roger thinks he picked the lock. Sheriff Franklin thinks he used his key."

"And you have a key to that lock."

His chuckle was sardonic. "Yes, ma'am, I do."

"Did Sheriff Franklin actually say he thought you did it? Or are you jumping to conclusions?"

"He actually said that he could find no signs of forced entry. He asked where I was from six o'clock last night until six-thirty this morning. I told him I was home alone."

She made a *tsk*ing sound. "Lying to a police officer. No wonder you get into trouble, Billy Ray. Did Sheriff Franklin also ask everyone else where they were last night?"

He answered grudgingly. "Yes."

Feigning surprise, she gasped. "So you were treated like

everyone else. You weren't singled out because of your hei-
nous criminal record, were you?''

He reached across and caught her hand, then pulled her
from her chair and onto his lap. ''Smart-ass.''

''I've been called worse,'' she taunted.

Brushing his fingers through her hair, he smoothed it back
from her face. ''I know. I was there.''

''You're referring to what Vickie called me on Monday
night.'' She grinned and leaned back against the security of
his arm around her. ''Actually, having lived the kind of life
I have, 'slut' is really quite a remarkable way to think of
myself. I always wanted a chance to be wicked and wanton
and wild.''

''And what worse names were you referring to?''

''Sweet Celine, the closest thing to a saint this town has
ever seen. Reliable Celine. Efficient Celine. The brainy one.
The nice one. The innocent and naive one.''

''There's nothing wrong with those descriptions. You *are*
sweet and reliable and brainy and nice and innocent.''

''Oh, please, they're so *bland*. They make me sound a
hundred years old and on my way to heaven. I'm young,
Will, and I'm *alive*. I want to be footloose and—'' Abruptly
she broke off.

''Fancy-free,'' he finished for her. ''Isn't that how it
goes?''

She gave him a chiding look. ''I know how it goes. I just
don't want to be fancy-free.'' Her voice dropping a note or
two, she added, ''I sure have taken a fancy to you.''

For a long time he just looked at her; then, when she
became aware of his erection, swelling and pressing against
her hip, he shifted her to one side and laughed. ''It's your
own fault people label you like that. You are so damned nice
and capable and innocent, and you look just like an angel.
But there's nothing wrong with those labels, little girl. I think
sweet is a damned fine way to be.''

''I think naked in bed with you is better.''

''In time.'' He wrapped both arms around her, holding her
still on his lap. ''I want to ask you something.''

She considered being uncooperative and deviling him into
the house. But here in the dark on a quiet evening with his

arms tight around her and his shoulder beneath her cheek was also a fine place to be, so she sat quietly.

"For sixteen years everyone has believed that I'm Jared's father, but I'm not. You know I'm not, and so does he."

"Is that what you two were talking about at the cemetery this afternoon?"

"Partly. He saw me at my father's grave, and he wanted to know about him. He used to have a lot of questions about me. Now he has them about a total stranger."

"That's too bad. He's such a good kid, and he could really use a decent father about now. He's always had a special relationship with Jock, but this summer that's gone into a tailspin. Jock was so angry about your coming back, and then Melanie. . . ."

He looked thoughtful, and she wondered if he was somehow looking for a way to take on the blame for Jock's problems, too, until he spoke again. "If I'm not Jared's father, Celie, then who is?"

"I don't know."

"It's got to be someone here in town. When Melanie wanted more money from him, she came here. She said he knew I was back in town."

Until she had become convinced Will was telling the truth, Celine had never considered anyone else to lay the responsibility on. After she'd started believing Will, the identity of Jared's father hadn't seemed to matter. There had been too many other things of importance in her life, such as Will and their lovemaking. Such as her love for him. Such as the future she faced without him.

"I was too young back then to notice much," she said softly. "Who else did Melanie date around that time?"

"I don't know. I didn't pay much attention to girls unless I was going out with them."

"Or to bed with them," she gently teased.

He responded with a light swat of his hand on her hip. "Has anyone in town shown any unusual interest in her or Jared?"

She gave his question careful consideration. Every one of Melanie's visits to town had brought the usual gossip, speculation, and name-calling. Everyone had remarked what a disappointment Melanie had turned out to be, no better than a prostitute, white trash, and how sad for Jock and Sally, how unfair for Jared. No one had been particularly vicious in attacking her, and no one had been particularly careful to avoid her. Her friends remaining in town were so few that Jared had felt compelled to ask Celine and Will to her funeral so there would be someone there to mourn and not to gossip.

"No, not at all," she replied. "No one's made an effort that I can see, at least, to keep tabs on Jared or anything."

"How many of the guys who went to high school with her still live here?"

"That's hard to say," she answered with a sigh. "Remember, I was merely a child back then."

"You're little more than a child now," he retorted.

"Would you do to a child the things you do to me?"

"You mean this sort of thing?" He slid one hand inside the demurely rounded neck of her dress and cupped her breast, tormenting her nipple with brief caresses. "Of course I wouldn't."

"They would lock you away for it."

Reluctantly he removed his hand and smoothed the fabric back into place. "Honey, they ought to lock me away for what I'm doing to you anyway."

"Hmmm, with chains and bars and restraints—that idea has potential," she said in a husky, throaty voice.

Will laughed. "Keep your mind on the subject and out of the gutter."

"It's not in the gutter. It's in the bedroom." But, with a put-upon sigh, she turned her attention back to Melanie. "A lot of people have moved away since you left. Some went to college and never came back. Some got jobs along the river and moved to be closer. Some lost their jobs when the economy went bad and moved elsewhere looking for new ones."

"Do any likely candidates for fatherhood spring to mind?"

She considered the men in the right age range, about thirty to thirty-five. For a small town, there were a fair number of them. For many people here, roots ran deep. Many of them had never considered leaving the way Will had, the way Celine sometimes wanted to. Harmony was their home, and, like it or not, it was where they stayed. Even many of those who had left returned often. Jobs and new lives had taken them to New Orleans or Baton Rouge or someplace in between, but family ties brought them back every weekend.

"I don't know, Will," she replied. "I don't know what kind of guy Melanie was attracted to. There are too many men, so many years, and not enough to go on. I can't even make a guess."

"Do you know anyone who could?"

She answered so softly that he almost didn't hear it. "Vickie."

He became stiff and hard. "No."

"She told me once that Melanie used to toss out hints about this special boyfriend. She may know . . ."

"It's not worth finding out. Besides, if she'd known who he was, she probably would have told you."

"Probably," she conceded.

They sat quietly for a time; then Will, his voice low and sensuous, made a welcome suggestion. "Let's go inside, Celie. Let's take off our clothes and get all hot and sweaty. Let's do things to each other that would make a prostitute blush. Let's live down to your sister's estimation of us and have a hell of a good time doing it."

She pretended to consider it for about five seconds, but before she could give her answer, he was getting to his feet, balancing her weight precariously, and carrying her toward the door. She gave a delighted laugh and murmured, "Mercy me, Will Beaumont, I surely have taken a fancy to you."

Will didn't get to work Thursday morning until after seven o'clock. When he had sneaked from the cottage to the guest-house, Celine had followed him, wearing a thin cotton robe and nothing else, and she had put her very talented mouth—good for a lot of things other than talking, she had once informed him—to work at proving just that. He couldn't remember the number of times he had come—the number of times *they* had come, because when she was finished with him, he'd given her his own version of pleasure. He had made her tremble and plead.

He had made her weep.

And damned if he didn't feel like crying himself when he came out of the woods and into the clearing where the Kendall mansion sat. Sheriff Franklin's car, along with another department car, was parked in the driveway behind Roger Woodson's truck. The three men were standing in front of the truck, just looking at the house at first, then turning as one to him when he approached.

"What the hell . . ." he whispered.

Roger left the other two and joined Will. "The sheriff had one of his men drive by a couple of times during the night. This morning he found this."

Paint—gray for the balcony floor upstairs, white for the house and the pillars and dark green for the shutters—was splattered everywhere. The new doors had been kicked in, the windows broken, an ax taken to the recently repaired columns. Even the bricked gallery, splashed with paint and smashed with a sledgehammer, hadn't escaped harm. All the work they'd done, all the money Miss Rose had spent, and the place looked worse now than when they'd started.

"You have any ideas who might not want work on this house to proceed?" Sheriff Franklin asked.

Will couldn't pull his gaze from the gallery, from the hours of hard, painstaking work he'd done, from the large sections of ancient brick now turned to dusty rose powder. "Raymond Kendall was against the idea from the start," he said numbly. "That's why Miss Rose didn't even tell him until we were already working."

Then, realizing what he'd said, that he'd all but accused Raymond of such malicious destruction, he abruptly swung around to face the sheriff. "I don't think—"

Franklin interrupted him. "That's my job, isn't it?" he asked quietly. "Anyone else?"

"A lot of people would like to see me gone. Maybe someone figures if he shuts down the job, I'll have to leave. It's a sure bet no one else around here is going to hire me."

"Maybe. So . . . where were you last night?"

Will glanced at Roger, then at the deputy. When he turned back to Franklin, he replied so softly the man could barely hear him. "Home."

"Can anyone verify that? Miss Rose, maybe?" Franklin

paused. "No, she's involved in church activities all evening on Wednesday. What about Miss Celine?"

He was blushing—Will could feel the heat in his face and on his neck—and he silently cursed himself for it. If Franklin didn't already suspect something between him and Celine, he would now. "I was alone," he lied.

Franklin gestured for him to follow, and they walked away from the others. "Look, Beaumont, I'm just doing my job. I've got to ask questions, and if I don't get answers from you, I'll have to ask elsewhere. I like Celine. I have a great deal of respect for her, and I'd really rather not go to the library this morning and ask her if she was alone all last night."

Will just stared at the ground, at the splashes of white, gray and green paint on the grass and in the bushes.

"Protecting a woman's reputation is admirable, but right now, Will, you need to be worrying about yourself."

He looked up then, his gaze narrowing on the sheriff. "I didn't do this."

"I don't think you did. But it doesn't change the fact that your fingerprints were the only clear prints we could lift off that lock on the storage shed. It doesn't change the fact that you're the only person working here with an arrest record. It doesn't change the fact that you're the easiest person in the parish to blame when something goes wrong. People believe you're capable of anything. They think you're dangerous." His voice grew softer. "They think you should be locked up."

Will stiffened, his gaze dark and stubborn, his jaw taut. "I haven't done anything wrong."

"Probably not. But you'd be good for the theft out here if I decided to pin it on you. I could make a case without even trying. The trial would just be a formality. Half the people in town would line up to see you go to jail."

He wasn't merely boasting, Will knew. With his record, with the enemies he'd made, with no one to back him up and no one to believe in him but the town librarian and a fifteen-year-old boy, he wouldn't stand a chance. "So what are you suggesting I do, Sheriff?"

He expected an invitation to leave the parish. He'd gotten

that before, in small counties and smaller towns. *This is a good place for decent people. Your kind isn't welcome here.*

But Franklin surprised him. "First of all, quit worrying about Celine. She's all grown. She can handle herself. Give her credit for that. Secondly, show some sense. Start spending *all* of your free time with her. You never know when you might need an alibi. Third . . ." He gestured toward the house with a nod. "Watch your back. Maybe somebody has a grudge against the Kendalls or Mr. Woodson, or maybe they just have a real mean streak. Or maybe it's *you* they don't like. Whichever, be careful."

Will remained where he was, near the gallery, as the sheriff walked away. A moment later, he heard the two cars start behind him, heard the sounds of them driving away, followed by footsteps approaching. He glanced around at Roger, who looked about as down as *he* felt.

"God, this is a mess."

Will didn't speak. The statement didn't require comment.

"What's between you and the sheriff? Does he think you're involved with this?"

He hated this, Will thought, squeezing his eyes shut on the vandalism. He'd hated it with Miss Rose when it had caught him off guard, and he'd hated it with Celine, and he hated it now. But Roger had a right to know. He should have known weeks ago, before they even started work. "I have a record," he stated flatly. "Cops tend to lean a little hard on you when they know that."

"Yes, Mrs. Kendall told me about that."

Will gave him a long look. "You knew. And you still let me work here."

Roger bent and picked up a long sliver of wood that had come from the nearest pillar. "First of all, you don't work for me, Will, even though you prefer to act like just one of the crew. Mrs. Kendall hired you to supervise the job, and she's paying your salary. But even if you did work for me, I'm not sure any of that matters. People make mistakes. As long as you don't make them here. . . ." He tossed the wood to the ground, then withdrew a set of keys from his pocket.

"Go over to the Kendall place and bring the old lady back here. I want her okay before we go on."

It took Will a few minutes to drive to the house, a few minutes more to come back with Miss Rose. He helped her out of the truck and stood beside her while she took in the damage to the house. She clutched his arm tighter, and her face paled, but she didn't say a word. She just looked.

After a time she released him and moved forward to meet Roger. They talked quietly, and he showed her around the house, where more damage had been done. Finally they returned to the truck where Will was waiting to take her home. When he would have helped her inside, she stopped him, her gaze searching his face. "Who would do this to us, Will?" she asked softly. "Who would willfully destroy what we're doing here?"

"I don't know." But he didn't declare his own innocence. This time she seemed to believe him without it, and if she didn't believe him, all the denials in the world wouldn't make a difference.

He had learned that lesson well.

"I just don't understand. . . . Who could have something to gain by stopping work here? How could the work on this house matter enough to someone else that they would do *this*?"

When he didn't say anything, she sighed heavily, then accepted his help into the truck. As he closed the door and walked around to the driver's side, though, he couldn't help thinking that the work here mattered to Raymond. Stopping it mattered. Saving all those precious Kendall dollars mattered. Getting rid of *him* really mattered to Raymond.

How badly did Raymond want to get rid of you? Celine's voice whispered in his mind. *Badly enough to frame you? Badly enough to steal from himself? Did he want it badly enough to steal from his own mother?*

He didn't want to believe it. He didn't want to believe Raymond hated him so much that he could hurt his own mother like this.

At the big house, he went inside with Miss Rose and saw that she was settled comfortably in the sun room with a cup of tea before leaving again. Even though it was early, Celine was probably already gone to work, he thought, with a disappointed glance at the cottage. She would hear about the latest trouble there.

She had offered him such trust—believing him without proof about Melanie and Jared, about the break-ins here and in Alabama, about the theft at the mansion. She would believe him about this, had to because she had proof, because *she* was his alibi. But how long before she started doubting him? If the sheriff's suggestion—that someone didn't like him—bore out, if the incidents kept happening, how long until Celine stopped believing in him?

How many times are you going to believe me when I say I didn't do it? he had asked her at the fireworks show. *When are you finally going to believe that I'm lying?* And she had answered so calmly, so serenely, so damn trustingly. *When are you going to start lying to me?*

But it couldn't be that simple. He had earned distrust from far too many others when he was totally honest. He had never lied to Miss Rose, but she hadn't believed him about Melanie. She hadn't even given him a chance to lie when she had asked about those robberies in Alabama. Knowing that he'd lost her trust had hurt like hell. Knowing that someday he would lose Celine's . . . that would destroy him.

Celine was standing on a stepladder, removing red, white, and blue crepe paper from the bulletin board, when Millie called her to the phone. It was almost lunch time, and she had been daydreaming about showing up at the Kendall mansion with a quilt and a picnic for two when she recognized her mother's voice on the line.

"Why don't you come over for lunch?" her mother invited.

Celine couldn't help but be mildly suspicious, wrapping the coiled cord around her finger as she delayed answering. Maybe Annalise's invitation was perfectly innocent. After all, Celine *had* missed the family Sunday dinners two weeks running. Weekday invitations generally came with strings attached, though: Annalise had lost something important—again—or she wanted a glowing appraisal of her latest work of art or she needed help straightening out one tangle or another.

"Celine? Are you still there?"

"Yes, Mama. Are the grandkids there?"

"No, just me. It's quiet today—a little lonely, in fact."

Her mother didn't sound at all pitiful, but that cinched it for Celine, anyway. She really did love Annalise, with all her flaws, and she hadn't seen nearly as much of her this summer as she normally did. "All right, Mama. I'll be over in about fifteen minutes."

It was a short walk to her parents' house, and she could see it when she was still more than a block away. The last time she'd been over, it had been painted a pretty, pale peach—a nice, normal color for a house in this neighborhood. But Annalise had been busy since then. Now the second story, all she could see above the neighbor's house, was blue, sky blue, and white. She squinted to bring it into clearer focus, then laughed aloud. The outside wall of the upstairs bedrooms that had once been hers and Vickie's was now a blue sky with puffy white clouds. If her mother could be convinced to retire her paint brush and scaffolding now, then no matter how bad things got, the Hunter family would always have blue skies.

Annalise was in the kitchen, up to her elbows in flour. "Need any help?" Celine asked after leaving her purse in the living room.

"Oh, no, dear, this is for dinner. Lunch is all ready and in the refrigerator."

"Want me to set the table while you wash up?"

Her mother glanced at the clock overhead. "Well, let's give her a few more minutes."

Celine stiffened just slightly. "Who, Mama? Who else did you invite?"

"Actually, she invited herself—and you. This was Vickie's idea. Not," she hastened to add, "that I minded. We haven't seen much of you lately, and I always like to spend time with my two girls."

Considering the way their last meeting had gone, what reason could Vickie possibly have for wanting to see Celine today? It certainly wasn't affection or concern. The only reason their relationship had survived Vickie's marriage to Richard was because Celine, out of family loyalty, had worked hard at it. Not because Vickie had cared.

She didn't have a moment to wonder, because Vickie arrived just then. She let the door slam behind her, then made her way into the kitchen, her smile for her mother sweet, the one for Celine tinged with malice. She had been a fool to work so hard at staying on good terms with Vickie, Celine thought stiffly. The blood in their veins wasn't reason enough to maintain a relationship with someone who held her in such low regard.

Annalise shooed them to the dining room table, then washed up and brought out bowls of pasta salad and fruit salad and a tall pitcher of iced tea. They were halfway through the meal with nothing more than small talk when Vickie got to the point of this impromptu gathering. "There was more trouble out at the Kendall mansion today," she announced, her smile fixed on Celine.

Of course. She should have known that somehow her sister's desire to share a meal with her had to do with Will. Silly Celine. She had thought maybe Vickie intended to hint to their mother about the scene she'd stumbled upon in the woods. It was more than that.

"I heard there were some things stolen," Annalise remarked, unaware of the tension between her daughters. "One of those heavy-duty staple guns and some saws. You know, I've been thinking about buying a power saw. It would certainly make my carving go much more quickly."

Celine shifted her gaze from her sister to her mother. "Mama, you don't do any carving," she reminded her gently.

"Well, I've been thinking of starting. I saw the most striking pieces—"

"Mama," Vickie interrupted. "We're talking about the Kendall mansion, remember? Richard had to go out there again today—he underwrote the work, you know. It seems that somebody tore the place up—did thousands of dollars' worth of damage. And do you know who the sheriff thinks is responsible?" She waited a moment, looking from Celine to their mother, then back again. "Billy Ray Beaumont," she announced with relish. "He is the prime—the *only*—suspect. You know, old lady Kendall is paying him a fortune for just hanging out over there and doing nothing, and the sheriff thinks he's sabotaging the project so it will take longer to complete so he can keep drawing that ridiculous salary."

Trembling inside, Celine laid her fork down, then meticulously folded her napkin and covered the fork with it, removing temptation from sight. "And when did Richard get to be on such good terms with Franklin that the sheriff would confide his suspicions to him?"

"Well, Richard *is* involved in the investigation," Vickie said importantly. "After all, his company stands to lose a great deal of money if Billy Ray isn't stopped." Then she grinned. "And we all know the only way to stop someone like Billy Ray Beaumont is to lock him away for a long, long time."

"I don't believe you," Celine said quietly. "I don't believe Sheriff Franklin would confide in Richard, and I don't believe Will is a suspect in this. I think you're lying, making up stories the way you always do, and I think you're doing it because you're jealous."

"Now, Celine," Annalise started, but Vickie interrupted her.

"Jealous?" she repeated with an astonished laugh. "Of what, little sister? Of you shacking up with that Beaumont trash?"

"Victoria!" their mother scolded. "We won't have that kind of talk in this house."

"Yeah," Celine retorted. "You're jealous because he's in *my* bed instead of *yours*. Because he never gave you a second look. Because he would rather be celibate than sleep with you."

"Girls, that's enough!"

"Do you think I would actually go to bed with *him*? That I would stoop to his level?" Vickie laughed again, but it was brittle, forced. "Oh, please, Celine, give me credit for better taste than that. Billy Ray Beaumont is a shiftless, good-for-nothing, white-trash bastard who doesn't deserve to even live in the same town as us."

"Then why were you out at Miss Rose's when he came

back, panting over him? Why did you lie and pretend that you'd had an affair with him before he left? Why did you tell me that you were going to have another affair with him now that he was back?''

"You're lying. I never said—''

Annalise shoved her chair back, stood up, picked up her empty plate, and slammed it down on the table. The dishes rattled and the tablecloth swayed, and the plate broke in a smooth line, curving slightly at each end, right down the middle. Startled, both daughters sat back, sullen and quiet, and waited for her to speak.

Once she had total silence, Annalise slowly sat down again and looked from one daughter to the other. "Celine, would you like to explain what's going on here? Are you seeing the Beaumont boy?''

Celine hesitated only a moment, knowing Will didn't want this to come out and knowing that, on this subject at least, she didn't care what he wanted. She stared, hard and cold, straight at her sister, then turned to her mother. "Yes, I am.''

God, that felt good! Even though Will had warned her that it wouldn't be so easy for her if others knew about them, she felt such a sense of relief at having admitted it. Secrets were shameful things, she had argued with him, and she wasn't ashamed of him. This relief, and the calm it brought her, just proved it.

"You're having an . . . affair with him?'' Annalise gave the word a distasteful twist, not so much because of Will, Celine suspected, but because she preferred not to know the intimate details of anyone's life but her own.

Celine looked at Vickie, whose anger and meanness distorted her face, leaving her far from pretty at this moment, then at her mother, collected and serious in a way she'd rarely ever been, and she sweetly smiled.

"Yes, Mama. I am.''

Chapter Thirteen

Annalise sighed softly as she pressed the broken edges of the plate together. "This is my favorite set of dishes," she remarked idly. "I made them myself, you know, when I became interested in pottery. That was before the glassblowing . . . or was it after?" Then, accepting the loss, she pushed the pieces away and looked at Celine again. "I must say, Will Beaumont is *not* the man your father and I had in mind for you."

"Who *did* you have in mind for me? Someone like Richard, who went to bed with another woman the first chance he got?"

"No," Annalise agreed. "Richard was no good for you, either. You needed someone stronger than him."

Having stayed quiet as long as she could endure, Vickie snapped, "That's my husband you're talking about, and he's perfectly strong enough."

"For you, Vickie," their mother agreed. "But not for Celine. You're fond of Will Beaumont?"

Vickie snorted. "Fond of his body and what he can do with it is more likely."

Annalise gave her a sharp look. "That's enough from you, Vickie. I'm talking to your sister now. Celine?"

She stood up, then scooted her chair back into place. Part

of her wanted to continue this conversation in private, to usher Vickie out the door before she answered her mother's questions. The stronger part of her, though, didn't care what Vickie heard, didn't care what she thought, what she repeated.

"I'm more than fond of him, Mama," she said softly. "I'm in love with him. I know he's not what you wanted for me. I'm not sure he's what I wanted for myself, because someday soon he's going to leave here, and when he does, he's going to break my heart. But I know that, and I love him anyway."

Annalise reached for her hand, squeezing it tightly, and Celine knelt beside her. "You can't change his mind and make him stay?"

"Stay for what? So people like Vickie can gossip and spread rumors about him? So he can be treated like some sort of outcast? So he can be blamed for everything that ever goes wrong around here?"

"Stay for *you*. So he can settle down with you. So he can have a family with you. So he can have a normal life."

Before Celine could speak, before she could swallow the lump in her throat that had appeared at the mention of a family, Vickie jumped up from the table. "Oh, Mama, you can't mean that! You would welcome that—that bum into our family? Are you as crazy as she is?"

"Vickie. . . ."

"He's no good," Vickie continued. "He lies and cheats and steals. Mama, he's got an arrest record. He's an ex-convict, for God's sake!"

Slowly Celine turned her gaze on her sister. "I suppose Sheriff Franklin also told Richard that."

"It's common knowledge, *Celie*," she said sweetly.

Her secret name in her sister's phony nice voice sounded sour, and it stung deep inside. "Common garbage, you mean," she said softly. "Trash. Like you."

Vickie leaned across the table, the sunlight catching and glinting off her red hair. "Trash?" she echoed, her voice deadly quiet. "Look who's talking. You should have seen them at the fireworks display, Mama. He had his hands inside her clothes. He was crawling all over her, and she let him.

That's what he's taught her, Mama—to act like a cheap whore right out in public—and you want to welcome him into our family.''

Celine freed her hand from her mother's grip and slowly stood up. ''Moral outrage doesn't suit you, Vickie,'' she said drily. ''Not when your own morals are so lax.'' Bending, she hugged her mother. ''I'm sorry about all this.''

Annalise caught her hand again. ''*Has* he been arrested?''

She swallowed hard, wishing for Will's sake that she could lie, but there were too many people out there who knew the truth. ''A few times, but it was nothing serious.''

''But—''

''Trust me, Mama.''

Her mother released her, then stood up. With a stern admonition to Vickie to wait where she was, Annalise walked to the front door with her. ''Your father and I would like to get to know him.'' She stalled Celine's protest with a raised hand. ''Even if he isn't going to stay. We would like to meet the man who can make our reliable, sensible daughter fall in love.''

''I don't know, Mama,'' Celine said with a heavy sigh. Knowing Will's feelings on the matter, she couldn't offer to bring him over, couldn't even promise her parents a casual meeting with him. He would never agree to it. And it was just as well. Her parents, absentminded as they were, would probably forget that this relationship was a short-term thing. They would probably try to start planning a wedding. They would forget that there wasn't going to be one of those. Not for Celine. Not ever.

It had been a week since the trouble had started at the old house. First there'd been the missing tools, then the vandalism. In spite of the security guards Rose had hired, over the weekend, the tires had been slashed on the company truck left there, and last night there had been another burglary.

Raymond swiveled his chair around to face the window. He should be pleased, Frannie had told him over breakfast this morning. Rose was distressed; she'd been unable to talk about anything else after church Sunday. She had even made a vague reference to stopping the construction.

He hadn't reminded his wife that stopping work on the house, while an added benefit, hadn't been the primary purpose behind all this. He'd wanted to get rid of Billy Ray once and for all. While everyone in town was pointing fingers at him in this latest round of trouble, neither Mitch Franklin nor Rose seemed inclined to lay the blame on him. Franklin had refused even to consider Billy Ray seriously as a suspect—*no more,* he'd said, *than I'm considering everybody . . . including you, Raymond.* The son of a bitch. As soon as Billy Ray was gone, Raymond had plans to take care of Franklin.

As for Rose—hell, he could hardly even talk to her these days. She'd come to dinner Sunday like always and had gone on and on about the damned house; but every time he'd mentioned Billy Ray's name, she had snapped out of her despondency, fixed a hard-eyed look on him and told him that was one subject she wasn't going to discuss. Whatever he had to say about Billy Ray, she wasn't listening.

She refused to listen. Every time he called her, she was just lying down for a nap; when he drove out to her house, she wasn't feeling well. It was all an act, he suspected. She was the most manipulative old woman he'd ever met.

And Billy Ray was the luckiest bastard. He had wormed his way right back into Rose's life, into the easiest life he'd ever lived. He had a place to sleep, food to eat, was getting paid a good salary for a make-work job, and he had sweet Celine on the side. There was talk about them all around town, started by that piece of trash sister of hers. Saint Celine had tumbled a peg or two in some people's estimation, but she hadn't fallen. She hadn't taken the great plunge Vickie had expected when she'd given the push.

Maybe Celine was just horny. Maybe she was just screwing Billy Ray because he was available and could satisfy her hunger. Or maybe, as her sister claimed, she really was falling for the bastard. That presented Raymond with another problem. No one could give Billy Ray some small measure of respectability as quickly, as easily, as Celine could. She was well liked and respected herself, and her conduct had always been above reproach. If she saw something good in Billy Ray

Beaumont, practically the entire damned town would take that as a sound reason to warrant a second, less-critical, more-forgiving look.

Either way, he couldn't trust her anymore. He would have to keep an eye on her, too, damn it. But in the meantime, Billy Ray's luck *would* run out. Raymond was sure of that. If the sheriff wouldn't build a case against him for the trouble at the house, then Raymond would find some other way. He had one plan already in motion, and he would come up with another soon.

There was a tap at the open door. He didn't turn around, but just asked, "What is it?"

"John Stuart's office called," his secretary said. "Your mother has an eleven-thirty appointment with him, and she's asked that you be present, too. And Mrs. Kendall called. She's on her way down to meet you for lunch."

"Thanks," he said absently. A glance at his watch showed that it was eleven-fifteen now. Leave it to Rose to wait until the last minute to inform him of this appointment. That way he couldn't get out of it. But that was all right. He and Frannie would stop by over there, he would sit through the meeting, and then they would keep their lunch date as planned.

What business, he wondered, did his mother have with John Stuart that involved *him?* They didn't share any business interests—she kept those separate and private, probably just to spite him. She knew he was curious about her income and investments, knew he wondered just how much she was worth, how much she was spending, how much she was leaving for him and Meredith when she died. However much it was, he thought bitterly, it was a lot less than before she'd gotten this damn fool idea to fix up the house. There was no telling what the old woman was up to now. But he would find out soon enough.

Will dunked one end of a towel in a bucket of water, wrung it out, and began wiping the dirt from his face, arms, and chest. Miss Rose waited patiently nearby, dressed for town, her hands clasped over the handle of her flat bag, her gaze politely directed elsewhere. "Tell me again why I have to take off work and go into town with you," he said as he dropped the towel, then picked up the clean shirt she'd brought him. It was the one he'd worn to Melanie's funeral, plain cotton, long sleeves, washed, and pressed.

"We have an appointment."

He rolled the sleeves to his elbows, then began buttoning the shirt. "And just who are you making appointments for me with?"

"Hurry up, or we're going to be late. When we're finished, you might even have time to have lunch with Celine."

He gave her a long look as he began tucking his shirttail in. "I see enough of Celine at night," he said evenly, although that was a lie. He *was* spending a lot of time with her, but it would never be enough.

"So I understand," Miss Rose said archly. "Come along now. You look fine."

Curious about that first remark, Will followed her to the car and got inside. So Miss Rose knew he was spending all of his evenings and most of his nights at Celine's cottage—and apparently, she wasn't too happy about it. Did she think Celine deserved better than him? Did she expect that he would hurt Celine? Or was she disturbed because he hadn't, to use Miss Rose's own words, made an honest woman of her? It was probably that last one. *Ask Miss Rose sometime what she would think about you and me together*, Celine had once told him. *The old lady just might surprise you.*

They drove into downtown Harmony, past the library and the Baptist church, and parked in front of the bank. Will gave the building a quick look, then turned to Miss Rose. Business at the bank? An appointment with Raymond? There was no way in hell—

"John Stuart's office is across the street," she said, stalling his protest before he could even make it.

Will climbed out of the car and followed her across the street. "A meeting with John Stuart isn't much more appealing than a meeting with Raymond," he said flatly. "What business do you and your lawyer and I have together?"

She stopped outside the doorway and faced him. "You haven't asked me lately why I brought you back here."

"I figured you would tell me when you were ready." And

Celine was entirely too pleasant a way to pass the time while he waited.

Miss Rose nodded once. "Today I'm ready." She laid her hand on his arm. There was something supplicating about the gesture, something that made the muscles in his gut tighten. "I want you to promise me something, Will. I want your word that you won't make up your mind right away, that you'll think about what I'm asking of you and remember what I've done for you."

The taut muscles and the creepy, queasy feeling in his stomach must be justified.

"Your promise, Will."

He didn't want to give it. He didn't want to promise anything except what he'd told her all along: that he wouldn't stay here, that he was leaving again sometime soon and never coming back.

But she was waiting and looking smaller, frailer, than ever before. Her blue eyes, usually so sharp and all-seeing, were faded now, cloudy. For the first time since he'd come back, it hit him how old she was. *Old.* Wearing down. Wearing out.

He covered her hand with his and gave the answer she wanted to hear. "I'll think about it, Miss Rose. I promise." He gave the promise knowing she would accept it, knowing there was a better than even chance he would break it.

Satisfied, she stepped back and let him open the door for her. Inside the secretary escorted them back to the attorney's office, opening the door, then moving back and closing it again behind them.

The first person Will saw was Raymond, seated in one of the chairs in front of the lawyer's desk. Beside him was his wife Frannie, looking elegant and cool in spite of the day's heat. She was pretty, Will thought, in a rich-bitch sort of way. When he had lived with Miss Rose, Frannie had always treated him decently enough, even though there had often been a lecherous, amusing-herself-with-the-young-bad-boy flavor to her behavior. She had made suggestive comments, had touched him too often, had brushed or bumped against him. She had made him uncomfortable sexually, which, of course, had been her goal. She never would have followed through, though, even if he'd been interested. Amusing yourself with trash was one thing. Getting down and dirty was another.

He hadn't taken more than a few steps into the room when the conversation stilled and all eyes turned his way. Just as Miss Rose hadn't told him that Raymond and Frannie would be here, she hadn't warned them of *his* presence. Frannie gave him a brief, cool glance, then pointedly turned away, as if he were beneath her notice. The lawyer's expression was wary, and Raymond's was malevolent. It was no less than Will expected from them all.

"Good morning," Miss Rose said, ignoring the tension in the room. There were two chairs left empty, and she took the one closer to Frannie. That left Will with a straight-backed chair set a little off to one side. The position gave him a nice view of everyone's faces.

"All right," Raymond said, his voice sharp with tightly controlled anger. "What is this about, John?"

John Stuart didn't say a word. With a vaguely uneasy smile, he gestured to Miss Rose. It was her show, and she played it. She sat erect in her comfortable seat, her head high, and that familiar, alert look was back in her eyes. Her hands were folded over the top of her handbag, but she wasn't clutching it. She wasn't revealing any tension whatsoever.

"I requested this meeting today because I thought it was about time I answered Will's questions. I asked him to come home to do something for me, but once he got here, I kept putting off telling him what it was. I wanted to wait until he was settled in, until the bad feelings caused by his return had settled." She looked regretfully at Raymond. "I wanted to wait until you quit behaving so badly toward him, but I know now that's not going to happen. You resented him before, and you resent him even more now. So . . . it's time for him to know, for all of you to know, why I brought him here."

Trying to ignore the apprehension spreading through him, Will glanced at each of the others. John Stuart knew what was coming, and he was sitting behind his desk pretending he wasn't there. Frannie was gazing at the floor, looking bored and disinterested, but her hands were folded too tightly in her lap for either emotion. Raymond leaned forward, anxious to hear his mother's announcement, certain he wouldn't like it, ready to react to it.

Will was certain he wouldn't like it, either. He wasn't sure what he had expected from Miss Rose—he hadn't given it much thought—but not something that required an attorney—or such melodrama.

After that brief silence, Miss Rose went on, this time directing her conversation to Raymond alone. "Between your own share of the Kendall money, your income, and Frannie's family money, you're more than comfortable, Raymond. Even as much as Frannie likes to spend money, you're always going to have enough to meet your needs. It's the same for your sister. Meredith's husband, as much as I disapproved of him, is a good provider. She and her children will never want for anything. That's why I've decided . . ."

The words trailed off, and for a moment she seemed to turn inward. Was she losing her nerve? Will wondered. He'd never imagined such a thing, but after all, she was an old woman—one who had apparently made a decision sure to have an explosive impact on her son. Maybe, finally faced with telling him, she was rethinking it. Regretting it.

Then she drew strength, straightened again and went on. "I've decided that, once a few bequests have been honored, the rest of my estate when I die will go into a trust, to be paid out to charitable organizations as the executor sees fit."

Raymond started to rise from the chair, his face turning shades of rose and purple. He opened his mouth in protest before she even finished speaking, sputtering incoherent complaints. Beside him Frannie was also in a rage, but instead of turning red like her husband, her face was deadly pale. The greediest people in the town of Harmony, Will thought with disgust. The old lady wasn't anywhere near dead yet, and they were already furious over getting only one-fourth of her estate instead of half. Under Louisiana's forced-heir laws, Miss Rose was required to leave one-half of her estate to be equally shared by her children, but the other half was hers to do with as she pleased. The state couldn't force her to leave them more, and, judging by the stubborn look on her face, neither could anyone else.

Sitting back and tuning out Raymond and Frannie's protests, Will relaxed. So this was what she wanted from him: she was leaving him something in her will, something that must come with strings attached. A piece of property? he wondered. Did she think a piece of land could make him stay in Harmony? No way. Not even if leaving meant forfeiting it to Raymond. If he settled here for any reason—which, of course, he wouldn't—it would be for a woman, not land. It would be for Celine.

"You can't be serious," Raymond said, finally putting a coherent sentence together. "You can't do this! That money, that property, belongs to me!"

Miss Rose arched one eyebrow. "I beg your pardon, but everything I have belongs to *me* right up until the minute I die. Don't worry about it. The law will see to it that you get your fair share—and that your sister, whom you seem to have forgotten, gets hers. Now . . . as to the executor . . ."

She paused briefly again, drawing in a deep breath. "I considered several people. Naturally I want someone who can be trusted to follow my instructions, someone who won't think giving money to charity such a waste. I want someone who won't consider himself or herself the most worthy charity around. I want someone who's understanding and compassionate."

Oh, shit. Will slowly sat straighter in his chair. She couldn't do this—not to Raymond and sure as hell not to *him*. He'd done nothing to deserve this. He was leaving Harmony soon, cutting all his ties, and he was never coming back, no matter what she did. Damn it, he was!

"It was disheartening," Miss Rose continued with a sigh, "how few people I'm close to fit those requirements. Not Meredith. Not Frannie. Certainly not you, Raymond. That's why I chose Will. He'll be my executor after I'm dead and my conservator before. So if you get any ideas about trying to have me declared incompetent, Raymond, keep that in mind. You still won't gain control."

Raymond got to his feet and advanced on his mother. "You can't do this! I *will* have you declared incompetent, and I'll get myself appointed conservator! I'll prove how he's influenced you. I'll show what a crook he is. I'll stop you, damn it! That money belongs to the Kendall family and, by

God, I won't let you give one more penny of it to that bastard! Do you understand?''

Miss Rose slowly stood up and faced her son. She was nearly a foot shorter, but she wasn't intimidated. ''You're the one who doesn't understand, Raymond,'' she said tiredly. ''Will hasn't influenced me on this. *You* have. I raised you the best I could, but you still turned out selfish and greedy and just plain mean. You don't care about anyone but yourself. You've had every luxury you ever wanted all your life, but you begrudged a ten-year-old boy a bed to sleep in and food to eat. You've never had a charitable thought in your life. Even now all you can think of is *me, me, me*.''

Her sigh was heavy, seeming to rob her of her vitality and to round her shoulders. ''Son, I've thought of you more than half my life. In my death, at last, I'll be thinking of someone else.''

As she turned away from him, Will got to his feet. ''Miss Rose, I—''

She raised one hand to stop him. ''You said you would think it over, Will. You gave me your word.''

And he'd known at the time that he probably wouldn't keep it. But he wouldn't break it here, not in front of Raymond and Frannie, who were looking at him with such hatred. He would think it over, but his answer would be the same. He wasn't taking on such responsibility. He wouldn't. He couldn't.

''Mr. Stuart.'' Miss Rose shook the lawyer's hand. ''We'll be back. Raymond, Frannie, I'll see you Sunday. Come along, Will. I'll treat you to lunch before you return to work.''

She slipped her arm through his and strolled out of the lawyer's office as if the meeting had been nothing—unimportant business pleasantly dispensed with. When Will started toward the car across the street, she waved it away and suggested instead that they walk to the lunch counter in the drugstore two blocks away.

''Miss Rose—''

''No discussion, Will. You haven't had time to think about it.''

''I don't need time. What you're asking is . . .'' *Too much.* He owed her a great deal, yes—probably his life—but did

he have to pay that debt by sacrificing the rest of his life?
By sacrificing Celine? Because if he agreed to the old lady's
proposition, if he stayed here, he wouldn't be able to stay
away from Celine, and sooner or later she would have to pay
for it. She would suffer for it.

"What I'm asking is no more than any parent would ask
of her grown child. I'm asking you to act like an adult. To
quit running away. To accept responsibility. To settle down
and fall in love and get married and have a family. To give
up this miserable life you've chosen for yourself and face
your problems and show some maturity."

He chuckled in spite of himself as they entered the drugstore. The restaurant was at the back, consisting of a counter
with barstools and four small booths. "When you ask for
favors, you make them big, don't you? What you're asking
is for me to completely change my life and become an entirely
different person."

"You would be happier here."

"What makes you think that?"

She gestured to the corner booth and the woman sitting
there. Waiting there. Celine.

Damn it, he'd been set up again.

She smiled when she saw them approaching and slid to
the inside of the bench, leaving plenty of room for him to
join her. Like bloody hell, he thought with a scowl. The
other three booths were occupied, and so were half the stools
at the counter. She was crazy if she thought he was going to
sit next to her under the watchful gazes of all these nosy
bastards.

Halfway there he saw another familiar face, this one at the
magazine rack that bordered the booths. "I'll be there in a
minute," he said, veering away and joining Jared on the next
aisle. He saw Miss Rose's scowl at his defection, saw Celine's
smile slip. "I thought you did all your reading at the library."

The boy looked up from his magazine and faintly smiled.
"Hey."

"You doing okay?" Will asked, deliberately not looking
in Celine's direction.

"Yeah, I guess. It's been nearly two weeks now." He
shrugged as if that brief passage of time meant something.

Will knew from his own experience with his father's death that it didn't. It would take a whole lot more than two weeks for the hurting to lessen. "I heard there's been more trouble out at the house."

"Yeah." Will scowled. "News sure gets around, doesn't it? Listen, are you interested in a part-time job?"

Jared gave him a solemn look. "Working with you?"

Will nodded.

After a moment, the boy nodded, too. "I'd like to get out of the house for a while. All Grandma does these days is lie on the sofa and cry. And Grandpa . . ."

Celine had told Will that Jock wasn't handling his grief well at all. He was going to work each day, but instead of working, he was slipping off to drink away his sorrow. He was close to losing his job, and how in the world would the family get by without it?

In a way Will sympathized with the old man. A child's death had to be hell and gone harder to deal with than a parent's, and the fact that Melanie had been murdered, as well as the knowledge that the person who'd done it was still free, had to make it even worse.

But Jock had other responsibilities. He had his wife. Hell, he had Jared. He owed it to the kid to get himself under control and give his grandson some sort of family life. Jared had never had a father, and now he'd lost his mother. He needed his grandparents more now than ever.

"Come out to the Kendall place tomorrow morning and we'll talk to Roger," he suggested. "I think we can work something out."

Jared nodded again, then glanced back at Celine and Miss Rose. "Hey, Will?" His voice dropped a few tones. "You talk about news getting around . . . The news about you and Miss Celine is sure getting around."

Will closed his eyes for a moment and exhaled heavily. Damn it, this wasn't his day. He didn't want to hear this, didn't want to hear that Vickie had disregarded his warning and started telling tales anyway. He didn't want Celine touched by the gossip and rumors surrounding him.

Opening his eyes again, he asked coldly, "What kind of talk?"

"That you guys are . . ." Flushing, Jared ended the sentence with a shrug. "You know."

The muscles in Will's jaw tightened until they ached. Yeah, he knew. Damn it to hell, he knew entirely too well. "Where did you hear it?"

"Everywhere. It's all over town." Jared gestured to the other diners in the restaurant. "They're all waiting to see what you do when you sit down with her, so they can go tell everyone." Then he shrugged again. "It's not like it matters, Will. I mean, it's no one's business but yours and hers, but . . . I thought you'd want to know."

With a quick glance around, Will saw that Jared was right—everyone was waiting—and he muttered a silent curse. It *was* no one's business but his and Celine's, but damn it, everyone knew. Everyone was waiting to judge her. But today they would be disappointed. There would be nothing to talk about. Nothing to whisper over. Nothing to damn her with.

Taking Jared's arm, he started toward the end of the magazine rack. "Come and have lunch with us. Sit with Celine."

"Great. Then, in addition to gossiping about you and her, they're gonna' be gossiping about you and me."

His words brought Will to an abrupt halt. He was right again. The dirty whispers about Celine would spread to take in Jared, too—comments like Raymond had made at Melanie's funeral. *Well, well, so you finally found some fatherly instincts. It only took you . . . what? Fifteen years?*

Slowly he released Jared's arm and took a step back. "Do me a favor, kid. Go back there and tell Miss Rose that I decided to head on back to work."

He expected Jared to trot off to obey, but he didn't. Instead, he gave Will another of those all-too-serious looks. "Why? You afraid of a little gossip?"

"I don't want people talking about Celine."

"They're already talking about her. They're already talking about me. So who cares? You don't like these people. Why does it matter to you what they think?"

Will dragged in a deep breath. His head was hurting like a son of a bitch, and he wasn't sure he could keep down any lunch he might manage to eat. All he wanted was to get changed, then go back to work where no one would bother him. At work no one gave a damn who he had lunch with or who he talked with.

But before he did that, he wanted to at least try to explain. "Look, Jared, all my life—"

Jared interrupted him. "People have treated you like shit. So screw'em. Who cares?" A look of disappointment sliding into his blue eyes, he shrugged. "Go ahead. Let them run you out of town again. Let them keep you hiding out there out of sight. I'll give Miss Rose your excuse."

Will watched him turn and walk away. Jesus, the old lady had just accused him of being immature and irresponsible, and now he was being called a coward by a fifteen-year-old kid. Today he couldn't win for losing.

Well, hell, maybe he was a coward, because he was going to do exactly what Jared had suggested: he was going back out to the Kendall place where he belonged. He was going to hide out there where he wouldn't have to hear the gossip, where he wouldn't have to endure the speculative looks. He wasn't going to make Celine a loser, too.

Will didn't come home from work at his usual time. Celine watched and waited, pacing back and forth to look out the front windows, then the back. Six o'clock, seven, eight, and he still wasn't home. The door to the guesthouse was still closed, the lights still off.

At half past eight, when wondering had changed to worry, she got her car keys and drove to the old Kendall place. The sun was disappearing in the west, and the encroaching darkness gave the site an eery feel. Tendrils of Spanish moss swayed in the slight breeze, and shadows from the trees moved disconcertingly across the white walls. Even the bird-calls—whippoorwills, bobwhites, and doves—that were comforting at her own house sounded low and mournful here.

Suppressing a shudder, she got out of the car and called, "Hello? Is anyone here?"

Two shadows—one Miss Rose's security guard and the other Will—moved out from beneath a giant live oak. The guard headed toward the house, climbing the steps to the gallery for a routine walkaround. Will came to meet her near the house.

"What the hell are you doing here?" he demanded, his voice as harsh and unwelcoming as his scowl.

"I—I was worried when you didn't come home. So much has happened over here, and I—I thought . . ."

He took her arm and pushed her back toward the car. "Oh, right. So much has happened over here, so what do you do? You get in your car and come over all by yourself after dark. Jeez, Celine—"

She cut off whatever he was about to say. "You could have come home, Will. All you had to do was say you didn't want to see me tonight. I would have left you alone." She said it with a smile, even though it hurt. Watching him walk away without so much as a word at lunch today—that had hurt, too.

Her words stopped him cold. Even in the shadows, she could see the regret that crossed his face, the anger, the apology. In his brief time in town today, had he heard the rumors?

She had. Friday at the library. Saturday at the grocery store. Today at the drugstore.

Have you heard about Celine carrying on with that Beaumont boy? And her always acting so sweet and innocent. Now we know what she's really like. Trash, both of them. Oh, her poor mother!

Of course, not everyone was malicious. There were some people who would think she had hung the moon even if she danced naked in the streets. There were others who thought, after a lifetime with her crazy parents and her selfish sister, after her experience with Richard, that she deserved to take her pleasure wherever she could find it. Most, though, just didn't care. They were idly curious. The gossip provided them with something to wonder about, something to comment on to pass the time. Last week it had been Melanie. This week it was her and Will. Next week it would be someone or something else. She understood that and could let the comments slide away without finding their target. Will couldn't.

He sighed, and his grip on her arm became more of a caress. She leaned into it, leaned into him, and his arms just naturally went around her. "I'm sorry about the talk," he said.

"I know."

"I never intended for anyone to find out. . . ."

She rested her head against his shoulder for one guilty silent moment, then finally looked up at him. "I did."

He had no response at all to that. His muscles didn't tighten. He didn't stiffen and put her away from him. "You did what?"

"I told Vickie about us. And Mama. Last week."

The response she had expected a moment earlier came now. He released her and took a few steps back to look at her. The moon was high enough now that its light touched her face, spotlighting her guilt while leaving Will in the shadows. But she didn't need to see his face to know that he was annoyed again. She could feel it in the tension radiating from him. "You told them," he evenly, cautiously, quietly repeated.

"Yes."

With his next words, his anger broke free of its restraints, sharpening his tone, increasing the tension tenfold. "Why, in God's name? You knew Vickie would talk! You knew she would tell everyone!"

She tried to smile, but her mouth couldn't hold the curve. "Actually," she began, her voice unsteady, "I was counting on that. In Harmony the best way to make a secret public knowledge is to tell Vickie. I knew that if I told her, everyone in town would know within a matter of days." Then she found the confidence she'd been searching for. "I told you, Will, that secrets are for shameful things, and I'm not ashamed of you or myself."

"They'll hurt you," he said flatly.

She shook her head. "They don't have the power." But Will did. He could punish her for going against his wishes on this. He'd had as much right to keep his secrets as she had to reveal hers, and yet she hadn't given him any choice in the matter. She had acted without regard for his feelings, convinced that once the damage was done and he saw that it was nowhere near as bad as he'd expected, he would understand and see that she'd been right. But maybe she hadn't been right.

"Are you going home soon?" she asked at last, her voice subdued.

He just stood there for a long moment, looking at her; then slowly he took her hand and pulled her close. "I suppose I'll have to eventually if I want to keep you out of trouble . . . or maybe get into more. Guess it depends on your outlook, doesn't it?"

He had just brought his mouth to hers, beginning a long, lazy kiss that was sure to turn hot, when the acrid scent of smoke tickled her nose. The security guard had lit a cigarette, she assumed, and the light night breezes were carrying the odor their way. But just as she realized that it was awfully strong for only one cigarette, Will suddenly released her. "Do you smell—"

Without finishing, he grasped her hand and pulled her around toward the back of the house, slowing only when she stumbled trying to match his long strides. The smell grew stronger, and just before they rounded the corner, the crackle of flames became audible.

"Oh, my God."

They both stopped abruptly, and Celine stared in horror, taking in the scene. A pile of lumber was blazing, lighting the night, burning so hot that she could feel the heat from a safe fifty feet back. It smelled smoky and faintly sweet, but it burned her eyes and made her skin grow feverish.

But it wasn't the fire that had drawn that soft, taut interjection from Will. It was the body dressed in dark blue trousers and a light blue shirt bearing the patch of the Baton Rouge–based security firm, lying on the ground near the fire.

She started toward the guard, but Will yanked her back. This time he ran with her back around the house, back to her car, jerking the door open and shoving her inside. "Go home and call the sheriff. Tell him to get an ambulance and the fire department. And call Roger over at the motel. Tell him what's happened. And *stay there*. Do you understand?" He was bent over, his face only inches from hers as she fumbled to turn the key in the ignition. "Don't come back here, Celie. And lock your doors. Promise."

Like hell, she thought, but this was no time to argue. "I promise." Just before he backed away, she laid her hand to his cheek. "Be careful." Then he slammed the door, waiting only for the click of the power locks before he disappeared once again behind the house.

Her car skidded in the soft sand of the driveway, but the ruts kept her on track. Once she reached the dirt road, she floored the gas pedal and worried all the way home. What if the man who'd started the fire was still around? What if he attacked Will this time? What if the security guard was badly hurt? How much more guilt would that add to the load Will insisted on carrying?

Miss Rose's house came into sight first. The lights were off, giving it an empty, abandoned air in the moonlight. Her own house across the lawn was well lit. She skidded to a stop in front, jumped out and raced onto the porch. She was too excited—too afraid—and her fingers wouldn't work properly. She had trouble separating the house key from all the others on the ring, had trouble fitting the serrated teeth properly into the lock. Inside, she dropped the phone twice before finally managing to punch in the numbers.

The dispatcher put the call out. Satisfied that help was on the way, Celine sat down for a moment, bending over and breathing deeply, forcing herself to calm down before calling Roger Woodson. That call took only a moment, then, without regard for her promise, she drove back to the Kendall place.

She parked her car to the side, where it would surely be out of the way of the emergency vehicles once they arrived, and hurried through the sultry dark night, giving shivery glances over her shoulders into the shadows, around to the back of the house.

Will had moved the security guard away from the flames. The man was conscious now, leaning against a pillar on the gallery. In the firelight, she could see the trickle of blood down his face, and he was gingerly probing the back of his head. Standing a few yards beyond him was Will, his hands on his hips. He was staring into the flames, his expression a mix of irritation and guilt, anger and hopelessness.

She left him there alone for a moment and knelt beside the guard. In the distance the wail of sirens picked up, growing stronger, sharper, more ominous. In addition to the fire truck and the ambulance, she knew there would also be Sheriff Franklin, probably every deputy working tonight and every other one who somehow heard about it. Serious crime in Harmony was so rare. Arson and assault—attempted murder?—would be something of a treat.

"I don't know what happened," the guard murmured dazedly when he became aware of her. "I had gone all the way around the house and was coming back this way when, all of a sudden, the wood just went up in flames. I started down the steps to do something, and . . ." He looked at her, pain and confusion on his face. "My head . . ."

She moved his hand away and gently touched the back of his head. There was the real injury—a sticky knot the size of her fist. The gash on his face had happened when he'd pitched forward unconscious and landed on something sharp. "You'll be all right," she said, raising her voice over the sirens that were arriving around front, shutting off one at a time in low, mournful whines. "The ambulance will be here in a minute."

There was the sound of running feet, then Sheriff Franklin, along with two of his deputies, came around the corner. The fire engine arrived next, followed by Roger Woodson and, finally, the ambulance.

At last Celine approached Will. He hadn't moved from his position at the top of the steps, hadn't shifted his gaze even once away from the beautiful, terrible sight of the flames. She touched his shoulder hesitantly, and he flinched. "I told you not to come back. You promised. . . ."

"And leave you here with some lunatic on the loose?" She leaned against the nearby pillar, watching him instead of the activity around them.

"How do you know *I'm* not the lunatic?"

"Oh, right. Or maybe it's Miss Rose. Maybe that little old lady is sneaking out of her bed in the middle of the night and coming over here to wreak havoc. Or maybe it's Jefferson

Kendall's wife. Maybe her ghost doesn't want work to progress here. Maybe she wants it left exactly the way it was
when she died.''

Finally he did turn to look at her. The fire, hissing now
and smoking heavily as water was sprayed over it, lit one
side of his face. The other was in shadow.

Neither side revealed anything to her.

"This is happening because of me, Celie. The thefts, the
vandalism, the assault—it's all because of me. Everything
was all right in Harmony until I came back. This is my fault.''

She hated his line of reasoning, hated the natural conclusion
if she let him go on with it: if the trouble had started because
he'd come back to town, then it would end when he left
again. "I hate to break this to you, Will, but not everything
in this town revolves around you. Most people don't give a
damn that you've come back.''

"*This* person does.''

Swallowing nervously, she didn't ask if he had any ideas
who he was referring to. *She* did. The instant he'd spoken
the words, an image had come to mind. A face. A name.
A man with reasons aplenty—or so he thought—for hating
Will.

"This person—''

Before he could say anything else, she reached up and laid
her fingers across his mouth. "Not here,'' she whispered.
"Not now.'' And only an instant later, as she drew her hand
away, Sheriff Franklin joined them.

"Hell of a mess,'' he said flatly.

Will held her gaze for a long, wary moment before turning
once again to watch the fire, leaving her to respond to Franklin's comment. "Yes, it is,'' she agreed grimly. "Is the guard
all right?''

"He got hit pretty hard. They're going to take him to the
hospital for X rays, probably keep him overnight.'' Franklin
glanced from her to Will, then back again. "I understand
you were here when this happened.''

"Yes. Will and I were around front.''

"Do you mind if I ask doing what?''

Seeing the muscles in Will's jaw somehow clench even
tighter, she smiled faintly. "Kissing.''

Franklin looked uncomfortable. "I didn't mean to be that specific. Why were you over here? Work stopped for the day hours ago."

"I stayed to finish up a job and to keep the guard company for a while," Will replied, not turning to look at either of them. "Celine came over to give me a ride home."

"Do you know what happened?" she asked, drawing the sheriff's attention to her.

"My guess is the guard came back around here before whoever did this had a chance to get away, so he cracked him over the head with something." He removed his hat, ran his fingers through his hair, then replaced it. "Seems odd that the guy would do it with you two out front. Of course, maybe he figured you had already left."

"Maybe," she murmured.

They watched the last flames sputter out, then, as soon as the water hoses were turned away, flare up again before the sheriff spoke again. "Miss Celine, I'd like to talk to you if I can."

She glanced at Will before following the sheriff away. He didn't even seem to notice them going. They walked to the end of the gallery, away from the deputies and the firemen, away from the heat of the flames. There Franklin removed his hat once more, running the brim between his fingers.

"You have any theories on who's doing this?"

Theories. That was just another way to say suspicions. *Do you suspect anyone in particular? Do you want to name names?* A lot of people disliked Will, though mostly more for the boy he had once been than for the man he'd since become. A lot of people didn't trust him, wished he hadn't returned to Harmony; but of all those people, there were only two she could seriously consider enemies. Jock Robinson was one, but there was no way he could be masterminding these incidents. Everything had happened since Melanie's death; and since then, Jock had been hardly capable of dressing and feeding himself. He couldn't plan a burglary, vandalize Miss Rose's property or injure an innocent man, and he certainly couldn't afford to pay someone to do it for him. But Raymond could.

Raymond could afford to pay some lowlife thug to come

in here and tear things up. He could afford to pay for a lot of things. Like assault, arson and blackmail.

Swallowing hard, she avoided Franklin's gaze and tried to sound casual as she replied, "I thought theories were *your* job, Sheriff."

"You and I both know Beaumont's not behind all this."

Silently she thanked him for believing that.

"But we also know it's got something to do with him."

"So you don't think it could be just random acts of violence or someone with a grudge against Miss Rose or Roger Woodson."

Franklin shook his head. "I considered that, but, no, I don't think it's likely. That leaves Beaumont. Who would profit most by getting rid of him?"

"Profit?" she repeated. "I'm not sure anyone would actually profit, Sheriff." But she was stalling, and he knew it. He knew the answer she would give if he pushed, the answer he was already considering.

"Then let me rephrase it. Who has a big enough grudge against that boy to want to get rid of him this badly?"

She hesitated a moment, then offered him a reluctant half smile. "It's not easy naming names or casting suspicion when we're standing here on Kendall property, when I'm living on Kendall property."

"No," he agreed softly. "It isn't, is it?"

She sighed hopelessly. "It would break Miss Rose's heart."

"Yes, I'm afraid it would."

They stood silent for a long time, watching. The paramedics took the security guard away, driving off with their lights flashing in the dark night. They would take him to a hospital in Baton Rouge, and tomorrow night the company he worked for would probably send two guards, maybe even three or four. Of course, Raymond would know, and he would plan things more carefully next time.

Next time . . . God, she had already tried and convicted him, hadn't she?

"Why don't you go on home, Miss Celine? And take him with you. I'm going to leave some of my men here the rest of the night."

With a nod, she started to walk away, but he stopped her before she'd gone more than a few feet. "Tell him to watch out, and not to hang around over here when the rest of the crew isn't here. Tonight the guy stopped with the guard. He could have as easily come after the two of you."

She nodded again, then approached Will. She expected an argument, but when she suggested they go home, he didn't even speak. He simply followed her to the car.

While he used her bathroom to shower, she fixed sandwiches and tea, then sat down at the kitchen table to wait. She felt all quivery and uneasy inside, the way she had on Will's first day back, as if a storm were about to break. She just hoped it didn't leave too much devastation in its wake.

Will found her there when he came out, feet drawn into the seat, arms around her legs. She looked young, fragile and curiously vulnerable like that. He wanted to wrap his arms around her and promise to protect her, but it wasn't likely that he could. Any danger she might face would be because of him. The only way he could save her from it was to walk away right now and never look back.

And, God help him, he couldn't do it.

They ate in silence. She looked troubled, and he felt it. A man had been hurt tonight, and he couldn't shake the belief that it was his fault. It would be safer all around if he left Harmony and never came back.

"What were you doing in town today?" she asked, focusing her attention on him as if anything had to be better than whatever she'd been thinking.

The details of Miss Rose's meeting in the lawyer's office, temporarily forgotten, came back sharply—her insistence on his promise, Raymond's and Frannie's anger, Raymond's threats. "Miss Rose finally told me why she brought me back here. In her will, she's leaving half her estate to Raymond and Meredith, and she wants the rest given to charity. She wants me to oversee it. Can you believe that?"

But Celine didn't look at all surprised. "I can't think of a better person for the job."

He could: her. When he told Miss Rose no—when he let her down once again—he would suggest that she change her will to leave Celine in charge. She was far better suited than he was for such a task. "Yeah, right," he agreed sarcastically. "With my background and arrest record, I'm just the person you'd want to put in charge of your hundreds of thousands—hell, I don't know, maybe even millions—of dollars."

"You're compassionate. You're intelligent. You understand better than any of us the problems of being homeless and hungry, of having no place to go and no one to turn to for help. And you're a good judge of character. You can tell when someone's trying to scam you—"

"Like now?" he interrupted with a scowl.

She ignored him. "Miss Rose made a wise choice."

"I'm not going to do it." Even though he'd promised to think it over, he was sure of that much. He didn't want the responsibilities the old woman was trying to force on him. He didn't want to give away her money, didn't want to be responsible for one penny of it.

Celine didn't look surprised by his refusal, either. Part of him wished she would argue, would try to change his mind, would say, "I want you to stay in Harmony." But she didn't. Of course, she'd known from the beginning that he wasn't going to stay. He'd made that clear, had told her every chance he'd gotten. Now she simply sighed and carried their dishes to the sink.

Eager to change the subject, Will asked, "What did the sheriff want to talk to you about?"

"He wondered if I had any theories about who's behind the trouble at the mansion."

"And?"

She gave rinsing the dishes more attention than the job needed, watching the tepid water flow from the faucet across the plates and down the drain. Finally she stacked the plates, knives, and glasses, then turned to look at him. "Remember what you asked me before—that if you aren't Jared's father, then who is?"

He nodded.

"We didn't ask the right question. Instead of which man in Harmony about Melanie's age might have fathered her baby, we should have been asking which man in Harmony has sufficient wealth to pay her blackmail demands."

A prickly feeling slithered along his spine, the same kind of feeling he'd gotten that Sunday when she'd told him about the robberies the night he left town sixteen years ago. An uneasy feeling that even thinking what she was thinking was wrong. A sick certainty that saying it would be a mistake they couldn't walk away from. Celine knew it, too. He could see it in the wariness in her eyes, in the air of tension hovering around her even though she stood absolutely motionless. She knew, but she was going to say it anyway.

"Everyone in town knew that she was planning to get some money—and lots of it—from Jared's father. The people who believe that's you probably thought it was just more of her wishful thinking. But I don't think it was. I think she truly believed Jared's father would come up with whatever she was asking for. So his age isn't the important thing here." Her voice softened, and her eyes grew shadowy. "His finances are."

He knew Melanie, knew she'd had big dreams, big expectations. She had planned to move away and make a whole new life for herself with this money, and that wouldn't have come cheap. The payoff she was asking for would have been substantial. And there were very few people in town whose financial situations were sufficient to put together a substantial amount of cash on short notice. Miss Rose was one. Raymond was another. Damn it, why did everything keep coming back to Raymond?

He shook his head in denial. "Don't say it, Celie. Don't even think it."

"Who committed two crimes and set you up to go to jail if you returned to Harmony?"

Raymond.

"We don't have any proof. . . ."

"Who was right there alongside Jock all those years ago, urging him on, encouraging him in his threats?"

Raymond. He and Jock had always been friends—an odd relationship, all things considered. Jock was older, blue-collar all the way, a laborer, with nothing more than a high school education and far removed from the social circles Raymond moved in.

"Melanie was sixteen years old when she got pregnant,"

he reminded her, his words gritted out through a tightly clenched jaw. "Raymond must have been about *thirty*."

"And married. All the more reason for him to lay the blame elsewhere. He convinced Melanie to name you, and then he got rid of you. He paid you to leave town, and he arranged it so that if you returned, you would go to jail."

"He was practically old enough to be her father." But he knew he was grasping at straws. As Celine had already pointed out, age wasn't a consideration here. Melanie would have been flattered to receive an older man's attention.

"He was a handsome man, Will, and charming as hell. I had a crush on him myself when I was a kid. And Vickie said that Melanie used to hint she had a special boyfriend but would never say who. In this town, how much more special could a teenage girl get than Raymond Kendall?"

How much more, indeed? he wondered. Raymond had always been the golden boy, the bright one, the privileged one. He'd always had money and class and everything he'd ever wanted. If he had wanted Melanie, if he had chosen her, had seduced her . . . Damn, she would have thought her life was complete. It would have been a toss-up which would have thrilled her more—catching the eye of a mature, wealthy man at the tender age of sixteen, or the things that mature, wealthy man could give her.

"How could he seduce a girl half his age?" he asked. "How could they keep that a secret?"

"Melanie proved that her silence could be bought," Celine gently reminded him. "She kept his secret sixteen years."

"Jared's father gave her money to leave town years ago," he said quietly.

"Maybe money that was allegedly stolen?"

That made sense, he unwillingly conceded. According to the official story, five thousand dollars in cash and another fifteen thousand dollars' worth of jewelry were taken in those burglaries. How much of it had gone to Melanie? Had Raymond sold the jewelry to raise more cash, or had Melanie been willing to accept only the five grand? It would have seemed like a fortune to her, and, going to live with an aunt as she had, she probably hadn't looked ahead to the need for more money. If that was the case, he probably still had the jewelry safely hidden away somewhere. A little something extra for himself when his mother died.

"When Miss Rose took us over to the mansion that first afternoon, you were surprised. You didn't know it was still standing. But Jared knew. He said his mother had told him about it."

At last she left her place beside the sink and came to sit across from him. She fixed her gaze on him, her sweet green eyes locking with his. "And maybe she knew because Raymond had told her. Maybe he took her there. Maybe that was where their affair took place."

Leaning his head back, he stared hard at the ceiling, wishing if he stared hard enough and long enough, all this would go away. He didn't want Raymond to be Jared's father. The kid deserved better than that, and, damn it, so did Miss Rose. But it made sense. The pieces fit. Except for one.

"All right," he said slowly. "So maybe . . . Jesus, *maybe* Raymond is Jared's father. Maybe he was so eager to get rid of me because it helped keep his secret. Maybe he paid off Melanie back then and was being asked to do it again. Maybe he was responsible for the vandalism at the house. But what happened tonight . . . Celine, that guard could have been *killed*."

A sudden shiver passed through her, one so strong that he could feel its chill across the table. A stricken look on her face, she replied in a barely audible whisper.

"Melanie was."

Chapter Fourteen

"*No.*" Will shook his head. "*No*, Celie. Raymond isn't a killer. He's a selfish bastard and a pompous ass and—"

"And he hates not getting his way. He would have sent you to prison for his crimes just to get rid of you."

"But *murder*? You think he's capable of murder?"

"We're all capable of killing to protect the people or the things we value most," she pointed out. "And what Raymond values most is money. He had to pay off Melanie when she got pregnant, and now she was back, asking for more money; and if he gave it to her, when it was gone, she would be back again. Blackmail is never-ending. He would have been forced to pay and pay again. Will, he was the only one who benefited from Melanie's death."

"Jared's father is the only one who benefited." Scowling hard, he leaned across the table. "We're talking about *Raymond*, for God's sake. Neither of us likes him, but come on, Celie. That doesn't make him guilty of *murder*."

Celine didn't like the idea, either, but she felt way down inside that she was right. Raymond was behind everything. He was Jared's father. He had framed Will sixteen years ago and was trying to frame him again, and he had been the only person with something to gain from Melanie's death. Maybe he hadn't actually killed her, but he had been responsible. Somehow, some way. She was right. And Will knew it.

They sat in silence for a time, staring at each other; then abruptly he rose from his seat and pulled her from hers. "Where are we going?" she asked as he dragged her along behind him.

"To bed," came his grim reply. "To forget."

In her bedroom with the door closed and the curtains open, with the lights turned off so that only moonlight filtered into the room, they undressed on opposite sides of the bed, then met in the middle. He was ready that quickly, though she suspected denial and the desperate need for distraction played as big a role in his readiness as desire.

They made love quickly, with an air of urgency, and then slowly, as if they had all the time in the world and nothing to do but this, and when they finished, he was still disturbed. Still edgy. Still unnerved. She sympathized with him.

"We don't have proof of anything." His voice was hard and unyielding in the night darkness, seeming far more distant than the opposite side of the bed.

"No, we don't."

"If I tell Miss Rose I don't want to be executor of her estate, if I leave town, *if* Raymond is behind the trouble, it'll stop."

She turned onto her side to face him, even though the shadows hid him from her. "If you let him run you off again—that's what you mean, isn't it? If you let him make you leave your home again, make you leave the people you care about."

A month ago, even a few weeks ago, he would have had some flip response to that about how he didn't give a damn about anyone. Now he simply said nothing. She waited, gave him plenty of time to come up with something, but he didn't even try. With a sigh, she rolled onto her other side, her back to him, and fluffed the pillow beneath her head. "Do what you have to, Will."

And so would she.

The Harmony Public Library had never been one of Raymond's favorite places. Once he finished college, he'd had little interest in books, not even for pleasure. Of course, he did have more than a passing interest in a certain librarian.

Celine's call asking him to come by the library after work today had taken him by surprise. He had written her off as worthless as a source of information. She apparently liked screwing Billy Ray too much to be of any help in getting rid of him. But she'd said she wanted to talk to him about just that, and naturally he was fair-minded enough to listen.

The sign on the library door said Closed, but the door was unlocked. It was Celine's habit to leave the locking-up until she was ready to leave—a careless habit for a pretty young woman, especially one all alone in a big empty building like this. She never knew who might slip inside, have a little fun with her, then let himself out the back door into the alley, disappearing sight unseen.

"Celine?"

There was a sound from the reference room in back; then she appeared in the doorway. She looked the way she normally did, wearing a frilly, full dress that hid too much of her body and her hair pulled back and tied with ribbons. The outfit gave her an altogether too innocent look that was intriguing as hell. For a time he had thought that her experience with men had stolen much of her appeal, but now he knew he'd been wrong. There was something erotic about a woman who could look as untouched and virginal as any child when he knew for a fact she was screwing no-good trash like Billy Ray.

He stopped at the counter, letting her come to him, and wondered what she was like in bed. Did she like it plain and boring or hard and rough? Was she into S&M, bondage, pleasure from pain? Did she like to get kinky? Did she give good head? Damn, the image of saintly Celine on her knees in front of him was almost enough to give him an erection right here. He forced his attention away from her sweet mouth and onto business.

"I was surprised to hear from you."

She circled behind the counter, keeping it between them, and rested her arms on it. "Why?"

"I've heard all the talk about you and Billy Ray." He

offered her a chastising smile. "Really, Celine. We always thought Vickie was the slut of the Hunter family."

She didn't respond to the insult. Her look remained level and cool. "Did you also hear about the fire at the Kendall mansion Tuesday night?"

"The whole town did. I understand the security guard is all right."

"Lucky for you."

"For me?"

"I don't think Sheriff Franklin will concern himself with a case of simple assault the same way he would with a charge of murder."

Raymond maintained his smile, but it took effort. "And why does that make me lucky?"

"Because you hired the man who assaulted the guard."

She spoke very calmly, very precisely, and, shit, he had to struggle to hide his alarm. She was just guessing, just repeating suspicions that she'd probably heard from Billy Ray, the bastard. She couldn't possibly *know*.

"Right," he replied, keeping his gaze locked on her, injecting just a note of sarcasm into his voice. "And I also kidnapped the Lindbergh baby and masterminded the Kennedy assassination. Really, Celine, this is pretty pathetic. I guess I can assume that the sheriff is starting to look more closely at Billy Ray. Are you so horny for him that you would make accusations against me to divert suspicion from him?"

"I'm not making accusations, Raymond. I'm simply stating what I believe. I think everything that's gone wrong out at the mansion can be traced back to you."

His laughter sounded almost natural. "Pray tell, Celine, why I—a respected member of this community, president of the local bank and only son of the revered Miss Rose Kendall—would want to sabotage the restoration of my ancestral family home."

"You disapproved from the start. You wanted the project stopped immediately because of the cost. You wanted to put Will out of a job. You wanted to convince Miss Rose that the risks were too great." She paused, smiled politely, and finished. "And you do have experience at this sort of thing, don't you? You set up Will to go to prison sixteen years ago by stealing from your mother and by faking a break-in at your house.''

Sweet Jesus. Why in hell would she even suspect that? In sixteen years no one had ever questioned him. No one had ever doubted that Billy Ray had been behind both thefts. And now this deceptively innocent-looking little librarian had just so calmly stated it. Jesus, how did she know?

''*Bitch*.'' He spoke the word softly, and it was all the more threatening because of it. The malevolence brought a moment of uncertainty, an instant of fear, to her eyes, in which he took sublime satisfaction.

She started to step back, but he caught her wrist, his fingers clenching viciously, biting into her soft skin. ''You're guessing,'' he accused.

For a moment, she pulled against him, then, too quickly for his satisfaction, she submitted and stood still. ''And you just confirmed my guesses.''

His fingers tightened enough to make her gasp; then he eased his hold. Damn her and damn himself. He'd been set up. This hypocritical slut, sweet Celine, all innocence and good, had set a trap for him, and he'd gotten caught. If he had played it cool, if he had laughed off her suspicions . . . But it was too late for *ifs*. The damage was done—and *he* had done it. Now he had to minimize it. He had to find out what she knew and how she knew it. He had to figure out how to control her. She had plenty of weak spots—her parents, Rose, Billy Ray, Jared. It would just be a matter of manipulating her through them.

''You have no proof.''

''No,'' she admitted. Using her free hand, she pried his fingers loose, and he let her. She looked at her wrist, drawing his attention to the purplish red marks forming there. Bruises and pale skin—one of his favorite combinations. Obviously resisting the urge to rub the pain away, she slid both hands behind her back. ''But I don't need proof.''

''You've got nothing to take to the sheriff.''

''I never mentioned going to the sheriff.''

''My mother won't believe you.''

''Trust me, I have no intention of telling Miss Rose.''

''So what is it you want?''

"No more trouble at the house. No more trouble for Will."

He considered agreeing, lying, assuring her that nothing else would happen. But if he lied, if he didn't tell her about the check in his office bearing Billy Ray's signature, the check that had cleared a Baton Rouge bank yesterday and had come through Harmony's own bank today, she would find out and she would be angry. She would be less agreeable, less willing to negotiate.

"Too late," he said with a casual shrug. "He's already going to be accused of . . . shall we say, misdirecting two thousand dollars from the construction account into his own pocket."

She scowled. "Meaning you forged his signature on one of the company checks and pocketed the money yourself."

Another shrug. He wasn't going to actually admit anything. Nothing he'd said so far could be used against him. Nothing she suspected could be proven.

"Stop it. Put the money back in the account and destroy that check. Do whatever it takes to make things right."

"And that's all you want." Grinning, he shook his head. "The bastard must be a real hotshot in bed. Jeez, Celine, if I'd known you were so horny all these years—"

"That's not all," she interrupted. "Let's talk about Jared."

"Jared?" he asked blankly.

"Nice act," she said drily. "Too bad you didn't perform it earlier when I mentioned those break-ins. Jared wants to go to college, maybe even to law school, but you and I both know his grandparents can't afford that."

"He's a smart kid. Maybe he'll get a scholarship."

"Maybe he will. But if he doesn't, you'll give him one." Raymond stared at her. "I'll what?" he repeated.

"Put him through college—and law school, if that's what he wants."

"Do you have any idea how expensive a law degree is these days?"

Her smile, still so polite, returned, bringing a grudging measure of respect from him. He liked a woman who could talk blackmail with such cool, quiet confidence. He liked knowing Celine could be bought. Most of all, he liked knowing that she wasn't going to get anything beyond the correction of that two-thousand-dollar error in Rose's business account. After that one concession, he was going to teach her about playing hardball. He was going to demonstrate a thing or two about threats and demands and blackmail. He was going to show her how people who fucked with him got hurt.

"I have no idea," she replied with that smile. "Thirty thousand? Fifty? Seventy? However much, it's no less than you owe Jared." She paused, let those words sink in, then added, "It's no less than you owe Melanie."

The obvious ploy would be to feign ignorance—to deny that he owed Melanie anything, to deny any sort of debt to Jared. But he wasn't a good enough actor to pull it off, and she was watching him too intently to even try.

"Damn, Celine, that little brain of yours has just been working away, hasn't it? Solving all sorts of little puzzles. All right. No more trouble for Billy Ray and a college education for Jared." Now he knew which two buttons to push to keep her in line. "Let's get to the real question here. What do you want for yourself?"

"I don't want anything . . . except one answer."

With an expansive gesture, he signaled her to ask the question, and once again she surprised him.

"Did you kill Melanie?"

He stared at her, his eyes wide, his muscles tightening. "For God's sake, Celine, that's not funny."

"Did you?"

"Jesus. Do you really think I could do that? Do you think she was important enough to me that I would murder her? Christ, Celine!"

"She was blackmailing you."

"She wanted fifty thousand dollars. That's *nothing*—small change. I wasn't happy about paying it, but, hell, I wouldn't kill someone over it. For Christ's sake, Celine, are you crazy?"

She looked at him for a long time, her green eyes unreadable; then she blinked and said, "I believe you."

* * *

I believe you, Raymond repeated over drinks with Frannie when he got home. "The little shit accuses me of murdering Melanie Robinson," he said scathingly, "and then says, 'I believe you.' Just like that, as if she knew. Damn bitch."

"Why would she suspect you of killing Melanie?" Frannie asked. "You only knew the woman through your friendship with Jock. You hadn't even seen her in . . . how long?"

"Sixteen years."

She gave him a drily curious look. "You remember so easily? Should I be jealous?"

But he wasn't in the mood to be teased. "I remember," he said acidly, "because she left Harmony a few weeks after Billy Ray did."

"Ah, Billy Ray. Now there's a name I haven't heard in . . . what? A few hours?" She smiled to take the sting from her taunt, then became serious again. She was so damn beautiful when she was serious. "So Celine knows you're behind the sabotage at the old place. What is she going to do with this information?"

"She *suspects*."

Waving his protest away, she said, "Same difference, darling. She may not have proof, but she knows just the same. What did she hope to gain by letting you know that she knows?"

He told her the terms Celine had set out and also told her that naturally he had no intentions of fulfilling any of them.

"And what if, when you fail to uphold your end of the bargain, she decides to go public with what she knows? You know how quickly gossip spreads in this town."

"She won't."

"How can you be so sure?"

"Celine's got more weak spots than anyone else I know. You notice she didn't ask anything for herself. She's blackmailing me, and yet her only demands were for Billy Ray and Jared. She cares about them, along with a few others. If she messes with me, they'll pay. All I have to do is explain that to her in terms that she can understand, and, I promise you, she'll forget everything she knows."

Frannie gave him a sultry sort of smile that said she was

bored with this subject now. "Here comes Mae. Dinner must be ready."

But it wasn't a call to dinner that brought the housekeeper hurrying to the side of the pool. The woman's face was pale, and she was wringing her hands together when she stopped in front of Raymond. "Mr. Kendall, you have to go quick!"

He gave her an indolent smile that soon slipped. "What's wrong, Mae?"

"It's your mama. Miss Rose has had a heart attack."

Raymond paced the waiting room. Frannie sat nearby, her hands folded together, her head bowed in a prayerful pose. Will stood motionless at the big picture window, watching the rain outside, and Celine waited beside him.

She had been on her way home from her meeting with Raymond when Will, driving Miss Rose's car, had skidded to a stop beside her. He had come home from work and found the old lady collapsed on the gallery, he explained, pulling her into the car and driving off again before her door was even closed. The ambulance was already on its way to Baton Rouge, where Miss Rose's doctors were waiting.

They hadn't talked on the way up here. There just hadn't been much to say. She couldn't offer him reassurance that Miss Rose would be all right. The old lady was seventy-one years old. Any illness at that age was serious. And she certainly couldn't tell him now that she'd confronted Raymond, that she had made a deal with him, that everything was going to be okay on that front, at least. This wasn't the right time. She wasn't sure any time would be right.

The clock high on the wall showed eight-fifteen. They'd been here more than two hours, but information on Miss Rose's condition had been slow to come. The only thing they knew was that she was still alive.

Celine couldn't help but wonder as they waited what life would be like without Miss Rose. The old lady had played such an important role in her life the last six years. She was closer to Miss Rose than to her own family. It would hurt too much to know that the big house was empty, to know that there would be no more lemonade and cookies or home-made peach ice cream on the gallery on hot summer evenings.

It would be too sad to go outside on Sunday mornings before church and find no one waiting to ride along with her. It would be too lonely to face the rest of her life without Miss Rose's companionship, her friendship or her all-too-wise advice. And she would be even lonelier without Will. He wasn't planning to stay around long once he'd refused Miss Rose's favor, and there was no way he would remain here when she was gone.

How could she lose two of the most important people in her life at the same time?

Beside her Will shifted restlessly. He had been quiet for so long, hadn't even shown a response to Raymond's annoyance at finding him in the waiting room. She knew he was dreading the news the doctors would eventually bring and that he was afraid. Miss Rose was the last of his family. Once she was gone, he would be all alone—except for Celine, and that wasn't quite the same. She wasn't included in that tiny circle of people he loved.

Staring sightlessly at the rain outside, she tried a silent prayer, but the words wouldn't come. All she could do was repeat the same phrase over and over. *Please, God, please, God, please. . . .*

Please don't let Miss Rose die. Please make her all right. Please don't let Will leave. Please don't break my heart.

She was ashamed of her selfishness at a time like this, ashamed that when that sweet old woman might lie dying, that when Will was facing the biggest loss of his life, all she could think of was herself. She refused to consider that it might just be Miss Rose's time to go. That perhaps, at her age, she would welcome death and being with her beloved Wynn again. That maybe, if her heart was giving out, it would be cruel to force her to hold on to life one minute longer than was natural. All she could consider was herself and how much she didn't want to let go.

Time dragged by. Shortly after ten o'clock, Meredith arrived from Houston. She greeted her brother with a hug and a kiss, spoke briefly to Frannie, said a polite hello to Celine and Will. Only a few minutes after that, the doctor, looking haggard and tired, came into the waiting room, drawing everyone into a ragged circle near the door.

"Mrs. Kendall is resting comfortably," he announced, and Celine's breath caught in a thankful rush. "She's in the cardiac care unit. We'll give her some time to get settled, and then you can see her. One visitor every hour for five minutes, family only. Which of you is Will?"

All gazes, including hers, turned toward him.

"She asked to see you first."

Beside her, Will stiffened, and Celine flinched a little. Miss Rose was too damn close to death, and she was still creating a stir. She must know Raymond would object to granting Will visiting privileges at all, and he certainly wouldn't want to see him go first.

Sure enough, after a moment of stunned silence, Raymond pushed forward a few paces, his expression belligerent. "*He's* not family."

Will didn't say anything. He just returned Raymond's angry, hard look.

Support came from an unexpected source. Meredith, her smile tired, her manner brisk, also stepped forward. "Of course he is," she disagreed. "Mama raised Billy Ray from the time he was a child. In her eyes, he's as much family as you and I."

Unwilling to let the conversation bog down into a family disagreement, the doctor looked back at Will and continued. "You can see her at eleven o'clock. The nurses at the desk will show you where to go. The rest of you can go in one at a time every hour on the hour as long as she's awake. She needs her rest, so if she's asleep, let her be. If you leave the hospital, please leave a number where you can be reached with the desk. Any questions?"

When no one spoke, he walked away, leaving them there in that loose little circle with nothing to look at but each other. After a moment, though, Raymond moved toward Will. "If you think you're going to take advantage of this—"

Meredith stepped between them, her hand extended to her brother. "If *you* think you're going to cause trouble here when our mother is lying in the intensive care unit down the hall, Raymond, you're crazy. Mama wants him here. She wants to see him, and that's her right. She can see who she wants, and she can refuse who she wants."

"It's easy enough for you to take his side," Raymond replied, never drawing his malevolent gaze from Will. "You don't know about her will. You don't know what this bastard has convinced her to do. You think you're going to get half of her estate, Meredith, and you know what? You're wrong."

She brushed that off with an airy wave. "I've known about the changes in Mama's will since she made them back in May, and I know she named Billy Ray her conservator as well as her executor. She made him responsible for her care, Raymond—not you and not me. And as for the money . . . Good Lord, you have plenty of your own. Do you have to have Mama's, too? Just once can't you let someone else share the wealth?"

"Not *him*," Raymond replied, stabbing his finger in Will's direction.

Abruptly, as if he were no longer interested in the conversation, Will turned and walked away, going to sit on the couch nearest the window. After a moment's hesitation, Celine left brother and sister to argue and followed him.

When the cushion sank beneath her weight, he glanced sideways at her. "Do you pray, Celie?"

"Yes, I do."

"How often?"

She smiled wryly. "I used to pray every day. Now . . . I guess whenever I think about it. Whenever I need to."

His own smile was just as wry as he looked away. "Maybe I've turned you into a sinner, after all."

She didn't bother to dispute that. She didn't say anything at all.

After the silence had drawn out comfortably, he asked, "What do you pray for?"

"Happiness. Healing. Peace."

"For yourself?" he asked cynically. "You don't need healing—or peace."

"No, but Miss Rose does. You do."

He tilted his head back to study the ceiling. "Don't waste your breath praying for me, Celie. It won't do any good."

"Oh, right. You think you're such a big, bad man—beyond help, aren't you?"

"Beyond salvation," he agreed, but there was no satisfaction in his voice. Without pause, as if it were simply the most natural follow-up to that line, he said, "I'm leaving, Celie."

Her chest tightened, making deep breaths all but impossible. She struggled to keep her voice even and normal. "When?"

"As soon as Miss Rose is home again."

"Where will you go?"

"I don't know. Away."

She forced her clenched fingers to relax, forced her lungs to fill with air; then she asked the question she'd been waiting all her life, it seemed, to ask. "Can I go with you?"

He closed his eyes on her question, and the muscles in his jaw tightened. He didn't brush her off, didn't hedge or equivocate. He answered her simply, coldly, finally. "No."

"Come on, Will. It would certainly make life easier. We'd have my car, and I have some money saved."

Will left the couch and went to stand at the window again. It was still raining, that steady kind of leaden rain that seemed as if it would never stop. It made for miserable traveling when your clothes were soaked clear through to the skin and your shoes squished and rubbed your feet raw with every step. It made for even worse nights: trying to find a dry place, ignoring the mud and the chill, pretending you couldn't sleep because you weren't tired and not because you were in absolute misery.

"You don't know what you're asking."

She left the couch and came to stand beside him. He didn't look at her, but he could see her anyway—could see her reflection in the glass, her white dress and her silky long hair secured with ribbons. He had used those ribbons—red, white, and blue—to tie her to the iron bed one steamy hot night while he took her hard and deep and, God, so good. She had trusted him enough to do that. And she trusted him enough to want to go on the road with him. She was a fool.

"I do know," she disagreed, looking at him even though he wouldn't—couldn't—look at her. "I know it's not easy. I know sometimes things get tough. I know—"

"You don't know shit."

She fell silent. If he looked, he knew he would see that wounded look in her eyes, and, God help him, he would go down on his knees to make it go away. Instead, he just continued to stare outside. "What about when the car costs too much to keep? What about when it breaks down and we can't get it fixed and so we have to junk it? What about when the money you've saved runs out? Or when I can't find work?"

He paused, but she didn't try to answer, and relentlessly he went on. "Are you going to sleep on the ground on nights like this? Are you going to steal food to eat? And what about the times—and, I promise, they will come—when the local law doesn't like the way you look and figures you're good for a few nights in jail?"

Lowering his voice, he made it silky and soft. "Or what if they like the way you look entirely too much and figure you're good for a few hours' fun? Are you willing to do that, Celie? Are you willing to sell your body for a place to sleep or the price of a meal? Are you willing to let any man who takes a fancy do whatever he wants to you because you're too damn desperate or hungry or afraid to tell him no or because you're just too damned unimportant for him to listen?"

She stood motionless, her silence damning him. He could feel the hurt and the frustration and the helpless need to argue shimmering around her. But before she could find any words, behind them, on the other side of the room, Meredith cleared her throat. "Billy Ray? Will? It's eleven o'clock. You can see Mama now."

He remained where he was for a moment; then slowly he turned to face Celine. Her eyes were dark, her expression startled, as if she'd been attacked from an unexpected source. Ignoring the response that look triggered, he spoke in a lazy, cold drawl. "Grow up, little girl. Behave like the sensible, levelheaded woman you are. Quit trying to push your way in where you don't belong."

And then he walked away, leaving her standing there. As he went, he wondered bleakly if she would ever welcome him back.

A nurse at the desk directed him to one of the glass-fronted rooms across from the nursing station. In that big bed, surrounded by equipment and wearing a cheap cotton gown that was too large for her, Miss Rose looked fragile, as if she just might slip away. A deep breath or a blink of the eye, and, poof, she would be gone.

Will swallowed hard over the knot in his throat and wished to hell he had never come back to Harmony so he would never have had to see her like this. All tiny and old, God, so old.

"You don't have to stand there in the door," she said acerbically. "You can come on in."

"I was planning on it," he replied, matching her tone as he crossed to stand beside the bed. He reached for her hand, small and cool, as light as nothing, and held it gently in his. "You have a bit of a theatrical flair, you know that? If you'd wanted a little attention, you could have just asked for it. You didn't have to go to these extremes."

She wrapped her fingers around his—he could see it—but he couldn't feel them. Her grip was so lax, so weak. "Did I frighten you?"

Choked laughter forced its way out. "Hell, yes, you frightened me. You frightened all of us."

"I suppose Raymond and Frannie are here."

"And Meredith."

"And Celine?"

He looked away from her penetrating gaze. "Yeah, she's here, too."

She pulled her hand from his and patted the mattress beside her. "Sit down here. I want to talk."

He eased onto the bed, careful not to bump her. Being so close made him all too aware of how frail she seemed. With a sudden clarity that he despised, he knew she wasn't going to be around much longer, and he wasn't sure how he could live without her. Even though he'd been gone for so long, he'd always known she was there, had always known he could go home and she would be waiting. What would he do when he knew she wasn't? How would he cope?

"I considered adopting you after your father's death. Did you know that?" She smiled faintly. "No, of course, you couldn't. I talked myself out of it. You were a Beaumont and proud of it. No matter how I tried, I never could have turned you into a Kendall. But in my heart, I always considered you my child, my second son. I always loved you.''

His answering smile was uneasy. ''I know. I always . . .''

She patted his hand and echoed his own words. ''I know. When you came back home, I had great hopes that you would stay, that you would settle down and be happy. I thought maybe this time I could hold you there. Lately I'd begun to believe that Celine surely could. Nothing would make me happier than to see you and Celine married. She's a lovely girl, and she thinks the world of you. She's good for you. And you're good for her.''

''Yes, ma'am, I've been real good for her,'' he said bitterly. ''People talk about her behind her back. They call her names to her face. People who have known her and respected her all her life treat her like trash because of me.''

She brushed him off. ''Gossip. It doesn't mean anything. They talk about her now. Tomorrow they'll be talking about me, up here with one foot in the grave. The next day they'll find someone else more interesting. It doesn't mean a thing, Will.''

''It does to me.''

''You've got too much pride. Celine says that's all right because sometimes pride is all you've had.'' With a huffy look, she added, ''And a stubborn streak a mile wide.''

The same nurse Will had spoken to earlier stepped inside the door. ''Time's up. You need to get some rest now, Mrs. Kendall.''

Miss Rose fixed a stony stare on her. ''When I'm ready, young lady.''

Seeing that the nurse was about to protest, Will raised one hand. ''Just another minute?''

She relented and went away again.

''You'd better not alienate these people. You're going to be depending on them for a while.''

''Then I'd best set them straight from the beginning, hadn't I?'' she asked scornfully. The haughtiness fading, she picked up his hand again. ''Will, you've lived much of your life acting on impulse or out of desperation. Don't do it this time. You've got too much to give up, too many reasons not to go back to your old life—and I'm not talking about what I've asked of you. You think long and hard before you break that girl's heart. You look at everything she can offer you, and you consider whether you can live the next fifty years without those things."

This time he didn't make any promises, didn't tell any lies. He simply stood up and bent over, kissing her powdery soft cheek, carefully hugging her. "I do love you, Miss Rose," he whispered.

When he straightened, the old lady looked tired, ready to rest, and the nurse was waiting once again in the door. He held Miss Rose's hand a moment longer, then gently laid it on the covers and went out.

He didn't go back to the room where the others waited, where Celine waited. Instead he got directions from the nurse to the cafeteria a few floors down and bought himself a cup of strong coffee. He took it to a corner table, sat down, and forced his mind to go blank. He wouldn't think about Miss Rose or Celine, leaving Harmony, going back on the road or returning to the life he hated. He wouldn't think about renting a shabby room when he could afford it or sleeping on the ground when he couldn't. He wouldn't think about the suspicion, the distrust, about bedding strange women for what they could give him.

He wouldn't consider what Miss Rose had suggested: whether he could live the next fifty years alone, the way he'd lived the last sixteen. Without Celine. Damn it, he wouldn't.

Celine stared out the car window as they drove along the road into Harmony. It was eight-thirty and already a sultry hot morning. Before they'd left the hospital nearly an hour ago, she had seen Miss Rose for five precious minutes, and they had listened to the doctor's reassurances that the old lady was going to be fine. She had certainly looked it. A good night's rest had put color in her face and sparks in her eyes.

Celine noted without humor that there was no color in her own face this morning, no sparks in her eyes. She and Will hadn't spoken since before his visit with Miss Rose. She had gone looking for him when he hadn't returned, had found him sitting alone at a table in the cafeteria, but she hadn't approached him. She hadn't forced her way into his seclusion, hadn't pushed her way in where she didn't belong.

Even now he might as well be a million miles away. He hadn't looked at her, hadn't touched her, hadn't even noticed that she was there. Was this what it would be like until he was gone? He had already left her in every way but physically.

Before they reached town, he turned onto the dirt road that would lead them past the Kendall mansion and to Miss Rose's place. When they got there, he would probably go to the guesthouse where he could shut her out even more thoroughly, and she would go to her own house. She would call Millie Andrews, she decided, and turn the library over to her, and then she was going to bed. She was going to sleep the day away. She was going to sleep last night away.

Will parked Miss Rose's car in its usual spot, and they got out. She thought about being sensible and inviting him for breakfast. After all, they had missed dinner last night. But there would be nothing sensible about inviting him into her house when he didn't even want to be in her life.

He stopped at her steps, looked as if he were going to speak, then shook his head and walked on to the guesthouse. A moment later she heard the screen door slam, followed by the thud of the door closing.

Her house was cool and dark inside. She called Millie, arranged for her to work, then sank down at the kitchen table. She was hungry, exhausted, heartsick. She wanted to go to bed, wanted to go to sleep. But she needed to do it with Will.

Showing none of the sensibility she'd long been credited with, she took half a loaf of banana bread from the counter and a bottle of Coke from the refrigerator, left her shoes where she'd kicked them off, her keys where she'd dropped them, and walked across the dew-damp grass to the guesthouse.

The door was open again, because of the heat, she imagined, and through the screen she could see Will, wearing jeans and nothing else, sitting on the bed with pillows propped behind his back. She knocked once and waited, then, deciding that he was going to ignore her, she let herself in.

"Bearing gifts, huh?" His grin was insolent, his voice mocking. "Or is that merely an excuse? You horny, Celie?"

"Breakfast." She set the bread and the Coke on the table, then slowly moved closer. "Are you not going to work today?" she asked, keeping her tone level and calm.

"I'm quitting soon. Why bother?"

Deliberately she kept her expression blank, offering no reaction to his reminder. "Certainly not because you have an obligation to Miss Rose and to Roger and Jared," she replied agreeably. "Go ahead and prove to them that they were wrong to trust you, wrong to believe in you."

His grin dissolved into a scowl. "I never asked for anyone's trust."

"But they gave it to you anyway—*we* gave it to you anyway. Not that you ever deserved it." She stopped beside the bed, beside him, and reached up to pull the ribbons from her hair. Her hair fell, heavy and confining, over her shoulders. "But that's all right, Will. Run away. Disappoint the only people who give a damn about you. Live down to the reputation you so carefully created for yourself. Sacrifice the rest of your life."

She let the ribbons drop to the floor, then began unbuttoning her dress. It was one of her favorites, white, sleeveless, the blouse fitted and trimmed with ribbons and lace, the skirt gathered and full. When she put it on yesterday morning, it had been ironed and starched. Now it was wrinkled and limp.

From the corner of her eye, she saw Will sit a little straighter in bed. He wasn't an arrogant smart-ass now. In fact, he was starting to look just a little bit anxious.

She had to bend low to reach the bottom buttons of the skirt. When the last one was open, she straightened again and slowly shrugged out of the dress.

"What the hell are you doing, Celie?" he demanded as she draped it over the headboard of his bed.

She still wore a lacy white bra, slip and panties. When she dropped her bra, he swung his legs to the floor. "You know, most women wait for an invitation," he said irritably. "Until they're wanted. They don't just push their way in."

Deliberately, offering him her own version of his damnable grin, she dropped her gaze to his groin. There wasn't any clothing in the world lose enough to shield his erection, and the jeans he was wearing were far from loose. He wanted her. He just didn't *want* to want her. But that was all right. This was for *her*.

She stepped out of the last of her garments, then knelt beside the bed. When she reached for his zipper, he tried halfheartedly to stop her—the spirit was willing to bring this to a halt, but the flesh was weak—but she pushed his hands away and opened his jeans.

Maybe she had that backwards, she thought with a faint smile. There was nothing weak about this flesh. His penis was thick and hard, throbbing in her hand when she gently drew it free of his jeans, throbbing in her mouth when she took it deep.

He slid his fingers through her hair, tangling them in the heavy strands, ostensibly to push her away, and he ground out a curse. "Jesus, Celie, don't do this," he groaned. "Don't . . . do . . . ."

She fed on him, teasing, sucking, licking, biting. She liked the taste of him, the incredible heat, the silkiness and the hardness. She liked the whole scene—being in control, doing this even when he'd insisted he didn't want it. She liked being on her knees—a position of submission if ever there was one—and exerting such power. She liked making him weak. In the end, even though he'd pleaded don't, he held her there, his fingers clenching spasmodically when he came, his semen hot and thick and alien to the taste.

His muscles still tensing, Will grabbed her shoulders and lifted her onto the bed. He wriggled out of his clothes with her all-too-eager help and, before the tremors had eased, before the shocky feelings had lessened one degree, he pushed himself inside her.

Raising himself on his arms, he stared down at her. She was smiling a smug, self-satisfied smile that he hated. "Damn you," he whispered viciously, but it just strengthened that smile.

But he knew how to take it away. He knew how to make

her need, how to stimulate every nerve in her body until his slightest touch was torment, until his sweetest kiss brought pain. He knew how to make her want until she trembled with it, until she thought she would die from it. He knew how to satisfy that need. And he knew how not to.

After a few long, deep strokes, he withdrew and shifted to the mattress beside her. He kissed and caressed her—her face, her breasts, her belly, even between her thighs. He slipped two fingers inside her and made her turn pale. He rubbed her everywhere, kissed her everywhere, except that one small, swollen place that would bring her relief. He entered her and got himself off again, all the while careful not to stimulate her enough to allow her the same pleasure.

She was shivering, pleading, weeping, when finally he took pity on her. His mouth at her breast, at last he slid his hand between her thighs, separating the damp curls there. He wet his fingertips inside her, then rubbed the heated, swollen flesh once, twice, three times, and the orgasm exploded through her.

Rolling onto his back, he held her, absorbing her shudders, his shoulder muffling her cries. When she finally became still, he used his free hand to tilt her face back so he could see. Her face was pale, her cheeks hot, her eyes glazed. She looked utterly exhausted. Even now, her body still occasionally racked with shudders, she was already about to fall asleep. Still, she managed to give him an accusing look.

"You're the one who wanted to make love," he pointed out in his own defense.

She settled more comfortably against him, and her eyes drifted shut. But before she fell asleep, she murmured one last thing that left him feeling raw inside.

"We don't make love, Will," she said with a yawn. "We fuck. Pure and simple."

Raymond sat in a chair pulled close to Rose's bed. She was still in the cardiac care unit, but because she was doing so well, her doctor had waived the rules regarding visits, and for the first time all day, Raymond had her to himself. Frannie had called a friend to take her home to Harmony, and Meredith had left only a few minutes ago to check into a hotel. No doubt Billy Ray and Celine would come back this evening, but for now Rose's attention was all his. More or less.

She was fingering a yellow carnation in an arrangement from some friend or another. Those were her favorite flowers, she had announced when an orderly delivered them. They were what she put on Wynn's grave every week, and they were what she wanted on her own. Raymond had brushed her off, had reminded her that the doctor said she was going to be fine. She didn't need to be worrying about dying for a long, long time.

She had simply looked at him.

Now she plucked the carnation from the arrangement and turned toward him. "We need to talk, Raymond."

She sounded so serious that immediately he got edgy. Whenever she got serious these days, it was always connected to Billy Ray, and that was one subject Raymond was *not* going to discuss here in this place. It was bad enough that he'd had to sit back last night and let the bastard come in here, just as if he were part of the family—which he wasn't, no matter what Meredith said. His sister was too kind for her own good. She didn't know what Billy Ray was really like. She had never really known him.

"What is it, Mama?"

"If I ask a favor of you, will you do it?"

He didn't hesitate. "Of course I will, Mama. You know that."

But she didn't ask right away. A distant look came across her face, and she sighed wearily. "That's one of the things I don't like about getting old, having to ask favors of people. Fortunately, I have the money to buy almost anything I want, so I don't have to rely on the kindness of others. But I'll buy this favor if I have to, Raymond. I hope I don't have to, but I'm prepared."

Now he was curious. There wasn't much he wouldn't do for his mother except give in on Billy Ray. If that was what she wanted, if she thought she could bribe him into treating the son of a bitch like family, she was going to be disappointed. Not even for every penny of Kendall money would he do that.

"What is it you want, Mama? Tell me, and if it's in my power, I'll do it." *Except that.*

She started to speak, sighed heavily, then, in a resigned sort of voice, said, "I want my diamond earrings."

He thought of the earrings, fat diamond studs, that she wore every Sunday to church, to every dinner and on every special occasion, and stifled a foolish desire to laugh. "Here? In the hospital? You can't wear them, and there's no safe place to keep them. When you get home—"

"I want the diamond earrings my mother and father gave me when I married your daddy," she cut in. "The diamond earrings that . . . God forgive us both, Raymond, the diamond earrings that you stole from me sixteen years ago."

He started to protest, started to get to his feet to pace and play out the biggest scene of his life. How could you even suggest such a thing? he would ask. How could you believe I would do that to my own mother?

But, halfway out of his chair, he sank back down. He had lied to her for sixteen years. Continuing the lie now would only damage their relationship irreparably. She would lose whatever respect and fondness she had for him, and he would never get it back.

"How long have you known?" he asked, subdued.

"I've suspected it for a long time."

"Why? No one else ever did." *Except Celine.* She had figured it out, too.

"I always had trouble with your theory that Will had committed the crimes. I don't doubt that, if he were desperate enough, he might steal money, but I cannot believe he would take anything that he knew I cared about. He knew the sentimental value of that jewelry far exceeded the financial value. He understands about that sort of thing. You never have."

He reached for her hand, and she let him take it. "I'm sorry, Mama."

"You have it all, don't you? Your father's ring. The emerald bracelet. The cameo brooch. Why, Raymond? Why did you hate Will so much?"

"Why did you love him so much?" he countered. "He's not your son. He's trash. His people used to work for ours, for God's sake. And you took him right into our house and tried to treat him like he was one of us."

"You were jealous?" she asked in dismay. "You tried to frame an innocent eighteen-year-old boy for your own crimes because you were jealous of him?"

"Because I wanted him gone. I wanted him out of our house, out of Harmony, and out of your life."

"And you wanted that badly enough to send him to prison?"

Absolutely. "You never understood, Mama," he said wearily. "He didn't belong. He didn't fit in. He was nothing but trouble from the beginning."

"And so you tried to destroy him."

"I tried to save you from him."

"By stealing from your own mother." She spoke with such disappointment, such resignation.

"Mama, I—"

Raising one hand, she stopped him. "Just bring me the earrings, Raymond. I want them tonight."

He tried one more time. "Mama, I never meant—" Seeing that she wasn't listening, that she wasn't going to listen anymore, he sighed. "All right. I'll be back with them in a couple of hours."

Satisfied, she closed her eyes and settled back in the bed.

It was all Billy Ray's fault, Raymond thought with a scowl as he left the hospital and headed for Harmony. If he hadn't come back this summer, none of this would have happened. Raymond wouldn't have been forced to hire someone to sabotage the construction site and injure the guard in the process. Celine never would have made the connection between him and Melanie, between him and the trouble at the site or between him and the burglary. Rose probably would never have made the connection, either.

Damn Billy Ray Beaumont to hell. If there was a God above, he would move Billy Ray right on out of Harmony—right off the face of the earth sounded all too sweet—and Raymond's life would return to normal.

The house was quiet when he got home. Frannie's car was gone from its place, and Mae was off in the kitchen, preparing dinner and listening to an afternoon soap opera. He didn't bother to let her know he was home or that he wouldn't be here for dinner. He just went straight to his office and the safe, built right into the floor behind his desk there.

There wasn't much in the safe, but all of it, he grimly acknowledged as he worked the combination, was damning. There were the blank checks from Rose's business account and the piece of paper covered with his forgery attempts. There was the name and number of the man he'd hired for the job at the mansion. There was a copy of Jared Robinson's birth certificate, old and yellowed, sent by Melanie from Georgia over fifteen years ago to show that she hadn't named him as the boy's father, in return for which she'd gotten five thousand dollars. There was also a slip of paper with a French Quarter address and a phone number that had accompanied her request for more money. And there was the jewelry, each piece wrapped in a square of velvet and all stored together in a leather pouch.

With the last number, the lock clicked open. He opened the door and reached inside, but abruptly stopped before touching anything.

The safe was empty. The papers, the addresses, the jewelry—all were gone.

Sweet Jesus.

For a moment he sat motionless, his heart thudding in his chest, and then he began opening his desk drawers. It was a useless search—he knew exactly where he'd left everything . . . but it wasn't there. None of it.

Leaving the safe open, the desk drawers open and in disarray, he left the office and headed upstairs. No one had access to the house but him and Frannie and Mae. Mae had no interest in his safe whatsoever. Safes and the things a person might put in them simply weren't a part of the housekeeper's life.

But Frannie . . . He'd never given her the combination, but if she were determined enough, she could have found out. She was a very intelligent woman, very devious, very wealthy. That was a combination that would get her anything.

He tore the bedroom apart, going through the nightstands, the dresser, the fancy French writing desk of hers that stood under a window. He moved on into her dressing room, empty-

ing drawer after drawer of stockings, lingerie, sweaters, and
scarves. He searched through shelves of handbags, gave the
rows of clothing a quick pat for a suspicious rattle or lump,
dumped shoes and cosmetics and toiletries.

Finally the top shelf of the closet, filled with boxes and
cases, was all that was left. He dragged a stool over and began
pulling down box after box, looking inside, then dropping it
to the floor. He found nothing until he reached the hatbox in
the middle.

It was oval and covered with a pretty floral print, and it
seemed heavier than it should if it held nothing more than
the hat it was meant for. As he stepped off the stool, he
shook the box and was rewarded with a glassy tinkle.

His hands were shaking, his palms damp. He cleared a
place on the floor and set the box down, kneeling in front of
it. His brain had to give the command to open it twice before
his hands obeyed. When he'd finally lifted the lid, he wished
to God he hadn't, wished he could put it back on, wished he
could forget what he'd seen in that brief glance and walk
away. He wished . . .

Oh, Jesus.

His papers were there, and so was the leather pouch . . .
among other things. It was a motley collection: a pair of
cheap earrings. A small tape deck. Five ten-dollar bills. And
a tacky Mardi Gras mask. They were things he had never
seen before. Things he had only read about in the newspaper,
had only heard about in gossip.

They were things that had been stolen from Melanie Robinson's apartment. Things that had been taken by the same
man—dear God, the same *woman*?—who had killed her.

At the bottom of it all were two photographs. Both were
old—about sixteen years old, he estimated—both black-and-
white and cut from a high school yearbook. He recognized
them both in spite of the big, black *X*'s that crisscrossed their
faces.

One was Melanie Robinson.

The other was Billy Ray.

Chapter Fifteen

It was a miserable day.

Will woke up late in the afternoon, when the day's heat was at its worst. He was tired and cranky, out of sorts with this change from his usual schedule. His head felt thick, his brain slow to function, and his throat was parched.

He rolled onto his back, and beside him, Celine shifted. She was a large part of the reason behind his black mood. He didn't like her coming here the way she did, doing the things she'd done. He didn't like the way he'd treated her in response. He especially didn't like what she'd said.

We don't make love, Will. We fuck. Pure and simple.

Damn her.

He sat up and allowed himself to look at her for a minute. She was lying on her stomach, her hair falling in a tangle over the pillow. Her skin glistened with sweat, and the combined scents of that and sex, earthy and musky, clung to both of them. He watched the subtle signs of her breathing, studied the long, lean lines of her body, her slender waist and her hips so nicely rounded out from there.

Damn. Just looking at her on a day too hot to even raise a hope, and he was getting hard. He could wake her slowly, could love her sweetly to make up for this morning and last night, could gently roll her over and slide so easily inside her.

We don't make love, Will.

Muttering a curse, he shook out his jeans and stepped into them, then went to the door. It was a quiet afternoon, the heat shimmering in the air. He wondered how Miss Rose was doing up in Baton Rouge. He wondered when the doctors would let her come home, and when he would be able to leave this place.

You think long and hard before you break that girl's heart.

He scowled hard. He had never lied to Celine. He had never given her reason to believe he would stay here, had never promised her any kind of future.

But she had believed in it anyway. She had thought that somehow he would change his mind—that maybe she or Miss Rose could change it for him—and he would spend the rest of his life in Harmony. She had thought he would spend the rest of his life with her.

It wasn't his fault she'd been wrong. It wasn't his fault she was greedy, wanting more from him than he could ever give. But it damn sure felt like it.

There was a curious stillness in the air, a sort of waiting. He wondered if they might get some rain to break this terrible heat, but the sky above was clear, a blue so thin it looked white. There wasn't a cloud of any substance in sight, and not so much as a whisper stirred the air.

Hellfire.

This time he would go west, he thought gloomily. He would put the entire state of Texas between him and Harmony. There would be plenty of small towns in New Mexico and Arizona, plenty of sheriffs he hadn't pissed off yet, plenty of jails he hadn't seen the inside of. Plenty of women he hadn't been inside, either. He would go west, and he would forget about this place, these people. He would manage some sort of life for himself.

The approach of a car from town distracted him from considering how hopeless his future was. When the driver slowed, then pulled into Miss Rose's drive, he glanced over his shoulder. "Celine."

She shifted, murmured, pushed her hair from her face.

"Wake up, Celine. We've got company."

Finally she sat up, and he turned to look out again, catching no more than a glimpse of her face, her long throat, the generous curve of her breast. He watched Frannie Kendall get out of the Mercedes and tried to ignore the sounds of Celine dressing behind him, tried to ignore the desire, unpleasant in its intensity, that vibrated through him.

Had Frannie come to pick up a few things for Miss Rose? Did she have news? Since he and Celine had slept together after all, they should have done it at her house, where the hospital would have been able to reach them if there was any change in Miss Rose's condition.

Frannie stood beside the car for a moment, creating a striking picture: the silver luxury sedan, the elegantly dressed redhead beside it. Then, seeing him in the doorway, she touched the handbag slung over her shoulder and started across the lawn toward the guesthouse.

Another look over his shoulder showed that Celine was in the bathroom now. He could hear the water running and thought longingly of a cool shower and air-conditioning and making love to her, and then he opened the screen door and stepped outside.

"How is Miss Rose?"

Frannie gave him a puzzled look, as if she hadn't expected the question, then shrugged. "She's fine."

"Are you here to pick up something for her?"

"No. Actually, I'm here to see you and Celine. Is she here?"

There was the pad of footsteps on the wood floor inside, then Celine was opening the screen door. It was obvious she had just gotten up—her eyes were hazy, and there was a sleepy air about her—but she had washed her face and used his comb to untangle her hair. Instead of looking more presentable, her efforts merely made her look sexier. "Hello, Frannie. How is Miss Rose?"

In a flat voice, Frannie repeated what she'd just said, then asked, "Can we go inside?"

Celine pushed the door open wider in invitation, but Will blocked Frannie with one upraised hand. "Why?" He didn't want her in his room, didn't want her to look at the bed with its sheets half-off, didn't want to see that damned smirk of hers when she realized what they'd done there.

"Because I want to," she replied. She moved, a very controlled gesture that drew Will's gaze from her face down to her purse. She had patted it when she got out of the car, as if making sure something—her keys maybe—was inside. Now he knew what.

The pistol looked ridiculously like a toy. It was small enough to conceal in a jacket pocket, definitely small enough to tuck inside a woman's purse. In spite of its size, though, he assumed it was deadly. He assumed it could do some nasty damage.

The idea that Frannie had come here to harm them was laughable. It was a lazy hot July day, good for nothing more than lying in the shade and drinking lemonade. The shimmery still air wasn't meant to be disturbed by anything more dangerous than a gnat. But she was here. And she was holding a gun. And she wasn't laughing.

Beside him Celine had gone absolutely motionless. He wondered if she felt even half the fear he did. He wondered, if he somehow distracted Frannie and gave Celine the chance, if she would have the presence of mind to slip inside and out the back. But where would she go barefooted on this terribly hot day? Where would she find safety from a nut case with a gun?

He swallowed hard and shifted slightly to his right, slightly in between the two women. "You mad at us about something, Frannie?"

"You never should have come back here, Billy Ray. You've done nothing but stir up trouble. The two of you . . . you're problems that must be dealt with. Raymond tried it his way, but it didn't work. No one believes you're causing the trouble at the house. Sheriff Franklin doesn't even consider you a suspect. He's certainly not going to arrest you for it."

He moved again, only an inch or two. "I'm leaving here, Frannie, as soon as Miss Rose gets out of the hospital. You won't have to worry about me causing any more trouble."

She wasn't impressed. "It's too late. The day you saw me in New Orleans, it became too late."

He stared at her, about to ask what she meant, to deny that

he'd seen her when he was in the city. Then, slowly, the muscles in his stomach tightening even more, the fear growing until he felt sick with it, he shifted his gaze to her car. A silver Mercedes. The day he'd gone to New Orleans for supplies, the day Melanie was murdered, he had waited for a parking space only a block or two from Melanie's apartment—a space being vacated by a silver Mercedes.

"Oh, Christ," he whispered.

Frannie smiled and shrugged. "Let's go inside now."

He looked at the gun again. She seemed familiar with it. She held it firmly, but not too tightly. It looked comfortable in her hand. It didn't waver nervously. As calm as she was, as at ease as she seemed, he didn't stand a chance in hell of disarming her. First move he made, she would shoot him, and then Celine. . . .

Oh, God, Celine.

"Leave her out of this," he stalled. He didn't want to go inside the guesthouse. He didn't want to die there. God help him, he couldn't let Celine die there. "It doesn't involve her. She doesn't know . . ."

"She knows practically everything, and what she doesn't know, she'll figure out. She's smart that way, aren't you, Celine?" Her smile was chillingly friendly. "All these years I've been the only one who knew all the secrets. In the beginning all I had were suspicions, but I found proof. I paid attention. I eavesdropped on phone calls. I acquired the combination to Raymond's safe. I used to follow him when he met that Robinson tramp over at the old Kendall place. I was hiding there when he paid her off the first time. I followed her there the last time, when she asked for more money."

A gnat buzzed annoyingly across her face, and she brushed it away with her free hand. The pistol, Will noted, never moved. "You're a very smart girl, Celine," she went on admiringly. "I never gave you credit. With none of my advantages, you figured it all out—that Raymond fathered Melanie's brat. That he faked those burglaries. That he was behind the trouble at the house. You were wrong about Melanie's death, though. Of course, you must have realized that pretty quickly. He told you he didn't do it, and you believed him right away."

Stunned, Will turned only his head to look at Celine. "You *told* him? You admitted that we knew what he'd done? My God, Celie—"

"I—I thought . . ." Her face was deathly pale, and her eyes were shadowed with pure terror. "I thought he would leave you alone if he knew that we knew."

"Another mistake—and unfortunately this one will be fatal. I already knew that I'd have to take care of you, Billy Ray. I was waiting, giving you a chance to leave, giving Raymond a chance to set you up again, but Miss Rose's little scene in the lawyer's office—to say nothing of her brush with death—added a new urgency. You have to die now, so she can be persuaded to make the necessary changes in her will, and Celine has to die with you." She motioned toward the door with the pistol. "Now, I'm through being polite. If you don't go inside now, Billy Ray, I'm going to shoot her right here. You can watch her die and know that it's because of you."

The cold, soulless look in her eyes left no doubt that she would do precisely that. Even though every instinct he possessed warned him not to, slowly he turned his back on her and, grimly gesturing for Celine to retreat, he walked into the guesthouse. She was a few steps ahead of him, her movements jerky and uncoordinated, and Frannie was a few feet behind, acting for all the world as if she'd simply come visiting.

He was near the bed when Frannie ordered him to stop. As he slowly turned to face her again, his gaze swept across the splashes of white on the floor there—his briefs, Celine's slip, panties and her sexy, lacy bra. Neither of them had taken the time to get completely dressed this afternoon, and that was how they would be found, with half their clothing discarded on the floor. It was pointless to regret, but Celine deserved better than that. Damn! He had brought her to this. She was going to die, and it was his fault.

For the first time since his father's death, he offered a silent prayer, fervent and short. *Please, God, let her live.* He didn't care what happened to him as long as Celine was all right.

"What are you planning, Frannie?" she asked, her voice

unsteady. "Do you think Sheriff Franklin will believe someone just happened along and killed us? He already suspects Raymond in the vandalism at the house. Do you think he isn't going to suspect him in this, too?"

"Raymond is in Baton Rouge with his mother. He won't be back until this evening. By then your bodies will have already been discovered. As for what the sheriff thinks, I don't care. He can suspect whomever he wants, but he won't be able to prove a thing."

She was probably right, Will acknowledged. The New Orleans Police Department hadn't made any headway on Melanie's murder, and they had a hell of a lot more going for them in talent and resources than the DeVilliers Parish Sheriff's Department.

"Frannie, you don't have to do this," Celine said. "We're reasonable people. We can work something out. You don't have to kill us. You don't have to—"

She drew back the hammer and pointed the pistol dead center at Will's chest. "Shut up, Celine," she commanded, and the frightened flow of words dried right up.

Slowly Frannie moved closer. She was enjoying this, he realized. She wanted to make it personal, wanted to make it intimate. She was sick—not crazy, as he'd earlier thought. Very controlled, very calm, and very sick.

Sounds from outside froze her only a half dozen feet from him—an engine, the skid of tires on shell, the slam of a car door, her husband's frantic yell. Help had arrived . . . but for them? Or her?

She didn't turn to look, but over her shoulder, Will could see Raymond. He started toward the cottage, then saw the open door and headed toward the guesthouse instead. His footfalls were heavy on the steps outside, his breathing labored when he came through the door.

He wasn't surprised, Will saw. He had known what he would find. Still, he looked sickened by it. "My God, Frannie, what are you doing?"

Still she didn't look at him. She didn't take her gaze from Will. "Taking care of your problems," she replied calmly. "You make messes, Raymond, and you never know how to clean them up. You would have paid Melanie the money she asked for; and when it was gone and she came back for more, you would have paid her again. You tried to get rid of Billy Ray, but all you did was put yourself at risk. If Celine could figure out what you were doing, then so can the sheriff. So can your mother.''

"But you don't have to kill them, Frannie," he reasoned, cautiously moving closer.

"He saw me outside Melanie's the day she died. He knows. They both know."

"So let them tell. We'll take care of it—your father and I. We'll take care of everything. We can do that, Frannie, but not if you kill them, too."

She emphatically shook her head, setting her sleek red hair swinging. "They have to die, Raymond. They *have* to. Don't you see? Once they're gone, our lives will be normal again. Your secrets will be safe. No one will threaten us again."

"If you kill them, our lives will *never* be normal again," Raymond disagreed. Moving slowly, he took the last steps necessary to place himself between Will and his wife. "If you kill them, Frannie, you'll have to kill me, too. It's all my fault. If I'd never had an affair with Melanie, she never would have gotten pregnant, never would have demanded money. It's *my* fault. I can't let you go on punishing other people for what I've done."

She studied him for a moment. Wavering? Will wondered. Or deciding how best to get him out of the way? Then she smiled, a slow, sexy, sultry sort of smile. "It'll be all right," she assured him. "Killing them solves everything. No one else knows that Jared is your son. No one else knows that I killed Melanie. With them dead, your mama will change her will back the way it was. He won't get control of her money. It solves all our problems, Raymond."

"I called the sheriff on my way out here," Raymond said flatly. "He'll be here any minute. Give me the gun, Frannie, please. Don't let him find you here like this."

She laughed, a sound so easy and normal that it raised chill bumps on Will's arms. "Oh, please, darling. You wouldn't call the sheriff on your own wife. You care too much about your reputation, about the great Kendall name."

With another of those sexy smiles, she added, "You care too much about *me*."

Will doubted him, too. There was no love lost between him and Raymond, none between Raymond and Celine. He wouldn't sacrifice his wife to save them.

But damned if just then Mitch Franklin, seemingly appearing from nowhere, didn't open the screen door and ease inside the room, his service revolver in hand. "Mrs. Kendall." He spoke quietly, soothingly. "Please give the gun to your husband."

For a moment she stood completely still, scarcely breathing. Then, with a shiver, anger flared in her eyes, followed by hurt, such hurt that she seemed to fold in on herself. She looked at the sheriff, then back at her husband. "Raymond, how could you?" she whispered, stunned by his betrayal. "I just wanted to protect us. No one would have cared if they died. No one would have cared!"

He moved to her then, taking the gun from her limp hold, laying it on a box. Wrapping his arms around her, he held her tight, stroking her hair, saying nothing, staring tight-lipped into the distance.

Franklin came forward and took the gun, sliding it into his pocket, then looked at Will. "I would have been here sooner, but I had to take a call from Miss Rose's daughter Meredith." He looked away, cleared his throat, then looked back again. "Miss Rose . . ."

Still holding Frannie, Raymond abruptly turned around, and the knot of fear in Will's gut began tightening again. He wanted to back away, to put his hands over his ears, to do anything at all to block out the sheriff's next words, because he already knew, oh, God, no, what he was going to say. But he couldn't move, couldn't shut out the news, couldn't stop the inevitable.

"A half hour ago Miss Rose suffered another heart attack," the sheriff said flatly. "Raymond, Will, Miss Celine . . . I'm sorry."

Celine stood beside the door in the guesthouse, leaning back against the wall, her arms folded across her chest. When they had returned from John Stuart's office a few minutes ago, Will had made it clear that he didn't want her company in here, but she had tagged along anyway. She wanted to watch him pack, wanted to see him take every piece of clothing from the armoire and place it in that battered suitcase of his. She needed to see for herself that he really was leaving.

The reading of Miss Rose's will this morning had been somber. Meredith had stayed over for it, although she was now on her way back to her home in Texas. Raymond had also been there, but Frannie hadn't. She was in a private psychiatric hospital somewhere around New Orleans, undergoing evaluation before her trial for killing Melanie. She wasn't going to be charged with threatening Celine and Will. Considering what she was facing in New Orleans, there just didn't seem much sense to it.

It was nothing less than amazing how Raymond had supported her. He'd taken a leave of absence from his job at the bank, had closed up his house in Harmony and moved temporarily to New Orleans to be close to her. The bastard really did love something besides money, after all.

Miss Rose's wishes had been pretty simple. She'd left one-fourth of her estate each to Raymond and to Meredith. She'd made some small bequests to Sophy Michaud and a few other friends, some to a few distant Kendall relatives. Some money had gone to the church, and some to the library, to be used as Celine saw fit.

A fund had been set up to complete the restoration of the mansion, with the deed then being transferred to the state. The cottage where Celine had lived the last six years was hers now, along with a tiny plot of land surrounding it, and the rest of the property here went to Will. Had Miss Rose thought the house or the huge sum of money he was supposed to distribute to worthy charities would hold him here in Harmony? She had probably only hoped—as Celine had. They had both been wrong.

They hadn't made love in a week—not since that morning here in the guesthouse. They'd hardly even spoken. They had gone to Miss Rose's funeral together Sunday afternoon, had sat side by side through the service, had stood next to Meredith at the gravesite, but Will had been so distant. He had totally shut her out. Nothing she said, nothing she did, reached him.

Laying the last of his belongings in the case, he closed it. He had inherited a nice little stash of cash along with the house, but he was walking away with nothing more than his last paycheck in his pocket. With nothing less than her heart.

"Where will you go?"

He didn't look at her. "Out west."

"No chance of changing your mind, huh?"

He didn't reply.

Her throat tightened. She had cried plenty of tears these last five days—for Miss Rose, for Will, for herself. She didn't want to cry again, not in front of him. "What about Miss Rose's wishes?"

"I don't have to be here to take care of that."

No, he didn't. John Stuart had been all too helpful explaining that. All he had to do was keep in touch with the lawyer. Anything needing his signature could be mailed or faxed, any instructions given by phone. Damn all lawyers.

"What about me?"

Finally he looked at her. It was the first time he had, she thought, since Miss Rose had died. His eyes were hard and cold, his expression blank. She wondered if he had cried for the old lady, wondered if there was any place left inside him where tears wouldn't freeze in the chill. She knew he had loved Miss Rose, knew he grieved for her, but he wouldn't show it. Maybe he couldn't show it.

"What about you?" he asked, his disinterest painful.

"What am I supposed to do?"

"What you've always done. Be the efficient librarian, the dutiful daughter, the long-suffering sister."

"And live the rest of my life alone?"

He glanced around, making sure he had everything, then picked up the suitcase and came toward her. "You'll meet someone, fall in love, get married."

"I love *you*, Will."

"Yeah?" He gave her a skeptical look. "You'll get over it."

"Damn you," she whispered, her tears blurring his relentlessly hard features.

"Yes, ma'am," he said agreeably. "I surely am damned."
He shifted his gaze from her to the quiet scene outside. For
a moment he just stared, his jaw set, his muscles rigid. Then,
regretfully, he looked back at her. "I'm sorry, Celine."

"No, you're not. If you were sorry, you wouldn't leave."

He came a step closer, brushed his hand over her hair,
smoothed a strand of it back from her face. She stiffened,
hating his gentleness, hating what it was doing to her inside.
Bending, he kissed away a tear from her cheek, and she
squeezed her eyes shut as the action unleashed all the tears
she'd been trying to hold in.

She didn't open her eyes again for a long time. Not when
she felt him moving away from her. Not when she heard the
floor creak beside her. Not when she heard the screen door
open, then close again. She couldn't watch him walk across
the yard, couldn't watch him turn onto the road that would
take him away. She couldn't watch him walk out of her
life.

After a time she slid to the floor, drawing her knees to her
chest, hiding her face in the folds of her skirt, and she cried
for the last time. These were the only tears Will would get
from her. When they were done, she would do exactly what
he said, what she always had. She would do her job efficiently, would go back to church every Sunday, would turn
her attention back to her parents and her friends and to Jared.
She would put Will out of her mind, just as he had removed
himself from her life. Even though she couldn't chase him
from her heart.

She would go back to boring, sweet Celine. Reliable Celine. Responsible Celine, sadder but wiser.

The sound of footsteps outside made her heart thud painfully. Had he changed his mind? Had he made it to town and
realized he couldn't do this? Was he coming back to her?

But it was Jared who came through the door, not Will.
Jared, his hair slicked back, his skin damp with sweat from
a morning's hot work at the mansion. He glanced around,
then down at Celine. "He's gone, isn't he?" he asked flatly.

She nodded.

"Damn!" His kick against the doorframe rattled the wall

behind her back. "I told him I wanted to say good-bye. I told him I would come over on my lunch break. Damn him!"

She dried her eyes, found a tissue in her pocket to blow her nose, and stood up, sliding her arm around Jared's shoulders. He remained stiff and unyielding, though, keeping a small distance between them.

"He could have stayed," he muttered. "He didn't have to leave."

"Maybe he did. It wasn't easy for him living here. You and I would have liked for him to stay, but . . . maybe he couldn't."

It wasn't easy for Jared living here right now, either. As she had predicted, she and Will were no longer the prime topic of conversation. Raymond was, and Frannie and Jared. The Kendalls had provided Harmony with the biggest scandal since Jefferson Kendall had murdered his wife and her lover nearly a hundred years ago, and, unfortunately, an innocent fifteen-year-old boy was caught right in the middle of it.

He didn't care, he'd insisted, when she and Will had sat down with him a week ago to explain everything that had happened. He didn't need a father. He didn't want a father, and he certainly didn't want Raymond Kendall for a father.

What he'd wanted then and now, Celine suspected, was the only father he'd grown up knowing about: Will. Even though there was no blood between them, the bonds were still there.

"Do you think he'll ever come back?"

She bit the inside of her lip. In spite of all of Will's warnings, she had somehow come to believe that he wouldn't leave. What would happen if she let herself believe now that he might come back? If she waited day after day for him to come walking down that road? If she spent the rest of her life, year after year after hopeless year, looking for a man who wasn't coming back?

"I don't know, Jared," she whispered. "But I don't think so."

At last he moved into her embrace. He leaned against her and bent his head to her shoulder, and she held him, comforted him. When he finally straightened and pulled away again, she smiled. "Come into town with me. I'll buy you lunch."

He considered refusing, then abruptly agreed. She was grateful he did.

Before they left the guesthouse, they closed all those wonderful tall windows, turned off the ceiling fans, and unplugged the only appliance—Miss Rose's old hot plate. Jared picked up the pile of laundry Will had left near the door—two sheets, two pillowcases, and a few towels—while Celine retrieved the key from the table where Will had put it.

Outside she pulled the door up tight, then twisted the key in the lock. For a moment she just stood there, her palm flat against the sun-warmed wood. Locking up seemed so final, so permanent. Now two of the three houses were empty. She would be living out here with nothing but ghosts for neighbors.

Then, with a deep breath, she stepped back and let the screen door close. She joined Jared at the foot of the steps, walked with him to the cottage to drop off the laundry, then to her car.

She had the rest of the day off—time for a leisurely lunch with Jared before returning him to work. Time to buy four bouquets of yellow carnations and make a visit to the cemetery, to Miss Rose's grave and to Wynn's, to Jared's mother's and to Will's father's.

There was time, too, to make an appointment. Time to gather her courage and go through with something she'd been considering all this long, hot summer.

It was time to keep a promise she'd made herself on a hot Fourth of July night.

Chapter Sixteen

*B*rushing dirt from his clothes, Will climbed the steps that led to the tiny one-room house—one-room shack, he thought uncharitably—that he'd been calling home for the last three days. The place needed repairs, but so did everything else on this run-down Oklahoma farm. Broken windowpanes had been replaced by squares of cardboard, and there were weak spots on the floor where the aged wood splintered each time he stepped on it. Leaks in the roof were dealt with by placing pots around the room to catch the rain. A rusty residue in the bottom of the pots, along with the dust that came through the cracks, told how long it'd been since rain had been a problem here.

If this were his place, he would walk away from it. The man who had hired him for room and board and a pitifully low salary was working himself to death here, and so was his wife. They were killing themselves for the crops that were dying in the fields. But at least they were doing it together.

Stubbornly closing the door on that thought, he sat down on the top step and unlaced the workboots the farmer had given him. They'd been left behind by the last hired hand. Beaten down by the futility of the job—by the futility of his life?—he had taken off one day. He hadn't taken anything with him, not even his clothes or his last week's pay, and no one had seen or heard from him since. Maybe he'd gone down the road to someplace better, or maybe he'd just given up. Maybe he'd walked until he couldn't walk anymore. Maybe come fall, when hunters filled these woods, someone would find what was left of him.

He kicked his boots off and poured little hills of dirt from them, then peeled off white socks turned nearly black. He was tired after days on the road, bone-tired after three days of working from before sunrise until past sunset. Still, he didn't want any time off. He didn't want time to think. He didn't want to remember how he'd spent his time in the last two months. He didn't want to remember being at home or seeing Miss Rose. God help him, he didn't want to remember Celine.

His jaw clenched, his face lined with a scowl, he went inside the house. He hadn't intended to come to Oklahoma, had instead wanted to put as much distance between himself and Louisiana as he could, but he'd gone where the rides had taken him, and where they'd taken him was right here: a dirty little shack on an unproductive farm in a place without hope.

Still, he'd stayed in worse places. The house had a bathroom, a bed, and a dresser. There was an easy chair with broken springs and a card table with uneven legs, and there was a sofa, set directly underneath the grimy double window and holding a bucket on the center cushion to catch any drips. He had lain there the last two nights, too tired to sleep, and studied the sky. Out here, a fair distance from the nearest town and miles from the nearest city, the night was dark and the stars and the moon hung low in the sky, almost close enough to touch, close enough to bring to mind a childhood nursery rhyme. *Star light, star bright, first star I see tonight . . .*

He dropped the boots just inside the door and tossed the socks on the pile of laundry in the corner. Stripping out of his clothes, he added them to the pile, then went into the bathroom to shower. The water was hard, the flow sluggish, the temperature tepid. It felt good against his heated skin. That completed, he dressed in his last pair of clean jeans and his only clean shirt, the white, button-down dress shirt he'd worn to Melanie's and Miss Rose's funerals, and he went to

e couch, setting the bucket on the floor, stretching out with
is head pillowed on the understuffed arm.

He'd gotten soft in the last two months. He'd forgotten
hat it was like to be on the road, had forgotten the isolation,
e loneliness, the weariness. He had forgotten that constant
ense of never being wanted, no matter where you went, and
e depressing certainty that, whatever troubles lay behind
ou, there wasn't anything better ahead.

Maybe he just wasn't willing to accept it any longer. Was
is the life he'd envisioned for himself? Miss Rose had
sked. Moving from town to town, never staying long, always
ving alone. He had lied to her, had told her that he was
appy with his life, that he'd lived it the way he wanted, and
e had shaken her head in disagreement. Her advice had
een so simple: Settle down. Find a job. Find a pretty girl
nd make an honest woman of her. So simple . . . and so
mpossible.

He had settled down in his two months in Harmony. He
ad stayed out of trouble, had stayed out of bars—mostly—
nd away from women and out of jail. He had found a job,
ne that he was good at, one he liked. And he had found the
rettiest girl of them all. But what had it gotten him? It hadn't
made things right. It hadn't made him a better man, hadn't
made him any more deserving. It hadn't made him the kind
f man Celine needed. It had just left him dissatisfied. Angry.
Without hope.

Reaching into his shirt pocket, he pulled out the keepsake
e'd tucked there for safety. The room was dark—he hadn't
et bothered to turn on the single lamp—but enough light
ame through the window to see. It was a loop, knotted
ogether a few inches from each end and braided in between.
t was satiny, already soft, and made more so by his frequent
andling.

Ribbons.

They were the ribbons Celine had worn in her hair that
morning in the guesthouse when, wanting her more desper-
tely than he had ever imagined, he had tried to push her
way, but she had come to him anyway. They were the
ibbons she had worn around her wrists that sweet night in
he cottage, the ribbons he had bound her to the bed with.

The ribbons she had bound him to her with? he wondere
humorlessly.

When he had packed to leave Harmony, he had found the
on the floor beneath his bed, dropped there and forgotte
when she had undressed that morning. Not wanting the mem
ories, he had pushed them farther under the bed, then ha
almost immediately pulled them back out and stuffed the
deep into his suitcase. He had acted on impulse, and the firs
time he had come across them in his bag, he had very nearl
acted on another impulse and thrown them away.

But getting rid of the ribbons wouldn't get rid of the memo
ries. Nothing short of dying would accomplish that . . . and
Jesus, sometimes he felt as if he were close. He had know
leaving her would hurt, but he'd told himself he could de
with it. The ache would be temporary. Any grieving he di
would be for Miss Rose. But he'd been wrong. Oh, he misse
the old lady, missed her like hell, but there was a sort o
finality to missing her. She was dead.

But Celine wasn't. God have mercy, she was alive, swee
and loving, alone and missing *him*. All he had to do was g
back to her. Go home to her.

His gaze drifted from the ribbons, mere shadows in th
night darkness, to the window and the stars beyond. *I wis
I may, I wish I might* . . .

If he were foolish enough to believe in wishes, what woul
he wish for? To be the sort of man Celine needed . . . eve
though he already was the man she wanted. To know that h
could make her happy, that he could protect her from whisper
and sly gossip. To know that he could make as big a differenc
in her life as she'd made in his.

Scowling, he tucked the ribbons back into his pocke
Wishing was useless. It couldn't change his life. It couldn'
make him a better person. It couldn't make him happy.

But Celine could, a silent voice whispered. God hav
mercy, yes, Celine could.

Across the barren yard, the dinner bell at the back door o
the farmhouse sounded, and he rose wearily from the couch
heading out the door, letting the screen door slam behin
him. He took his meals over at the farmhouse, sitting at th
kitchen table with the farmer and his wife. They were a youn

couple, not long married and determined to make a go of this farm that had been in his family for three generations. Will understood the man's attachment—his father had loved his land, too—but he wondered why it mattered to the wife. She clearly wasn't cut out for this kind of work. She was pretty, young, and liked to laugh, and it was obvious that she'd come from a better life. The way she dressed, the way she acted, the way she talked—all were giveaways, to say nothing of her ignorance of farming.

She could find an easier life someplace else, could find another man who would take better care of her someplace else. So why did she stay here? Why did she sacrifice comfort for hard work, security for uncertainty? What was it about this place that held her here?

Only a few yards from their house, he came to a slow stop. The kitchen windows and the door were open, casting yellow light into the night, and music drifted out on the warm evening air. Inside the table was set for dinner, but neither the farmer nor his wife were eating. Instead they were dancing around the kitchen, keeping time with the slow song on the radio, their attention focused on each other. He was gazing down at her, and she was smiling at him in a way that made Will hurt just seeing it. It was an intimate sort of smile, full of promise and passion. Full of joy. Of love. It was the kind of smile Celine had smiled for him.

Was it that simple? he wondered. The woman loved her husband and so she gladly accepted the hardships that being his wife brought? She didn't mind the long, weary days because the nights were spent with him. She preferred this difficult life over an easier one someplace else because at least she was sharing it with him.

Maybe it was. Celine could have had her pick of men—easier men, respectable men, men any parents would be happy to welcome into their daughters' lives—but she had chosen *him*. She had tried relationships with other men, but they hadn't satisfied her. They hadn't made her happy. They hadn't given her passion. *He* had.

Maybe it was so simple. Maybe, like the farmer's wife, Celine would rather have *him* than the comfortable life she'd always lived. Maybe respectability was a poor companion on long hot evenings like this. Maybe sainthood wasn't enough to fill the empty places in her life. It was hard to swallow because his mouth had gone dry, but he managed, and even though it scared him like hell, he forced one last thought into words.

Maybe *he* was.

It was Sunday, the last day of a record-breaking hot July, and there was still August to come. All the good people of Harmony would be in church this morning, playing their hypocritical roles. Will wondered as he gazed out the window of the truck if Celine was there, if she'd gone back since Miss Rose's funeral two weeks ago or if he'd ruined her forever for that. No, not ruined. He hadn't ruined her. He had livened up her hot summer. He had brought her passion and pleasure and a great deal of satisfaction.

He had loved her.

Rubbing his fingers over the braided ribbons, he shifted in the seat. The man who'd picked him up forty miles back was quiet, lost in his thoughts. He hadn't spoken beyond asking where Will was headed and acknowledging that he'd be passing right through. The silence suited Will. It gave him time to think—and for the first time in his life, he was thinking about the future. He was making plans. Miss Rose had left him her house and some money, and chances were good that he could get back his job with Roger, at least until work on the Kendall mansion was finished. He might even earn a permanent spot on Roger's crew. They worked all over the state of Louisiana and occasionally in southern Mississippi, but it wasn't such a wide area that he would ever be far from home.

He would never be far from Celine.

There wasn't much traffic on the road, but the truck traveled at a steady fifty miles an hour. They passed through one nothing town after another, places he knew even if he'd never been there. Places exactly like all the other nothing towns where he'd lived out his life. They were comfortingly familiar.

The road rounded a bend, and a gas station appeared up ahead. There was a welcome sign across from the station, a sign that he had always known somehow excluded him. This morning he didn't give a damn.

"This where you're heading?" the driver asked.

"Yeah. If you could let me out a couple of blocks ahead, I'd appreciate it."

A tense feeling growing in his gut, he tucked the braid into his shirt pocket. He hated coming into towns, hated the attention it brought him. But this nervousness had nothing to do with the town or the curious looks he was sure to get. It had to do with coming home. God help him, it had to do with Celine.

He saw her little blue car parked at the end of a row in the First Baptist Church lot, and he directed the man to let him out there. After thanking him, he left his suitcase beside the car, then, counting the chimes as the church bell struck twelve, he started toward the main doors.

The service ended a few minutes later. Leaning against the lightpost near the sidewalk curb, he watched as the big double doors opened and people began coming down the broad steps. They looked at him, and he looked back, keeping his gaze steady and even, searching for one face in particular.

Jared came out first, saw him immediately and came to such an abrupt stop at the top of the steps that the woman behind him, her attention directed elsewhere, bumped into him. She looked up to apologize, and the muscles in Will's stomach tightened. It was Celine, and, oh, God, her hair . . .

The day you leave I'm cutting it all off, she'd told him one night in bed, *even shorter than yours*, and she'd done a damn good job of it. It was short and sleek, curving over her ears and ending inches above the lace collar of her dress. It was so short, so different, so . . . He chuckled softly. So damned sexy.

"In a crowd like this, Jared," Celine said with a laugh as her mother walked into her, "the idea is to keep moving, not see how many people you can pile up behind you." Sensing that he wasn't listening to her and feeling the intensity of his gaze, she looked to see what he found so riveting, and her heart skipped.

Dear Lord, it was Will. Wearing faded jeans and that white dress shirt with the sleeves rolled up, leaning against the streetlamp as if he owned it, he looked perfect enough to be the answer to the prayers she had just prayed through this morning's service.

"Go on," Jared said, drawing her around and giving her a little push. "He's waiting for you."

She slowly started down the steps, reaching the bottom all too soon, crossing the ten feet of sidewalk that separated them. Stopping a few feet away, she gave him a long look. "I knew you would come back," she lied and saw that he knew it was a lie.

He grinned that smart-ass grin of his. That dear, sweet grin. "You were sure of that, were you?"

"I wished, hoped." She sighed softly. "I prayed. Will . . ."

Suddenly serious, he stopped her. He moved away from the post and a step toward her. "This is your last chance, little girl. In another thirty seconds, I'm going to kiss you right here in front of God and everyone else, and then—"

She interrupted him with her smile. "Promises, promises, Will."

His grin returned, and he touched her then, taking hold of her wrists, pulling her slowly into his arms, snug against his body. She knew they had an audience. She even heard the disgust in Vickie's voice as her sister asked, "What is *he* doing here?" But she had never cared about audiences. Will had. Will had never wanted to touch her in public, had never wanted to expose her to mean-spirited gossip. He had always wanted to keep their relationship secret.

But not now. Oh, mercy, no, not now when his mouth was on hers and he was kissing her, hard and hungry, and he was holding her tight as if he intended to crawl right inside her.

Finally he raised his head, and for a moment they simply looked at each other. Gently, wondrously, she touched his face, his throat, then rested her palms on his chest. It was then she saw the brightly colored braid sticking up just a bit from his pocket. "What's this?" she asked delightedly, recognizing her ribbons right away.

"I took them with me. I wanted . . ." Sheepishness gave

way to seriousness. "I wanted a way to find my way back home. Celie . . . Did you mean it?"

He had been gone ten days and ten lonely, lonely nights, but she knew immediately what he was asking, what one thing she'd said his last day here that mattered. Holding him tightly as if she could keep him there with no more than her embrace, she answered, "I meant it."

His gaze dark and intense, he searched her face. Satisfied, he said, "I love you, Celie. God help me, I do love you."

She thought she had cried her last tears over him, but her eyes were filling now. "I love you, too, Will."

Oblivious to everyone around them, he tenderly touched her cheek. "I want to stay here. I want to live with you. I want to get married and fill Miss Rose's house with babies and spend the rest of my life with you."

"Yes."

He shushed her. "I haven't asked yet."

"You usually don't. You usually don't need to."

"I want to this time. I want to do this properly. I've never done much right in my life, but this . . ." He broke off, swallowed hard and solemnly, heartachingly asked, "Will you marry me, Celie? Will you be my wife?"

Equally solemnly, she replied, "I would be honored."

He considered her answer, and his expression lightened by degrees until he was smiling, until his wicked dark eyes were laughing. "Honored. Oh, no, Celie, the honor is all mine."

As he kissed her again, she heard another comment from someone passing by. "So Billy Ray Beaumont's back in town . . . again."

He heard it, too, and broke off the kiss to look at her. "But this time," he said softly, promised softly, "I'm home to stay."